Mary Cowden Clarke

# The Girlhood of Shakespeare's Heroines in a Series of Tales

Vol. 3

Mary Cowden Clarke

**The Girlhood of Shakespeare's Heroines in a Series of Tales**
*Vol. 3*

ISBN/EAN: 9783337023485

Printed in Europe, USA, Canada, Australia, Japan

Cover: Foto ©Andreas Hilbeck / pixelio.de

More available books at **www.hansebooks.com**

# THE GIRLHOOD

OF

# SHAKESPEARE'S HEROINES

IN

## *A SERIES OF TALES*

BY

## MARY COWDEN CLARKE

*Author of the Concordance to Shakespeare*

* * *

New York

A. C. ARMSTRONG AND SON

51 EAST 10th ST., NEAR BROADWAY

1891

# CONTENTS.

✠✠✠

# KATHARINA AND BIANCA;

## THE SHREW, AND THE DEMURE.

## TALE VII.

# KATHARINA AND BIANCA;

### THE SHREW, AND THE DEMURE.

' The one as famous for a scolding tongue,
As is the other for beauteous modesty.''
*Taming of the Shrew.*

"But I must and will go to church to-day, Antonia ; it is the Santa Lucia ; and the altar is to be decked—and there is to be a procession—and all the world will be there—and I tell you, I must go.''

"But our aunt is worse to-day, you know ; she must not be left alone. And remember, it is my turn to go out to-day, Claudia ; and Camillo will be so disappointed, if I do not meet him ; for I promised him I would, as I knew to-day was my Sunday abroad, and——''

"O, if it be to meet your betrothed, of course, I must give up ;'' retorted Claudia. "No doubt, a pious duty ought to give way to a love-meeting.''

"Nay, you are unjust, sister ;'' replied Antonia. "I merely pleaded for my turn, thinking of his disappointment, and my promise ; but I must not be selfish. My aunt shall not be left, yet you shall have your wish. Go to church, dear. It is a laudable motive ; you shall pray for me ; and above all, for our poor sick aunt. Fetch your veil, my Claudia, and I will arrange it for you.''

"You are a kind creature—you always were ;'' said Claudia, as Antonia arranged the folds of the veil, and fastened it with the silver pins, and ivory comb, so as to set off her sister to the best advantage ; "and if I should happen to see Camillo in my way, I'll give him your love, and tell him the reason you couldn't come. Poor old aunt ! I fancy we shan't have to nurse her long. Heigho ! I'll pray for her. Camillo will forgive your disappointing him, for the sake of the kindness it proves in you, staying to watch by her. He says it's that unselfish goodness in you, Antonia, which makes him adore you as he does. So you'll only add to his love, you see, by stopping away to-day, after all. Good-bye !"

Antonia smiled, sighed, kissed her sister, as she returned the "good-bye." Then when Claudia had tripped away, and closed the door behind her, the sigh was repeated ; and for a few moments, the young girl remained lost in thought, looking through the window. But rousing herself, she said :—"I won't think of his disappointment, or my own. Let me go up to my aunt ; and see whether she be ready for her 'bollitura.' "

Antonia and Claudia were two young Genoese girls. When their parents died, they had no relation, but an aunt, a widow, in a thriving way of business as a fruiterer. This aunt had taken charge of her two orphan nieces, and for some years, entirely supported them, her trade sufficing to maintain them all three in comfort. But as the sisters grew towards womanhood, the aunt's health declined, and it became the duty of the two girls to return a part of the kindness they had received at her hands, by devoting themselves to the care and nursing of their sick relation.

This duty was cheerfully as well as strictly fulfilled by the elder of the two nieces, Antonia. But Claudia, the younger, felt a constant attendance by the bedside of a woman, whom age and infirmity made somewhat peevish, irritable, and exacting, to be a most irksome penance, which she made no scruple of avoiding, as often as she possibly could. The sort of means she took to avoid it, have been already hinted, in the dialogue which took place between her sister and herself.

Claudia was very much prettier than her elder sister, Antonia ; but it was strange,—and truth to say, strangest of all to herself,—that the plain Antonia had had many suitors, nay, was actually betrothed to one, her own choice, while the pretty Claudia had never been able to boast more than a few passing flirtations, —heart-smitten admirers of a week or so,—but not one bona-fide proposal. She thought so charming a face as she beheld every day in the glass, needed but to be more seen, to bring a host of lovers ; and this it was which made her so anxious to frequent the most crowded places, when she did go abroad.

The church of San Lorenzo, on a saint's day, was sure to be the most thronged, and most fashionable of all resorts ; and besides, Claudia was quite a devotee,—in her way ; she knew all the embroidery on the priests' robes by heart ; was enthusiastic in the fineness of the lace round the altar-cloths ; doted on the velvet with which the pulpit was hung ; was thoroughly versed in every pearl in the waxen madonna's necklace, and every gem on her petticoat ; was learned in processions ; could tell every saint's day in the calendar, off-hand ; and was ready for every feast, moveable or appointed, long before its arrival. Nay, she saved up her pocket money scrupulously, to put into the ‘ tronco dei poveri ;’ only, it sometimes happened, that a bright ribbon, or a tempting new kerchief, would dwindle the destined ‘ liri ’ into a few ‘ soldi’.’

On the day in question, she had no sooner entered the church, than she perceived that her usual seat was occupied by a remarkably good looking young man ; who, however,—on her approaching with a helpless, embarrassed air, plainly bespeaking her perplexity and its cause,—immediately gave up the place he occupied, drawing one of the rush-bottomed wooden-backed

chairs from the nearest stack, and setting it for himself not far from her.

This courtesy on the stranger's part, necessarily
produced some on hers. She offered her missal, seeing that the young gentleman was unprovided with a
book. She held it between them ; and when some of
the little coloured prints (of saints with up-turned
eyes, or of several small fat, flaming, cross-laden
hearts, toiling up a hill, with dabs of crimson to represent bleeding footsteps) that were put into the missal as markers, occasionally fluttered out upon the
pavement, as they would do, and as they seemed to
take a perverse pleasure in doing, Claudia would hurriedly stoop to pick them up ; and then the young
stranger would gallantly prevent her ; and then, when
he recovered it, and attempted to replace it, Claudia
would help him so awkwardly, and with such trembling fingers, that the little picture was in danger of
tumbling down again, and then Claudia would colour
a good deal, and look in a terrible state of pretty confusion.

All this improved their acquaintance amazingly ; so
that by the time mass was over, nothing seemed more
natural than that the young gentleman should offer to
see her home ; and when she protested she could not
think of giving him so much trouble, he could do no
less than assure her that it would be something very
different from trouble to him ; and when she said :—
" Well it was not far, to be sure," he was called upon
to say that " were it situated at the very farther extremity of Genoa city, he should only be the better
pleased ;" and after many of the like remarks—no
less unexpected, than brilliant and original, she permitted him to escort her to her aunt's house ; which
led to a request on the young gentleman's part that he
should be allowed to call on the morrow, to enquire
after her health, and that of her sick relation. In
short, this day's church-going produced what Claudia
had so earnestly desired—an offer of marriage.

The young man announced, that his name was Baptista Minola, son of signor Minola of Padua ; that he was now at Genoa on business for his father ; that he was about to return home ; where he would be sure of a double welcome, could he bring so charming a bride in his hand.

The match was concluded ; madame Minola took leave of her aunt and sister, and set forth with her husband for Padua, protesting with much obliging unction, that she should be always glad to hear of their welfare ; that she wished her aunt's speedy restoration to health, and hoped it might not be long ere her sister was married to her lover, Camillo. " He is not a gentleman born, to be sure, like my Baptista ;" said she to Antonia, in the flow of considerate feeling towards her sister, inspired by her own superior good fortune ; " but he is a very worthy young man—an excellent workman, I dare say ; and his exertions will doubtless suffice to support you both very comfortably, when you marry. I hope it may be soon for your sake, Antonia. Nothing is more distressing for a girl than a protracted engagement, and a long deferred wedding. I trust you'll soon be able to send me word that you are a happy wife—as I am."

" My aunt's state of health, will not allow of my thinking of quitting her : and heaven forbid, that I should owe my happiness to the death of one who has been so good to us, as she has been ;" sighed Antonia. " I fear Camillo and I must not think of marriage for a long time yet awhile."

When the bride and bridegroom were departed, the sick woman called her niece to her bed side, and said —" You are grieved at parting with your sister, my Antonia ; but we must not regret her, her happiness is assured. It is the thought of yours, and of how it may also be secured, which occupies me now. I know your attachment for Camillo ; his for you. I know how it has been made subservient to your dutiful attention towards one who has had it in her power to benefit you. I know how often you and he have given up your natural desire to be in each other's so-

ciety, that you may not let my comforts, or my tendance, be lessened. This ought not to be. But I
have not the courage to give up my nurse, my Antonia, my dear niece. I have thought then, that if
Camillo will endure the presence of one whom age and
infirmity render less patient than she ought to be,—
if he will consent to the infliction of a burden for the
sake of the girl he loves,—if he will help her to share
its weight, that he may secure her society, without
withdrawing her from the duty which gratitude and
her own good feeling impose upon her,—if, in short,
he will receive us both to his home, I have considered
how it may now be arranged that your union shall be
no longer delayed. The amount of my hoarded sav-
ings I had intended to bequeath in equal shares to my
two nieces. Claudia's marriage with a man so well off as
her husband is,—the son of a rich Paduan gentleman,
—renders it unnecessary that any of my money should
go to her ; and the two portions combined, together
with what Camillo's skill and industry can command,
will amply suffice to maintain such a home as your
moderate wishes could desire. Why then tarry until
death shall have put you in possession of this destined
sum ? Why not accept, instead of inherit it ; and
give me the happiness of enjoying it with my children,
instead of the barren comfort of leaving it to them
when I am gone ? Let us induce Camillo to think
with us, and then we may all live as happily together,
as an enfeebled frame, and the task of ministering to
its wants will permit."

It may well be imagined that the young couple were
not slow to avail themselves of their generous relation's
offer ; and they determined that the affection and zeal
with which they would make her future happiness
their care, should best prove their gratitude, and make
her feel that she had gained double tendance by the
kindness with which she had given up her nurse to be
the wife of the man she loved. In the wedded home
of Camillo and Antonia, the sick and aged aunt was

rewarded for the protection she had formerly bestowed on the two orphan girls.

Upon the occasion of her marriage, Antonia wrote to her sister at Padua, informing her of her happiness ; and expressing trust that its knowledge was the only thing wanting to complete that of Claudia.

Claudia sent a congratulatory letter in reply ; which concluded with a hint that her sister had proved her wisdom in abiding with a relation who had wherewithal to recompense attachment. " But do not let the thought of having deprived me of my share of our aunt's property, disturb you for a moment, Antonia ;" the letter concluded ; " I assure you, I have the greatest pleasure in ceding to you whatever portion might have been mine, could I have resolved to pain a worthy man's heart by refusing to be his, on a plea of staying to watch by a sick relation. I should wish you never to reproach yourself with having supplanted me in my aunt's affection ; I have that of a kind, an indulgent, husband, to console me. Nor would I have you reflect upon yourself for having been the sole recipient of her bounty. You want it, I do not. I dare say a turner of olive wood does not make so large an income, but that a generous aunt's contribution to the household must be a consideration—an important advantage. I rejoice that you have it, sister. As for me, I have an establishment far beyond what my poor humble merits could have entitled me to. And lately, signor Minola's death has made us even richer than we were before. The good old man left my Baptista all he was worth—and if ever there was a saint in Paradise, that dear good old man is surely gone there. That you may enjoy the result of your assiduity and vigilant care, unalloyed by one sting of self-reproach, my dear Antonia, is the sincere wish of your

Affectionate sister and humble servant,<br>CLAUDIA MINOLA."

For some time, no farther communication took place

between the sisters.　After a period of a year or two, however, another letter reached Antonia from Padua. It ran thus :—

    " Dear sister,
      " Although so long a time has elapsed without your having found time or inclination to write to me, I will not reproach you with your negligence, or do you the (perhaps) injustice to believe that you are indifferent to what concerns me.　On the contrary, I will flatter myself that the news of a circumstance I am about to impart to you, will give you as much gratification as it does me.　My husband's position and fortune, the importance of his connections, and the considerable wealth he possesses, makes it very desirable that he should have an heir.　Hitherto, my hopes of bringing him one, have been frustrated.　At present, I have a prospect of their being realized.　My daily and nightly prayers have been granted ; my unwearied applications to the saints, strengthened and directed by the pious exhortations of my confessor, father Bonifacio, have been at length heard, and through their holy intercession, I am about to be blessed and to bless my husband, with offspring.　We had some thoughts of asking you and your husband to stand godfather and godmother to the expected baby ; but we have since felt it our duty to offer the compliment to a neighbour of ours, a landed proprietor, and octogenarian.　His name is signor Gremio ; he has only one son, a tall sickly man, who has overgrown his strength, and whom the doctors think unlikely to live. What a terrible thing, the prospect of losing an only son !　I already feel by anticipation the power of sympathising with poor old signor Gremio.　To lose an only child, must be almost as bad as to be disappointed in the hope of having an only child at all !　I am sorry to hear that you, sister Antonia, have no prospect of becoming a mother.　Ah, my dear ! it is a blessed prospect, believe me.　If you or your hus-

band should think of treating yourselves at any time
with an excursion to Padua, with what joy I shall
place my dear little expected son in your arms. But
I suppose you will not think of leaving our dear aunt,
poor old soul ! Well, you do quite right not to give
her up ; she has made it worth your while to show
your attachment to her. You were always a wiser-
headed girl than your poor little sister, Claudia. Discretion, gravity, steadiness and prudence in the dis-
charge of your worldly duties, were always a part of
your character, Antonia. Humility, with a meek
hope of recommending herself to the guardianship of
the saints, was ever the utmost aim of her who sub-
scribes herself

Your devoted sister,<br>
Claudia Minola.''

With unfeigned pleasure, Antonia received these
tidings of her sister's prosperity ; though the old
smile was repeated as she read Claudia's self-compla-
cency under the guise of self-depreciation ; innuendo
under that of commendation, triumph under that of
pity ; while the old sigh was breathed again, as she
owned that the pity was needed. The one blessing
of children had been denied their home ; and the want
of that one blessing had rendered their domestic joys
incomplete, even in their fulness.

But the happiness they had hitherto possessed was
suddenly interrupted by the death of the good aunt.
She was sincerely mourned by Antonia ; who, attached
to her by the double tie of gratitude, and affectionate
care, felt her loss deeply.

Camillo therefore, was well pleased when another
letter arrived from madame Minola, inviting her sister
to Padua to stand godmother to the baby that was
now born ; as an unexpected circumstance had altered
their views with respect to asking old signor Gremio's
sponsorship.

" I suppose they have found out the old gentleman's

coffers to be less well stored than they imagined ;"
thought Camillo ; " or possibly, the son may be pronounced in better health, or be about to marry, and
the estates discovered to be entailed—or some equally
potent reason for making the senior signor Gremio a
less eligible godfather to the heir of the Minolas than
was at first supposed.  But however that may be, I
am not sorry they have asked my Antonia to be gossip
on the occasion ; as the change will do her good.  She
shall set out for Padua immediately."

Antonia would fain have had her husband accompany her ; but he pointed out that he had not been
included in the invitation,—that he could not well
manage to leave business for a mere pleasure-trip,—
and that it was as much as they ought in prudence to
afford, the cost of her journey, and the necessary outlay for a christening gift.

" Thy sister is quite right in supposing that an
' ebanista ' is no rich trader, Antonia ;" said he smiling ; " but it makes the compliment her affection pays
us, all the greater, in wishing to have thee for her
child's godmother ; I'm right glad to see Claudia hath
so much good feeling.  Her babe shall have the rich-
est carved cradle I can send her."

Antonia was received with much show of hospitality
and kindness by Baptista Minola and his wife ; but
it struck her, that in her sister's manner there was a
strange embarrassment, when she begged to see her
child.

" I long to see the little fellow—to clasp him in my
arms—to hug him, and tell him how glad I shall be
to have him for a godson, dear Claudia ; where is
he ?"

" The child shall be brought forthwith—sit down,
Antonia—thou must needs be tired with thy journey.
Some wine and fruit shall be set here in the orchard,
till the more substantial meal be ready."

But at this moment, the nurse approached, bearing
in her arms a small recumbent individual, swathed

into a stiff bundle, adorned with knots of ribands, who could be no other than the heir of the Minolas. It was plentifully be-hung with relics in proper preparatory christening-trim ;  and had been duly deluged with holy-water, until the necessarily deferred ceremonial could take place.

Antonia exclaimed, "Here he is ! Give him to me, nurse !"

" ' He,' ma'am ! It's a she, ma'am ! It's no him, but a blessed her—a little girl, ma'am !" said the nurse.

" Yes, it's too true, Antonia ;" said her sister. " My expected son proved to be a little girl, after all. It's a sad disappointment ; we could not think of asking signor Gremio to be godfather to anything less than an heir, you know ; so we put off begging him to become sponsor till another time. Next baby, we shall hope to be more fortunate.  But we thought you wouldn't mind a girl, and so———"

Madame Minola stammered, and left her speech unfinished ; but her sister hastened to relieve her, by the assurance that the baby would be no less dear to her for being a girl than a boy, and that she was quite as much delighted with a goddaughter as with a godson.

" How like the world that is !" murmured madame Minola.  " It takes but a one-sided view of most things—a limited—a merely selfish view ! Of course it can signify little to you, as a godmother, whether your godchild be a girl or a boy ; but you forget what a mother feels on such a point.  True, you are not a mother yourself, and can therefore little enter into the force of a mother's feelings.  Still, I think, you might have expressed a little more sympathy with your sister's disappointment, Antonia.  You might have felt, that she naturally sighed to present her husband with an heir to his large property ; but you always were cold and prudent—vastly more so than your poor sister, who cannot help feeling warmly where she loves.  I own I am so attached to my husband, as to regret bitterly not having brought him a son—but doubtless you are wiser in your coldness, than I in my warmth.  Besides, it is the saints' will—(at least, this time)—and to that I submit."

"And how do you mean to name the little creature ?" said Antonia, bending over it, to conceal whatever emotion her sister's words might have called forth.

"Why, Baptista at first thought of calling it by yours, as a compliment to godmamma ; which, of course, was all very kind and considerate on his part ; but I told him I knew you had too much good sense to feel hurt, if I preferred having it called according to a very particular wish of my own."

"And what is your favorite name, my sister ?" asked Antonia.

"O it is not a mere favorite name—one name is well-nigh as pretty as another, for that matter ; it's no such frivolous motive as that, which determines me, I assure you, sister ;" said Claudia with a look of injured innocence ;  "I should have liked your name very well—as it's the same with our blessed St. Antonio of Padua—the patron-saint of our city ; but as the babe was born on the feast of Santa Katharina, I should like her to be called after that holy martyr. So my husband has consented to give up his whim in deference to my wish.  Certainly, its proceeding purely from a pious motive, entitles it to some consideration."

Claudia paused, for some assent to her last proposition ; but as her sister offered none, she proceeded.

"It is rarely that I find any one take things in the same fervent point of view that I do ; I remember of old, Antonia, you never sympathized with my ardour for church-going,—my zeal in the endeavour humbly to fulfil my religious duties ; it is scarcely to be attributed to you as a fault ; we are not all constituted alike ; some are of a more enthusiastic temperament than others,—and certainly, the phlegmatic rationality, and cool-judging prudence of your character is far more philosophical, and far more useful, in a worldly point of view, than my ardent and impulsive disposition. But I am content to be as I am, and to set my heart upon things not altogether mundane."

She here heaved a soft sigh of self-satisfaction, and paused again; but finding that Antonia still preserved silence, she went on.

"As I was saying, few people contemplate things in the far-viewed and earnest way that I do. Now, if I thought that calling my child Antonia would propitiate the patron saint of our Padua, so that he would send me a boy next time, to present to my husband, I would have her baptized by that name at once ; but upon mature deliberation, and after frequent consultations with padre Bonifacio, I am induced to think there is more to be hoped from naming her after the holy virgin-martyr, Santa Katharina, on whose festival she was born."

However, madame Minola's hopes of a son were destined never to be realized. Whether owing to an error in the naming of her first-born, or not,—certain it is, that her second child was also a girl. The poor lady took this reiterated disappointment (looking upon it as really quite a pointed thing on the part of Fate and the Saints, after she had taken such anxious pains to discover the best means of conciliating them) so much to heart, that she sank into weak health ; and even her boasted energy in church-going could not avail to rouse her from her easy chair, which she thenceforward constantly occupied. But she solaced her pride of devoteeism, by continual interviews with her father confessor ; in padre Bonifacio's presence, in his ghostly exhortation, in his comfortable counsel, she strove to cherish that warmth of zeal, on which she had always so much plumed herself.

By the time her two little girls had reached an age most to require her active superintendence, she had become a confirmed invalid ; never leaving her arm-chair, but for her bed ; or her bed, but for her arm-chair.

The elder of the two, Katharina, was a spirited, lively child, whose unchecked sallies were fast becoming flippancy ; whose glibness of retort, and unbridled freedom of tongue were speedily leading her into insufferable pertness.   At first, the child's quickness caused her to be laughed at, and encouraged in her proneness to make saucy answers ; but gradually they were found to be annoying, rather than amusing ; rude, instead of droll and pretty.   But there was no judicious mother, to train the insolence into sprightliness, to subdue the malapertness into harmless mirth, and to soften the character, by teaching her to mingle gentleness and kind-meaning with her native vivacity —which might thus have been mere pleasant and winning playfulness.

Instead of forming her child's disposition, and giving a wholesome tendency to such points of character, as might have grown into attractive qualities, with proper restriction and worthy culture, madame Minola was deep in some controversial discussion with father Bonifacio on the relative merits of St. Poppo and St. Macarius ; as to whether the latter saint's pious zeal in courting gnat-bites, or St. Simeon Stylites' singular taste in lodgings, deserved the greater reverence, and emulation ; in doting upon the humility of St. Anthony, who took to mat-making, or the never-sufficiently-to-be-admired St. John Chrysostom, who, with a conscience more queasy than his stomach, ' used the same stinking oil for his food as his lamp ; ' and sometimes she would discuss another holy man's bland opinion respecting the span-length of those infant souls condemned to an eternity of torture.   While she should have been watching the defects in her child's temper, and striving to counteract them by substituting or developing better feelings, she was engaged in reading the lives of the saints, or listening to a history of the miraculous transit of the house of Loretto.

When the defects had ripened into faults, for want of early discipline and care ; when, of the child who might have become a merry-hearted creature, with enough of roguery in her sallies to keep all those about her on the alert, and who might have won all their loves with her raillery and playful replies, was made a pert unpleasant chit,—then she punished. Punishment, strict, summary, and inexorable, was resorted to, for a cure of those evils, which ought rather to have been timely prevented.

Bianca, the younger, was a child of totally different disposition. She was quiet, watchful, and unopposing. That which exasperated her more petulant sister into angry retort, or furious defiance, she would receive with a meek shrug, or a placid remonstrance. She shrank from contention ; avoided scrapes ; evaded difficulties. She seldom provoked censure, and always contrived to escape correction. She was so passive, that she seemed to have no will ; but she could be meekly stubborn, and had a remarkable method of getting her own way. She made no show of determination, but she rarely failed of compassing anything she desired. She seemed incapable of resistance, yet generally succeeded in effecting none but her particular plans. She never appeared to contest a point with any one, but somehow, all yielded to her wish. She had quite a neat little faculty of her own for gaining her ends, together with the good will and liking of everybody. She was a general favorite ; her unthwarting manners, her innocent air, her mild speech, her soft, deprecating looks, rendered her popular, and secured her a universal good word. All were ready to give her a good character. She passed for very obliging, though she used little exertion for any one ; but then she never offended any body's prejudices. She had a reputation for gentleness and modesty ; for she scarcely seemed to have an opinion of her own— and certainly never bluntly expressed one. People thought her full of sweetness, because she had none

of her sister's tartness,—which always particularly
shocked her ; and found her very amiable, since she
never affronted them, or wounded their self-love.

Bianca's being so shocked at Katharina's defects,
gained her immense credit in public opinion ; it placed
her beyond all suspicion of sharing or countenancing
such misconduct, and avouched her own superiority.
Public opinion ranked the one sister as highly, as it
rated low the other.  It took the two girls on their
own estimate of the value of its regard.  Katharina
cared little for the world's opinion,—slighted it,—set
it at defiance ; while Bianca bent to it,—deprecated
its censure—courted its approval, in her every demure
word and look.  The world requited each of them,
accordingly.

One of the persons who especially excited Katharina's dislike, and who, in consequence, was frequently the object of her impertinence, was padre
Bonifacio.  She did not dare treat him thus in her
mother's presence, knowing how highly esteemed the
confessor was by madame Minola, but she took every
other opportunity of marking her contempt.

If he passed her, coming in, or going out, of the
house, in return for his murmured " Benedicite,
child !" she would make the ' jettatura ' at him, or
look over her shoulder towards him, and say :—
" You're there, are you ?  How do ?" or nod slightly,
without so much as glancing up, saying :—" Good-
day ; good-day !"  This, the worthy gentleman scarcely
observed ; partly, because he was deaf ; partly, because he thought the pertness of the child not worth
notice ; partly, because his spirit of meekness forbade
resentment.

Once when he called her towards him, and, placing
his hand on her head paternally, gave her some message for her mother, she slily put up her hand, and
held her nose, while he continued speaking.  The
good man did not perceive her having done so ; but

her sister Bianca did ; and when he had departed, asked Katharina what was her reason.

"The odour of sanctity was too much for me ;" replied she. "I'm not worthy to stand so near it, I suppose. Of course, the reason friars wear baize gowns, is because woollen retains fumes well—the fume of holiness."

"For shame, sister !" exclaimed Bianca ; "what would our mother say ?"

"She would have me whipped, to teach me a keener relish for wholesome smells ; but it'll take a great deal of whipping to make me bear the same amount of sanctity that she can. But then, she's so very good, you know ; and I'm always naughty—at least, if I'm to judge by the many whippings and penances I get."

At last, Katharina forgot herself to padre Bonifacio in her mother's presence. She was running into her mother's room to call Bianca to dinner. Seeing the confessor there, she exclaimed "Ah, you're there, are you ? How do ? How do, and good-bye,—for dinner's serving, I'm hungry, and the sooner you're gone the better."

"How now, child ! Is that the way you speak to the holy father ! I'm amazed at you ! If ever I hear such a style of addressing his reverence again, you know what shall be your punishment."

"Yes, yes, I know ;" then turning to the padre, she repeated "Good-bye, good-bye ! And good-bye to my dinner too ;" added she ; "for I know I shall have to dine off dry bread now."

Dry bread for dinner was so frequently her punishment, that she tried to strip it of its terrors, and to vent her indignation against it, by turning it into jest, and inventing witticisms upon the subject. On one occasion, when her father bade her to come to table, she curtsied saucily, and said, "Thank you, pa' ; but I don't dine at home to-day ; I dine at my ordinary."

"Thine ordinary, child ! What dost mean ?"

" Dry bread ; that's my ordinary ; I ordinarily dine upon it ; and ordinary fare it is, I can tell you !"

Once her sister passed her, while she was eating her allotted portion in a corner, and she said :—" Look here, Bianca !  Here's bread ! such dry bread—bread that I don't ask for—but they give me a stone ; it's as hard as a stone.  Hardly I'm used by these stony-hearted creatures !"

" Remember, you speak of our parents ;" said Bianca.

" I thought parents were to treat their children tenderly !" retorted she.  " Here's tender treatment ! Here's tenderness for you !—no,—for me !  Here's softness !  Here's delicacy !  Why it's like a brick ! I can't get my teeth into it.  I shouldn't be surprised if it were to break them.  Marble or granite,—more fit to pave a church, or build a bridge, or a jail with, than to feed a daughter upon !  It's a week old, if it's a day.  No wonder it makes me ·crusty ; I shall turn into a crust, if they·give me much more of it."

Another time, she gave her mother a hint of her disgust, by inserting a clause in the prayer she was repeating by her side.  Madame Minola was very scrupulous in hearing her children repeat morning and night a long string of words arranged into prayers ; but which she never gave herself the trouble to explain to them, nor thought to ascertain whether they understood the spirit and meaning of that which they uttered.  They were even allowed ignorantly to parrot the most divine of prayers.

Now, when Katharina came to the petition for ‘ daily bread,’ she added :—" with meat to it."

" Profane child !" said her mother.

" Well, I do wish I could now and then get my daily bread with some butter upon it, or·a handful of fruit, to help me down with it ; it does stick in my throat so, day after day, you can't think ; it is so very dry and daily."

In short, poor Katharina was becoming, fast, a settled naughty child ; a little reprobate, hardened in her contumacy,—her rebellious ways of thinking and speaking. Always in disgrace ; never repenting. Perpetually being punished ; never amending. Her insolence, her pertness, her bad-temper, seemed to be given up as a hopeless case. She was looked upon as incorrigibly perverse, altogether disagreeable, and incurable. A domestic nuisance—but irremediable, though intolerable. People shrugged their shoulders, and endured her—as well as they could. She became an object of universal dislike and avoidance.

About this time, her godmother, aunt Antonia, came to Padua on a visit.

Madame Minola made many pathetic complaints to her sister, respecting the plague Katharina's unhappy disposition was to them all ; bemoaned herself that she should have given birth to such a wayward wicked child ; and wondered what she had done to deserve such an infliction.

"For an infliction she certainly is, sister. Her naughtiness makes her odious to every one. But, I fear, there's no help for it."

"Why so, sister ? She may be reclaimed, and made a comfort to you and her father, as well as to every one else, herself included. For the poor little thing, as she is, cannot be very comfortable or happy —to be thus at variance with all her friends."

" Oh, as for her—I've no concern for her discomfort ; she don't deserve that I should. A perverse, ill-conditioned, troublesome little hussy ! I've no patience with her !" said the mother.

" I fear so ;" answered the aunt quietly. " But I cannot see why she might not be made a better child ; she is naturally high-spirited—full of vivacity—these form an admirable basis for character, if only directed properly. A friend she could esteem and respect might do much with that nature, or I'm greatly mistaken."

" Esteem ! Respect ! She has neither, for any

one ! Why, she does not respect her parents—or even padre Bonifacio ! She minds nobody—she's utterly graceless and worthless ; and hasn't a notion of obeying anything but her own whims of pertness and insufferable rudeness."

" Might not some better notion be instilled into her ? Might she not be taught regard for others ;— deference, obedience, docility ? It is hard to set down one so young as incorrigible. It is dangerous to give a child a character for any particular fault ; it too frequently fixes the attribute. A child hearing itself constantly called sulky, or indolent, or headstrong, or pert, will learn to consider itself so, and come to act upon the character it has received. It acquires the habit of thinking of itself thus, and to believe that there is no use in attempting to be otherwise. It finds no better expected of it, and becomes confirmed in its original defect ; which probably, by other treatment, might have been destroyed,—or at any rate, weakened."

" It's all very fine talking, sister ;" returned madame Minola ; " you were always famous for thinking you could perform a duty better than any body else. But try the child yourself ; and you'll soon see whether she's to be made anything of, except the pert rudesby I've told you she is."

" I will try, my dear sister, since you give me leave ;" said Antonia ; " I will try to win her confidence—to see if I can't bring her to speak a little with me. She may be more tractable than you imagine. We have not seen much of each other, hitherto ; but I am not without hope of leading her to love her aunt and godmother."

" Do as you please, sister ;" replied madame Minola. " I'm sure, if you've any fancy for taking a troublesome brat in hand, I shall not hinder you. But you always were famous for liking to undertake disagreeable tasks. You found your account in one, certainly ; I wish you equal success in this."

Antonia was a staid sensible woman, with an inexhaustible stock of patience. When her niece Katharina found that she bore with her pert manners, never reproached her about them, never made them matter of remark, but answered her words quietly, and with entire disregard of the flippancy which too often accompanied them, she gradually dropped her insolent tone, when they spoke together ; this led to a greater ease ; the ease to a sense of comfort ; the comfort to a feeling of liking for the person with whom she was thus comfortable ; and so on, until she grew to entertain a stronger regard for her aunt Antonia, than she had ever before felt towards any human being.

When Antonia perceived that she had established this feeling of preference and confidence in her niece's mind, she ventured gently to remonstrate with her, as one friend might do with another, upon such points of her character, as most needed admonition.

"My dear child, what makes you behave so contemptuously to padre Bonifacio ?" said she to Katharina, one morning, as they sat together at work in the parlour, through which the father confessor passed on his way to madame Minola's room, upon observing the little girl give him one of her impertinent nods.

"I don't behave contemptuously to him. I don't care a fig about him. I detest him."

"Why should you detest him ?" said her aunt ; contenting herself with replying to one only of her inconsistent sentences.

"O, I don't know—I hate him—he has such a smeary voice ; such nasty wheedling ways ; such a creeping step. When he throws back his cowl, he has drops dotted all over his bald head—like rain on a cabbage-leaf ; and he wears such a filthy old baize gown. I hate the very sight of him."

"But have you never considered that his presence gives your mother great comfort ; that she esteems and reveres him ; and that it must give her great pain, to see him treated with rudeness ?"

"I don't treat him with rudeness—that is, I don't care how I treat him,—for I loathe him—a dirty old man !"

"But your mother sees something in him besides a dirty old man. She sees an attached friend, a faithful guide, a kind pastor ; one to whom she is accustomed to look up for counsel and assistance ; one whom she regards with veneration and gratitude. Ought not you to behave towards him a little more in accordance with her opinion of him, than with yours? Do you not think it would be well to try and see him in the light that she does, for her sake ?"

"Why should I try to oblige her, when she's so cross and unkind to me ?" said Katharina. "I never go near her but she scolds me, or finds fault with something I say or do. Why should I do any thing to oblige her ?"

"Because she's your mother ;" said Antonia emphatically.

"I know that, of course ; but"—Katharina was proceeding ; but as she looked up, she caught her aunt's eye fixed steadily upon her. There was a grave earnestness in its expression, that the child could not withstand, and her own eyelids drooped beneath the gaze.

Presently she said in a low tone :—"Mother's so peevish."

"So might you be peevish, had you as much pain to bear, as she has. Night and day,—day after day, and night after night, your mother suffers many hours of racking pain. When you are calmly sleeping in your bed, she tosses to and fro, restless, weary, wakeful with her pain. When you are running about the garden, happily playing, your limbs in action, your spirits gay, she is confined to her invalid-chair, vainly seeking to find a respite from pain, even in repose. Well may she be fretful, having to endure so much, from which there is scarcely a prospect of release, save in death. The time may come, my dear Kath-

arina, when, too late, you may wish that you had
never been the means of adding to all this pain she
has had to undergo ; that you had borne her fretful-
ness better ; that you had never been guilty of disrespect towards her. You will then regret having ill-
treated one whom she regards."

" I will try and think of this, when next I see padre
Bonifacio ;" sobbed the little girl ; for she was crying now, at her aunt's words ; " I'll try and behave
better to him ; indeed I will."

" Come to me, my dear child ;" said her aunt,
soothingly. " I would not have given you this pain,
but that I knew it would rouse you to better feelings,
and better conduct. My little Katharina does not
want for an affectionate heart ; and that will teach her
to be all we could wish, in time."

And so, perhaps, it might have been ; had that
heart continued beneath the guidance of the judicious
friend who now sought to awaken its gentler impulses.
But the attempt had scarce been made, ere it was un-
avoidably abandoned. Antonia was suddenly recalled
to Genoa by a summons from her husband, who had
injured his hand with a sharp-edged tool ; it was
feared, so deeply, that there was a doubt whether he
would ever recover its use sufficiently for future work.
Thus it proved ; and Camillo's inability to labour for
their support, involving the necessity of his wife's ex-
erting herself to earn bread for them both, prevented
her ever returning to Padua.

By this unfortunate occurrence, the first beneficial
influence that had ever been exercised over Katharina's
mind and heart, was withdrawn ; the patient care, the
winning kindness, the gentle yet earnest words which
might have curbed all that was wrong, while they
fostered all that was generous and right, were removed ; and the poor little girl, in the weakness of
unaided childhood, soon fell into her former petulance,
and wrong-headed ways.

Before, however, the effect of her aunt's visit upon

Katharina had faded, her mother suddenly died. The unexpectedness of the event ; the remembrance of her aunt's words ; this speedy fulfilment of what they had hinted at as probable, combined to overwhelm the child with remorse. She felt with all the keenness of her vehement nature. She suffered the tortures of an accusing conscience, when she remembered her frequent insolence to the mother who was gone for ever. She writhed with the pangs of self-reproach and unavailing repentance, as she recalled how often she had been disobedient, rude, and disregardful to the suffering invalid, who would never return to the sick chair she had so long occupied, and before which Katharina now flung herself on her knees, in a transport of vain sorrow.

She abandoned herself to the most passionate grief. Her pillow that night was literally wet with her tears. She flung herself to and fro in the terrible unrest of remorse,—even worse than that of sickness, which had been her mother's. But as she thought of the many wakeful nights that mother had passed, thus, like herself, unable to get peace or ease, her tears and sobs burst out afresh.

Her sleepless night sent her with white cheeks, swollen eyes, and choking throat, next morning, to the breakfast-table.

Her sister placed food before her.

"How d'ye expect me to eat, when my throat's full ? I can't swallow," she said.

"Thy grief's too shrewish-violent to last, I fear me, Katharina ;" said her father. "Thou wert ever too untoward with thy mother when she lived, to let us think thou mourn'st her very sincerely now she's dead. Dry thy crocodile tears ; and have done with this show of grief."

O words of reproach ! No mustard-grain seems smaller seed, yet what fearful sowing is yours ! Words of reproach lightly let fall, yet yielding poisonous blossoms ! Words of reproach, dropped unheeded, yet bringing forth deadliest fruit ! And no soil so fatally sure to nurture them into this baleful maturity as the domestic hearth. Let those who would preserve home in peace and happiness beware of even the shadow of reproach. It is thistle-down for seeming insignificancy—but of like insidious propagation. It is gone with a breath—takes flight, and is forgotten by him who carelessly puffs it forth ; but it scatters mischief and generates evil.

Her father's reproach roused all that was bad in Katharina's disposition. Those tears of hers, might have been turned to gentle account ; her young sorrow might have been the means of drawing her to softening thoughts, and worthy resolutions ; but she was taunted with them as insincere, when she knew them to be genuine ; she was reproached with them as a pretence, when she felt they were only too true ; and she resolved henceforth to hide them,—to struggle with them,—to crush and repress her sorrow as something that was misunderstood by others, and painful to herself.

As a natural consequence, she grew more hard and saucy than ever. She was not only acerb and disrespectful in speech ; but she indulged in all sorts of perverse contemptuous ways. She would go about the house on a Sunday, between mass and vespers, with a needle and thread stuck on her side, or with her knitting-pins peeping from her apron-pocket ; and if remonstrated with, would reply :—" Well, I haven't been working, you know ; I've been to mass as well as you."

On a fast day, she would make a parade of throwing a beef-bone, or a mutton shank to the dog ; and when the expostulation came, which she hoped would follow, she gloried in answering :—" The dog has no soul, I suppose ? Where's the harm of letting him have a meal of meat ? He needn't fast ; it's quite enough, methinks, if we do."

A letter addressed to her father, was allowed to

wait several hours in a corner on a table ; and when he asked her why she had not mentioned it to him, she said :—"You told me to hold my tongue, this morning ; how should I speak to you, or tell you anything ? How did I know but you might bid me be silent again ; or chide me for being officious ?"

Another time, when a lad brought him a message, Katharina happening to open the door, slammed it to again in the messenger's face ; and afterwards this was her excuse ; "You said you wouldn't be disturbed ; how should I dream you didn't mean what you said ? If you knew your own mind a little better, I might know how to please ye, mayhap !"

"Thou hast a parlous curst temper of thine own, girl, that's a sure thing ;" said her father. "Why canst not take pattern by thy sister ? See how biddable and mild she is. Canst not try to be like her ?"

"No, I can't ; and what's more, I won't. I wouldn't be such a piece of bread-and-butter goodness as she is, even if I could. Why, if a wasp were to settle on her hand, she'd allow it to stay and sting her, rather than brush it rudely away. She'd let a mad cow toss her, before she'd frighten the poor thing by flirting a kerchief in its face. Her toes might be trodden upon till they were smashed flat, ere she'd hurt a person's feelings by begging they'd mind where they were stepping. None of your spiritless milk-and-water virtue for me, I thank ye, pa' !"

"Better an' thou hadst a little of her want of spirit, perhaps ; thou hast far too much of thine own, child. But thou'lt never be as good as she is !" said the father.

"Heaven forbid !" she replied.

"Thou pray'st amiss, wench ; well would it be for thyself—and still better for us all, were thou likely to be but half as good. But e'en that much, thou'lt never be."

"Never !" she exclaimed. "Never ; so long as you keep holding her up as a pattern and a model to me.　I hate model people.　They're odious in themselves ; odious in their popularity ; for ever perched up on a brazen pedestal of conceit and approval."

" Go to ;　I'm weary of thy froward humours ;" said Baptista.　" Begone, I say, and send thy sister hither to me."

" Thank you, pa', for dismissing me ;　I'm as weary of my stay, as you can be.　You don't send me from you more willingly that I go, I promise you."

There was a large entertainment given at the country-house of signior Gremio, to which signior Minola's little girls, among other young people, were invited. The old gentleman had made the party a juvenile one, in compliment to his son ;　whom he considered still a boy, though he was past forty years of age.　The octogenarian had so long been in the habit of looking upon him as a child, compared with himself, that he really thought of him in no other light.　The son had always been called young signior Gremio, to distinguish him from his father ;　and this had farther helped the notion.

There was to be dancing ;　sports and games of all kinds ;　and a tent was spread in the grounds, with refreshments, and a cold collation.　The old gentleman bustled about with as much animation as his tottering limbs would allow ;　rubbing his hands, and taking great interest in seeing that all his young guests were duly amused.

" Where's my boy ?" he would exclaim at intervals ; " Oh, yonder ;　I see him.　Among that group of lads, watching their game of mora ;　but he should be over here, helping me to receive his young lady guests. But he'll be here presently, my dears ;　never fear, never fear."

" I don't ;" said Katharina.

" That's very good of you, my dear.　And when he comes, I'll make him get up a dance, and he shall be your partner.　But, you see, I don't like to disturb him from what amuses him ; it's natural for young people to amuse themselves ; yes, yes, I can make allowances ; young people will be young people."

"Not always,—sometimes they're elderly ;" said she. "But I suppose you can make allowance even for elderly young people. When he's as old as you are, perhaps he'll be more steady ;" added she, glancing at the old man's shaking head, and trembling hands.

"I'm afraid you're a bit of a rogue, Miss Katharina ;" said the good-natured old gentleman, not willing to perceive any malice in her observation ; "you're a wit, quite a wit, I declare,—and wits are apt to be sad rogues."

"That's not saying much for their liveliness ;" said she. "But here comes your middle-aged man,— your boy, I mean."

"My dear boy," said his father, "here are some young ladies dying with impatience for a dance. Set one afoot, pr'ythee ; and set their pretty feet in motion, as soon as may be,—there's no time to be lost."

"No truly ;" said Katharina ; "our dancing days may be too soon over."

"Will miss Bianca favor me with her hand ?" said the son, with a flourish of his hat under his arm.

"My sister has too much grace, to like to see grey hairs stand uncovered before her ;" said Katharina. "Pray put on your hat, signior, lest you take cold in your head."

"Fie, sister ; how can you ?" murmured Bianca, as she put her hand into the gentleman's arm ; who led her away, looking mightily disconcerted.

"You mustn't be left without a partner, my dear miss ;" said the old gentleman to Katharina. "Let's see what we can do for you. Here, Giulio !" cried he, calling to a young lad, who was cracking and eating 'pignoli' at a little distance ; "come hither, child ; and offer thy hand to this young lady.'

The lad lounged towards them, glanced at Katharina's face, and said, " I'm afraid."

" ' Afraid !' I shan't eat it ;" said she.

" I don't know that ;" he answered. " You look as if you'd snap at anything, that comes in your way. I shouldn't wonder if you'd bite my nose off, an' I said anything you didn't fancy."

" Like enough ;" said she. " If you deserved it, you'd catch it, I promise you ; I'm not one to stick at anything when I'm affronted ; I care not who knows as much."

" ' Catch it ?' Catch what ? Some of your bites or scratches, I suppose ; but as I've no fancy for scars, I shan't trust my skin near you, nor offer my hand to any such miss Miscetta, I thank you, miss Minola."

" Do you call me a cat, sirrah ?" said she, with sparkling eyes.

" Gently, gently, my good master Giulio ; are these your manners to a lady ?"

" I see no lady ;" said the lad.

" Well, well ; to this young gentlewoman."

" Nor gentlewoman neither ; certainly, no gentle woman."

" Well, well ; to this little girl. Dear, dear, what am I to do with these quarrelsome children !" exclaimed the old gentleman in great perplexity. " My dears, will you do me the favor to be good, till somebody comes to help me make you friends ? will you be so obliging as to keep quiet, just for a minute, till I can call somebody to part you ? O, here, son Gremio !—I'm glad the dance is over ; you're come in happy time to preserve peace. Our young friends are falling out, I fear me."

" Come you with me, Giulio ;" said the younger signior Gremio ; " let you and me go seek some refreshment for these young ladies ; they must need something cool after all this heat and dancing."

" Bring some ' cedrata,' or ' limonata ;' they are iced, and will be pleasant ;" said his father,

" Better a little ' semata ; ' are not the others too sour, think you, sir ?" said Giulio ; " we have acid enough, already."

" Be off with ye, child ; and do as my son would have you. He'll find what is fitting, and nice, I'll warrant me ;" said the old gentleman, pushing the boy away by the shoulder ; but unable to forbear smiling.

" Pert monkey !" muttered Katharina.

" Never mind him, my dear ;" said her host. " He doesn't mean any harm, bless you ; it's only his joke. Giulio's always full of his jokes. My son don't mind him. My boy rather likes him ; they're quite friends and comrades."

" I wish he'd keep his jokes for his friend, then,— and for those who like 'em—I don't ;" said she ; " and if he treats me to any more of them, I shall just—— "

She was interrupted by the return of the younger signior Gremio with some fruit and cakes, which he presented to the sisters.

Katharina had no sooner helped herself to some strawberries, than master Giulio stepped forward, and pouring some cream over them, said mischievously, " mew, mew ; have a little milk, pussy ?"

The next instant, the whole contents of her plate were chucked in his face.

" My dears,—my dears,—pray—pray !" said the old gentleman.

" Now why should she be so enraged when I liken her to a cat, if she didn't feel the truth of the portrait ?" laughed Giulio, who had burst into a roar of enjoyment, as he received the deluge of strawberries and cream. " I'll be bound her sister wouldn't be angry, though, if I should tell her she were like a cat, —and yet she has nearly as much of a cat in her, as 'tother."

" Who, I ?" said Bianca, in soft wonder.

" Yes, you, you ; mew, mew ;" said the boy,

mimicking her way of speaking. "You sit there, with your fore-feet primly before you ; your eyes opening and shutting, demurely winking ; your sleek looks, and your pur-pur-purry voice. And then you've got such velvet paws ;" said he, touching the back of her hand.

They couldn't help laughing, Bianca included.

"Are they so very soft ?" said she, smoothing her hand against the boy's ruddy cheek.

"Yes ; I hope they conceal no claws ;" said he.

"Don't make too sure of that ;" said Katharina ; "velvet paws can put forth talons as sharp as razors, —and that, when you think it least."

"At any rate, they're kept in reserve ;" said he ; "they don't appear till occasion calls them forth ; even that's better than those horrible claws which are displayed at all seasons, unsheathed, and menacing, ready to rip and rend on the slightest provocation ; those frightful cats, with their green eyes, swollen tails, and backs always up ; constantly prepared to spring upon you at a moment's warning."

"At any rate, they put you on your guard ;" said Katharina, "which is more than can be said for the velvet-paws. The one makes no secret of her being ready to fly at you, if you offend her ; the other lies in wait to attack you, and give you a sly gash, when you least expect it."

"But I confess, of the two, I prefer the velvet-pawed cat, to the fierce, green-eyed, spread-clawed cat ; if you'll permit me a choice, miss Miscetta Mi-nola ;" said he.

"I have heard that men prefer the animal that creeps stealthily and demurely, all innocence in her looks, pretending to be thinking of nothing, while the whole time she's watching how best she may pounce upon his weaknesses ;" returned she ; "and I suppose you, sir boy, affect to ape their taste. I care nothing, not I, for your tastes or your preferences ; but I'll thank you to call neither my sister nor myself, a cat, any more ; and I give you fair warning, that if you hint at such a thing again, I'll give you as sound a box o' the ear, as you can well imagine, with all your fine fancies, of claws, and paws, and green eyes."

"No, will you really, Miscetta ?" said he.

Slap came a swinging cuff against the side of his head ; but as he only laughed, and repeated " puss, puss, puss," a shower of blows followed ; and grasping a few clumps of his hair in one hand, she fairly belaboured him with the other, until signior Gremio the younger, assisted by one or two of the other guests, came to the rescue, and drew her off.

Giulio was still roaring with laughter, as he shouted, " O never mind, let her alone, she'll soon tire herself. See, the bird is still unwounded by Kate Cat ! He has strength left to fly out of pussy's reach." Saying which, he sprang up, caught hold of some low branches of a tree just above his head and swung himself up among them. Here he remained carelessly dangling his legs, and whistling ; while he pulled some more ' pignoli ' out of his pocket, and sat contentedly cracking and eating them.

By-and-by he varied his amusement by pelting the company with the shells ; slily contriving that the major part of them should hit Katharina.

She looked up wrathfully. " How dare you ?" she said.

" You'll see how I dare. Don't ye like it, Miscetta ?"

" If you do it again, or say that again, I'll have my revenge ;" said she furiously.

That same second, the words were repeated ; and the next, a large stone that lay at Katharina's feet, was picked up and flung violently into the midst of the tree.

It hit him. It struck his temple ; and stunned, he fell forwards. There was a rustle among the boughs —they fortunately broke his fall—and then the lad dropped to the ground. The guests started up, in consternation ; ran towards the spot ; and raised him in their arms.  Blood was oozing from the wound in his head ; but he was insensible.

This incident abruptly broke up the party.  The guests withdrew, holding up their hands, and exclaiming at the ungoverned temper of the little girl who had occasioned the accident ; the young lad was lifted into the house, and laid on a couch, while a surgeon was sent for to examine his hurts ; the two signior Gremios deplored the unfortunate conclusion of their entertainment, and addressed themselves to the recovery of their young friend, despatching a servant to conduct Katharina and Bianca home.

As they walked along in silence, Bianca whispered :—" What a shocking thing to have happened !  I shall dread it coming to father's ears ; he'll be so angry.  Yet it's my duty to tell him ; for I suppose you won't ?"

" Why should you suppose so ?  I shall ;" said Katharina.

A pause.

" He's badly wounded, I fear ; did you see the bleeding dent upon his forehead, where the stone hit him, sister ?" said Bianca.

Katharina shuddered ; then recovering herself, she said :—" What did he torment me for, then ?  I told him I'd be revenged,—if he went on so any more. He had fair warning."

" If the boy should die ?" murmured Bianca.

" How can I help it ?  It's his fault—I told him I'd have my revenge ; and I took it.  But don't be afraid—he'll not die—such disagreeable hateful boys as he, never do die."

" But if he should ;" softly persisted Bianca.

" Pshaw ! he won't, I tell you.  How you worrit, Bianca ; and harp upon a thing, when you've once said it.  He'll not die, never fear."

" I have no cause ; it's you who have to fear, sister, and who ought to fear ;" said Bianca.

"But I don't, you see ;" said Katharina.    And here the matter ended for the present.

However there it could not end, eventually.    The boy, thanks to his youth and his good constitution, did recover ; but signior Baptista was so shocked at the injury that his daughter's rashness had caused ; he was so much vexed at the scandal, which this public exposure of the violence of her temper occasioned, that he resolved upon a step which he hoped might have the good effect of reforming her, while it offered the present advantage of removing her from the observation of society.    He determined to place his two daughters as pensioners in a convent, for the finishing of their education.

There were two convents near ; both highly famed for the young ladies' schools attached to them.    One had the name of extreme simplicity, even to plainness, in its appointments ; of strictness and rigour, even to austerity, in its ordinances.    The other was said to be more lenient in its regulations ; and consequently was more fashionable, more in favor among those who styled themselves ' the leading and genteel families ' of Padua.

At first, signior Baptista, in hesitating to which of these convents he should send his daughters, rather inclined towards the austere one, as more likely to effect the cure which he desired in his contumacious child ; but at length, considering himself to be among ' the leading men ' in his native town, and wishing his girls to take their place among the genteel young ladies of Padua, he decided in favor of the more fashionable establishment.    In his deliberations, he did not ostensibly shape his conduct by these motives ; on the contrary, he told himself that it was because he did not think it was fair to punish Bianca for her sister's faults by sending her to a rigorous school, though such a one might be advisable for Katharina ; and as for the latter, why, he could always hold the more austere convent as a threat in reserve, should the other fail in bringing her to a suitable state of decorum.

Katharina and Bianca were accordingly placed as boarders among the ladies of the Holy Petticoat; such being the name of the fashionable sisterhood, in honor of a relic of great virtue and sanctity, which they possessed,—a portion of a sacred garment miraculously preserved and bequeathed; while the rival con‑vent was known as that of the Sisters of Humility.

On the first introduction of the two daughters of signior Minola, they were presented in great state to the lady Abbess, who was condescendingly affable; and made a little speech to them, full of affectionate unction, and coaxing patronage, telling them she was sure they would prove shining ornaments to the holy community of which it was now their privilege to form a part.

"We're not going to become nuns—don't think it;" abruptly exclaimed Katharina.

"You would not be fit to become a nun, my child, with that rebellious tone of yours, which I fear betokens something of a rebellious spirit. But we'll soon set all that to rights; we'll soon tame down that wicked little lion of a spirit, till it becomes a lamb, a very lamb." And the lady Abbess smiled through her set teeth, and smiled through her half-closed eyes, as she looked at Katharina with a placid consciousness of power.

"There's very little of a lamb in me, as you'll find;" said Katharina; "a lamb ends by becoming a sheep, and I've no notion of settling down into a fleecy fool, to be sheared, driven, slaughtered, roasted, and eaten up."

"'Very little' there may be; and I fear, 'very little' there is; but that little we'll find out, my child, depend on't; for all our sakes. Saint Agnes be praised! thou hast been blessedly sent hither, amongst our holy flock!"

"Not to be a nun, I tell you!"

The lady Abbess again smiled through the row of teeth between her slightly parted lips, and smiled through her half-closed eyes, as she surveyed the figure of the child, standing there with clenched hands, flushed cheek, and defiant look.

There was something in the expression of quiet, assured triumph, with which the Abbess sat thus regarding her, in silent superiority, that galled Katharina to the quick.

She stamped her foot, and repeated "Not to be a nun, I tell you !"

"Umph ?" said the Abbess in a silvery tone of enquiry, as if she had not heard what had just been said, in the loudest and most violent of voices.

"Not to be a nun, I tell you !" was again repeated in a shriek.

"Sister, sister, remember it is the reverend lady Abbess you are speaking to !" interposed Bianca.

"What's that to you ? or to me ?  Why need you interfere ?"  And a smart slap of the face followed.

"Tie that little vixen's hands behind her ;" said the lady Abbess in a bland voice, to one or two of the nuns who stood nearest. Katharina kicked and struggled ; but it was done.

"It was my intention to have given a little feast to welcome these two young ladies among us ;" resumed the lady Abbess ; "but since the elder has seen fit to conduct herself in a manner as unexpected as it is reprehensible, she shall not be permitted to partake of the festivities, but shall be satisfied with dry bread."

"Ah ha !  Dry bread !  My old friend—or rather, foe !  But it's too stale a punishment to frighten me.  I'm become accustomed to it.  ' Satisfied with dry bread ! '  Why, it'll be quite a regale to me, for old acquaintance' sake."

"And not only shall she have no other dinner than dry bread," proceeded the Abbess, with the same smile, and in an even tone, as if she were conscious of no interruption to her last speech, but were going on in continuation,—"not only dry bread, which in itself, as an inaugural dinner, would be disgrace enough to a child of feeling ; but you will be so good as to see, sister Brigida, that she eats it in presence of the whole school, while they are enjoying the dainties I have provided for to-day's little festival."

"See if I eat it, though ! I'd rather starve," said Katharina.

"And now, remove her ;" added the Abbess, with her smile, and her even tone.

The scene in the refectory was such as had never before been witnessed in that place of discipline and order.

First the young ladies were marshalled in, Bianca among them, and took their places at the dining-tables ; a nun presiding at the head of each, a teacher at the other end, with lay sisters in attendance, to hand the plates, and fill the drinking-mugs.

Then the prisoner, Katharina, was ushered in, between two meek-looking nuns ; she was brought to the centre of the room, and placed at a small table, upon which was a thick slice of bread upon a trencher.

But the moment her hands were untied, that she might commence her dinner, the first use she made of them was to skime both bread and trencher to the other end of the hall.

There was a look of amazement at her daring, upon all the school-girl faces turned towards her.

The meek-looking nuns refastened the knots upon her wrists, picked up the trencher and bread, and brought them back ; but no sooner replaced before her, than table, and all, were knocked over with one kick of her foot.

The school-girl faces expressed increasing interest in this singular exhibition of bold and persevering defiance.

"Reverend mother insists upon her eating it ; she enjoined me to see her will performed ;" said sister Brigida.

The meek-looking nuns again picked up the bread ; broke it into morsels, and put some of them to Katharina's lips.   She took one into her mouth, chewed it hastily, then sent forth the fragments in a shower of crumbs.

There was a titter ran through the ranks of scholars.   The nuns began to feel there was danger to the solemnity of their supremacy, rather than salutary terror, in the example.   They hastened, therefore, to put an end to the scene, by procuring an order from the Abbess, that the refractory new-comer should be lodged forthwith in a certain solitary chamber, devoted to the reception of culprits convicted of heinous offences.

Here, shut up in darkness, and debarred from all society, she was left to reflect upon her errors, and to learn repentance.   She did neither ; but she suffered intensely.   The confinement enraged her ; the silence oppressed her ; the darkness dismayed her.   At first she tore about the narrow space like a little wild thing, thumping at the doors, wrenching at the windows, and beating madly against the walls ; then uttered shriek upon shriek, demanding in frantic shouts and screams to be let out ; then she sobbed passionately, and flung herself upon the floor, striking and scratching at it, as if she would have dug herself a passage through.   Then she raved aloud again ; and then listened for an answer :—but when no sound reached her, in reply to her outcries, the echoes of her own voice seemed to mock her, and the silence that followed was like an insult.   It irritated her with its mute contempt ; it so completely baffled her spirit of resistance, her love of contest, and opposition ; she would fain have had it take a tangible shape that she might have struggled with it ; she ground her teeth at it in impotence of rage and defeated will.

Gradually, its continuance frightened her ; it seemed to vanquish her by its sheer passive pertinacity ; she felt quelled and subdued by its monotony.   Its effect was aided by the darkness which surrounded her.

Her screams subsided into moans, her sobs into sighs ; and she lay panting and trembling, cowering down in a corner. But she never once repented of her fault—she never once confessed to herself that it was her own violence which had incurred this punishment ; she only blamed their injustice, accused their tyranny, who had subjected her to such cruelties, and resented their having the power to inflict them. She would not own that her misconduct had caused her this suffering ; but she resolved that in future she would be more guarded in her behaviour. She did not intend to set about curing herself of insolence, or insubordination ; but she thought she would henceforth take care so to keep them within rule, as not again to draw upon her the terrors of that dark solitude.

She kept her resolution tolerably well. She put severe constraint upon herself, so that her outbreaks should not come beneath the immediate notice of the lady Abbess, or any of the nuns who were mistresses in the school. She with great difficulty reined in her tongue when she came in contact with the former ; for there was something in that smile through the half-closed eyes and teeth which peculiarly stung her. When she met it, directed towards her, she felt every fibre tingle, every pulse quicken, every drop of blood throb and rush to her fingers' ends. But she learned to master the show, at least, of contumacy, lest she should offend one who had power to order her to the dark room. Her violence of temperament was smothered ; but it was not extinct. Radical cure of a bad passion is not effected by such means. Subjection is not conviction. Fear may induce the show of submission ; but through reasoning affection alone, is genuine compliance obtained. Tyranny but inculcates the meanness of hypocrisy—the expediency of apparent yielding. Love only can truly subjugate a haughty spirit. Through love alone and its divine teachings are evil feelings to be eradicated, and virtuous emotions implanted in their stead.

There was just now another chance for this little girl to have been redeemed from her defect of disposition ; but like the former one, its influence was lost to her.

In the chapel belonging to the convent, there hung a picture of the marriage of St. Catherine. It represented the virgin saint, kneeling at the feet of the infant Saviour. By her side was the symbol of her martyrdom, the torturing wheel ; but her face shone with holy fervour, hope, and extacy, as she bent to receive the ring of espousal from the hand of the sacred Babe, who leaned from his mother's lap to place it upon her finger. First, Katharina came to regard this picture with curiosity, as being that of her patron saint ; then she came to admire it for its great beauty, and the glories of its painting ; then she loved to linger near it, and gaze upon it, for the sake of the benign expression upon the maternal countenance, for the sake of the radiant sweetness in the smile of the Babe, and for the sake of the happiness she felt in watching the look of hope, of joy, of heavenly aspiration on the face of the virgin-saint, her namesake. It seemed a comfort, a delight, to let her eyes rest upon so much of tranquil, unearthly gladness as shone there. She felt the turbulent sensations that usually agitated her soul, lulled and soothed, and set at rest, by looking upon this picture. She felt better, as well as happier, while she gazed ; and she would often linger behind her companions, when they left the chapel, that she might stay and enjoy the delicious frame of mind into which the contemplation of this picture threw her. She would sit like one entranced, forgetful of time ; the nuns, her schoolfellows, her daily vexations, her petulances, grievances, ill-humours, all and everything, faded from her view ; she beheld nothing but the picture,—felt nothing but the beatitude it inspired.

One evening, after vespers, when her schoolfellows had all retired, she remained thus absorbed, and was sitting in her usual trance of delighted contemplation, opposite the picture, when one of the nuns, who had missed her, returned to the chapel in quest of her.

" So, you are here, my dear child ;" said the nun, in the confidential whisper peculiar to her vocation ; " neither sister Fidelia, nor sister Brigida, nor sister Lucia, could imagine where you were ; and they want you in the school-room ; and they sent me to seek you ; and to tell you that——"

" I wish you wouldn't hiss so ;" interrupted Katharina, to whom the whispered chatter of the nun was insupportable, jarring as it did with her then mood of mind ; " can't you speak out what you have to say— and not ish-sh-sh-sh there, like a serpent."

" A serpent ? Holy mother forbid !" ejaculated the nun, crossing herself hastily. " Far be it from me to bring anything belonging to the enemy of mankind here. Not even the hiss of the old gentleman ought to approach this place. But you know, Katharina, my dear, it isn't seemly to speak loud in chapel ; so I must whisper what I have to say."

" And what have you to say ?" said Katharina.

" Why, I told you before ; only you're so pettish you never give yourself time to listen to what's said. They want you in the school-room for evening lessons."

" Pshaw ! lessons ! I was studying better here. I wish they wouldn't disturb me."

" Studying ? you mean, praying, I suppose ; chapel isn't the place to study in. Ah, I see ! you were praying to your patron saint, blessed Santa Katharina. Only you should kneel to her, and not sit lounging there in your chair, when you pray."

" I wasn't praying ;" replied she.

" What were you doing here, then, child ?"

" I told you ; studying. I was studying that glorious face, to get it by heart. It does me good ; and I should like to have it always with me."

" What do you mean, child ? Studying a saint's

face ? getting it by heart ?   What bold, heathenish
ideas !   But it's of a piece with your sitting, when
you ought to be kneeling before the blessed picture."

" It is a blessed picture ; but I feel its blessedness
better when I'm sitting, than when I'm kneeling.   My
knees get stiff and cramped, and the pain distracts me
from the sensation I have of the blessing of looking
upon that face,—upon all the faces, for they are all
beautiful and blessed."

" What a strange way you have of talking, child !
Somehow, you shock me, with your odd manner of
expressing yourself."

Katharina did not reply ; she was again lost in rapturous contemplation of the picture.

Suddenly she said :—" I have found why the face
of the Madonna so delights me.   It is just such a
kind, gentle, good face as my aunt Antonia's.   It is
very like her.   It never struck me till this moment ;
but it is very like her."

The nun started ; again crossed herself ; and exclaimed—" Santissima Madre !   What are you saying ?   It absolutely horrifies me to hear you attach such
mundane notions to the picture of our blessed lady.
Come ; let us leave the chapel.   If I hear any more
such profanity, I shall have to report you to the
Superior."

Although the nun did not actually carry a formal
complaint to the lady Abbess about Katharina's profane ideas respecting this picture, yet in the tittle-
tattling way which grows upon those nuns whose orig-
inally-limited supply of brains dwindles down to a
mere nothing, in the round of trifles to which it is for
the most part confined in its exercise, the matter soon
got wind.   It was whispered about, that Katharina
had strange fancies of her own about the picture in
question.   A grand mystery was made of it—as of
all occurrences there, however trivial.

In a convent, as on board a ship, during a long sea-
voyage, minutest incidents become important ; the

slightest events assume interest ; insignificant things are magnified into marvels of curiosity and investigation. A gull flying near the mast-head—a knot of sea-weed—a passing cloud—are noteworthy objects to passengers, weary from very idleness, on the look-out, and prepared to be grateful, for anything that may vary the monotony and inactivity of their watery journey. So, a frown of the lady Abbess, a significant cough of one of the nuns, a hem more than usual, or more than can be accounted for by a cold, from one of the teachers, is sufficient, to put a whole convent-school in a state of animated discussion for days. " Is it a bead mis-told ? Can it be that inadvertent gape of Laura Pigrizia, last evening at complin ? Do you think it was observed ? Foolish thing ! How could she do it ? Or was it that careless toad, Nina Trascura ? Did you hear what a lump she let her missal fall, t'other morning ? just as father Pietro was beginning the ' Asperges ' !" &c. &c. &c.

With still keener interest was the rumoured story of Katharina's odd notions about the picture discussed. There was a general huddling together, a closing of bended heads, with whispered confabulations, and stolen glances in her direction, when next the school-girls repaired to the chapel.

Katharina felt that she was observed,—watched ; her wrath was rising ; but she stifled her indignation as well as she could, knowing that such an indecorum as an outbreak in chapel would be severely punished. She sat therefore, biting her lips, swelling, and swallowing ; compressing her hands till the nails cut against the palms,—almost to pain ; casting, now and then, scorching glances at her companions, in return for their inquisitive looks.

But the moment service was over, and the chapel was quitted, she flamed out.

The tribe of girls was pouring forth into the play-ground, down a flight of stone steps which led into it ; they tripped by twos and threes, some hand-in-hand, some with arms clasped round each other's waists, some flying alone, but all rushing onwards, eager for play, and chattering at the top of their voices.

Presently, high and shrill above them all, sounded that of Katharina Minola.

"Stop!  Come back, all of you! I want to speak to you!  Stop, I tell you!"

Involuntarily they checked their steps, and stood in groups around the base of the stone staircase, at the head of which was Katharina, surveying them.

"What were you all staring at?"

A pause ; while the troop of school-girls looked at each other, disconcerted.

"What were you all staring at, I say, in the chapel to-day?"

Still no answer ; while five or six girls who had unwittingly lingered behind their companions, and were thus standing near Katharina, suddenly made a dart past her, and flew down the steps to join the rest.

"Just like sheep, I declare!" laughed she, scornfully ; "what one does, the other does.  But what were you all staring at, to-day, I ask you once more ? I should say you stared as hard as eagles, if anything so sheepish could look like the king of birds."

"I suppose you mean to say you're like the sun, if we stared like eagles ;" screamed a giggling voice from among the crowd below.

"Who said that ?" said Katharina, darting a piercing glance into the midst of them ; "let her come up, whoever it was, and say it again, to my face, and see if I won't pitch her right down from top to bottom of the steps."

"It's all very fine, twitting us with staring ; why you yourself will outstare an eagle,—or any body else, when you're in one of your tantrums !" said the same giggling voice, which was echoed in such myriad giggles and titters, running through the bevy of school-girls, that it was impossible for Katharina to distinguish the speaker.   All at once, the giggles subsided ; and a sudden gravity stole over the up-turned faces.

Katharina, who was scanning them eagerly, per-ceived the change ; and also, by the direction of their eyes, saw that it was caused by some object immedi-ately behind herself.

She turned, and beheld the lady Abbess ; standing close to her elbow, with arms folded, and person drawn up to its full height. Confused thoughts of flinging herself against the reverend mother, of upset-ting her, and tumbling her headlong down the flight of steps,—even a keen sense of the pleasure it would be, to see one so dignified and imperturbable, bundling helplessly over,—flashed wildly through the brain of the child ; but a second glance at the face and figure of the Superior, sufficed to show even her impetuosity the folly of any such attempt. The shrewd glassy eye, all the more stern for the cold smile with which it gleamed through the quivering half-closed lids ; the compressed lips, the set teeth, the folded arms, the firm erect mien, all told the utter futility of hoping to move—either physically or morally—such a woman.

She stood thus for some moments, transfixing her with those sharp slantwise glances ; until she seemed satisfied with their effect, and knew that they had gained her the mastery. Then she said, in her even voice :—" I have heard something of this. And so you do not like to be stared at, Katharina Minola ? Then you should learn to comport yourself a little less singularly, my child. We will take order that it shall be so. You shall learn to pray before a holy picture, as other people do, not study it ; and then perhaps when you affect no singularity, your companions will not be disposed to wonder at you, or stare at you ; you will be spared that, my child, if it affront you. I am willing to spare the feelings of all my flock as much as may be, and I expect, in return, that they will not offend me by affecting singularity, which I hold to be a sinful and dangerous vanity,"

" I don't affect—I hate affectation—I——" stammered Katharina.

" Be silent, my child, while I speak ;" interrupted the lady Abbess. " In order that you may obtain an insight into your error, and learn to regard that picture in its proper light, I desire you will repeat a thirty days' prayer, together with the seven penitential psalms, upon your knees, morning and evening, fasting, in front of that sacred picture ; and may this penance serve to cleanse you of your past sin, and inspire you with better and more fitting thoughts for the time. Pax vobiscum ; et benedicite, my child !"

" But I can't,—I won't"—began Katharina passionately.

" You will either perform the penance I enjoin you, or go into solitary confinement for a week ;" said the abbess, as she withdrew. " I would fain be lenient. I give you your choice, my child."

Nothing less than the threatened terrors of the dark room, would have induced Katharina to go through with the other penance. As it was, she performed it ; but how ? In a spirit of repugnance, of mutiny, of all that was destructive to salutary effect. She kneeled, it was true ; but with heart unlowly, unreverential, full of indignation and rebellion. She repeated the appointed words, but it was with distracted attention, thoughts wandering and inappropriate. She resented the compelled utterance of what she felt to have no consonance with the ideas she attached to the picture. She abhorred the mechanical repetition of these sentences that carried with them no one echo of the emotions inspired by gazing on those sublime countenances. In the constantly recurring unwillingness, and disgust of her task, in the sense of its unsuitableness, its uselessness, its very mockery, as it seemed to her, she learned to associate feelings of discomfort with the picture itself ; and by the time her thirty days' penance was concluded, she had come to look upon it with nearly as much reluctance, as she had formerly gazed with eagerness. The holy awe, the tender fascination, with which this painting had once inspired her, might have been made the source of chastening self-examination, of worthy endeavours ; but it had been turned into a means of tyranny and wrong teaching, and the opportunity for future good was lost. Passionate temperaments are apt to be influenced by Art. Their very ardour and susceptibility render them peculiarly open to impressions for good or evil through the senses, the imagination, the intellectual faculties,—all of which are appealed to, in high Art. A fine painting, a solemn strain of music, might produce powerful effects upon such a disposition as Katharina's ; while upon one of softer mood, it should produce nothing beyond a perception of beauty. Had the strong hold which that picture originally took upon her feelings, been carefully fostered, wisely aided, and holily directed, it might have wrought her incalculable benefit, remoulded her character, and developed its excellences ; but a pernicious bias had been given, and the very strength of her original impressions had made the harm done, the greater. Ever after that period, Katharina as earnestly shunned, as she had formerly sought, looking upon that picture.

And now the annual distribution of prizes was about to take place. For many weeks previous, the school was in a bustle of preparation. There was to be a grand exhibition of the works of the school ; recitations of poetry, and singing in parts, were to be given by the young ladies. Parents were to be invited, that they might see their children show off, and receive the rewards of merit, and of emulation ; to say nothing of those that might be due for vanity, envy, and malice.

It was a striking feature in this display, that all works of utility were omitted. Nothing but fancy-works, works that would *show* well, were included among those got up for the occasion. Of course, during the long period of preparation for all this, every kind of useful lesson or solid acquirement was set aside, to give time for the heaps of show-things that it was necessary to achieve.

Nothing was to be seen but pieces of satin, and silk, taffeta, lute-string, and brocade ; beads, coloured papers, tinsel, gilded bordering, spangles, gauze, palettes dabbed with the gaudiest of paints, drawing-boards, cards, fillagree, bran, embroidery, floss-silks, worsteds, wools, ribbon, ivory, shells, feathers, wax, lace, pencils, paint-boxes, silver and gold wire, thread, cat-gut, gum, paste, varnish, bugles, gilt-foil, muslin, tissue-paper, velvet ; all kinds of smarteries in material,—all possible variety in bits, shreds, scraps, morsels, and small quantities.

And then, by degrees, this mass of trumpery was formed, modelled, and made up. Beneath the diligent fingers of the young ladies, aided by the skill and invention of the nuns, it shaped itself into innumerable objects of almost indescribable appearance, and of utterly indescribable and undiscoverable use, but which were collectively to be displayed as the works of the school—and to form that grand exhibition, upon which the hearts of the young ladies and their parents were so fondly fixed, as the result of their year's schooling, and the source of the forthcoming prizes. There were pincushions—vast numbers of pincushions—of every size and shape ; but the favorite kind of pincushion was a singular fabric of crimson satin crammed with bran, fashioned three-corner-wise, the two upper points of which being strained across the top and fastened together, the whole was supposed to form a striking resemblance to that mysterious organ, the human heart. This,—to be dangled at the side, by a long ribbon,—was considered a useful present to a faithful servant, or favorite nurse ; at the same time that it afforded an affecting typical assurance of the fond attachment for home maintained by the young lady during her school-life.

Upon the whole, perhaps, the pincushions were the
most useful objects there ; at any rate, there was a
definite and specific use to which they might be put.
But for the most part, the articles constructed, were
purposeless ; utterly devoid of any conceivable aim or
avail whatever. There were boxes so small that they
would contain nothing ; boxes so fragile that they
would hold nothing ; boxes with such inadhesive sides,
insecure handles, and limp, inteniblc bottoms, that
they were fit receptacles for nothing but dead flies or
dust. There were heaps of artificial flowers, with
nearly as little the shape, or hue of nature, as the
smell ; set under glass cases. There were waxen
effigies of lambs, or babies, embedded in myriad fillagree curls, closely wedged in flat boxes with glass lids.
There were ' suonarelli,'—or rattles, made with patch-
work, and gilt tape. There were ' pazienzi,'—non-
descript things, supposed to be of great virtue, hung
on the side, or round the neck ; square bits of cloth,
ornamented with sewing-silk, and trimmed with col-
ored ribbons, and pen-and-ink miniature figures of
saints. There were more than one ' Presepio ' of
large size ; a sort of holy peep-show, representing
Bethlehem Stable, with wax figures stuck about.
There were worsted-worked prodigal sons, with black
and white stitches, for eyes ; and a speckled wool calf
in the distance : embroidered Ruths, with blue and
white floss silk eyes, and pink floss cheeks, and yellow
floss sheaves of corn framed and glazed. There were
certain fabrications, popularly believed to be meant
for watch-pockets (were a watch among the family
possessions),—or for reliquaries ; these were fashioned of all conceivable varieties ; octagonal, hex-
agonal, square, oval, round, and diamond-shaped ;
quilted, quilled, frilled, and rosetted ; but invariably
finished off with such slender hanging-ribbons, that on
putting these frail and treacherous pouches to the use
for which they were professedly adapted, the watch
or relic would disappear behind the bed's head—smash

on to the floor. There were shell-work bags that would not bear anything put into them heavier or stronger than flue ; feather, and rice, and wafer-baskets, that mightn't be touched, lest they should come ungummed, or unpasted, or unfixed. And then the things, by courtesy, called paintings ! Daubs of heads, with mouths out of drawing, chins awry, eyes askew, nostrils formed by a dot or a scratch.

On the eve of the appointed day, the whole was collected, sorted, and disposed to the best advantage, preparatory to the important occasion ; and the young ladies were permitted to enjoy the sight of their accumulated labours. While the rest had been eagerly inspecting the arrangements, Katharina had remained in a quiet corner, diligently plying her knitting-needles.

"And is it possible you don't take any interest in the sight of all these beautiful things, sister ?" said Bianca. "Do come and look at them, now they are arranged."

"Truly, not I ; I don't care for 'em ;" returned she.

"An't you pretending ? Don't you really care ?" said Lisa, one of the youngest of the pupils.

"I never pretend—nothing's worth the trouble of making a pretence about, that I see. I don't mean these things, but things in general ; there's nothing worth pretending to feel what one don't feel. I'm a bad hand at pretending ; I might get on better if I did, perhaps. But I can't ; and moreover, I don't think I wish I could ;" said Katharina.

"But don't you admire these beautiful works ? I think them lovely ! I only wish I could make any one of them—but I'm too young ;" sighed Lisa. "Perhaps next half, sister Maria-Josepha says, I may be able to try an iron-holder ; but I fear I shall never succeed. O you should see the glass-bead dew-drop on Celestina's plum pincushion ! O, so natural ! And the bloom ! Oh dear ! If nobody rubs it off by accident, before the time comes—it will be so praised !

And oh ! you should see the caterpillar Alicia has worked upon hers. It makes my flesh creep, it's so real ! And as for the lady-bird, and the beetle, on the leaf, they're perfect little darlings !"

" Carolina Ariotti has painted such a beautiful tear on her Hagar's cheek—it seems to be actually running down her face ;" said Bianca.

" From the glance I ·had, it seemed to be stuck upon her nose ;" said Katharina.

" But you surely admire Anna Berini's group of flowers ; and Luisa Romelli's landscape ?" said her sister.

" Neither one nor t'other ; one's all blue passion-flowers, and pink lilies ; and the other's all lilac skies, red trees, and brown water. That's how you always go on, Bianca,—picking out the very worst things, and bepraising them most. It's just as if you praised in spite,—over-praised, to draw more attention to the defects."

" There's some truth in that ;" remarked one of the young ladies, aside.

" They say, the Sisters of Humility have such exquisite works this year ;" observed another of the scholars. " I suppose they're trying to cut us out, as usual ; but I don't think they will."

" It's really very mean of them to be always vieing with us. Sisters of Humility, indeed ! That's not much like practising the virtue, methinks !" said a third.

" I hear they're working a splendid altar-cloth, with a lace border that depth," said the other ; " and the pattern's to be wheat-ears, vine-leaves, and grapes. But we can match it with our banner for the Easter procession. Why, the gold rays alone, round the Agnus Dei, are worth all they can do in the way of lace-work."

Most of the young ladies here went away, to take another view of the assembled works ; little Lisa alone remaining near Katharina.

"Why don't you admire those things?" she said, after a few minutes watching the knitting.

"They seem to me trumpery, tawdry, frippery; not worth the time and trouble that have been wasted on them; certainly not worth the spite, and jealousy, and petty envy that they have created. Did you hear what they said about the works at the rival convent?"

"Yes. It's a pity they do that; but they don't know any better, I suppose. They've never thought of it in that way. They're taught to strive all they can to out-do the Sisters of Humility, and to work as hard as they can to get a prize. I wish I could get a prize! I wonder whether I shall ever work well enough to get one. Why didn't you do some pretty work to get a prize, Katharina? Don't you wish for one?"

"No; I like knitting stockings better than fancy-work; and I don't wish for a prize."

"Is it possible!" exclaimed Lisa, with a look of wonder, as if she found it very difficult to believe what she heard.

The grand day arrived. An ecclesiastical dignitary of eminence had promised to honor the proceedings with his presence. He was to be seated on a kind of throne, temporarily erected; hung with garlands of artificial flowers, and plentifully besprinkled with spangles. In the body of the room were ranged benches, for the accommodation of the parents and guests, who formed an eager and expectant crowd. The upper end of the room was fitted up with a kind of dais, or raised platform, on which stood a well-thumped set of virginals, that had seen severe service beneath the fingers of daily relays of practising young ladies; on it also were rows of school-forms; and around hung a great deal of festooned drapery of white and sky-blue calico, intermingled with wreaths of pink paper roses.

The guests, on arriving, were conducted through a suite of rooms, in which were long tables, covered with the school-works, set out with elaborate care, so as to display them to the best advantage, and with slips of written paper pinned on each, bearing the name of the gifted young lady whose work it might be. There was, of course, much lingering, and inspecting, and admiring, on the part of the visitors, as they passed along through these importantly-laden tables ; much congratulation, approbation, laudation, from them ; much whispering, confidential hinting, and delicately insinuated flattery to certain parental ears, from the nuns,—teachers in the school,—who glided to and fro among the lady-friends of their young charges,—mothers, doting aunts, affectionate cousins, or wondering younger sisters, brought by especial indulgence to this scene of juvenile glory and achievement. Now and then, a side-door would open, and a young lady or two, of the school, would slip in among the arrivals, to give a surreptitious welcome to their own particular party. On the stairs, on the landing, here and there along the ante-chambers, might be seen some of these adventurous spirits, flitting amidst the crowd of gaily dressed worldlings, conspicuous by their white frocks, blue sashes, and veils, their hushed voices, their pretendedly-apprehensive glances at the nun-teachers (secure, all the while, of their connivance) ; while squeezes of the hand, furtive kisses, and stolen hugs, were plentifully exchanged between them and their delighted relations.

Suddenly there is a whisper runs among the crowd : —" Monsignore is arrived !  Make way ! make way !" The crowd draws back—there is a passage formed, through which Monsignore and the troop of attendant priests pass, in great state and dignity, towards the great room. The nuns disperse, the stray school-girls vanish, the crowd close in behind the ecclesiastical train, and hurry forward to secure seats. Monsignore is ushered to the throne ; the attendant priests sit around him ; the visitors push and struggle for the front benches ; the nuns attempt to marshal them

into order, and to prevent some of the ladies from
occupying three-fourths more space than is necessary,
with the skirts of their gowns. By dint of a great
deal of coaxing, smiling, whispering, nodding, nudg-
ing, and pointing, this is, in some degree, effected ;
and the majority of the guests are seated. But there
are still many standing ; some flattened against walls,
others jammed in recesses ; while through the door-
ways, there appear vistas of straining heads, which,
from their occasional bobbing disappearance, sudden
re-appearance, and renewed popping down again, suggest the idea of their owners being on tiptoe as long
as nature will second the efforts of their anxiety to
behold the exciting scene they imagine to be taking
place.

For some time, however, there seems to be nothing
of very thrilling interest going forward. There is a
pause, during which, Monsignore applies himself to
his pouncet-box, and whispers the priest seated next
him. Several of the tonsured heads bend forward, and
endeavour to partake of the remark that falls from the
reverend lips ; which, by the smile they wear, proclaim it to be a humorous one. Then the smile is reflected upon each pair of lips belonging to the tonsured
heads, obsequious to his reverence's clerical jest.
Then there is a troublesome cough affects Monsignore ; which the lady Abbess perceiving, she hands
him a box of choice sweetmeats. He takes one, with
such a look of saintly suavity, that it is positively
touching to behold.

Presently, a door in one corner of the platform
opens, and the young ladies of the school enter two
and two, with their white veils drawn on each side of
their faces, their eye-lids cast down, and their hands
folded before them. At this point of time, there is a
great stir among the straining heads ; the tiptoes are
perseveringly sustained ; and some of the flattened
and jammed against the walls and in recesses take the
opportunity of stepping on to some of the benches

which their former occupants have in haste abandoned, in order to get a better sight, peering over the heads of those in front. There is much whispering, and pointing out of individuals among the just-entered school-girls, who take their seats upon the very edges of the forms, and remain with their eyes fixed upon the floor, while one of their companions, together with one of the teacher-nuns, goes over towards the virginals, which they proceed to belabour with certain blows supposed to form a musical duet. As this progresses, the veiled young ladies venture to raise their eyes, cast sidelong glances into the room ; and as they gradually discover their friends, bite their lips to prevent smiling, then risk another glance, then smile more openly, then nod, and at last, not only interchange looks of recognition with those they know, but actually take courage to stare at Monsignore himself.

The duet ended,—prolonged applause from the guests (of admiration from those connected with the young lady player, of relief from all unconcerned in her) marking its conclusion,—six other young ladies rise from their seats, advance to the front of the platform, and sing a piece of music, in a tone both squeaky and nasal ; at certain intervals, elevating their eyes, and lifting their hands—alternately the right and left —in a style imagined to be indicative of feeling, animation, and appropriate action.

At the end of the vocal piece, Monsignore is again seized with a fit of coughing. The box of comfits is once more offered ; but this time, the Abbess's courtesy is declined by a gesture of the white and jewelled hand of the polite ecclesiastic ; who has an eye to the coming collation, and thinks it as well not to injure his appetite with the cloy of sweets.

Then four young ladies stood up in a row, and engaged in a French recitation. It consisted of long speeches gabbled by the several young ladies in succession, as rapidly as their organs of articulation would permit ; and as, now and then, a hand was raised, a head was nodded, a chin was tossed, and a body was jerked forward with a little petulant motion from the waist, it was presumable that the dialogue was to be understood as consisting of some very smart, witty, and jocose hits.   From the circumstance, too, of Monsignore being observed to condescend a gentle smile, which was instantly followed by a corresponding one upon the faces of the attendant priests ; and from the obliging titter which ran through the two front rows, those occupying them being sufficiently near to distinguish (not the sense or meaning, for there was little or none of either—but) the words of the gabbled recitation, there could be no doubt that it was intended to be comic, and highly facetious,—so accordingly, the audience were kind enough to laugh.

Then came the bestowal of the prizes.   The candidates—those happy selected young ladies destined to receive them, came one by one, and stood before the throne of Monsignore, who addressed a short speech, in a mild snuffle of mingled admonition and encouragement to each ; a tinsel crown was placed on her head, the prize was given into her hands, as loud a congratulatory crash as could be banged out of the old virginals, followed ; and then she was permitted to join her friends in the room.

A cold collation succeeded : fruit, cakes, and wine, for the visitors.   A banquet of all that could be collected of rarest and most exquisite in both eating and drinking, for Monsignore and his train.

" Do you see who is one of the priests in attendance on his reverence, sister ?" whispered Bianca, as the ecclesiastical train left the room where the prizes had been given, for the one in which their refection was spread.

" Yes, yes ; I see.   It's father Bonifaccio ;" was Katharina's reply.

" Oughtn't we to go and speak to him, think you, sister ?" continued Bianca.

"You can go, if you think fit; I shan't. I never could endure that filthy old creature, with his carnying way of speaking. I don't know which I used to hate worst—his stinking baize gown, or his sincary voice."

"Fie, sister; you should try and forget his personal defects in his holy office;" said Bianca, with a little prim air peculiar to her.

"Pooh! His defects and my disgust are too strong to be stifled and out-perfumed, even by church-incense. There's one thought, indeed, which might make me tolerate him; but——"

"Tolerate him, sister! Is that the way to speak of a member of holy church?"

"It's my way of speaking, you hear, my demure sister;" said Katharina; "and that's enough for me; and it must be enough for you, too. I never stay to pick my words for any one."

"Pity but you did, perhaps;" said Bianca. "But what was the one thought which might bring you to endure—no, to tolerate the good father? Tolerate, forsooth!"

"Ay, tolerate; that was the word I used. And truly, it demands obtuser senses than I can boast, to let him get the wind of me, for more than the space of ten seconds or so; a minute would upset me quite. I might be subverted,—never converted."

"But your one thought, sister!" pursued Bianca.

"My one thought? Oh, it's gone—it's over—it's past; like most of my good thoughts, it's evanescent —off like the wind. No thought serves to restrain me for a longer time than the summer air takes in blowing the shadow of a cloud across a corn-field; the impression it produces is as fleeting—as transient—as insubstantial."

She fell into a fit of musing; in which Bianca left her, to go and join her schoolfellows. Katharina remained alone; her eye unconsciously watching the dancing of the reflected light from some water in a cut-glass goblet, that had been left untasted by Monsignore, when it was brought him to still his cough. The sunbeams caught the crystal of the glass and water ; and threw flickering lights upon the floor at Katharina's foot.   Her eye followed their undulations, but she was not noting them.   Her brow was knit ; her nether lip was drawn in, and held by her front teeth, which pressed upon it ; while her thoughts flew back to the time of her mother's death, of her remorse, of her aunt's words which had foretold both, while they had opened her mind to its first perception of a higher rule of action than self-will.

"Had she been here to-day, she would have given me a motive for bearing with him ; even for being glad to see him ; she would have bade me try and look upon him with toleration, for the sake of one who regarded him ;" something like this, was her course of thought ; " she would have led me to associate this idea with him, until it overpowered the old disgust, or at any rate taught me the endeavour to lessen my repugnance, as a deed of expiation towards her memory, whom I have so often fretted and angered on this very man's account.   But all this is very fanciful.   Why should I trouble my head with it ? After all, he is a nasty filthy old man ; and my going and speaking to him, won't retrieve my offence to my dead mother.   What have I been dreaming of ?"

Childish dreams of good and noble things !—unripe perceptions of wiser and more generous impulses !— imperfect visions of the better nature stirring within ! —why are ye not more frequently, and more sedulously, watched for, fostered, and developed, by those who have the tutelage of youth ?   Why was there no gentle friend at hand, with the sense of patience of the good aunt, to bring forth and assist these faint struggles towards good, in Katharina's soul ?   Is it because girls' schooling is mostly held to be comprised in the teaching of knick-knack making, accomplishments, and housewifery, with but little regard to the heart and mind which may one day be a wife's—perhaps a mother's ?  Was it that these nuns—like many other school-teachers, were too intent on the culture of external qualifications, to pay any attention to the inward workings of their pupils' natures ?  Certainly, those of Katharina's were unnoted and unaided ; and, left to themselves, they were insufficient to effect the redemption of her character.

Several successive vacations,—with their prize-distributions, their work-displays, their pincushions, their recitation-gabbles, their chorus-squeaks, their tinsel-crowns, their paper rose-wreaths, their frivolous anxieties, their important trifles, their absorbing insipidities,—had followed each other as the years came round.  But the end of that time found the young ladies of the school little changed.  They had grown up, indeed, from quite little children into tall girls of from fifteen, to seventeen, or eighteen,—some even older—quite young women, in age and appearance : but, in point of mind—in all matters of faculty, or judgment ; in heart,—in all matters of principle or sentiment ; they were as completely children as ever.

Their brains had remained stunted, while their bodies grew ; their characters had been permitted to remain undeveloped ; their ideas had been cramped and compressed into shell-baskets and rice-paper boxes ; their thoughts had been pinned down to pincushions ; their intellects had been put under glass cases with artificial flowers,—dwarfed and confined beneath glass lids with waxen effigies, and gilt fillagree ; they had never been suffered to entertain an opinion on the subject less flimsy than floss silk, catgut, or gauze ; to speculate upon higher subjects than paste, wire, and gum ; or to exercise their invention upon things of graver weight than feathers,—of greater moment than spangles, foil, and tinsel.

In all, save increased dexterity of finger, they were veriest babies still.  Some of the most energetic among them, who had been prompted by natural activity to take advantage of the lessons going on at

those times when the preparation for the prizes did
not engross all attention, had gained a smattering of
grammar, a notion or two of geography, (about as
much, perhaps, as to know that their native Italy was
pink, and shaped like a boot ; that France was blue,
Portugal green, Spain yellow, and the British Islands
a smoky brown,) could write flourished alphabets in
three or four different texts, and add up sums the
whole length of a slate ;—but these were looked upon
as the prodigies of the school—quite geniuses ; girls
almost unfemininely clever.

The same rivalry went on between the two convents
year after year.  The school conducted by the Ladies
of the Holy Petticoat, maintained its pre-eminence as
a fashionable seminary ; while that under the superintendence of the Sisters of Humility was still cited
for its strict discipline, its propriety, and its excellent
system.  Many particulars of this system became
known to the rival school, by the secession of one of
the young-lady boarders, who coaxed her guardian into
letting her come over to the milder and more modish
establishment.  She was received with delight by her
new schoolfellows.  Her acquisition was a matter of
triumph.  Her stories of the community she had left,
were devoured with avidity.  She was urged, encouraged, courted, to relate every petty minutia concerning it.  They dwelt, with the pertinacious interest of
little minds, upon the most insignificant details ; and
seemed never weary of hearing and canvassing the
most trivial circumstances.  The appetite for gossip,
induced by paucity of food of a higher kind, is as
craving as it is irrational.  It increases in proportion
as it is gratified.  It seems absolutely insatiate.  No
amount of gossip suffices your gossip-lover.  No
amount of the aliment—frothy in itself, to be sure,—
will produce repletion.  A true gossip-lover will gorge
it with hungry eagerness—with an ever-gaping maw,
that only such fictitious appetites know.  The appetite
for gossip is a morbid taste, one of those unwhole-

some, unnatural relishes,—such as they fancy for crunching slate-pencil, green gooseberries, cabbage-stump, and raw turnips,—very apt to grow upon ill-regulated school-girls ; and it is almost sure to be engendered by frivolous instruction, a teaching of handiworks rather than of ideas,—insufficient mental culture. Give a girl silly things to do and to think of,—occupy her fingers, and leave her mind unsupplied,—and the natural consequence is, inanity, with its almost universal concomitant, an inordinate love of gossip.

To see the way in which her schoolfellows flocked round their new associate, Elvira Blangini, at recreation time ; every voice full of eager enquiry, every eye fixed upon her, their looks beaming with interest, their lips apart and breathless, their chattering hushed while she spoke, it might have been supposed that some object of vital importance was in operation, profoundly affecting them all. But no ; they had only been questioning her about the regulations observed at meal-times, at bed-time, and during play hours, in the school of the holy Sisterhood of Humility.

" At five ?  O, impossible !" exclaimed half a score of voices.

" Hush ! let's hear !" screamed a score and a half. " Let her speak !  Tell us, Elvira ! tell us !"

" Quite true, I assure you !" replied she.  " Five, winter and summer.  And expected to be down in the school-room at half-past ; washed and dressed, too, I can tell you ; or there was a sum that height, to add up, for our pains."

" Shameful !" ejaculated the half score.  " We never have to get up here, till seven ; and early enough too, I'm sure !"

" Hush !" screamed the rest.  " But how about dinner, Elvira ?  Were you allowed to send up your plates twice ?"

" O yes, as often as we liked, but it was such nasty mess ; that eternal ' polenta ;' plain soup and ' bollito,'

or simple ' arrosto ;' no nice dishes,—nothing savory,
—nothing dainty in the way of sweets ;—all so dis-
gustingly insipid—and stupidly wholesome.    Pah !
It makes me sick to think of it !''

"Pah !   Ugh !'' echoed her new schoolfellows.
" No wonder you wished to leave, and come to us.
We have such nice things—all the new-invented
dishes, and most delicious sauces ; and such pud-
dings !''

" It's a pity we're only helped once, though ;  I
could often eat more ;'' murmured the voice of a
little girl ; but it was drowned in the farther enquiries
of the crowd.

" Nothing but water ?   Oh dear !''

" No, nothing but water ; reverend mother used to
say it would make us fair ; and that she didn't mind
about our drinking, so that we did but eat well.   She
said, eating heartily was the best thing growing girls
could do ; and used to beg the teachers to see that
we had sufficient ; but, you know, it was impossible
to eat enough to satisfy oneself, of their nauseous
' bollito ' and ' arrosto.'   I'm sure I couldn't.''

" How did you manage ?'' said the little girl who
had before spoken.   " You must have starved ; only
you don't look very thin.''

Perhaps Elvira didn't hear her ; at any rate she
didn't answer her ; but went on to say :— " You can't
think what a pack of absurd rules they had there.
One was, that if any young lady talked at meal-time
she was to give a fine to the poor-box ; if she was in-
attentive, or saucy, or disobedient, always a fine, and
always put into that never-ending poor-box.   Then
there was another ; if you left off any portion of dress
that was too old, or that you had out-grown, it was
added to the bundle always accumulating for the out-
of-work among the poor ; then they made us scrape
lint for the poor, and make baby-linen for the poor,
—at least, they called it *allowing* us to work for them
—as if it were any such vast privilege to bore oneself

with taking trouble for a tribe of people whom one never saw."

"O, but for the poor, you know !" exclaimed Bianca, and one or two others.

"Yes, yes, it's all very well ; I don't mind helping the poor, of course ; giving them money, doing charity, and all that ; but I have no notion of giving oneself trouble for 'em, you know ;" said Elvira. "That's rather too much of a good thing."

Katharina gave a short laugh. "Too much for you,—or for them ?" she said.

Elvira only stared in reply, and went on :—"Then they were so tiresomely moral, and strict, and straight-laced ; appealing to our own feeling, and duty, and that kind of thing. We were all to be upon honour, as they styled it, with regard to our faults ; and to tell of ourselves, if we were conscious of having done wrong, or deserved punishment. A likely thing, indeed ! They talked about reasoning with us, and trying to convince our good sense—and a parcel of ridiculous stuff of that sort ! Perfect nonsense, you know !"

"La, yes ! All we have to do here, is just to obey ; that's all. They settle for us what's right, and what's wrong ; we have only to believe what we're told, and to do as we're bid. And really, it saves trouble ;" said one of her hearers.

"Then they were so frumpish and fogeyish in their ways !" continued Elvira. "Because they're called Sisters of Humility, I suppose, they won't allow a bit of ornament any where about the rooms ; the walls are white-washed, the floors are all plain brick,—no ornament,—no ' battuto.' There's an iron grating in the receiving parlour ; but not a picture, not a flower, not a morsel of drapery. There's not even a bell in the house ; but when a summons is needed, it is given by striking a couple of iron rods, or small bars, to-gether ; and this, it seems, is merely because it has been an old custom, from time immemorial, and therefore thought to be more primitive, and less pretentious. The Sisters of Humility are very proud of their primitive simplicity ; and affect, in all things, merest neatness and utility. They plume themselves on their meekness, and hold their heads high on the strength of their lowliness and purity.''

'' Is back-biting one of their purities ?'' said Katharina ; '' do they inculcate spite and slander among their meek precepts ?''

'' What does she mean ?'' said Elvira, with a slight shrug, and a look of enquiry at her companions.

'' O, we none of us ever mind Katharina ; she's allowed to be as cross as ever she likes—it's her way —she can't help it, poor thing !'' tittered. Carolina, one of the school-girls.

'' Gramercy for your forbearance ;'' said Katharina ; '' only, as you give me credit for none, don't be surprised if I pay you out, the next such sneer you treat me to. Remember ; I warn you !''

'' Fie, sister !'' said Bianca, interposing ; '' Carolina meant no harm, I dare say ; you only prove her words, in being so cross with her. Why do you lose your temper ?''

'' Quite right, my smooth sister !'' said Katharina ; '' Carolina meant no more harm than you do, I'll be bound. You two, deal in the proprieties and safeties of inuendo, and affected pity ; while I prefer outspeaking. As to losing my temper, I can't well lose what I never had.''

'' What a queer girl your sister seems !'' said Elvira to Bianca, as Katharina left the room. '' How tartly and snappishly she takes one up at every word ! She seems a regular spitfire !''

'' I mustn't listen to my sister's dispraise, or allow you to call her names, to my face ;'' said Bianca, in her prim way. '' But I will own to you in confidence, —for I've quite taken a fancy to you, Elvira dear,— quite should like you for a friend,—and we can't help liking friends for companions even better than sisters, you know, sometimes—I will own to you that she has an unhappy temper, and that she's been more than once called what you called her just now."

" Spitfire ?" said Elvira.

Bianca nodded. " Yes ; shocking, isn't it ? And worse than that !"

" La, what ?" said Elvira.

" Shrew ;" said Bianca with an emphatic pause. " Dreadful, isn't it ? Really dreadful, you know, for a girl to have a sister known as a shrew and a spitfire ; and to be called so, too ; and not able to contradict them, when they call her so ; for certainly, it must be owned, she is a shrew and a spitfire both. Oh, if you did but know——"

" What, what ? Speak out, Bianca ;" said Elvira, and two or three of the other girls.

" But perhaps I oughtn't to speak of it, as it was my own sister who did it ;" said Bianca.

" Did what ? Do speak out—do tell us."

" Really, it was too horrible—he might have died —if you had but seen the wound on his temple—and oh ! the blood ! Oh !"

" Good gracious, Bianca ! wound !—blood ! Goodness me, did she ever murder any one ?" And the girls drew round Bianca eagerly ; and never ceased plying her with questions till they had drawn from her the story of the boy and girl squabble between Giulio and Katharina ; of the stone thrown into the tree ; of his falling to the ground wounded and insensible. " But of course she didn't mean it, you know ;" concluded Bianca ; " you mustn't think more hardly of my sister, than you can possibly help. She has an unfortunate temper—that's all."

" Ah, but who can like a girl with such a temper as hers, I should be glad to know ?" said Elvira. " It's impossible to like a girl who could behave in such a way as that !"

" I oughtn't perhaps to have told about it ;" said Bianca.

" Then why did you ?" said one of the girls.

" I am sure I would not set you against my sister,
on any account ;" said Bianca.    " I should be very
sorry to do that ; but every one can see that she's un-
governable, hasty, and apt to be passionate and wilful."

" To be sure ; every body can see that !   A disagreeable, cross, overbearing spitfire !  that's what she
is !   I shall take very good care *she* shall never be my
friend.   Very different from her sister, my sweet
darling Bianca ;" said Elvira.

" Still I shouldn't have mentioned about Giulio if
I'd thought you'd have thought the worse of Kate for
it ; with all her faults, she's my sister, you know ;"
said Bianca.

" Did you think we should think the better of her
for it ?" said the same girl who had before spoken ;
and who, having formerly been a great friend and
favorite of Bianca's, felt jealous of the liking which
had evidently sprung up between her and the new-
comer, Elvira ; and seemed bent on revenging herself,
by asking teasing questions.

" Never mind, Bianca ; you had a right to tell
what you did ;" said Elvira.   " An't I your friend ?
And we ought to have no concealments from our
friends, you know."

" Very true ; and you're my dearest friend ;" said
Bianca ; " my bosom-friend.   I liked you from the
very first ; and I feel now, I shall always like you."

" I wonder how long the ' always ' will last ;" said
the other girl, laughing contemptuously, as she turned
away, and left them together.

" I hope all our life ;" said Elvira.   " I've taken
quite as strong a fancy to you, Bianca darling, as you
have to me ;" she continued ; " and when the holidays come, you must spend them with me.   I shall
write and ask your father to spare you to me ; and I
shall tell him he mustn't think of refusing me, for
I'm accustomed to have my own way in everything.

My old guardian lets me do just as I like ; excepting
that he would have me go to school at last, because
he said it was only what every young lady did,—and
certainly it would be awkward not to know anything
at all ; of course, that would be tiresome—more tiresome, even, than going to school,—so I went."

" To the convent of the Sisters of Humility ?" said
Bianca.

" Yes ; one of the nuns is a relation of my guardian's ; and she persuaded him to send me there.
She talked him into a notion that I had been spoiled,
—let to run wild ; that my education had been
neglected,—ruined ; therefore he consented that I
should try what a finishing-school would do for me.
But I was hipped and moped to death with those old
frumps ; so after trying it a little time, I got guardy
to change my school,—and here I am ; and I'm sure
I shall like this one,—at least, as well as any school."

" Don't you like school ?" said Bianca.

" Like school !" exclaimed Elvira ; " why, of
course not ; who does ? stupid teaching, and hum-
drum learning, and dull lessons, and all that,—instead of doing as one likes all day, and idling away
as much time as one pleases, sauntering in the garden,
and so forth, as one can do at home. Besides, Hortensio says I'm too old for school now ; and so I am.
I shall be nineteen next birth-day."

" I didn't know you had a brother ;" said Bianca.

" I haven't ;" said Elvira.

" Then who's Hortensio ? I thought, perhaps, he
was your brother."

" My brother ? La, no. He's—he's—a—a—
friend ; a neighbour of ours. His father's house is
next door to us ; and the garden joins ours. When
I'm at home, he comes sometimes, and sits with me,
in the summer-house ; that is, if I give him leave ;
for he never ventures to climb over the wall without
my permission."

" Climb over the wall !" said Bianca.

"Yes; there's a wall between the two gardens;" said Elvira; "so he's obliged to climb it, when he comes to have a chat with me."

"He could go round through the house, couldn't he?" asked Bianca.

"O dear, no! Guardy don't know that I know him. That is, he don't know that we know each other more than as mere neighbours, and all that. Guardy and Hortensio's father are not on speaking terms; so he don't think we're a bit more intimate than they are, don't you see?"

"I see;" said Bianca.

"And I hope you'll see Hortensio himself, next holidays;" said Elvira. "He is so handsome, you've no idea! Such black eyes and hair! Such loves of white teeth, and such a darling aquiline nose! He is the very handsomest boy I ever saw! I know you'll admire him."

"I'm sure I shall, if you do, my dear friend;" said Bianca.

"I wish the holidays were come; I quite long to show him to you!" said Elvira. "What an endless time it does seem to wait."

In spite of the endless-seeming time, it came to an end at last; and Elvira Blangini obtained her wish of having her friend Bianca Minola to spend the holidays with her. She also very soon had her other wish fulfilled, of showing Hortensio. For not long after the two girls had arrived, and were still in all the delight of unpacking their school-boxes, and arranging their dresses and the rest of the school-girl possessions coming under the comprehensive term,—"things," in their own rooms, when suddenly Elvira exclaimed in a sort of breathless excitement :—"Come here, come here, Bianca to this window! stand behind this curtain with me, and peep out, and you'll see him. There! Look! Walking in the next garden, with a mandolin in his hand. It's he, himself!"

"Who?" said Bianca.

"Who, child? Why, Hortensio, to be sure! Dear fellow, there he is! He little thinks who's looking at him."

"That! That, Hortensio! Why, that's a man!" exclaimed Bianca.

"A man? Why, of course! La, child, what do you suppose he was?"

"A boy; you always spoke of Hortensio as a boy; and I was foolish enough to expect to see a little fellow with curly black hair, and rosy cheeks; and now I see a tall young man,—quite a tall young man;" said Bianca.

"Ah, I see how it is;" said Elvira laughing. "Yes, yes, he was quite a boy when I first knew him; and I've known him so long, and seen him so frequently, and so intimately, and easily, and all that, you know, sitting and chatting with him like neighbours' children, together, in the summer-house, down yonder, that I've always kept on thinking of him as a boy; and have talked of him to you as a boy; I suppose."

"Yes, you certainly did;" said Bianca. "You gave me the idea of quite a boy, by your manner of speaking; for you said he was a handsome boy, you know—and yet,—yet,—he actually has—actually—a moustache! and—and—a—a—tuft!"

"Well, I suppose that don't hinder him from being handsome, does it?" said Elvira, still laughing. "For my part, I think they make him look handsomer than ever. I'm glad he wears his moustache; and don't shave it off, as some of the effeminate young fellows nowadays have taken to do. But come, Bianca, get a fan—I have mine—and we'll go down into the garden and see him. He'll be so astonished to find I'm come home. Why, how you blush! What a bashful thing you are!"

"Am I?" said Bianca.

"Are you? why, to be sure you are! A regular school-girl,—out of countenance at everything. Didn't you colour up to the eyes, when I first presented you to my old guardian, this morning ? As if he could be anything to blush at. The idea of blushing about guardy ! Why one would as soon think of changing colour for the bronze statue of holy St. Anthony !"

"If I blushed at all, it was from surprise, I believe ;" said Bianca. "I was astonished to see your guardian looking so young ; I had imagined him, from your words, to be an old gentleman."

"Why so he is ! He's fifty at least—quite an old fogey ; I shouldn't wonder, if he were fifty-two or three."

"I somehow absurdly fancied he was about eighty. I expected to see a tottering old gentleman, with a crutched stick ; and he's a smart beau—quite gallant, and attentive ; and I thought seemed particularly so, to his fair ward ; eh, Elvira ?"

"O, if you mean he admires me—you're quite right there ;" said Elvira, whose cheeks certainly evinced not the slightest tendency to change colour, and bore full testimony to the truth of her thinking it wonderful that guardy should be a subject for blushing ; "the old fellow hasn't lost the use of his eyes ; he can see a pretty girl clear enough—and knows that I'm one— and would only be too glad to marry me to-morrow, if I'd have him."

"How you talk, Elvira !" said Bianca.

"Ay, my dear ; I'm out of bounds, now : I can be as prim as you please—as demure-looking and as demure-spoken as yourself, when I'm in school. But school's one thing, and home's another ; and that's why I like home best—as I've often told you. But come ; don't let's stand chattering and dawdling here any longer ; let's go down into the garden."

When they reached the summer-house, Elvira gave Bianca a bit of fancy-work, to hold in her hands, and took up some herself ; but presently flung it down, and took up a book, turning over the leaves, and reading a line or two aloud, here and there ; stopping,

and listening occasionally, between whiles ; then with
an air of vexation, tossed that aside also, and snatched
up a guitar, struck a few chords, going close to the
open window as she did so.

Presently a voice was heard, at a little distance,
saying :—" I did not know you were returned home,
signorina ; may I come over ?"

Elvira stepped to the entrance, smiling, and graciously bowing her head ; and, in another instant, Hortensio leaped the low wall, and came forward to the summer-house.

Elvira Blangini presented him to her young school-
friend, on seeing whom, the young man, at first, looked
much embarrassed ; but what with the absence of all
embarrassment on the part of the young hostess herself, who seemed in the height of good-humour and
spirits, and what with the extreme shyness of her
friend Bianca, he soon gained courage ; grew talkative
and gay—rattled on—rallied the young ladies on their
notable dispositions—gave his opinions on silks—
shades of colour, &c. &c.; and in short, made himself
quite agreeable, and at home with them,—ending by
offering to play either the guitar or the mandolin to
them as they worked.

" No, perhaps best not ;" said Elvira, giving a
peculiar look in the direction of the house ; " you may
read to us, if you like—here's Ariosto."

" La, do you read poetry, Elvira ?" said Bianca ;
" I thought it was forbidden."

" Oh, ay, at the convent, child ; it's all very well
there ; but here, I read what I like. We're school-
girls there ; we're women here, my dear ;" said
Elvira.

" And very charming women, too ;" replied Hortensio, with a gallant bow and glance. The words,
the bow, and the glance, caused her such a hot rush
of confusion, as Bianca had never before experienced.
She knew not which way to look ; while her friend
exclaimed,—" What a shamefaced moppet thou art,

Bianca ! Shut up in that dowdy old convent, thou hast heard nought but chidings, from teachers and nuns. But in the world, child, thou'lt hear quite other phrases ; commendation, not chiding, is the mode here abroad.''

'' And the signorina Bianca must learn to bear hearing her own praises ; she'll hear little else, I fancy, when once she has exchanged the convent for the world ;'' said Hortensio, with another bow, and another glance.

Whether because the words, the bow, and the glance, were now addressed solely to Bianca, without including herself, certain it is, that there was something in them which made Elvira rejoin—'' Yes, my dear, you must learn to listen to praise in the world, without letting it turn your little head ! You'll give up blushing at fine speeches, when you discover that they mean just nothing at all. You'll soon care no more for the praises, than we used to do for the chidings ; and that was little enough, I believe ! But hush !— what was that ?—I thought I heard——''

She put her finger on her lip—listened—then pointed stealthily in the direction whence Hortensio had come. The gesture was so significant, and so instantaneously obeyed by the young gentleman's sudden retirement over the wall, that Bianca could not help seeing it must have been a signal in frequent use between them on former occasions of the like kind.

The next moment Elvira's guardian appeared in one of the garden-walks, approaching them ; and Bianca, if she had had courage to look up, might have perceived still farther and edifying proof, in the unmoved colour and expression of her friend's face, that she had said truly, she thought blushing for guardy a preposterous idea. Not even the gross deception she was playing off upon him could excite one faintest reddening. On the contrary ; with hard glassy eye, and hard brassy voice, set in the detestable firmness of triumphant, as well as habitual deceit, she said ;

"I'm glad you're come, guardy ; I want to consult you about the dance you have promised me to give my schoolfellows.　When shall it be ?"

" Whenever it best pleases yourself to appoint, my charming Elvira ;" said the gallant guardian, raising his ward's hand to his lips ; " only whenever the time fixed, remember that I claim this fair hand for the first dance."

" We'll see about that, guardy ;" said Elvira, half coldly, half coquettishly withdrawing her hand, and giving him a pat on the back of his ; " you know I don't approve of such ways !"

" I know you are all discretion and propriety, my sweet Elvira ;" said he, with a fond look, so different from the fatherly one it ought to have been, from a guardian to his ward, that Bianca could not help thinking he really did look, after all, very old and horrible.

" Bianca darling, you take this sheet of paper, and write down the names of the guests we mean to invite, while guardy and I dictate them to you.　Guardy shall tell you the young men, and I—no, stay,—I'll select the young men, and guardy shall name the young ladies we'll have.　Of course we must ask your sister Katharina, Bianca dearest ; or she'll feel herself affronted, and I should be sorry to do that for your sake ; otherwise I'd rather be without her ?　What say you ?"

"O, she'd be highly affronted, if she were left out ;" said Bianca ; " she'd fret and fume for a week, and lead my father such a life !　For his sake, we must have her."

" If we must, we must ;" said Elvira.　" And now, guardy, for the rest of the young ladies."

While she bribed his attention and good-humour by letting him name all the prettiest girls of their acquaintance, she made out her own list of sparks ; artfully contriving to insert Hortensio's name, with a passing remark, uttered in a negligent off-hand way, to the effect that they could not well omit asking so near a neighbour, as they wanted all the eligible young men they could muster, to make up the requisite number of partners.

An early day was fixed ; the interval being devoted by Elvira and Bianca to consultation upon the dresses they should wear, and to consideration and discussion of the mode in which they might altogether most becomingly set themselves off for the occasion.

"Not that I care for dress, you know, my dear Elvira ;" said Bianca. "It is even sinful vanity, and waste of time, to bestow much time on adorning one's person ; a simple white frock and a few flowers in her hair and bosom are the utmost ornaments a young girl needs ; but I would fain put them on as advantageously as might be, that I may do honor to my friend's ball."

Elvira laughed. "Vastly well, my little sancti-mony ! That speech of thine would do mighty well for the convent ; and befits thee, who has just come thence. But I doubt me, Bianca darling, whether thou be'st not in good sooth, as arrant a little sly-boots, as the worst of us wicked worldlings."

"Nay, Elvira ; I know not what thou mean'st. Sly-boots ! I ?"

"Thou'rt right, sweetest ! That little innocent air of thine will do wonders with the men, by and bye. It'll tell, amazingly. They'll think thee a miracle of artlessness, meekness, and all-charming modesty."

"What wild thoughts thou hast, Elvira ! I care not for attracting men's commendations, not I. How can'st thou think such wicked things ?"

"I think them, because I know them. I know, that however we may see fit to make a pretence of bashfulness and pretty confusion, at the bare idea of a man's admiring us, it's the idea that creeps nearest the heart of all us school-girls from the very first moment we make out what's in a mirror. And de-pend on't, between ourselves, it's just such quiet girls as you and I, who know how to carry it demurely before nuns and teachers in the convent, and before duennas and guardians in the world, who most think of our looks, and of the impression they'll make. An out-speaker, a reckless doer, like your sister Katharina, now, though she seem to court attention by her violence of manner ; cares, in reality, little to attract, far less to secure admiration.''

"She wouldn't be so negligent of appearances, certainly, if she cared to win liking ;" mused Bianca.

"Exactly, my dear ; you can see clearly what I mean, I perceive ;" said Elvira. "Best be candid between ourselves, whatever we may be to others.''

"Owning a thing to an intimate,—to a bosom-friend, is of course very different from showing our secret feelings to all the world ;" said Bianca.

"Precisely, darling ; so now let's determine what flowers we'll wear. I think I shall have oleanders ; and you shall have a wreath of pomegranate-blossoms.''

"A simple lily will do for me ;" said Bianca.

"Well done, simplicity !" laughed Elvira. "Your meekness knows full well, that a single white flower will set off your golden curls better than a whole garland of scarlet showiness ; eh, Bianca ?"

"Red never did suit me ;" said Bianca. "It's too staring—too gaudy—I don't like to draw notice upon me, by wearing such very bright-coloured flowers.''

"Stick to the truth, my dear ; it popped out at first. Red don't become you !" answered her friend,

"How can you, my dearest Elvira ? But come, let us plan how you shall wear your oleanders. Shall they be placed on one side, in a drooping bunch ? Or twisted into a chaplet round the head ?''

The party assembled at the ball was a very large one. There were all Elvira and Bianca's favorite schoolfellows, as well as a goodly company of young

people of both sexes,—neighbours and acquaintances ;
besides whom, were some elderly members of the same
families.    Among the latter, was a madame Ciarla,—
known to all Padua as an inveterate gossip, though a
good-natured woman.

On her first arrival, she found herself near Bianca,
who had just advanced to receive her sister Katharina,
and dutifully to ask news of her father.

" Well, young ladies, I'm delighted to see you once
again ; and so grown and improved, I declare !   All
Padua misses two such ornaments to its society as the
signorini Minola, I can tell you."

" Why should you flatter us ?" said Katharina.

" Flattery ?   Not a bit of it !   You are both very
handsome girls ; and as you'll soon be told so by all
the young gallants, it's as well the news should be
broke to you first by an old woman like me.   And it's
no such unwelcome news, either.   To be told that
you have hair as black and as glossy as a raven's
wing ; and that your eyes sparkle like diamonds, is
no such hardship to hear, surely.   And there's your
sister, miss Bianca, quite a different style of beauty,
to be sure ; but still, with her gold locks, and blue
eyes, and pink cheeks,—and then with that modest
glance—and that white frock, and pure lily—she looks
so nice and so pretty one could eat her."

" A dainty compliment !" said Katharina, with a
short laugh.

" If you think me pretty—I mean good-looking—
that is, not ugly," said Bianca, " what will you say,
when you see my friend, Elvira Blangini ?   She is
indeed a lovely girl—a perfect beauty, isn't she,
Kate ?"

" Far from it,—and you know it, Bianca ;   but
that's just your way ;" said Katharina.   " Your
praise, when you give it, is such over-praise, that it
seems like malice.   When you tell people that Elvira
Blangini is lovely—a perfect beauty—it's more likely
to do your friend harm than good : for their feeling,

when they see her, will be disappointment ; and they'll be inclined to find her even less pretty than they would have done without your insidious praise."

"I didn't see you at church last Sunday, miss Katharina ;" said madame Ciarla, anxious to effect a change in the conversation.

"I never go to church, if I can help it ;" said Katharina. "It makes me feel so irreligious."

"Fie, sister !" said Bianca ; "what a strange girl you are !"

"Irreligious ?—going to church make you irreligious ? My dear young lady, what can you mean ?" said madame Ciarla.

"I mean that when I'm there, I see so much staring about them, so much irreverence, so much attention to everything but what they ought to be attending to, on the part of the congregation ; I hear such odd things said, I see such strange things done, that it puts me into a fever of anger, and of inclination to scoff, and doubt, and question ; makes me so undevout, so irreligious, so impious, that I avoid going to church on principle. I don't want to make myself worse than I am ; so I stay away."

"I don't understand you, my dear ;" said the old lady. Then, after looking for a moment more, in a wondering, puzzled way, at Katharina, who offered no farther explanation, madame Ciarla continued :—"I was quite disappointed not to see you there, with your father, good signior Minola ; and so were others, I fancy, who had heard wonders of the growth, and improvement in beauty, of his two fair daughters, since they've been so long away at school. There was signior Gremio, who had lost his old father, by-the-by, at last, and is, I hear, on the look-out for a pretty young wife, to help him spend his large inheritance. And then there was young signior Giulio, who's grown quite a tall handsome young man ; he shows no signs of the weakness and deformity that were predicted he would grow up with, if ever he reached to man's estate, in consequence of that terrible fall he had, when a boy. But, bless me, I beg your pardon, miss Katharina ; I forgot all about it's having been you who caused that accident. Your turning so red, reminded me ; but he bears no malice about it—he never speaks of the matter, and seems to have forgotten that such a thing ever took place at all."

" He was an ill-bred, teasing brat, and deserved all he got ;" said Katharina. " That's all I remember of him. I've forgotten him, quite as much as he has me."

" I dare say he hasn't forgotten you, my dear miss Katharina ;" said the old lady ; " indeed, I know he hasn't, for the other day, I heard him say——"

" Best not speak of him ; my sister dislikes him ; it only irritates her to mention his name ;" said Bianca.

Her sister gave her a strange look, and seemed about to speak ; but she checked herself, bit her lips, and forced herself to listen to what madame Ciarla was going on to say.

" Well, we'll speak of a gayer subject. It seems that signior Gremio is determined to celebrate his coming into his fortune, with a grand party,—quite a festival."

" He's of age, certainly ; though a good deal more than twenty-one ;" sneered Katharina.

" He is old, it must be owned ; said madame Ciarla ; " nearer sixty than fifty, I take it ; but, as he's only just come into his birth-right, and on the look-out for a young bride to share it with him, I dare say, there won't lack for pretty girls, at this grand party of his."

" Very likely ;" said Katharina.

" I suppose we shan't see you there, miss Minola ;" said madame Ciarla ; " for young signior Giulio will certainly be asked ; and as you've such a pique against him still, perhaps you won't like to meet him."

" I shan't stay away on his account, depend upon it ; I care too little about him, to let his presence prevent me from going wherever I like ;" said Katharina, with the same sudden colour in her cheeks, as had flashed into them, on the first mention of his name. As she turned away, Bianca said to the old lady, " What a pity it is, my sister retains her animosities so bitterly, and so long. She never can bear that young man's name repeated,—though so many years have elapsed since their boy and girl quarrel,—without turning scarlet. I've remarked it frequently, whenever I've happened to revert to the subject ; which I have done sometimes,—quite inadvertently, of course."

At this moment, Hortensio made his way up to Bianca, saying :—" There is such a crowd, I have only just been able to reach you, signorina. Pity my Tantalus torture ; I have been watching you from a distance without being able to get near enough to beseech your hand for the dance."

" Where is Elvira—will not she expect—where is Elvira ?" said Bianca, looking down, and picking the tip of her glove.

" She is dancing this measure with her guardian ; let us find places anywhere ; the dancers are so numerous, we cannot be fastidious ; nor shall I feel inclined to be so, were it the worst place in the room, with my present partner,—except, perhaps, for her sake."

" Who is she ?" said Bianca, looking up with an air of unconsciousness worthy of one who had left school many years, instead of a few days.

" The charming Bianca ; when she deigns to accord me this fair hand." He seized it, and hurried her among the dancers.

" Look at my friend Elvira, yonder ; how exquisitely beautiful she looks, does she not, in the full bloom and animation of the dance ?" said Bianca to Hortensio.

"It strikes me she looks a little sulky, at this moment :" he replied laughingly.

"Ah ! can you wonder, with that ugly old man for her partner ?" said Bianca, casting a moment's glance at her own young dashing one, then casting her eyes down upon her spread fan.

"He's an odious wretch certainly, to aspire to youth and beauty for a wife, which I fancy he does ;" said Hortensio.

"Yet he's almost warranted, by the great temptation. Is she not passing lovely ? Did you ever see more brilliant carnation on a cheek ? Or hair more flowing, in its graceful disorder ?" persisted Bianca.

"Her cheeks are even too florid for my notion of perfect beauty ;—and her hair is disordered indeed ! —untidy, I should call it ; with the exertion of dancing, I suppose. And what could possess her to put such odious flowers in her hair ?—they make her face look all of a colour with themselves !"

"You are a connoisseur in beauty and dress, I perceive, signior Hortensio ;" said Bianca, with a playful smile, and another furtive glance.

"I hope I can recognize true loveliness when I see it ;" said Hortensio, with an unequivocal look of admiration towards herself. "The pure and colourless modesty of the lily, has more charms for me, I confess, than all the oleanders that ever glowed."

"Oh, but you really mustn't criticise my friend's looks, or her dress, too severely, merely to show your judgment, signior connoisseur. I cannot allow that. I think Elvira's wreath remarkably well-chosen."

"Inasmuch as harmony of colour constitutes tasteful choice ;" replied Hortensio. "The flowers match the cheeks precisely, it must be owned."

"Fie, saucy critic that you are !" said Bianca. "See, Elvira has finished her dance, and is coming this way ; go and make atonement by engaging her for the next, or I'll never forgive you."

" On that condition, I obey your mandate ;" said Hortensio, as he bowed, and quitted her.

" I've performed my duty-dance, now for my pleasure-dance ;" said Elvira, holding out her hand to Hortensio, as he approached. " Who have you been dancing with ? Oh, I see ; my school friend, Bianca Minola. A dear little innocent milk-and-water thing, isn't she ? Talks bread-and-butter,—lisps white-of-egg ; but she's a darling creature, for all that ! I can endure her insipidity, for the sake of her sweetness ; she really is very sweet. But see here, what I have received ! An invitation for signior Gremio's grand party, next week. Mind you get one, also. The entertainment will be none to me, unless you're there ; so, be sure and come."

" How can I fail, with such flattering inducement ?" said he.

" Go along with you, wicked pretender ; it's you are the flatterer, I fear ;" she said, as she went on to take her usual vivacious part in the trifling that followed up the previous specimen.

Signior Gremio's party was to be of the most attractive description. The company were to assemble in the beautiful grounds of his estate, where means were amply, and in tasteful variety, provided for spending the day in one round of pleasant out-door amusement. There were, dancing, ball-playing, battledore-and-shuttlecock, archery, and all kinds of active sports, at the option of the young people ; there were swings put up among the trees, for such as preferred more lazy amusement ; and there were shady seats, and turf banks, and tents, and a pavillion containing tables spread with ices, fruit, coffee, ' cedrata,' and all sorts of preserves, sweetmeats, and cakes, for those who preferred entire repose and refreshment.

Among the earliest arrivals were Elvira's guardian, with his fair ward and her friend Bianca. Then came Baptista Minola, with his daughter Katharina. Then Hortensio ; then madame Ciarla, with many others ; and then the rest of the guests poured in, in quick-succeeding groups. The host received them all with smiling courtesy ; and seemed bent on playing the young heir, just come into his estate.

Some one of the guests, of a waggish turn, ventured to remark that it was generally understood, signior Gremio had convoked that fair assembly, to choose from among its fairer portion, the fairest, for his future bride.

" Whenever I choose my future bride, she shall be the fairest, depend on't ;" said signior Gremio, fixing his eyes as he spoke, on the light golden hair that fell in profusion round the pretty face of Bianca Minola. It was really edifying to see the innocent way in which she sat, plucking up the wild flowers on the turf beside her, looking the picture of soft unconsciousness—such as might have become a child of a few years' old, or a practised coquette of thirty ; and after a pause, looking up into his face, and saying : "I hope you won't be very angry with me, signior Gremio, for despoiling the sward of these little ducks of daisies, will you ?"

" All here is at the command of my fair guests, for their special behoof and gratification ;" answered he ; " they cannot confer a greater favor on me, than by appropriating them to that end ;" and he concluded by throwing himself on the turf beside her ; which act of gallantry caused his senile joints a pang that would have twisted his features into a grimace, had he not covered it with the nearest thing to a smile he could muster.

There was a large group dispersed round the grassy bank on which Katharina, Bianca, and her friend Elvira, had seated themselves. The gentlemen lounged at the ladies' feet, or lay a little in the rear, or leaned against the surrounding trees ; while light talk, gay jests, and repartees, sometimes of compliment, sometimes of raillery, flew from one to another, and were bandied to and fro.

Suddenly signior Gremio said, "I expect Giulio Vinci here to-day; he's not long returned from Naples, where he has been spending some time with an uncle of his, a captain in the marine service."

Katharina's face flashed scarlet.

"And who may Giulio Vinci be?" said Elvira.

"A young friend of mine, for whom I've a great value. I rejoice that he has returned home time enough for my entertainment;" said Gremio.

"He's the boy I told you of, whom my sister was so unfortunate as to injure;" said Bianca in Elvira's ear; pressing her friend's arm, to draw her attention to Katharina's change of colour.

Katharina overheard the words, and said loudly and passionately :—"If ever you speak of that again, I'll make your meek blue eyes as red as a ferret's, with my nails."

There was an awkward pause. The company shrugged their shoulders, and exchanged significant looks, at this evidence of Katharina Minola's unabated violence, and shrewish tongue; and then, by degrees, they broke up into little separate parties, talking low among themselves, or proposing strolls among the trees, or joining the dancers, the ball-players, and the other sporters.

"I shall despatch guardy to the house to fetch me a veil, or something, under pretence of the heat;" whispered Elvira to Bianca; "and then take pity on Hortensio, who has been leaning against a tree this half hour in hope of catching my eye, to beseech for a ramble together. I mustn't disappoint him, and make him despond altogether, poor fellow!"

Bianca had some notion that the impatient glances of Hortensio had been directed rather towards her own colloquy with signior Gremio, than towards her friend's with her guardian; but she uttered no iota of her thoughts. Only nodded, and said :—"Very well, dear;" and then resumed the smiling attention she was paying to the old gallant at her side.

Presently, signior Gremio proposed adjourning to the lawn, where the dancing and ball-playing were going on. He offered his arm to the two sisters to conduct them thither, saying :—" I'll find you a partner, Miss Katharina ; as for Miss Bianca, I hope she will favor me by becoming mine."

" Never mind me ; I shan't dance ;" said Katharina ; and when her companions had left her, she stood lost in thought, with her eyes fixed upon a certain tree, that she well remembered. Gradually, her eyes drooped, and fell to the ground ; her nether lip was compressed beneath her set teeth ; a frown gathered ; her nostrils sank and dilated, dilated and sank ; she breathed hard, and held her hands closely clenched, as she remained absorbed in reverie.

Presently, a gay, hearty, good-humoured laugh reached her ear, and a few words were spoken.

She started violently.

Then she heard the voice say :—" She's here, is she ? Object to meet her. To be sure not ; why should I ?"

" How contemptuously he speaks !" was her hurried thought.

Then, accompanied by signior Gremio, Bianca, and others, Giulio Vinci came towards her. She was making up her mind to repulse him haughtily, should he offer to shake hands with her, as she thought that would be from his wish to assume superiority over her, and to show his magnanimity of forgiveness ; when, on her turning round towards him he merely made her a passing bow, and turned to speak to some one else.

Soon after a game of ball was formed. A great number of the company engaged in it ; and it proceeded with spirit.

Giulio Vinci had just made a long run after the ball, and was tossing it up into the sky as high as he possibly could, and catching it, while he returned to the spot whence he was to pitch it into Bianca's hand,— her turn being to throw it next.

As she caught it from him, she said :—" How active you are, signior Giulio ! what a mercy it is, that you've no lameness—no weakness remaining from your accident ! we ought to be very thankful."

The words were hardly out of her mouth, before Katharina snatched the ball from her sister's hands, and flung it over the wall. " I warned you not to allude to that again !" she exclaimed.

" Hey-dey, miss Miscetta ! Are these your tricks still ?" exclaimed Giulio, turning suddenly towards her. Then, seizing her by the wrists, he cried out : —" Run, some of you, and fetch the ball. I'll hold this little fury fast till you return." She writhed, and struggled ; but not one jot could she move her wrists in his firm grasp. He laughed at her fruitless efforts to free herself, and said :—" You had to deal with a boy, then ; I'm a man now, Miscetta, and stronger than you are."

" I care not for your strength. Let me go, I say !" she exclaimed.

He unclasped his hold, saying :—" There, you are free ; but if you interfere any more with our game, you spoil-sport, I'll take care and prevent you effectually."

She laughed a short mocking laugh, and her eyes flashed, as she said :—" I make no promises !"

" But I do ! and you'll see that I'll make them good ;" said he.

The ball was brought back ; and the game was resumed ; but the instant it became Bianca's turn to throw the ball, Katharina seized it from her, and threw it over the wall as before.

She had no sooner done so, than Giulio caught her up in his arms, and ran with her to a tree, at a little distance, near to which lay a cord that had been used for one of the swings. With this he proceeded to bind her to the tree, in spite of her frenzied stamping and struggling ; while the company half laughing, half concerned, at the scene, looked on, expecting to hear her flame out with her usual violence.

But not a single word did she utter.

At first, she panted, struggled, and strove her utmost to prevent his effecting his purpose, her face, all the while, crimson with rage. But, after a time she grew deadly pale. For while Giulio was binding her to the tree, she suddenly became aware that it was the same from which her own violence had caused his fall, years before ; in his exertions to secure her, the hair became pushed back from his forehead, and she caught sight of the deep-seamed scar that marked the place of the wound her hand had given him.

A quite new and strange set of emotions overwhelm her, and hold her, as it were, paralysed in speech and motion. A perplexing feeling of shame and surprise takes possession of her, at finding herself completely overcome,—*mastered.* As the strong, manly arms, hold her firmly, constrained there to abide his will, she feels her spirit as well as her body give way, and own itself vanquished. One of the most singular features of this new state of feeling, is, that the sense of defeat, for the first time in her life, is not altogether painful. As her woman's frame involuntarily yields to his masculine strength—as her feeble limbs bend beneath his will, and submit to his power, there is an inexplicable acquiescence, an absence of resentment and resistance, altogether unwonted, and surprising to herself.

Her silence, her turning pale, her ceasing from struggle and opposition, made Giulio, in his turn, relent. " Say you'll not meddle with the ball again, and I'll undo the cords ;" he said.

She looked into his face ; but was literally unable to speak.

Taking her non-reply for stubbornness, he turned on his heel, saying :—" When you're tired of your bonds, you can cast them off by a word. Call to me, —promise to let the ball alone, and I'll come and release you.''

When he returned to the ball-players, he found

several gentlemen standing round Bianca, engaged in bewailing the scratches which her sister's rough seizure of the ball from her hands had inflicted ; she, with pretty shrinkings, and delicate hesitations, now winding her handkerchief about them, and now unwrapping and showing the scarce perceptible red marks, and lines, which made the little dainty trembling hands look only the whiter—a fact of which she was of course unconscious.

" Let me give you my arm to the pavillion, signorina Bianca ;" said signior Gremio ; " a little iced water with wine in it will restore you."

" A glass of water, then ; for I own I feel a little faint ;—perhaps, with the loss of blood. But a glass of water merely—no wine—I never touch it—I couldn't think of such a thing."

The sympathetic train of gentlemen attended her, as she proceeded to the pavillion ; and the rest of the bystanders took the opportunity of following their example, to obtain some refreshment.

Giulio was following the crowd ; but he turned back, went to the tree where he had left Katharina bound, and unfastened the cords. When he had released her, he drew her arm within his, and led her to the pavillion with the rest. There was something in this silent attention on his part—in the quiet decision of his manner—relieving her of all necessity for aught but passive acceptance, that was strangely pleasant to Katharina. She walked unresistingly by his side,—obeying his impulse, his intention.

But as they entered the pavillion, some one said : —" Here comes signior Giulio, with his fair enemy. He has given her quarter ; and there's a truce to hostilities, for the present. Let's hope peace will last."

" See, he has linked his captive to his chariot wheels ;" said another. " Or is it the generous support accorded by a conqueror to his vanquished foe ?"

" I need no support ;" said Katharina, withdrawing her hand suddenly from Giulio's arm, and pushing

him from her with an angry gesture.   But she belied
her words, by dropping on a seat, as she spoke.

"My friend Giulio is making the most of his time,
in gallant behaviour to his fair enemies on shore, as
he is so soon to encounter the enemies of his country
on sea ;" said signior Gremio.   "My friend has just
obtained a commission on board of one of our war ves-
sels.   He leaves us, to join his ship, this very evening."

A smothered cry burst from the lips of Katharina.
To Hortensio, who happened to be handing her some
cakes, she said :—"What's the use of holding the
plate to me ?   Don't you see I can't take any ?   My
hand's useless ; my wrist is sprained."

"My poor sister !   It's all owing to you, I fear,
signior Giulio ;" said Bianca ; while her sister cast a
burning glance at her.   "You would bind her hands
so tight round the tree.   I'm really afraid you've hurt
her wrists with the cords."

"No matter ;" replied he, laughingly ; "it'll do
her good—teach her to take heed when she's spoken
to, another time.   She don't mind hurting and scratching others.   Besides, she shouldn't have struggled as
she did at first, if she didn't want the cords to hurt her.
It'll be a good lesson to her how to obey ; she'll learn
what a man's power is,—and that a woman's best
policy, to say nothing of her best interest, is to submit gracefully, and of her own accord, to that which
can extort submission from her inferior strength."

But presently, under shelter of the talk and laughter
of the other young people, which was speedily resumed, Giulio came round to the spot where Katharina
was sitting, and said :—"Let me look at your wrist ;
I didn't mean to hurt you seriously.   I hope I haven't
really hurt you."

She raised her eyes to his face, with a strange expression of eagerness and scrutiny.

"Let me look at it, I say.   I should be sorry if
your wrist were really sprained, though you are a sad
tigress, Miscetta."

" Don't touch it ! Let it alone !"     And she snatched the hand away, which she had just before extended towards him.

He laughed.   " You are a sad tigress, now, an't you ?   A wild cat,—a cat-o'-mountain,—anything fierce, and savage, and fury-like ?"

" What people make me out to be, they may take me for !" she said ; and she leaned over the sprained hand, and held it to her bosom, and rocked herself to and fro ; while a hot tear or two fell upon it.

Giulio saw them ; for he was looking earnestly at her, watching her with curiosity and interest ; and the thought came into his head, whether she might not be in some measure right—that the character of scold and shrew, so universally given to her, wrought the very evil it ascribed—that it worked upon such a disposition as hers in making her worse than she naturally was—that it made her sore and irritable, and chafed her into fury, rudeness, and violence.   He saw that taunts and reproaches were so far from correctives, that they but served as stimulatives to her temper ; when, to proper controul, and a firmly maintained authority, it might probably be taught to yield. He was getting so far as to wonder whether by some one whom she could respect, and who would in return respect her foibles,—or rather treat them with toleration and forbearance, yet with judicious restraint,— she might not be reclaimed ; when Hortensio called to him, and begged him to show the company the letter he had had from his uncle the ship's captain, who had given him an appointment on board his own vessel.

Giulio joined them ; took out his letter, and began reading it aloud.   It contained some very kind expressions of his uncle's pleasure at his having chosen his own favorite profession ; promised to undertake his outfit ; and gave him some good advice.   Thus Giulio was proceeding, when one of the young gentlemen present, seized with a fit of caprice, or a fit of jealousy, exclaimed : " Come, we have had enough of the old admiral's prosing. I wonder you an't ashamed of repeating so many praises of yourself, Giulio. Here, away with it ! And let us have some more ball-playing on the lawn." Saying which, with a fillip of the finger and thumb beneath the open sheet of paper, he sent it spinning out of Giulio's hand. The air caught it, and was blowing it across the room towards an open window, when, just as it passed Katharina, and Giulio made an eager exclamation, she sprang up, and seized it, just in time.

" She has caught it with her sprained hand, I declare !" remarked Bianca.

" And after all the fuss she made about her hurt !" said Elvira. " It could not have been very painful, one would think, if she could use her hand so nimbly as that."

At these words, Katharina darted an angry look towards them ; and, crumpling up Giulio's letter in both hands, flung it right in her sister's face.

Giulio laughed ; fetched his letter, and while he smoothed it out, and folded it up, to put it into his pocket, he said :—" I thank you, nevertheless, signora Katharina, for saving my letter ; though you might have returned it to me in a more gracious manner."

Bianca meanwhile was making a vast deal of the blow on the lips she had received from the paper missile ; calling upon signior Gremio and Hortensio to see how swollen her lip was ; and receiving from them many assurances that the protuberance she pointed out to them, was only its natural pretty pouting rounding and fullness—that it was coral-red, and by no means black-and-blue, &c. &c.

Then Giulio took leave of his friend signior Gremio, saying it was high time he should be on his journey. He addressed a few farewell words to some among the company that were known to him ; and at length came up to Katharina.

" Come ;" said he to her ; " let you and me part friends, for all that's past and gone between us. Shake hands with me—to show you have no malice."

She stood up, trembling violently, but made no answer ; and kept her eyes fixed on the floor,—her face, neck, and arms, one glow of crimson.

" Thou'rt a strange creature ;" he said.   " But come, it may be for the last time ; shake hands."

She seemed immovable.

" If you won't, you won't ; I can't help it, Miscetta."

At that word, as if stung, she exclaimed,—lifting her eyes, and flashing them upon him,—" I hate you !"

" I know you do ; you've proved that long ago ;" he said, laughing ; " but I owe you no grudge.   Farewell !"

He turned away to the rest.   Stationed them at the window from which they could see him at the last visible point on the road he was about to take.   " And then, when I turn, and wave my hat, do you all give me three loud cheers.   And mind you marshal them, Hortensio ; and see that the girls don't huzza out of time ; they always will cheer badly,—either starting off before any one else is ready to begin,—or else raggedly, one after the other,—dropping in with a little additional scream when every body else has done."

He dashed out of the room, exclaiming " Goodbye all !"   And then there was a huddling round the window, and a pressing, and crowding, and chattering ; and little exclamations, from time to time, of " I see him !   No, do you ; where ?   O yes, there ! Now he's going out of the gate—now he's going along the road—now he's coming to the turning—now he's reached the point.   I see ! he turns, and waves his hat !   Huzza !   Huzza !   Huzza !"

As the echo of the last cheer rang through the pavillion, and died away in the distance, a deep sob was heard.

The party of young people started, and turned round. Bianca pointed stealthily to the seat on which Katharina lay at full length, with her face buried in her arms.

"Well ;" said Elvira ; " I think it is most unfeeling, not to say very selfish, of Katharina,—you'll excuse my saying so of your sister, Bianca, my love,—but it certainly is very unfeeling and selfish of her, to be lying there, moaning and groaning, over her sprained wrist, instead of rousing herself to give a parting cheer to such a nice fellow as Giulio. Why didn't you join in the huzzas for the young sailor, Katharina ?" added she, raising her voice that Katharina might hear what she said.

" I can't huzza ;" said Katharina in a thick husky voice.

" She can't huzza *for him ;*" said Bianca, in a low tone. " That's it. She can't bring herself to huzza in his honor ;—she never could bear him,—quite as a child."

" I remember ;" said madame Ciarla ; " when both were children, they quarrelled dreadfully, and——"

She was interrupted by Katharina ; who started up, saying :—" And you,—all of you,—how came you to be able to huzza for your friend ? Mighty fond of him you must be, to be sure, to cheer and huzza at his going away !"

" O, if you're going to quarrel, Katharina, I'm off ;" said Elvira. " You know there must always be two to a quarrel ; and I never choose to quarrel with you —I should be sure to get the worst of it."

" You always have the worst of it, you should say, in your meanness, your sly pretences, your mock-modesties, and your show-offs of meekness, propriety, forbearance, and all the rest of the maidenly decorums which you and my hopeful sister affect ;" said Katharina.

Elvira only shrugged her shoulders, and went away with Bianca, softly tittering and whispering together ; followed by their train of gentleman-admirers.

For some days afterwards, Katharina remained more than commonly silent, and lost in thought ; peevish, and tart, if spoken to ; and very restless in her mood.

At this period, Bianca's visit to Elvira concluded ; and she returned home to her father's house. By a compact between the two friends, they contrived to coax their respective household authorities,—Elvira, her guardian, and Bianca, her father,—into the persuasion that any farther schooling was unnecessary for them ; and they were, in consequence, to return no more to the convent. Masters were henceforth to be engaged, that their education might receive the finishing polish. Bianca professed her love for study, books, and music, with an enthusiasm, which quite charmed her father, signior Minola ; but which might have called forth some sneer from Katharina relative to the slight amount of either, that sufficed her sister at the convent, had not her attention been wholly absorbed in other thoughts.

In one of her restless moods, not a week after the entertainment at signior Gremio's, Katharina took a rambling walk down the road that skirted his estate. On one side of this road, there was a sort of dry ditch, or grass-grown hollow, that sloped upwards with a low green bank, surmounted by a hedge, which enclosed the extensive grounds belonging to him.

By some impulse,—unacknowledged to herself,— Katharina climbed up this bank, and crept into the hedge, holding by a young olive tree which grew there, while she looked earnestly into the enclosure. She soon distinguished the tree which grew upon the lawn ; and for some time kept her eyes fixed upon it, her thoughts recalling the scenes with which it was associated. Again she saw the laughing boy seated there, idly cracking nuts, and carelessly swinging his legs ; —the rustle among the boughs,—the fall—the bleeding temple—the pale face—the insensible form, borne away apparently lifeless. '' I owe you no grudge— I owe you no grudge,'' her lips murmured,

Then she beheld the struggle, when he bound her there, to its trunk. She felt the clasping masterful arms—she saw the scar gleaming beneath the locks of hair—she felt once more that sight, and the force of manly strength and will, bending her to a half-reluctant, half-pleased yielding, beneath their combined potency of influence. And again she murmured ;—" I owe you no grudge—Farewell !"

At that instant, voices approach along the road. Katharina shrinks closely within her leafy covert, holding fast by the olive sapling. The voices come nearer ; and one of them,—which Katharina recognizes for that of madame Ciarla,—says :—" Yes, indeed, a frightful piece of news ! Frightful in itself—frightful in its suddenness. So young ! So full of life and hope ! His first voyage, too. Just as he joined his ship—while he stretched forth his hand to seize the rope by which he was to scramble up her side to the gangway, the boat beneath him gave a lurch, and the poor young fellow fell overboard, sank, and was drowned. It is supposed, he struck his head against the keel of the vessel, for he never rose to the surface after he once went down."

" It's a shocking thing indeed, though I don't know the young man ;" said the other voice ; " What did you say his name was ?"

" Giulio Vinci.—Bless me ! what was that ? A groan ?"

The speakers stop, and listen. " No ; nothing." The voices die away ; and Katharina dropped from the bank into the grass-grown channel at its foot. She lay there some time, as if stunned. At length she returned to a sort of half-conscious, dreamy state, in which she got up and went home. The action of walking in some measure restored her ; but she was still frightfully pale ; which attracted her father's attention, and caused him to reproach her for being so perverse as to go out in the sun, during the heat of the day.    .

In the afternoon, just as the family were going to sit down to their collation of fruit, eggs, coffee, and bread and butter, Katharina happened to cast her eyes through the window, and saw madame Ciarla approaching the house. She instantly felt that the visitor was come to tell the fatal news.

Katharina went to the table, seized up a knife, and began cutting bread and butter. In came the gossiping old lady ; and not a minute elapsed before she was launched into the midst of her story.

" Yes, too true ! Poor dear young man ! Drowned ! Dead !"

Katharina dropped the knife, and held her clasped hands close beneath her chin. " What's the matter now ?" said her father.

" Poor Kate's crying ;" said Bianca ; " Though she couldn't endure him, yet she's shocked to hear of his death."

Katharina gave her one of her fiercest looks.

" What's amiss with your hand, miss Katharina ? There's blood trickling down your arm ;" said madame Ciarla. " Why, you've cut your finger ! and mercy me !—very deep too ! Let me bind it up. See how it's staining your frock !"

" You see, Bianca, my girl, you gave your sister credit for too much feeling—at least, too much feeling for others ; she's crying over her own cut finger, not the poor drowned lad," said Baptista Minola.

" Nay," said Bianca, " I think it was Giulio's death, for——"

" How can you—how dare you, repeat his name ? Take that, to remind you never to do so again in my hearing." And Katharina dashed a cup of hot coffee smack into her sister's neck.

Bianca screamed.

" Plague of my life ! You've scalded your unoffending sister to death. Come hither, my Bianca. As for you, shameless, spiteful hilding ! Begone to your room ! and let me see no more of thee, until thou can'st behave less like a fiend, more like a christian."

Katharina flung out of the room—rushed up to her own chamber—locked the door—threw herself on the bed,—and wept long and bitterly.

The intimacy between Bianca Minola and Elvira Blangini, continued as strongly as ever. Not a day passed, but the girls met at each other's houses. Now it was some flower, or some gossip, or some new stitch, or some new fancy, that had to be shown, imparted, and discussed. They were as profuse as ever, of their epithets of " dear," and " darling," " sweet," and " love," to each other, as they had always been. They kissed each other as fondly, they sat together as closely, they whispered to each other as confidentially as before. But notwithstanding all this, there was a feeling of mutual restraint ; and a sense of hollowness in their friendship, that grew upon them more and more. Perhaps for this very reason, they increased in outward demonstrations of attachment, and professions of regard ; so that every one remarked, how beautiful was the affection between these two young girls, and how touching to see their school-liking still preserved in such strength and constancy.

In secret, however, the hollowness grew and grew, until scarcely more than the mere empty husk of their sworn bosom-friendship was left. It was like the rind of a pear, eaten out by wasps and earwigs ; all the pulp and sweetness sucked forth, while the worthless outside remained—a mere show and semblance of the fruit it once was.

Elvira's whole stock of vanity—and it was by no means small—could no longer blind her to the fact that she had ceased to be the sole object of Hortensio's attentions. She had so long been accustomed to believe them exclusively her own, that it was very difficult to persuade herself, that he was any other than her devoted though unavowed adorer. She for some time continued to look upon his gallant speeches to

Bianca, as only a sort of reflection of the admiration which he felt for herself ; a kind of liking for her friend, for her sake. But when they were not only repeated and multiplied, but assumed more and more of warmth in tone and manner, and were accompanied by significance of look and expression that were almost unmistakable, she began to think of some strong measure for recalling him to his allegiance, such as her self-love, and her long belief in his attachment, would not suffer her to imagine could fail.

She determined to bring to a decided avowal the long-hinted sentiments of her guardian ; doubting not that, when her younger lover should be threatened with the chance of losing her, by a definite proposal of marriage from another it would frighten him into a summary declaration of his own passion.

With so unscrupulous a coquetry as hers, with so cold a heart, so artful a nature, and so wily a tongue, it may be supposed that she was not long in effecting her purpose, so far as her elder prey was concerned. The amorous old gentleman, her guardian, caught only too eagerly at the bait held out to him. He snapped at once ; made his proposal in form ; offered to make what settlements she chose ; and entreated her but to follow up her kind encouragement by forthwith promising to be his.

She, with well-affected modesty and discretion, required a few hours to consider of his proposal ere she gave her final answer ; and then, having made sure of his absence from home, by entreating him to pay a visit to a friend whose estate lay at some distance, on the plea of wishing to have complete solitude for the important self-consultation which was to decide the happiness of her life, she took her way to the summer-house in the garden, and was not long in contriving to summon Hortensio to her side.

In the conversation that ensued, she found, to her dismay, that she had entirely miscalculated the aim of his affections. He plainly told her they were fixed

on her friend Bianca ; and by pretending not to see
the amazement caused by his announcement, he effectually turned the tables on her own duplicity.

Her pride enabled her to make some show of con-
cealing her disappointment, her resentment, and the
crowd of conflicting feelings that tormented her ; but
the moment she decently could, she dismissed him,
left the summer-house, and retired to her own room,
where she threw herself into an arm-chair, and medi-
tated on what should now be her course of conduct.

Her first feeling was of despair at having so fatally
mistaken the sentiments of one, whom she now felt
she loved but too fondly.   Her next, was one of rage,
that he should have so fickly transferred to another,
that preference, which she flattered herself was fixed
upon herself.   Her next, that of detestation at the
arts and blandishments of the little flirt who had lured
him from her.   In her despair, she wrung her hands,
and vowed she would die.   In her rage, she ground
her teeth, and vowed she would turn her love into
hate.   In her detestation, she bit her lips until the
blood sprang, and vowed she would have revenge.
But at length, her despair, her rage, her detestation,
found consolation in the thought that she would best
satisfy them all three by an immediate acceptance of
her guardian's offer of marriage.   By this act, she
would proclaim her indifference to the treachery of her
lover and her friend ; and by the wealth and importance it would secure, give her the means of eclipsing,
mortifying, and triumphing, over them.

The thought of this, enabled her to meet her guardian on his return home with spirits sufficient to play
him off a scene of coquettish compliance—of affected
coyness, hesitation, reluctance, pretty diffidence, and
young-lady fastidiousness, with a pretence of smothered liking beneath all, that put the old inamorata into
a fever of admiration and delight.   On the strength
of it, he, of his own accord, gave directions to the no-
tary that, in case of his death she should be secured

mistress of all his wealth, by a no less ample jointure, than by constituting her his sole legatee.

Elvira was not long in giving herself the first of her proposed indemnifications for the sacrifice she considered she had just made of her youth and beauty. She called upon her friend Bianca Minola, to announce her approaching marriage.

"To your guardian! My dearest creature," said Bianca, "how could you think of accepting him? he's old enough to be your father. It is an absolute sacrilege to think of giving such passing loveliness, as yours, my darling Elvira, to such a battered old beau as that!"

"I must entreat you to remember, my sweet Bianca, that you speak now of my future husband; and I really cannot permit your partiality for your friend to lead you into the sin of injustice and disrespect towards my lord and master."

"I do him but justice, surely, when I say he is too old for my beautiful Elvira?" said Bianca. "O my dear! Don't let the phantom of riches dazzle you to the misery of devoting yourself to a silly disagreeable old man."

"He is neither silly, disagreeable, nor—so very old;" said Elvira.

"Is he not silly in wishing to purchase a young wife with his money? Is he not disagreeable in his attempts to play off the young lover and husband? Is he not old enough to be your father? And oh, my dear, darling, sweetest Elvira, consider how little can money compensate for disparity of years. See here, darling, what a beautiful string of pearls, and what a handsome Venice chain, and what a rich damask silk, I have had sent me by a suitor of mine. But in spite of all these fine gifts, I assure you, I don't mean to be tempted—nothing should induce me! He's too old for me—it would be wrong, quite wrong; and therefore I shall refuse him."

"And who is he?" said Elvira; unexpectedly in

the position of hearing her friend's triumphs, rather than detailing her own.

" Old signior Gremio ; he pesters me out of my life. So does signior Hortensio. I shall certainly have to complain to my father if these suitors persist in plaguing me so. Not a day passes but one or the other of them is sending me some fine token or other, of their troublesome attachment."

" Troublesome ! Hortensio's attachment troublesome ! Why do you encourage him, then, if you find his attachment so troublesome ?'' said Elvira.

" Encourage him ! Goodness, I don't encourage him. But how can I help it, if he will admire, and besiege me, and load me with attentions, and presents, and protestations ; swearing that he worships me, and me only, and that he's dying for me."

" He swears that, does he ?'' said Elvira.

" O la, yes ! And fifty absurd things beside, of the same kind. But I'm not so silly as to believe a word of it, you know, darling, of course."

" Of course not ;'' said her friend rising to depart, and giving her a farewell kiss on the forehead. " You, so honest, so transparent, so innocent, so truthful, so artless, and so modest, know better than to credit the flatteries, insincerities, and false praise, of such men as Hortensio,—of such beings as suitors. They're all alike."

" That's the only merit of an old one ;'' said Bianca ; " they're more sincere, perhaps ; but then they're in every respect so odious. Goodbye, dearest darling ! Since you are bent on having your ancient spouse—although (excuse the partiality of a friend) I think you're wrong—may all felicity,—all possible felicity,—attend your nuptials !''

" Hollow, deceitful, treacherous toad !'' ejaculated Elvira, as she left her friend's house.

The marriage was,—in deference to the bridegroom's impatience—to take place in a few days. And immediately after the ceremony, the new-married couple left Padua for a beautiful villa they possessed, a few miles out of town.

A week after the wedding, madame Ciarla paid a visit to the Minolas, full of news she had just received. It was no other than that on the previous day, Elvira's husband had been seized with a fit of apoplexy, which after a few hours' duration, had put an end to his life.

" Shocking, isn't it ?  Not a week married, and already a widow !  So young too, poor thing !'' said madame Ciarla in conclusion.

" How interesting she'll look in her widow's weeds, poor darling thing !'' remarked Bianca.

" Ah ! you deserve to be a beauty yourself, as you are, my dear Miss Bianca ;'' said the old lady, who was more good-natured than deep-sighted.  " You are never backward in praising the beauty of others.''

" I hope I know my duty better than to be envious, or anything that is wrong and wicked ;'' said Bianca.

" Dear young lady ! you are famed far and wide for your mild behaviour, your beauty, and your modesty.  Well would it be if your sister would take pattern by you.''

" O, but she dislikes taking pattern—and she says she hates model-people.  Poor dear Katharina !'' sighed Bianca.  " She disdains to imitate excellence. She does not wish to be good.  She has not the least virtuous emulation.  Poor dear Kate !''

Time went on.  The young widow remained in wealthy seclusion at her villa.  Bianca's character for sweetness, and artless modesty increased ; while Katharina,—her temper irritable and morose, her manner violent and abrupt, her voice harsh, her words in-solent,—gained the reputation of being a confirmed shrew.  Her father, Baptista Minola, tired out with her conduct,—yet forgetting how much of its cause might be traced to his own habit of reproach, and to his having failed to see that she was surrounded with proper and curative influences of education, in moral and mental discipline,—found himself perpetually longing to get rid of her presence, by her marriage with some one who would remove her out of his way, out of his house, out of his daily seeing and hearing.

About this time he learned the views of signior Gremio and signior Hortensio, with regard to his youngest daughter, Bianca. But he informed them, that until his eldest was disposed of in marriage, he could not think with parting with her sister ; adding, that either of them were welcome to take Katharina. This intimation,—as might be expected from its unfatherly want of delicacy,—was received slightingly and with open disrespect by the two gentlemen. Their proposals, Baptista Minola's reply, and the rejoinder, happened to be made in both the daughters' presence ; and, enraged to hear herself thus treated, Katharina turned sharply to her father, saying :—

> *" I pray you sir, is it your will*
> *To make a stale of me among these mates ?"*

The conversation going on angrily, Bianca says, first to Katharina, then to her father :—

*" Sister, content you in my discontent.*
*Sir, to your pleasure humbly I subscribe :*
*My books and instruments shall be my company ;*
*On them to look, and practise by myself."*

---

How the shrew is tamed into the submissive wife ; how the scolding tongue becomes schooled to duteous accents ; how the beauteous modesty and maiden mildness, show in their demure intrigues, their clandestine flirtations, their sly construings, with music-master and book-man, and in their open unmasking, and native insolence of self-assertion, the moment the marriage-tie is knit, and the husband secured ; are all set forth by one to whom the author of this poor story says :—

> *"* Well, you are come to me in happy time,
> The rather for I have some sport in hand,
> Wherein your cunning can assist me much."

# OPHELIA; THE ROSE OF ELSINORE.

TALE VIII.

## OPHELIA ; THE ROSE OF ELSINORE.

" O Rose of May !
Dear maid, kind sister, sweet Ophelia !"
*Hamlet.*

THE babe lay on the nurse's knee. Could any impression have been received through those wide-stretched eyes, that stared as wonderingly as if they were in fact beholding amazed the new existence upon which they had so lately opened, the child would have seen that it lay in a spacious apartment, furnished with all the tokens of wealth and magnificence, which those ruder ages could command. There were thick hangings of costly stuff to exclude the keen outer air and chill mists of that north climate. The furniture of the room was constructed of the rarer kind of woods, and fashioned with the utmost skill and taste in design then attained. The dogs that sustained the fir clumps blazing on the hearth, were of classical form and device ; and the andirons on either side, were of a no less precious material than silver. The sconces round the apartment were of the same metal ; while the spoon, cup, and other utensils appropriated to the infant's use were of gold. Could any dawning sense of external objects yet have made its way to the brain through those wide-stretched· violet eyes, they might have noted that a tall figure, of graceful mien, of gracious aspect, frequently came to bend over, and utter murmured words of joy and tenderness, and breathe mother's blessings upon the little baby head.   They might have perceived that another figure of less gentle aspect, but kindly and fond, would come to look upon the little daughter lately vouchsafed to him ; and that still another, a young boy, would advance on tiptoe to peep at, and touch very carefully, the strange baby sister.   Of the large broad good humoured face that more constantly hung over it ; of the huge splay hand that enclosed its own diminutive one in the recesses of the crumby palm ; of the white amplitude of warmth, and softness, and comfort, and repose, against which the babe buried its nose and nestled its cheek, and from which it drew forth delicious streams of nourishment, the wide-stretched violet eyes probably gained clearer perception ; for they learned to look eagerly for these evidences of the presence and the ministry of the good peasant woman, who had been engaged to perform the office of wet-nurse and foster-mother to the little Ophelia,—daughter of the lord Polonius, and of the lady Aoudra.

There were extensive gardens belonging to the nobleman's house ; and in these the good nurse Botilda would carry her baby charge up and down, during the more genial hours of the day ; while by the side of child and nurse, gambolled the young boy, Laertes.   When the violet eyes learned to distinguish objects upon which they rested, they grew fond of dwelling upon the lively brother, of following his antics, of watching his sports ; and then baby would crow, and spring, and leap in the nurse's arms, with sympathetic delight at his active movements.

When the sun faded from the gravel-paths, and the shadows lengthened, and the watchful nurse knew that the mists and dews of evening were stealing on, to take the place of the earlier afternoon warmth, she would carry her nursling in-doors, and lull it to sleep upon her lap, and hush it against her bosom, crooning ends of old-word ditties, and scraps of antique ballads, such as she knew.

The lady Aoudra's attendant, Kraka, one day saw fit to call the rustic nurse to account for the subject of one of these songs, which struck her town-bred notions as somewhat lacking in the matter of decorum. "Hast thou ne'er a cradle-song, or proper nursery-rhyme, good Botilda, to chant to my lady's baby? The songs thou choosest for the child's lullaby, are none of the most seemly for the purpose, to my poor thinking."

"I choose them not;" answered the peasant; "my stock of songs, God wot, is none so large, that I may pick and choose. I'm fain to sing such as I know; I care not for the sense, so that the sound serves to lull my little one; it matters not for the meaning, which is none to her, so that the tune helps to keep her quiet and to close her eyes."

"There's no knowing how soon a babe may catch a meaning," said the lady's maid, tossing her head: "meanings,—'specially naughty meanings,—are sooner caught than you, in your country rudeness, might suppose, good mistress Botilda. There's no telling how early a child may spy out wickedness in words—they're so 'cute in listening, and pretending not to understand, and all the while making out a deal that they oughtn't. There's much more o' that going on, than you'd think, mistress Botilda."

"Of a surety, children are not the only ones to spy out wickedness, and catch naughty meanings, where no harm's intended; and then making a pretence of over-innocence,—the more's the pity;" replied the nurse. "But as for my poor foolish old songs, I can't think they'd do mischief to any one that isn't set upon seeing more in 'em than's meant—let alone a sucking-babe, that makes out nought of the words but the chime and the rhyme they make."

"No harm? no mischief?" exclaimed Kraka; "why, there's that tawdry nonsense you sing about St. Valentine's day. I should like to know what you make out of that; good mistress Botilda?"

"I leave it to you, to make out what you have a fancy for from it, mistress Kraka;" said the nurse quietly. "I can only say, as I said before, no need to mind the words of my song, so that the tune soothes my baby; no call to take heed of the matter, so that the murmur pleases her; it's no matter to me; and certainly no matter to the child, that can't make matter out of it."

"What stupid animals these country folks are!" muttered the waiting-maid; "little better than swine, in their brutish ignorance of what's what, and in their obstinate sticking to what they've once said."

"Let them that like to ferret out filth, find what they have a mind to, in my old songs;" said the nurse to herself; "only don't let 'em go and give their nasty notions to my innocent child; who, if ever she should chance to catch up the words by-and-by, from hearing me repeat 'em, would only do so, like a prattling starling, for the sake of the sound, and without a thought of any bad meaning."

Before the little Ophelia could run any risk of learning either words or meaning of the foster-mother's songs, inasmuch as it was before she could speak, the good Botilda's office of wet-nurse ceased; she returned to her peasant-family, her native country-home; while Ophelia's own mother, the lady Aoudra, gladly took the charge of her little girl upon herself. She had hitherto neglected to fulfil the most important maternal duty, solely from the physical cause of disability. Not long, however, did she enjoy this new delight of cherishing and watching the infant growth of her child. Ophelia was yet a little toddling thing, when her father, the lord Polonius, received an appointment as ambassador in Paris, and was compelled to quit the Danish court for an uncertain period.

So distinguished an honour, as this official dignity conferred upon him by his sovereign, was a matter of high self-gratulation to the ambitious courtier; and he determined to fulfil his mission with such pomp with such unsparing profusion of outlay, as should best prove how worthy he was of the office for which he had been selected. He resolved that, as the representative of royalty, his travelling appointments should be princely in their richness, their magnitude ; and for the like reason, his household and retinue, when established in the French capital, should be of even regal magnificence. In order the better to carry out his views of making his embassy as complete a semblance of royalty as might be, he determined that his wife should accompany him, remarking that a court without a queen, an embassy without an embassadress, were shorn of half their splendour and influence. His lady, dreading the lengthened separation from her children which this would involve, made an attempt to dissuade him from the arrangement, begging to be left behind in Elsinore with her young son and daughter, until such time as they should be old enough to travel with her ; when they could all three join him in Paris together.

But Polonius gave several weighty reasons why this could not be done ; alleging that the first impression was the most important ; that he was convinced greater effect was produced by the presence of a lady —that it attracted other ladies ; that the more ladies attracted and attached, the better, inasmuch as the influence of woman's wit and woman's beauty had ever been acknowledged to be some of the most potent agencies in a court atmosphere ; together with several other sage and worldly observations in support of his views, and ending with an intimation that, in short, it was his will she should go with him at first and at once. Without further opposition, therefore, to her husband's will, the lady Aoudra prepared to obey by making arrangements for the suitable placing of her children during their parents' absence. For Laertes, the boy, there was the protection of his uncle ; a wealthy old bachelor, and retired general ; who found the seclusion and repose of his arm-chair to be the

sole refuge for which his wounds and their consequent
infirmity had left him fitted.   For the little Ophelia,
her mother determined she should be confined to the
care of her former nurse, Botilda.   She resolved to
risk the want of refinement in the peasant home, for
the sake of its simple food, its pure air, its kindly
hearty foster-care.   She trusted to the child's extreme
youth—scarce beyond babyhood—for security that
she should not acquire coarse habits, or imbibe unseemly notions.   She hoped herself to return to Denmark before the time when it was necessary to begin
the inculcation of principle, the inspiring of ideas,
the formation of heart and mind.   Meantime she
thought health of body, vigour of frame, activity of
limb, the main things to be secured for her child ;
and this she thought could best be done by sending
the little girl to the cottage of Sigurd and his wife
Botilda.   She knew they had children,—although
they had lost the youngest, the one whose early death
had procured Ophelia the wet-nurse services of the
peasant,—and she thought with them, her own child
would be brought up in health and hardihood, in exercise and open-air pursuits, and in kindly affection,
even if somewhat roughly and unrefinedly nurtured.

The lady Aondra determined to place her child herself in the arms of its foster-mother.   She ordered
her litter, and set forth on her short journey, consoling herself with the thought that she should at least
see the spot in which she was about to leave her
youngest darling ;  where she might picture her to
herself hereafter, during the long tedious period of
absence.   She did her utmost to combat the sorrow-
ful feelings, the half-defined fears that beset her as the
thought of that absence pressed upon her ;  she strove
to dwell upon none but cheerful thoughts and hopeful
fancies for the future, that the present moment might
remain unclouded in the remembrance of her little
girl, who sat beside her, looking in her face, and asking her questions of the new places and strange objects

among which they were passing. She exerted herself to entertain the child, that no suspicion of her own grief might interfere to mar the pleasure and enjoyment of this first journey, so full of delight and curiosity, and interest to the little one. At length the excitement, the constant demand upon her attention, the many hours past in the open air, which made its way through the curtain of the litter, caused the little Ophelia to fall into a profound sleep. Then the lady allowed herself to drop back among the cushions, and give way to her emotions at the thought of the parting that was so soon to come between her and her child. Weeping, and in silence, the poor mother travelled the remainder of the way,—praying earnestly.

All that she saw at the cottage of Botilda confirmed her in the previous conviction she had felt, that its advantages would outweigh its disadvantages. It was a clean wholesome place ; its inhabitants were homely but kindly ; and the lady Aoudra felt that her child would be healthfully and affectionately tended—the two great requisites at her age. She found, too, that the little Ophelia's chief companion would be Jutha, the only daughter of the peasant couple—a young girl of some fifteen or sixteen years of age, of the most winning appearance, gentle-mannered, sweet-tempered, and extremely beautiful. This afforded peculiar comfort to the lady-mother, as she knew how attracted children are by beauty ; and how happy their existence is made by gentleness and even-temper, in those who have charge of them. To Jutha then, she especially recommended the care and tendance of her babe ; knowing how superfluous it was to bespeak more of that which already so lavishly flowed in devoted affection towards it, on the part of the good nurse. And then the mother, assisted by these two, —who were in future to supply her place,—laid the sleeping babe in the rude wooden cot, and took a weeping farewell of her treasure.

" Let not the hot tears fall on the babe, my lady ;" whispered the foster-mother ; " they'll disturb her, an they drop upon her face ; a mother's tears are not to be felt without bale and smart, even by one so young. Besides, parting tears bring no good luck ; they're no blessed shower to sprinkle your babe with. Let her have a kiss and a smile, an ye can muster one, my lady, as a keepsake for the child, until ye come back to give her kisses and smiles the whole day long, as plenty as lips can give them."

An earnest pressure of the nurse's arm, told how well the kindly intent of her words was understood by the lady. By a strong effort, she succeeded in mastering her grief sufficiently to bestow a better-omened caress upon her child. The last kiss she gave it, as it still lay in a deep sleep, was almost cheerful, for she cast her eye up hopefully, and commended her little one to heavenly guardianship. Over the face of the babe, as it slumbered, crept a soft answering smile ; and then the mother, accepting the angelic token, turned silently away, and stepped into a litter, more serene at heart than she could have hoped.

For some hours after her mother had left her, the unconscious Ophelia slumbered on. The journey, the passing through the air, caused her to sleep soundly ; and there she remained, perfectly still, drawing soft regular breathings, with one hand beneath the peachy cheek, the other lying plump, and dimpled, and white, on the coarse coverlet. The rough wooden cot in which she lay, had been the resting-place of all the peasant-babes born there in succession. It was rudely fashioned but strong and safe, raised away from the ground upon high legs, which prevented the hostile approach of any wandering cat or other more formidable animal. It was furnished with bedding, coarse and homely, but clean and sweet-scented from the open bleaching ; and,—by the care of Jutha, whose pride it was to see it always kept neat and nice—a pretty object in the family sitting-room. As Sigurd and his two eldest sons, Harald and Ivar, came in from their daily labour, at eventide, they went and peeped at the little stranger who had become their inmate. Sigurd said some kind words to his wife Botilda, of his being glad she had the little lady-babe to take the place of the one she had lost ; and that it would do them both good to see the cot filled once more. The two tall lads, who looked like friendly ogres, or good-humoured giants, looked at the sleeping child, as if she had been a young bird, or a half hidden spring-flower nestling beneath a hedge.

"What a bit of a thing she be ! she looks as easy to be blown away, easy to be looked through, as sweet and as blooming, as a handful of rose-leaves, don't she ?" quoth Harald.

"Ay, she do ;" said Ivar. "She scarce looks like a baby, such as you or I once was. What a pretty creature 'tis !"

The family sat down to their evening meal ; while Botilda showed her husband the purse of money and the presents the lady Aoudra had given them to take charge of her child ; told him of the engagement she had made, to forward them each month a sum for its maintenance ; that the lady wished them to increase their own comforts at the same time ; and that in consequence, she, Botilda, had provided an extra supper for them to make a sort of feast in celebration of her own little lady-babe's coming among them.

Meantime the infant Ophelia continued to sleep on. But as one of the good-humoured giants happened to forget himself, and give a louder laugh than he had hitherto done, the sound disturbed her ; she turned, and opened her eyes, and lay awake. She was none of those fretful children, who, the very first thing they uniformly do upon waking up from sleep, is to roar ; on the contrary, she lay silent and still for a moment or two, and then raising herself softly against the side of the cot, rubbed her eyes, and looked over. It was a strange scene she beheld ; quite different from anything that had ever met them before. Instead of the spacious apartment, lighted by silver sconces, and hung with rich tapestries ; there was a raftered low room, a rough deal table, round which sat some uncouth figures on wooden chairs, eating by the light of a single oil-fed iron lamp. There was an elderly man, with a weather-beaten face, and grizzly locks ; there was an elderly woman, whose face seemed known to the child who was staring at them ; there were two very tall young men with bushy beards, rough hair, and good-natured faces ; there was a boy with large hairy hands, a fell of shock hair upon his head, shaggy eyebrows, from beneath which gleamed a restless pair of grey eyes, and a huge bare throat that swelled, and moved, and showed the big morsels which he was shoveling into his mouth, as they made their way along the gullet to the stomach. The staring baby's eyes, after dwelling sometime with a kind of uncomfortable awe upon this object, saw, lastly, that there was another figure at the table,—that of a young girl, beautiful and pleasant to look upon. The little Ophelia was still silently gazing upon all this ; when the hairy boy gave a grin—mutely writhing his face ; and then he pointed stealthily towards the cot, saying in a low growl, singularly harsh and discordant, though not loud :—" See ; 'little court-lady's awake."

" My baby awake, and I not notice it !" exclaimed Botilda, about to hurry towards the cot, in fear that the child would cry, and be startled at finding itself among strangers.

" Let her be a bit !" said Sigurd, laying his hand on his wife's arm ; " and let's see what she'll do : she don't seem a bit scared like, at all us new faces."

On the contrary, the child seemed entertained ; and continued to look from one to another, patting her hand on the end of the cot, and humming a little song to herself ; they all watching her the while with quiet, amused glances.

By and bye, she drew a long breath, looked round, and said :—" Mamma !"

Botilda and Jutha both now went towards her ; doing their best to distract her attention from the thought, which had at length evidently struck her. With the facile spirits of childhood, this was no difficult task. She was brought over to the table to take her first rustic meal of bread and milk, which she did with much relish,—despite the absence of the gold service which had hitherto administered her refection, —and with much apparent contentment, leaning against the familiar bosom of her nurse, frolicking and making acquaintance with the smiling beauty of Jutha, and graciously allowing the burly peasant Sigurd to curl her miniature hand round his great big horny forefinger. In short, the little lady-babe seemed at once to take to her foster-family, and make herself at home with them.

After this inaugural meal, however, when Botilda had, as a matter of course, taken charge of her nursling, Jutha contrived to secure the exclusive care of the child from that time forth. She had it to sleep with her, in her own little bed, the wooden cot serving for a day-couch merely,—she fed it, she washed and dressed it, she amused it, she danced and tossed it, she held it on her knee when she sat, she carried it about with her when she went out. She dedicated herself entirely to its comfort and happiness, and made it in return her own joy and delight. She would have been its servant, if such willing ministry as hers could be called servitude ; she would have been its slave, if such voluntary bondage as hers could be slavery ; as it was, she was the little creature's fond devoted girl-mother ; she had that peculiar affection which young girls have for a baby,—the childish, fondling, protective feeling, mingled with a sense of power, as towards a doll, or a plaything possession ;

the tender, thoughtful solicitude, the instinct of motherly feeling, as towards a little being dependant on her for life and welfare.

On the morning after Ophelia's arrival at the cottage, she was sitting on the young girl's knee, in that half drowsy state of quiet, which is apt to succeed a violent game of romps. Tired with laughter, panting with exertion, she lay back to enjoy complete rest and silence ; while her eyes fell dreamily upon a figure on the other side of the room. It was that of the hairy loutish boy. He was lying half crouching, half kneeling, in a recess in the wall opposite, killing flies. As the insects buzzed and flitted to and fro, he eyed them from beneath his shaggy brows, with snorting eagerness, and tongue out-lolling ; ever and anon taking aim with his hairy paw, and at each successful dab that sent a crushed and mangled fly to swell the heap which already lay there, the lout gave a grin. Sometimes he would chop among the mound of dead, with a knife that lay beside him ; sometimes he would seize one of the living ones by the wing, or the leg, and hold it between finger and thumb, watching its buzzing struggles, and grinning at its futile flutterings ; then let it go again, to pounce upon, and deal it its death-blow. The child lay looking at him in a sort of bewitched inability to remove her eyes from an object that filled her with uneasy wonder ; while Jutha, accustomed to the uncouth cruelty of her idiot brother, Ulf, had not perceived that the child's attention was fixed upon him. Presently, Botilda's voice sounded from an inner room, desiring Jutha to come and help her with some household matter that she had in hand. Jutha placed the little Ophelia softly on the floor, put some playthings near her, and bade her sit still for a few minutes till she came back. The child sat, with her eyes unmoved from the fly-killer. Presently he turned, and spied her. He gave one of his silent grins.

" Are you one of the Elle folk ?" he said.

No answer.

" Or the Trolls ?" asked he again.

No answer.

" You're little enough ; and pretty enough. But I remember, you're the little court-lady." He continued to stare down upon her, grinning ; as she kept her eyes fixed upon him. " Come to the bear !" he exclaimed presently, in his discordant tones ; " come here, and shake hands with me."

No answer, but a shake of the head ; as she eyed the huge paw held out to her. ." Come to the bear, I tell ye !" growled he. " I shan't eat ye. Only hug ye. Come to the bear !"

" No !"—desperately ; with a more vehement shake of the head.

" What if I threw this at ye, and knocked off your legs like one of them ?" said he, pointing with his knife to the heap of dead and dying flies stripped of their legs and wings.

Ophelia gave a startled scream.

In ran Jutha and her mother.

" Little court-lady's proud ; and won't shake hands with Ulf, the bear ;" he said, lolling out his tongue, and grinning.

" What have you been about, brute ?" said Botilda. " Frightening my baby, I shouldn't wonder. Take care how you ever do that, once for all, mind ; or I'll beat you, as long as I can stand over you."

" And that an't long, now ;" grinned he. " I get bigger, and beyond your strength ; you hurt your own hands, more than you do my shoulders, when you thump me now."

" You limb !" said his mother, shaking her fist at him ; " but mind my words. You dare not frighten my baby ; and if ever you do, it'll be the worse for you. She's the great lord Polonius's child, sent here to be taken care of—not to be harmed or frighted ; and he'll punish ye, if I can't, should his child be hurt."

" I didn't want to hurt her ; I wanted to hug her
—and she wouldn't let me."

" Don't touch her at all, Ulf dear, to hurt, or to
hug her ;" said his sister Jutha.  " She don't know
that our bear's hugs are harmless.  She don't know
you're called in sport, Ulf, the bear.  Let her get
used to you, before you try to make friends with her.
She got used to me, before she'd come to me from
mother, you know, last night."

" You always make me do what you will, Jutha ;"
grunted Ulf.  " But I don't mind pleasing you ; you
please me, and give the bear things he likes, sweet
food—good eating."

Sigurd's cottage was situated in a pleasant spot ;
one of the most fertile in all the island.  It overlooked
a green valley, embosomed in swelling hills ; and
towards the north-east it was screened by a thick and
lofty forest of primæval trees.  The soil in the immediate neighbourhood of the cottage was favourable to
vegetation ; but among the hills, it was rocky and
sandy—more in keeping with the prevailing character
of Danish ground.  The air was generally temperate,
though moist, being subject to mists ;—which, in the
more inclement seasons, became dense fogs ; and in
the winter there were fierce winds, with frequent
snow, hail, and sleet.  But during the summer and
autumn months, the climate was far from ungenial ;
and Jutha took care that her charge should then enjoy
as much of the open air as possible.  They would go
forth at quite early morning, and with some food in
Jutha's basket, would ramble abroad all day long.
Sometimes, they made exploring expeditions among
the hills ; now stopping to sit among the craggy
rocks ; now loitering in some curious cavern or grotto,
watching the plashings and oozings of the water that
made its way through crevice and fissure, down-drop-
ping amid the moss and lichens, and long stalactites,
and bright spars that behung the roof and sides.
Sometimes they would wander in the green depths of

the forest ; and sit on the moss-grown gnarled roots
of some old oak or elm-tree, or beneath a spreading
beech or tall feathery ash, while the young girl-mother
would bid the child mark the shape of the leaf, and
branch, and bark and bough, of rugged trunk and
smooth bole, until she learned to know tree from tree,
and to amuse herself by distinguishing one kind from
another. Jutha would point out, with rustic taste,
the luxuriant masses of foliage that enriched the monarch oak ; the noble strength and amplitude of its
sturdy body ; the vigorous growth of its giant arms ;
the strange grotesque forms into which its ramification
spread, in sinuous and angular branches ; the deep
indentation of its leaves, the curious cup, and smooth
fruit of its acorns ; the mottled red and white of its
apples ; the pearly berries of its parasite mistletoe.
She would show her the straight smooth-rinded stem
of the beech-tree, and how the pointed glossy leaves
grew in palmated branches, and flat fanlike sprays,
ever up-inclined, like huge sylvan hands raised heaven-
ward. She told her which was the stately elm, with
its graceful height, and amplitude of leaf and bough.
She taught her to know the towering ash, with its
light waving plumes of green ; the birch, with its
pensile sweeps of slender twigs behung with small
round leaves ;—the alder and elder, with their close
dwarf clusters ;—the firs and pines with their upright
stems, brown-coned and sober in the sullen season,
emerald-tufted and cheerful in spring-time ;—the sal-
low, with its downy catkins ;—the willow, with its
sad-drooping tresses, mirrored in the stream. She
would take her to bowery thickets in the wood, where
the pansy and the columbine grew wild ; and they
would peep among the grass, for shy lurking violets,
and pile up their basket with bright daisies, and bring
home roots of rosemary, fennel and rue, for the herb-
corner of their garden. Sometimes, Jutha would lead
the little one as far as the sea-shore ; where they
would pick up shells, as they strayed along the smooth

sand ; and when the billows came tumbling in, crested
with foam, rolling over one another in huge monstrous
frolic—like lion whelps at play—and when the sea-
breeze blew freshly, and the spray flew over the rocks,
bounding, and tossing, and breaking against them,
flinging itself wildly apart, and abroad, in silver
showers, as it caught the gleaming sunlight, the young
girl would tell the child how these vast waters of the
sea, that now looked so bright and gay, grew dark,
and threatening, and angry, when the stormy winds
of the north lashed them into fury.  She told her of
the adventurous men who put forth in search of the
fish that abounded on those shores ; she told her how
they braved the dangers of shoals, sunken rocks,
banks of quicksand, and whirlpools, to gain a bare
livelihood ; and how, sometimes, their boats were
sucked in, and buried beneath the waves that now
looked so buoyant and sparkling,—then murky,
tumultuous, menacing ; fraught with danger and
doom.

For a few moments, the little Ophelia would stand
with her eyes fixed upon the wide expanse of sea,
surging, and heaving, and swelling before her ; while
a feeling of awe would creep over her, at the thought
of a watery death—of the whelming billows, of the
down-sinking struggle, of the stifled breath, of the
stopped sight and hearing—of the heart-despair of
those poor drowning souls, of whom she heard tell—
the brave fishermen ; then, with the true happy ease
of childish spirits, incapable of long dwelling upon a
mournful idea, she would turn once more to her shell
collection ; admiring their pretty colours, and curious
shapes, and putting some of the larger ones to her
ear, that she might listen to the sea roaring within
them—as it were, distant, yet close beside her.
These rambles abroad with Jutha were the pleasantest
periods of the little Ophelia's sojourn among her
foster family.  When she was at the cottage itself,
she was dull, uncomfortable, uneasy, with a vague

feeling of disquietude and timidity, almost amounting to a sense of harm and danger. She felt herself strange and apart, among so many people nowise suited to her. After the first interest and curiosity excited by the vision of the little lady among them, Sigurd and his two elder sons, Harold and Ivar, took little notice of her, beyond a passing nod, or a good-humoured grin, when they were at home,—which was not often, or for long. They rose before it was well-nigh light, and were out and off to work by day-break; taking with them the means for their noon-tide meal, and returning to the cottage only in time for the supper, which immediately preceded their retiring to rest.

Botilda was ever occupied with household drudgery, in which she frequently enlisted the services of Jutha; so that neither from the nurse or her daughter, could the child obtain much companionship, when within the house. She was thus thrown entirely upon her own resources; and these were few or none for pro-curing entertainment, never having learned to play, or to amuse herself, from any child of her own age. Children, from each other, learn the sports, as well as gain the ideas, proper to their time of life : and it is seldom that a solitary little one either thinks, acts, or amuses itself like those who have been brought up in the society of others. She would, for the most part, when at the cottage, sit still, watching Ulf, the idiot boy, with a sort of helpless, fascinated, involuntary attention. She had never been prevailed upon by his attempted advances towards an intimacy between them, any more than on the first morning, when she had observed his hideous sport, and he had sought to lure her towards him to be hugged ; but although she would never go close to him, or suffer him to approach her, yet she seemed to derive a sort of desperate pleas-ure, and uncomfortable gratification, a strange, half-excited, half-dreading enjoyment in hovering about his vicinity, watching fearfully and wonderingly his uncouth ways. She looked tremblingly loath, at the very time she gazed upon him ; shrinking and averse, while she hung about near his haunts ; but it seemed as if she could not refrain from noting what possessed such mingled attraction and repulsion for her. It was with a kind of dismayed interest, that she would stand aloof, silently ; or sit, perfectly still and motionless, to watch, with fixed eyes, and suspended breath, the ugly odious Ulf. Once, he was squatting near the hearth, with a huge foot clasped in each of his large hairy hands, his chin resting between his knees, his leering blood-shot eyes staring greedily towards a string of small birds, which were dangling to roast, by the wood embers.

" Have some ?" said he abruptly, turning to the child, as he became aware of her presence ; " they'll soon be done."

The little Ophelia shook her head.

" But they're nice, I can tell ye. They're nice to sing—but they're nicer to eat." And he smacked his great broad lips, that were drawn wide from ear to ear.

Ophelia shuddered.

" Hark, how they frizzle !" said he ; and his large flapping ears moved and shifted as he spoke. " Sniff, how savory they smell !" And the black bristly nostrils gaped and expanded, while the blood rushed into his face, as was its wont, when he felt pleasure ; and all the lines of his countenance were contorted, writhing to and fro, as he gave his peculiar silent grin.

Presently, he clutched the roast in his fist, and exclaiming :—" they're done ! they're done !" held it out towards the little girl, repeating, " Have some ? you'd better !" while his eyes gloated beneath his shaggy brows, at her, and at the viands.

" Isn't it too hot for you to hold ?" asked the little Ophelia, as if she couldn't help putting the question —from wonder to see him grasp the burning food.

" Ha, ha ! the bear's paw is too tough to be scalded ; and I like my victuals hot ;" said Ulf, thrusting one of the birds into his mouth, whole, crunching it through, bones and all, and then bolting it, at one gulp.

As the child listened to the noise he made, his fangs champing into the bones and mangled flesh, and looked at the savage greed with which he crammed, she thought he seemed some wild beast, ravening his prey.

There was something cruel, and malicious in this idiot-boy's mode of doing even simpler things than eating singing-birds, or killing flies, which gave an air of horrible meaning, in the little girl's eyes, to his acts. She saw him once tearing up a rose ; and it seemed a tyranny and a barbarity, as if inflicted on a sentient creature. Leaf after leaf fell, as if they were rent limbs. When he held up the bare stalk, the stripped calyx and yellow centre looked like a skeleton ; and he twitched out the golden stamens, as though they were eyelashes, or teeth. He appeared to take a ferocious delight in ripping up and destroying flowers ; and would pluck off the winged petals from sweet peas, as if he loved to deprive them of their seeming power of fairy flight. The vindictive satisfaction with which he exercised this power upon things of beauty and fragility, and the air of triumph with which he gloated over his work of ravage as he leered at her after each feat of the kind, made the little girl always feel somehow as if she were herself the bird, or the fly, or the rose, or whatsoever other object might chance to be the victim of Ulf's destructive propensity. And yet, he expresses liking for her, not enmity ; but it seems to her as if his liking were destruction. More than ever she shrinks from his approaches ; yet still she cannot resist watching him. Dread and disgust she feels ; but withal a strange irresistible excitement, which impels her to look upon that she fears and loathes.

However, this is only when bad weather keeps her

in-doors.  When the sky is clear, and neither snow falls, nor winds howl, nor mists hover, nor rain-showers threaten, the little Ophelia coaxes Jutha abroad ; and again they sally forth together for a long ramble through forest, field, or valley ; among the rocks, or along the sea-shore.

And then the young girl amuses the child with telling her quaint tales, and singing her old ballads, such as she has heard from her mother.  There is one strange legend of a princess who was shut up by the king her father in a high strong tower, to be safe from the bold seeking of an adventurous young knight who loved her well, but who had no other inheritance than his good sword and his brave spirit, to entitle him to match with one of so high degree.  Nowise daunted by the difficulty of obtaining his mistress, the knight lover set forth for the strong tower, re-solved to try if fortune and his own valor might not avail to rescue her thence.  His road lay through a ' wild district where the storm-gods have their dwelling. He encountered successively Snorro, the divinity who holds the snow, hail, and sleet, at his command ; Frore, he who scatters the crisp and sparkling rime upon the branches of trees, hangs frost-diamonds upon the leaves and weeds, and upon every blade of grass, and bedrops the eaves of houses, and roofs of cottages, and mouths of caverns, with long, slender, down-pending icicles ; Drondror, he who bids the cataracts take their rushing leaps over crag and fell, and the mountain torrents their roaring, tumultuous course through rift and gully, sweeping all before them ; and lastly he met Dumbrunderod, the mighty ruler of the thunder, the dread wielder of the destroy-ing bolts, the speeder of the fatal lightning-stroke. But not all the terrors of the storm-gods—not even the flashing glance, and fire-darting nostrils of the thunder-ruler, who rolled angrily and threateningly by, in his war-chariot, casting furious glances, and hurling scoffing words at the daring mortal who ventured thither, could cause the brave heart of the knight to blench one jot in its stout courage and determination.  He restored the fierce glance, and gave back defiant words in reply to the storm-gods' contemptuous ones ; saying that all the terrors of earth, air, fire, water, of the sky above, and of the dark regions beneath, would vainly strive to conquer his resolution, or to extinguish his love.  That so long as life and limb were uninjured, his spirit would remain unvanquished, persisting still in its purpose to win his mistress, or die in the attempt.  The storm-gods burst into a loud peal of mirth, that shook the surrounding hills.  They could not but laugh to hear the puny mortal declare his small mighty will in opposition to theirs.  The hearty laugh exploded with a crash, that sent a thousand echoes roaring through upland and valley, while Dumbrunderod swore that the human pigmy was a fine fellow of his inches, and showed a spirit becoming a better race ; that, for his part, he knew how to allow for these fiery natures, hasty in their anger, prompt in their deeds, indomitable in their will, inevitable in their undertakings. He vowed that so far from resenting the knight's defiance of his and his brother storm-gods' power, that he applauded his ardor of courage and of love, and that it deserved the assistance it should receive.  At first the knight thought this promise of friendly aid and protection was strangely evinced, for there suddenly arose a tempest of such violence that it seemed threatening to carry all before it to destruction, himself included.  A hurricane of wind tore up trees by their roots, and scattered them far and wide ; the torrents and cataracts pelted down the hills, as if they would have inundated the whole face of the plain ; the heavens poured forth a deluge of snow, rain, sleet, and hail, all at once, while incessant claps of thunder rent the air, and sheets of lightning glared fearful illumination upon all this scene of gale and tempest. But when, at length, the knight succeeded in forcing

his way through the storm-blast, he found that it had
done its masters' work of beneficent help right well ;
for upon reaching the strong high tower, he saw it
leveled to the ground by a friendly thunder-bolt ;
which had struck it, leaving his mistress unharmed,
who stepped forth from the ruins, flung herself into
his arms, and fled with him that instant to a far distant country, where they lived happily thenceforth,
safe from royal tyranny.

There was another story of Jutha's, which told of
a wicked steward ; who,—left in his master's castle,
with charge to watch and guard from harm the lord's
only child, a passing fair daughter,—proved false to
his function of protector, stole the lady away from her
home, and would fain have forced her into a marriage
with his own unworthy self.   But the unhappy maiden,
resolved to die rather than suffer the degradation of
such a union, flung herself from the window of the
high chamber in which the false steward had confined
her ; and so, untimely, perished.   Then the lord, her
father, returning home to his castle, and hearing how
it had been despoiled by the miscreant in whom he
confided, ceased not until he had discovered his
wronger, whom he caused to be tried for his heinous
offences, and sentenced to death.   In consideration
of his treacherous breach of trust, and the death his
deed had caused, the false steward was broken on a
wheel, and died in cruel tortures.

One fine noon-day, when the heat of the sun had
compelled Jutha and the little girl to seek the shade
of the forest depths, Ophelia interrupted the story
then telling, by exclaiming suddenly :—" Look,
Jutha !   See there !"

Jutha looked in the direction of the child's pointing
finger, and saw to her surprise, a milk-white horse,
saddled and bridled, coming leisurely along beneath
the trees, cropping the grass, and looking as if he had
strayed from his fastenings.   " The beautiful creature !" exclaimed Jutha, rising from the seat Ophelia

and she occupied, on the spreading root of a tree ; "What costly housings it has ! It looks like a fairy horse,—the steed of some of those gallant princes in the stories ! And it is gentle, too ; see how it lets me lay my hand upon its bridle, and pat its neck. It is well trained, and belongs to some noble master, doubtless. But who can he be ? And where ?"

The young girl held the rein, and looked about her in perplexity, while the white horse tossed its arching neck, nearly jerking the curb from her hand, pawed the ground, and neighed shrill and loud.

"Look, Jutha !" once more exclaimed the child. "There among the trees—on that mossy slope—do you see ?"

"He is sleeping !" said Jutha, in hushed answer ; "and soundly, too ; not even the neighing of his good horse can disturb him."

The girl and the child crept a little nearer to the figure they saw lying there. It was that of a man, in a rich hunting-dress. His plumed hat had been placed so as to shade his eyes during sleep ; but it had fallen partly aside, and showed a face finely shaped, with features marked and handsome. One hand supported his head ; but the other, ungloved, was white, bore more than one jewelled ring, and lay carelessly, near the half-open bosom of his vest, as if it had slipped thence in slumber.

"A fit owner for such a gallant beast !" murmured Jutha, as she turned to pat once again the neck of the steed ; for the docile creature had suffered the young girl to retain his rein, and to draw him after her to the spot where his master lay. "Sure, a prince—no less ; such a prince as they tell of in the wondrous tales I have heard. How passing beautiful he is ! What can he be ? Where can he have come from ? From fairy-land—or from the court, surely ;" added she, as she looked again upon the handsome stranger.

"Are there such princes at the court ?" whispered

Ophelia. "I came from the court, they say ; but I remember none such princes there. I remember no one but my own papa,—my dear mother,—my brother Laertes—and those but faintly."

"You were little more than a baby, when you left them to come hither. It can hardly be, that you should remember them ;" said Jutha.

"But I do ; though only dimly—as if they were a long way off in the distance. And so they are ;" added the little Ophelia, musingly. "They are across the wide, wide sea ; far away from me—but perhaps one day I shall see my own mamma again—I remember how she looked, well, when she leaned her face close to mine, as we sat together, journeying here ; and how sweet her voice sounded, and how soft her arm and her side felt, as she hugged me close round, against her. I wish I could have her to hug me close again—I wish she would come. I want to see her ! I want my own mamma !" And the child looked and spoke plaintively,—impatiently.

"Hush, dear child !" said Jutha, soothingly ; "Look at this brave stranger. See how bright and handsome his clothing. Look what a goodly, beauteous face he hath ! He is as glorious to behold, as the king's son, who had a fairy for his godmother !"

Whether it was the plaintive tone of the child, or the animated one of her companion, which penetrated the drowsed senses of the sleeper ; they were, together, sufficient to awaken him. He opened his eyes, and beheld the two young girls standing there, opposite to him, with his courser between them, the bridle-rein in the elder's hand.

"I have brought you your horse, sir ;" said she, dropping her simple curtsey. "He was straying."

"And a fairer damsel to bring errant-knight his palfrey could not be found in all the realm of enchantment ;" said the stranger, springing to his feet, and receiving the bridle from her ; "surely I have wandered upon charmed ground, and you are one of its denizens.''

'' A plain country-maiden, none other, sir ; and this her mother's nurse-charge ;'' said Jutha, curtseying once again, and presenting the little Ophelia.

'' Still a charmer ;—an earthly charmer, if you will—yet no less bewitching ;'' said the handsome stranger. '' Pr'ythee, tell me thy name, pretty one, and I will tell thee mine.   It is Eric.''

'' And mine is Jutha, sir, at your service.''

'' Nay, an thou volunteer'st to serve me—to do my bidding, pretty Jutha, thou must call me by my name, as I call thee by thine.   So, if thou wouldst pleasure me, thou wilt no more say ' sir.' ''

'' I would please you, indeed, sir,—Eric,—an I knew how.''

'' It pleasures me, believe me, to hear mine own name spoken with an artless tongue, and with a blushing innocence of face like that I look upon.   Truly, thou seem'st an opening rose, Jutha, and yonder quiet little thing a close-furled bud, that promises to be just such another flower of beauty as thyself, when she shall have reached thine age of bloom.   In good faith, I may thank my lady Fortune, who brought me wearied from the chase to cast myself down in an enchanted wood, that I might dream a waking dream such as this.''

'' You were hunting, then, sir Eric ?'' said Jutha ; when, as she spoke, a mounted horseman rode up, and addressing the stranger in a tone of respect that showed them to be servant and master, announced that the chase was concluded ; adding that his majesty had noticed the lord Eric's absence, and had desired some one to search the wood, and collect stragglers from the hunting-train, as the royal party was now returning.

'' 'Tis well, Trasco ; ride thou on ; I will speedily overtake thee, and attend his majesty,'' said lord Eric.   Then vaulting into the saddle, he raised his hat, kissed his hand, and saying "I must obey the king's command now, but I shall find a time to see more of my wood-nymphs," gave the spur to his horse, and was gone.

There was an end of the story-telling for that day. Jutha could talk of nothing else during the rest of the ramble, but of the noble stranger, of his handsome face and figure, of his gallant bearing, of his milk-white steed, of his unexpected appearance, and of his speedy departure. Perhaps it was because she had so thoroughly exhausted the subject, in thus discussing it with her young companion ; or perhaps it was because they found on their arrival the thoughts of all at home engaged with other matters,—Botilda being busy scolding Ulf, and preparing the evening meal,—and the rest bent solely upon having the supper ready as soon as possible ; but certain it is, that the encounter in the wood was never mentioned at the cottage by either Jutha or Ophelia. The young girl seemed satisfied with the interest it awakened in herself ; and the child was of a quiet, retiring nature, which seldom induced her to communicate much with those around her. She was habitually silent ; observant, rather than given to make remarks in words : contented to look on, to listen, to notice what was passing, and to let others speak and act, while she held her peace. Her nurse, Botilda, had long left her wholly to the care of Jutha. The good woman saw that the young girl and the child sufficed in companionship to each other ; while she herself had ample employment in the care of her idiot son, Ulf, whose gormandizing propensities, and mischievous pranks, required her utmost vigilance.

At one time he was found in the dairy, scooping the cream off the pans with the palms of his hands ; holding some out in his great hairy paw to the little Ophelia, who stood there as usual, half quakingly, half wonderingly,—then supping it up himself, lest it should trickle and waste before she would advance.

His mother cuffs him soundly, nay, gets a stick, and belabours him as long as she has breath ; but the lout only pretends to blubber, "Hav'nt ye done yet, mother ?" while by his sly grin, he shows that her woman's arm fails to inflict any very severe chastisement.

"Cub that thou art ! thou shalt feel the weight of thy father's cudgel, an I catch thee at any more of thy pilfering tricks !"

At another time, he was discovered in the storeroom, stealing the honey-comb that had just been collected from the bee-hives. Ophelia finds him there, lurking in a corner sucking his paws, with greedy joy gleaming in his eyes. "They call me Ulf the bear. Ha, ha ! The bear's fond of honey !" he said, with a grin, as he swilled and licked the handfuls of streaming comb.

"Taste ! It's luscious-nice ! Taste some of the bear's honey." And, with his usual uncouth wish for her to share, he held some towards the child.

She shrank back. "It isn't yours. Best not touch it."

"Hush ! Mother'll hear."

But his mother had already heard. She fetched Sigurd, who happened that day to be at work upon something that wanted doing at the cottage. And in a few minutes more, Ophelia stood scared and trembling at the terrible sounds that reached her ear, of the father's blows, of Ulf's cries, more like the howls of a wild beast, than anything human.

Among these rough cottage people, more and more did the child feel herself alone and apart. Her shyness and sparing speech grew upon her. She was not unhappy ; but she became grave,—strangely quiet and reserved for a little creature of her years, and so confirmed in her habit of silence, that she might almost have passed for dumb. She might be said to feel her uncongenial position without understanding it ; she did not comprehend what made her serious, but she was rarely disposed to cheerfulness ; she did not know why she was disinclined to talk, but she seldom met with any inducement to open her lips, and insensibly she kept them closed.  With her sweet, earnest eyes, her placid though unsmiling countenance, and her still demeanor, she had a look of reflection,—of pensiveness, that better becomes womanhood grown, than childhood.  Childhood should be free from heed ; light-hearted, undreading ; encouraged in its frankness, its confidence, its every hopeful, eager, thought and word.  Still, however, she had one resource—her one companion, with whom she could assimilate, and feel at ease.  With Jutha, rambling abroad, she was never dull, never sad ; with her, her heart knew no heaviness, no misgiving, no loneliness ; with her, her spirits rose to gladness, and she was, for the time, unreservedly happy.  She used to spring forth into the open air like a young bird newly franchised, escaped from restraint, and soaring into its native element of buoyancy and freedom. With her hand in Jutha's, she would bound along, eager to take her fill of liberty, body and mind.  Her spirit, no less than her limbs, seemed to revel in this season of unrestriction.  For she then knew the joy that knows not how it is joyful ; she felt the glee that asks not why it is glee,—the joy and the glee of that age which should know no shadow of care.

For some reason best known to herself, Jutha now invariably took the way towards the wood.  Their former walks among the rocks, or along the sea-shore, were all abandoned, on some pretext or other, in favor of the path which led through the forest ; and the little Ophelia, loving the mysterious grandeur of its high-arching trees, was well pleased it should be their constant resort.  On one of the first mornings they returned there, they had strolled far into its woody recesses, Jutha, as usual, entertaining her young companion with tales and marvels ; but her tone was hurried, her attention seemed elsewhere ;

and her look, expectant at first, grew every moment more thoughtful and vexed.

Suddenly, it brightened ; and Ophelia, following the direction of her eyes, saw, coming towards them, the figure of lord Eric, on his milk-white horse. He threw himself from the saddle the moment he descried them, and eagerly approached. He seemed overjoyed to meet his nymphs of the wood, and sauntered long by their side, leading his horse by the bridle, talking and laughing animatedly. He shared their grassy seat, when they stopped to rest from the noontide heat ; he shared the contents of their basket, when they produced their noontide meal, declaring he had never tasted daintier fare ; he gave himself up to the spirit of the forest ramble, as though he could wish no pleasanter enjoyment. Morning after morning, he returned to make one in the wood-party ; and never had the hours thus spent, seemed to fly by so lightly. Certainly, Jutha found it so ; for the shadows of evening would steal upon them, with warning to return home, ere she could well believe it to be afternoon. The little Ophelia was less charmed with this addition to their society. She cared not that the stranger should come ; she had always found sufficient delight in listening to Jutha, in walking and wandering with her ; and though this gentleman was a very sprightly companion, and talked gaily and good-humouredly, yet as his conversation was chiefly addressed to Jutha, and was often carried on in a voice that scarce reached beyond her ear, it soon became productive of little entertainment to the child. Gradually, it grew to be exclusively confined to the two others, and the little girl was left to entertain herself, as she best might, with her own thoughts, or her own resources. She by degrees perceived that they were too much occupied with each other to be able to give much attention to her. She had hitherto been accustomed to have every question answered, every enquiry satisfied ; her friend Jutha had till now been always ready to furnish her with replies, and even to supply her with fresh store of amusement from her own talk ; it was otherwise, since this stranger had intruded upon their pleasant wood rambles. Jutha had now no look, no word but for him. But then she herself seemed so contented, that her child-friend could not altogether find in her heart to regret what made Jutha so evidently, so radiantly happy. She had never seen her look so full of joy, so full of spirit. Her eye sparkled, her color rose, her voice had exultation in its tone, as she took her way, with Ophelia, to these rambles in the wood—where they were sure to be joined by their new acquaintance.

Once, on meeting him, the child saw his face assume a vexed look, as it rested upon her. He turned to Jutha, and pointing to a nosegay she wore in her bodice, he said, " Why bring flowers ? I can gather you some fresh, here. Leave them at home, I beseech you, another time ; especially the rosebuds."

He said the last words with emphasis, though he dropped his voice as he uttered them. But Jutha answered simply, as she drew the flowers from her bosom, " I brought them for you ; I thought you would like some of our garden-blossoms. They are but wild-flowers that grow here in the wood."

He took them from her offered hand. " I love wild-flowers,—wood-flowers, best of all. Yet I thank thee, that thou thought'st of Eric in gathering these," said he, in his low-breathed tones. " Still, canst thou not still farther pleasure him, by omitting to bring with thee the green, unopened bud ? Thou know'st, the blowing rose, with its rich beauty of colour and fragrance, is the one he could look upon, never tiring, to the exclusion of every flower else."

He glanced for an instant at Ophelia, as he pronounced one part of this speech, with a look, which she had before noted in his face ; and which had told her plainly enough that he not only ceased to include her in the conversation he addressed to his nymphs of the wood, but that he would be heartily glad to have her out of hearing, nay, to be rid of her presence altogether.

The child thought to herself,—"He wishes me away ; but till I see that Jutha does, also, I shall not go. I wish *he* were away ; Jutha and I were very happy together, till he came ; I know what he means, about the rosebud ; but, till I find Jutha wants me out of hearing, I shan't stir."

So far from Jutha wishing her to leave them, Ophelia could hear that she was resisting lord Eric's urgently repeated request that she would " send the garden rosebud to gather wild ones," with such sentences as, " I dare not, indeed, my lord ; my mother gives her to my care ; I must not let her stray out of sight."

He seemed still to plead against these objections ; to over-rule them by asking what harm could come to her charge, in this quiet, solitary place ; adding, " Send her from us ; I cannot speak to you as openly as I would, sweet Jutha, with that child listening to every word I utter.  I want to speak to you fully— entirely."

" What can you have to say to me, my lord, that she may not hear ?  You can have naught to tell me, that"———Jutha's voice trembled, and a bright color stole into her face.  Then in a voice that strove for more firmness, but which still hesitated, she went on : " Were I to send her away, she would be sure to come back in fewer moments than your lordship thinks ; she does not like to be from me long."

" For however few moments,—for however short a space ; I would have you to myself, were it but for one instant.  Do not refuse me, Jutha."

The young girl seemed still to hesitate ; and the child could hear him mutter some reproach about " want of confidence, and not trusting him ;" which seemed to have more effect in moving Jutha than anything he had yet said.  She stopped, hung her head,

and faltered something in reply.  Lord Eric led her
to a seat on the turf beneath a goodly beech-tree ;
then turning to Ophelia, he said, in his most persuasive tone of gaiety and good-humor, as he unfastened the knot of a bright silken scarf, which hung
across his shoulder, "Here, take this, my little
maid ; I give it thee for a sash, an thou wilt go gather
me all the gay crow-flowers, king-cups, and daffydown-
dillies thou canst find in the forest, to make a chaplet
for this queen of the woods,—thy fair friend Jutha."

"I don't want the sash ;" said the little Ophelia,
drawing back, as he attempted to put it round her.
"Nor do you want the flowers.  You want me to go
away,—out of hearing, while you tell Jutha some
secret you have for her.  I do not care to do what you
wish, because you tried to make me believe the pretence of the flowers and the sash, instead of asking
me at once to leave you.  But I do care to please
Jutha ; and if she tells me she wishes to listen to your
secret without my hearing, I will go away at once."

Jutha said nothing ; but there was the bright color
in her cheek, which Ophelia could see, though the
young girl still hung her head.

"Jutha *is* curious to learn the secret you have to tell
her ; I can see she is !" said the child, peeping under
her friend's drooping face.  "I'll go then ; and I'll
stay away a long while, that you may have your talk
out freely."

The young girl made a faint attempt to detain her ;
but it was unperceived by Ophelia, who walked
straightway among the trees, bent upon relieving them
of her presence.  Once out of sight and hearing of
her late companions, the child strolled on more leisurely ; now pulling some stray twig or blossom that
caught her eye as she rambled along ; now stopping
to peer into some briery tangle of close underwood,
some leafy brake or thicket, where she fancied she
would spy a bird's nest ; now halting to watch some
scrambling squirrel, that would dart up the barky

trunk of a high tree, till he reached the topmost bough, whence he would slyly peep down at her in triumphant security. And still as she wandered on, trying to amuse her thoughts thus, they would ever and anon recur to the question of what could be the secret the gentleman had to tell Jutha. " Yet why should I ponder farther upon it ? It is clear, they did not wish I should know it, or they would not have sent me out of the way while it was telling. If I endeavor to find it out by guessing, it is almost as bad as trying to do so by listening. I won't guess any more. I won't even think about it. I'll see if I can find the beautiful white horse ; and amuse myself by feeding him.''

And many times after this, Ophelia was glad to find in the noble horse a source of entertainment during her solitary rambles. For her walks in the forest were all solitary now. Whatever might be the secret lord Eric had to tell, it was evidently not to be told in one conversation ; for, time after time, he made pretexts to send Ophelia away, while he and Jutha talked alone ; and the child, finding that her friend no longer sought to detain her by her side, left them together undisturbed. Though she herself could not feel so happy, separated thus frequently from her kind girl-companion, with whom she had formerly spent such pleasant hours, yet, so long as Jutha seemed the happier by the arrangement, Ophelia could fancy that it contented herself.

But after a time, Jutha's look of joy faded ; her spirits, that at first seemed almost too exuberant,—as if they must needs express the secret gladness she hoarded at heart, in bright looks, and a mirthful tone of voice that, finding speech too sober, would often break forth into bursts of song,—varied frequently ; the air of inward ecstacy, and conscious rapture involuntarily betraying itself in a thousand vivacious gestures, was exchanged for an appearance of anxiety and uneasiness. There were moments when her joyful looks rekindled ; her exuberance of gaiety returned ; but it was fitfully ; her spirits fluctuated ; she was alternately at height of glee, or lost in thought. She would still, in her cheerful moments, break out into snatches of the song which was her favorite at this time ;—" For bonny sweet Robin is all my joy ;" singing with an eager look, and exulting expression of voice ; but there was solicitude mingled with the eagerness ; there was forced mirth in the tone of exultation. These periods of cheerfulness grew rarer, and less lasting. They were more often replaced by fits of thoughtfulness, and brooding anxiety. The sparkling, bright up-look, gave way to a downcast expression ; or when the eye was raised, it was with a beseeching appeal in its tearful sadness.

The altered manner of the young girl escaped the notice of the cottage inmates ; but the child observed the change in her friend, and sorrowed wonderingly. Once, returning to the bank where she had left Jutha seated in one of her saddest moods, Ophelia found her restored to sudden gaiety. Lord Eric had arrived, while the child was away, and was talking cheeringly and encouragingly to his companion, while one of his arms was thrown about her, holding her close to him.

Jutha withdrew from the clasping arm, as the child approached, looking bashful and embarrassed ; but at the same time so happy, and so much her bright, former self, that Ophelia in her innocent affection for her friend, could not help hoping that their forest acquaintance might always come and console Jutha, with his kindness of word and manner, when she should be out of spirits.

But time goes on ; and the young girl's dejection increases. Ophelia finds her one evening, sitting by the rivulet, wringing her hands, and sobbing. The child soothes her fondly ; asking what grieves her.

Jutha attempts to deny that she has been weeping ; but Ophelia replies :—" You bathe your eyes in the water of the stream, that I may not see the tears, but

I know that you have been crying. Tell me what makes you cry, Jutha ?"

Jutha only shook her head, trying to stifle a sob that would be heard.

"If you care not to tell your grief to such a little thing as I am, who can comfort you with no help, or council, why not tell your mother what grieves you? I often wish I could tell my own mamma what I think and feel. Tell our good mother, if any thing grieves you, Jutha."

"But nothing grieves me—I can't tell her;" faltered the young girl.

"Then tell our friend of the wood—your friend— lord Eric ; he seems kind, and fond of you, Jutha."

"So long as he is fond of me—so long as he is my friend—nothing can grieve me ;" said Jütha. "But nothing does grieve me. Come, what are we talking of grief ? Let us return home ; and I'll tell you a story by the way."

"I shall like that ; it is long since I heard one of your stories, Jutha. I shall love to hear one again."

Jutha rejoiced to find that she had succeeded—as she had hoped to do—in turning the child's attention from herself to the promised tale. But though Ophelia looked up in her friend's face, with the eagerness of expectation, it did not prevent her from noting, with the sorrowing acuteness of loving perception, the many tokens of altered mien to be read there.

She remembered Jutha's brilliant color ; her beautiful face with its sunny look of health and liveliness ; her easy, alert gait ; the spotless nicety of her neat-fitting garments ; and though so young a child, Ophelia perceived the contrast they presented with the thin, white cheeks, the hollow eyes, the slouching heaviness of person and carriage, the disordered dress, the general air of depression and self-abandonment.

The change, although so great, had been so gradual, that the parents and brothers of Jutha, in their obtuseness of perception, and care of other matters, had still not observed it ; but it had long attracted Ophelia's eye ; and now it smote upon her heart with more painful force than ever.

"How the wind howls !  What a dreary autumn evening it is !" said Jutha, looking round her at the darkening sky.  "See how the leaves whirl, and fall !  The trees will all be bare soon ; and then comes winter—cold, cold, winter.  No more forest walks, when the trees are bare !  'They bore him bare-faced on the bier,'——That's not the song I am thinking of," she muttered.

"You think of sad songs now, Jutha ;" said the child.  "Where are your merry ones ?"

"Where indeed ?  Gone !  All gone !  'He is gone, he is gone, and we cast away moan.'  Ay, that is it !"  And she began to chant in a mournful voice :—

> " ' 'And will he not come again ?
> And will he not come again ?
> No, no, he is dead.
> Go to thy death-bed,
> He never will come again.' "

"Who is dead, Jutha ?  You frighten me ;" said the child.

"No one is dead ;" said the young girl, quickly.  "Who said he was dead ?  They say dead and gone ; but we may be gone, without being dead, mayn't we, little one ?"  She spoke in a sharp, abrupt tone, as if she would fain have made it sound jestingly.  Then she hurried on—"Do you hear the owl hoot ?  See, yonder she flies, with her flappy wings, and mealy feathers.  I'll tell you a story about dame owl.  I promised you a story, you know.  Listen."

"I am listening, Jutha."

The young girl told her the legend as she had heard it.  She told her that when He who had pity in his heart for the veriest wretch that crawls—for the dying thief—for the erring sinner—even for her whose sins were many ;—when He who taught divine pity and charity above all things, walked the earth in human shape, and suffered human privation in the plenitude of his merciful sympathy with poor humanity, it once upon a time befell, that He hungered by the way, and seeing a shop where bread was baking, entered beneath the roof, and asked for some to eat. The mistress of the shop was about to put a piece of dough into the oven to bake ; but her daughter, pitiless of heart, declaring that the piece was too large, reduced it to a mere morsel. This was no sooner done, than the dough began to swell and increase, until, in amaze at its miraculously growing size, the baker's daughter screamed out, like an owlet, ' Woohoo—hoo—hoo !' Then He who had craved food, held forth his hand ; and, in the place where she who lacked charity had stood screaming, there was a void ; but against the window, beating its wings, hooting, and struggling to get out, was a huge mealy-feathered owl. It forced a way through, took flight, and was seen no more ; excepting when some night-wanderer descries the ill-omened bird skulking in the twilight wood, or obscure grove ; and then he murmurs a prayer, to be delivered from the sin of uncharitableness, as he thinks of the transformed baker's daughter.

That evening, on their return to the cottage, it seemed to Ophelia, that those at home, first became aware of the change in her friend Jutha, which she had so long perceived and lamented. But it also strangely struck her that instead of this discovery awakening kindness and compassion towards the sufferer, it appeared to excite rather anger, reproach, and even invectives. Their voices were raised in a confusion of questions, threats and expressions of wonder, with which they assailed the young girl, in an incoherent clamour, from which the child could make out nothing clearly. The mother bemoaned her own and her daughter's fate ; the father murmured deep curses ; the two elder brothers, strode angrily to and fro with menacing looks, ground teeth, and clenched hands. The idiot boy sat jibbering, and croaking a harsh wailing cry in one corner; adding to the general discordance. Jutha had flung herself upon a chair in the midst; upon the back of which she leaned, burying her face in her arms. From time to time she uttered convulsive sighs; heavy sobs burst from her, each seeming to rend her frame asunder; but else she preserved a sullen, despairing silence, as sole reply to the clamorous enquiry that surrounded her.

Ophelia crept away softly to bed, unable to make out the meaning of this distressful scene; and marvelling much why they should show displeasure instead of sorrow at Jutha's illness; why they should seem to resent, rather than to compassionate; why they should overwhelm her with reproaches in the midst of her unhappiness, instead of seeking to comfort and console. For some time, she lay pondering on these things; full of concern and wonder; wishing Jutha to come to bed, that she might assure her of her sympathy, at least; and longing to see if caresses, and loving words of pity and tenderness might not avail to lessen her poor friend's grief. But the hours crept on, and the little one's affectionate anxiety yielded to drowsiness. She slept; but it was an uneasy sleep, full of dreams, and haunting ideas of wretchedness and perplexity. From this slumber she awoke strugglingly, and with a beating heart. It was pitch dark; she felt that many hours had elapsed, and that it was dead of night. She stretched out her arms, to feel for Jutha at her side; but no Jutha was there. In alarm, she started up. What could have kept her away? Was she worse? Was she unable to move? Was she still in the midst of that confusion of angry voices? The child listened. All seemed still below. What then could prevent Jutha from coming up to her room,—to lie down, and to get the rest she so much needed?

In alarm for her friend, in an irresistible desire to learn how she was, and what detained her, Ophelia stole out of bed, and groped her way down stairs. On reaching the door of the sitting-room, she saw a bright streak from the crevice at the bottom, which showed her there was light in the room. She felt for the latch above her head ; and succeeded in finding, and unfastening it. She pushed open the door ; but the blaze of light from within, suddenly contrasted with the obscurity from which she had emerged, made her pause. She stood on the threshold, gazing in, trying to distinguish the objects the room contained. On the large table, which occupied the centre of the apartment, lay something extended, which was covered with a white cloth. At one end were ranged as many iron lamps as the cottage household afforded, burning in a semi-circular row. Amazed at this strange sight, the child advanced ; and with an uncontrollable impulse, walked straight up to the table, and raised the end of the white cloth, nearest to the lamps. Their light fell full upon the object beneath. Startled, and shuddering, the child looked upon that which was so familiar, yet so strange. Could that indeed be the face of Jutha ?—that white, still, rigid thing ?—with those breathless, motionless lips, and those eyelids, that looked fixed, rather than closed ? And what was that, lying upon her breast, encircled by her arm ? A little, little face—a baby's face ! It looked so transparent, so waxen,—so pretty, though so strangely image-like, that the child involuntarily stretched forth her finger, and touched its cheek. The icy cold, shot, with a sharp thrill, to her heart, and she screamed aloud, as she turned to Jutha's face, and flung herself upon it with wild kisses and tears.

Botilda, hearing the cry, came running in. She used her best efforts to calm the mourning and affrighted child, carrying her up to bed, lying down by her side, folding her in her arms, and speaking fondlingly and soothingly to her, until she dropped asleep.

But it was long ere this was accomplished ; and for
many successive nights, the nurse had to sleep in the
room with her charge, that she might be won to rest.
The shock she had received, was severe ; and long
left its effects upon her sensitive organization.  Naturally gentle, she became timid.  She shrank about,
scared, and trembling ; fearful of she hardly knew
what, but feeling unassured, doubtful, full of a vague
uneasinesss and alarm.

Ulf's hideousness shows more horribly than ever in
her eyes.  He seems to her some fiend-like creature
as he crouches there, drawing the flaps of his ears
over till the tops reach beneath his chin ; pulling his
nether lip down, and turning it inside out, till it lies
stretched, and spread, displaying his cankered gums,
and his yellow and black teeth,—some flat, like tomb-
stones,—some long, narrow, and sharp, like the fangs
of a dog.  His manner to herself puzzles and torments
her ; for it is capricious, and varies accordingly as he
meets her alone, or with others.  When the family
are present, he treats her roughly ; speaks of her
jeeringly as the little princess, or the little court-lady ;
and twits her with pride,—complaining of her silence
as haughty, her keeping him at a distance as arrogant
and insolent.  When, however, by any chance, they
are by themselves, he becomes cajoling, and tries all
means to effect his purpose of approaching her, or
getting her to come to him.  He spares neither fair
words, wheedling tricks, or shy devices, to lure her
within reach of his paws ; but neither fawning nor
stratagem succeed.  Now, more than ever, she resists
his advances, and contrives to elude his contact.  The
former curiosity which had mingled with her disgust
at this idiot boy, exciting her to observe his uncouth
ways, yielded entirely to the loathing she felt for
him ; and she now dreaded and avoided him as sedulously as she had once watched him.

Upon one occasion, however, her vigilance in pre-
venting his coming near her, was frustrated.  He was

close upon her before she was aware. She had been wandering out towards the wood,—it was winter now, and the frost hung its glittering fretwork upon bush and briar,—she had been thinking how cheerless and desolate all seemed, in despite of the brilliancy of the white tracings around, since her companion Jutha was lost to her, and could never more come thither, to share her admiration of winter frost, spring buds, the rich luxuriance of summer leaves and blossoms, or the mellow hues of autumn ; she had been pondering upon the mystery of her friend's change of spirits, her sadness, her illness, her death ; and then, as there were no flowers to be found in that sullen season, she gathered a branch of wild-rose, which bore its winter fruitage of scarlet haws in bright profusion, that she might place upon Jutha's grave the best semblance that might be of a tributary garland.

The child repaired with her offering, to the quiet nook, where she knew her friend was laid ; and there, tired with her walk, oppressed with sad thoughts, and numbed into lethargy by the cold, she threw herself upon the low mound, and slept. Not many minutes after, she was perceived lying there, by Ulf, who crept stealthily towards her.

"It's little court-lady ! And fast asleep !" he muttered, with a grin. "No airs now ! The bear shan't be balked of his hug, this time !"

He leaned down over her. The hot breath reached her face ; like the rank fumes of a charcoal-furnace, it seemed to stifle her with its tainted oppression. She struggled and woke, to find that loathly visage hanging just above hers. Instinctively, to ward off its fearful approach, she clutched at the nearest thing at hand. It was the branch of wild-rose, which, beside its scarlet berries, was thickly studded with thorns ; and this she thrust with all her force against the impending face. The sharp appeal was effectual. The lout drew back, smarting and bleeding.

"The rose is prickly as well as pretty !" he said,

with a leer of idiot slyness ; "but we'll see if we
can't pluck away its thorns, and smell its sweetness,
in spite of 'em."

But in raising his hand to free himself from the
obnoxious branch, which had rendered her such good
service, Ulf gave the child an opportunity of slipping
from his grasp.  She was not slow to avail herself of
the advantage ; but dexterously pulling her skirts
from beneath his knee, which in his rude eagerness
he had set fast upon them, she succeeded in raising
herself away from him, scrambling to her feet, and
setting off to run at her utmost speed.  It would have
availed her but little, had he pursued her : but it happened that she had not gone many paces, before she
was joined by Botilda, who had come out to look for
her ; and Ulf, at sight of his mother, slunk away,
like a cur that fears detection.

That night, Ophelia lay awake,—a prey to fancies
and terrors that would not let her close her eyes.
Botilda, after sharing her bed for many nights, thinking that the child had by this time recovered the late
shock, had left her, to return to her own room, after
seeing her softly drop off into her first sleep.  But
from this, the little girl had suddenly started, broad
awake, trembling and agitated, with a frightful dream
she had been dreaming ; of digging down into Jutha's
grave, with a mad desire to look upon her face once
more,—of finding it, only to see it change into that
of Ulf ; who, raising himself from the coffin, groped
among the mould, and drew forth a little baby's white
arm, which he fell to scratching and marring with
briars.  The horror of the sight awoke her ; she
struggled into a sitting posture, stared through the
dim space, and found herself alone in that dreary
room.  She could just distinguish the blank square
spot where the window was.  There was deep snow
upon the ground—which cast a sickly glare, the moon
partially shining from amid haze and clouds.  The
familiar objects in the room looked shadowy and

spectral in that uncertain light ; and the child could get no assurance, or steadying of her thoughts, from looking upon them. At length it seemed to her, that among them,—there—yonder—at the farther end of the room, she saw something move. It was dark, and stole along without noise ; shapeless, indistinct, scarce seen, but horribly present. She shuddered ; and shrank beneath the bed-clothes. Her heart beat violently, and her head throbbed,—so loud that she could have counted the thumps of each. She had a confused notion of trying to do this, amid the distraction of hearing her teeth keep a bewildering counter-current of strokes, in a rapid timing of their own. Presently, she clenched them firmly, that she might listen to something that caught her ear beside the tumult of her own pulses. She thought she heard a muffled sound, as if something swept against the cover-let of her bed. In desperation, she held her breath, to listen the more acutely, for what she so much dreaded to hear. Yes,—again the sound, as of some-thing softly drawn along the side of the coverlet, was repeated ; and this time she felt the bed-clothes brushed by the passing substance. She would have shrieked aloud ; but her parched throat refused to give utterance to the cry of terror that choked her. Could it be an animal ? Was it anything alive ? Or were there indeed wandering shapes of evil permitted to visit the earth in night and darkness, as wild tales hinted ? The child's dismay hurriedly pointed to such questions ; but on a sudden, her attention was attracted to quite a different source. There was a noise of trampling feet in the snow outside ; a sound of many voices ; a loud knocking at the door of the cottage ; and upon her finding courage to look from beneath the bed-clothes, she could see the light of torches flashing and gleaming through the window. Then there came a stir in the house ; a hurry below ; hasty steps ascended the stairs ; and in another mo-ment the door of her room was flung open, and in the

midst of the stream of light that poured in, a figure
appeared, which rushed forward to the bed where she
lay, exclaiming, "My child ! my dear, dear child !
My little Ophelia !"

"Mamma !" was the instinctive reply, as the child
felt herself gathered into the soft security of a mother's
bosom.

In the confusion, no one had remarked the cowering
form of Ulf ; who darted from a lurking place by the
bedside, and made his way out through the open door,
just as the others passed into the room.  It was he,
who, in his brutish pertinacity of desire to obtain the
hug he promised himself, had alarmed the child by
prowling stealthily about her chamber in the dark.
But now, no more fear, no more harm, she was surely,
happily sheltered.

The lady Aoudra could not sufficiently feast her eyes
upon her daughter's face ; again she scanned every
feature, noted every particular of look and expression,
—sought eagerly each mark of remembered appearance, and traced east vestige of growth and alteration.
As she gazed, she became aware of the burning spot
that glowed and deepened in the young cheek, the too
bright sparkle of the eyes, the unnatural restlessness
of the lips, which at length wore an almost vacant
smile, while the fingers idly played among the long
curls of her mother's hair, drooping over her.  In
alarm, the lady caught her child's hand in hers ; it
was feverishly hot.

" I have been culpably unheedful—inconsiderate ;
I shall have only my own rash selfishness to blame,
should the surprise have been too much for my darling.  Yet who would have expected such sensitive-
ness—such susceptibility in one so young ?  Dear
child !  Mother's own treasure !  Mother's little tender one !"

Fondly, gently, she set about repairing the mischief
she feared she had done.  She shaded the light away
from the too eager eyes ; she coaxed them to close,—

to cease to look upon her, by clasping one of the hands
in hers, that the child might know she was still there ;
she lay down beside her, parting the hair back upon
the heated forehead, giving her from time to time
cooling drinks, and suggesting none but peaceful
happy thoughts, in the low soft talking she murmured
the while in her ear. Lulled thus, the child fell into
slumber ; but for some hours it was a disturbed, uneasy one, giving the lady many a pang of dread and
self-reproach. Violent startings, abrupt twitching of
the limbs, talking in her sleep, muttered ends of songs
and mournful tunes alternately alarmed the watcher.
Once, the little girl sprang suddenly up, trembling,
and looking about her with a scared eagerness of expectation, clinging convulsively to the arm stretched
to receive her ; but when she felt herself enfolded
within a mother's embrace, when she found herself
safe nestling against a mother's heart, cherished by a
mother's affection, guarded by a mother's care, she
yielded tranquilly, blissfully, to a sense of perfect repose. Lapped in that balmy atmosphere of maternity,
she sank into profound rest.

Holy mother-love ! nearest semblance vouchsafed
to mortals of Divine protection ! Benignest human
symbol of God's mercy to man ! There is a blessed
influence, a sacred joy, a plenitude of satisfaction, in
the very presence of a mother, that plainer speaks the
mysterious beatitude of Heaven itself to earthly intelligence, than aught else in existence.

The little Ophelia awoke next morning from her
healing sleep, revived ; and quite herself. She was
so free from the feverish symptoms which had so
much alarmed her mother, overnight, that Aoudra
thought she might venture to remove her at once to
their home at Elsinore.

The complete change proved the most beneficial
thing that could have been devised. In the new scene
to which she was introduced, the child acquired unwonted spirits. She gained more of the carelessness

befitting her age ; she lost that look of uneasiness, and irresolution, which had struck her mother so painfully at first ; she seemed no longer oppressed by a vague solicitude and dread which had appeared to haunt her, and hang its weight on her spirits. The only time there was any trace in her of a recurrence to such impressions, was when there happened to be allusion made to her past existence. She appeared averse from speaking, or even thinking, of the period she had spent at the cottage. She never reverted to it of her own accord ; never mentioned any of the names of her former associates, or recalled any circumstance that occurred among them ; and her mother, perceiving how distasteful the subject was. took care never to revive it in her child's mind. It was avoided altogether ; the lady Aoudra only regretting that she had ever been compelled to leave her little one in what had evidently been so uncongenial a home.

Her chief care was now to surround her child with none but pleasant, healthful influences, of person, scene, and circumstance. She kept her as much as possible in her own society, and in that of her father, —the lord Polonius,—whenever his court duties permitted him to be at home. Her young son, Laertes, was with them, for a period, until the time should arrive for his going to the university. Meantime, masters were engaged ; and the children pursued their studies together ; though the lady Aoudra chiefly superintended those of her little girl herself. She appointed the one of her own women to whom Ophelia seemed to have taken the greatest fancy, to be the child's particular attendant. Guda was a lively, good-tempered girl ; and her cheerful companionship was one of the wholesome accessories by which the mother hoped to effect a removal of any sinister impression that might remain upon her child's spirits of byegone discomforts.

The affection that now had full opportunity of taking its natural growth between father and child, contributed greatly to the happiness of Ophelia's new existence. Polonius became dotingly fond of his little girl ; and she in turn reverenced him with all duteous affection. She would watch for his home-coming ; soon getting to know the hours of his return from attendance at the palace ; and then she would set his easy chair, and bring his slippers, and the furred gown, for which he exchanged his court robes, when indulging in domestic ease ; and then he would pat her cheek, or pass his hand over her fair young head, and say some fondling words of rejoicing that he now possessed so pretty a living toy at home as his little daughter, to beguile his leisure hours.

He was a good-natured man, of a kindly disposition, with much original shrewdness, and a great deal of acquired worldly knowledge. He was an odd compound of natural familiarity, and assumed dignity ; of affability and importance ; of condescension and dictatorialness ; of garrulous ease and ostentation. He was often jocular, and would twinkle his half merry, half astute eyes, rubbing his hands with a chuckling air of enjoyment, as if he had not a thought beyond the relish of the immediate jest ; but, some time after, as if willing to show that it was the mere momentary unbending of the great statesman, he would knit his brow, lean back in his chair, with his hand supporting his chin, and look meditative. He used a pompous enunciation for the most part ; but occasionally, his opiniated eagerness would run away with him—hurry him into forgetfulness of the main thread of his subject, until he was brought suddenly to a check—a pause, from which he sought hasty refuge in the resumption of his didactic style.

He was fond of parcelling out his speech into formal divisions ; of putting forth his opinions in set phrases ; he was full of precept ; sententious in speech ; and uttered his axioms in an authoritative voice. He spoke perceptively. He would talk to his wife in manner of an oration ; clearing his voice, and pausing

a little, as if to bespeak full attention ere he began.
He liked to see those around him performing audience
to his dicta.    He would address the guests at his
table, as if they were a committee, or a board of council ; and harangue, rather than converse.    He prided
himself on great foresight and perspicacity.

He ordinarily prefaced with a hem ; and empha-
sized, as he went on, with one hand in the palm of
the other, or by reckoning off each clause, successively, on his fingers.    He collected attention by canvassing glances ; gathered it in by sharp espial upon
those in whom he perceived symptoms of its straying ;
and kept it from wandering by a short admonitory
cough. · He was accustomed to ask, in a triumphant
tone, when any prediction of his was ever known to
fail in being verified by the event.    He affected diplo-
macy and expediency in action ; mystery in expression ; craft in device.    He had a habit of laying artful schemes in conversation, for entrapping those
about him into betrayals of characteristics such as he
had ascribed to them—and then would exult in the
proofs of his accurate judgment.    " You see !   What
did I say ?"    He piqued himself on ingenuity in compassing his ends ; and, in their accomplishment, preferred contrivance and cunning to the commonplace
means of straightforward procedure.

Policy was his rule of action ; statesmanship his
glory of ambition.    He would complain of the fatigues
of office ; of the onerous demands of a court life ; of
the cares of government ; but secretly, official dig-
nities, a courtier's existence, and ministerial power,
formed the sum of his desires.

His wife, the lady Aoudra, understood his character
well ; but both her affection for the good qualities he
possessed, and her conjugal duty, taught her to ac-
quiesce in his peculiarities, forbearing to show any
unmeet consciousness of them. She would gravely
listen, when he told her of some deep-laid plot he had,
for bringing about what she, in her singleness of

mind, thought might have been effected by much simpler means ; she heard in silence, yet with attentive sympathy, his plans of ambition, his projects for advancement ; and she took active interest in his schemes for the national welfare, even when she felt them to be more subtly devised, than practically applicable.

But she could not forbear smiling—though to herself only—when she saw him carry this system of policy into his domestic sway. When she saw him exercise his authority as husband, father, and master, by a sort of trick ; when she found him securing her wifely obedience,—that obedience which would have been spontaneously yielded, without inducement,—by management and winning artifices ; when she found him governing his children, ruling his household, regulating his affairs, nay ordering his servants by a calculated method of stratagem, she could do no other than smile. Beyond all else that provoked her smile, was to see how the innocence of childhood—the unconscious simplicity of his young son and daughter set at naught the diplomatist's skill,—frustrated and rendered null his intrigues by an ingenuous look or word.

Instead of openly forbidding or reprehending certain deeds, he would lay snares for discovering whether they had been committed ; and while the process was going on, his penetration was baffled, by the artless behavior of the children. His guile was futile against their candor ; and was more frequently proved at fault than they. His sagacity was always aiming at detection, where no delinquency existed ; ever bent on discovering some concealment, where there was nothing to conceal. It was almost comic to see the searching frown he would bend on one of those clear, open countenances held up to him in confident unreserve, conscious of no shadow of blame. The questioning eye, the shrewd glance, the artfully put enquiry, seemed absurd, directed against such transparent honesty.

In consequence of this system of their father's, his praise was sometimes as mysterious and unexpected to the young Laertes and Ophelia as his reproof.

On one occasion, he called them to him and commended them highly, for never having been into a certain gallery which he had built out into his garden for the reception of some pictures, bequeathed to him by a French nobleman—a friend of his—lately dead.

Seeing a look of surprise on their faces, he added :—" Ah, you marvel how I came to know so certainly that you never went in.  But I have methods deep and sure,—a little bird, or my little finger,—in few, you need not assure me, that you never entered that gallery ; for I happen to be aware, beyond a doubt that you never did.   And I applaud your discretion."

" But we did go in ;" said Ophelia.

" What, child ?  Pooh, impossible !   Come to me ; look me full in the face."   Not that she looked down, or aside, or anything but straight at him ; but he always used this phrase conventionally, when he conducted an examination.   " I tell you, you never went into that gallery ; I know it for a fact.   There's no use in attempting to deceive your father.  I should have discovered it, had you gone into that room without my permission."

" But did you not wish us to go there ?  I never knew you forbade it ?" said Laertes.   " If we had known you had any objection, neither Ophelia nor I would have——"

" I never forbade it certainly," interrupted his father ;  " but I had strong reasons for wishing that you should not go into the room  till the pictures were hung.   You might have injured them.   No, no ; I knew better than to let heedless children play there ; so I took means to prevent your entering the gallery without my knowledge."

" But we did play there, every day, father ;" said Laertes.

" Yes ;" said Ophelia.

" And I tell you, impossible ! Listen to me ; I fastened a hair across the entrance. The invisible barrier is yet unbroken. So that you see, you could not have passed through that door without my knowledge."

" But we didn't go through the door, papa ; we got in at the window !" exclaimed both the children. " We didn't know you wished us not to play there ; so, finding a space which the builders had left, in one of the windows that look into the garden, we used to creep in there, and amuse ourselves with looking at the new pictures. We did no harm ; only admired."

Time went on. Laertes, now a tall stripling, was sent to Paris,—then famous as a seat of learning. The motives which swayed Polonius in the choice of the university to which he decided upon sending his son, were characteristic. He owned to his wife, that he should have preferred sending the youth to Wittenberg, where the king's son was a student ; such an opportunity for intimacy with the prince being a great temptation ; but there was a certain personage, highly influential with the court of France, who had exacted a promise from him that Laertes should be educated at the university of Paris ; and as it was of the utmost importance that the friendly relations with France which he had established during the period of his embassage there, should be carefully maintained, he resolved that nothing should interfere with his son's being placed at college in that country.

Ophelia grew into delicate girlhood. Ever quiet, —ever diffident, in her retiring gentleness and modesty ; but serene, and happy. A tranquil-spirited maiden, unexacting, even-tempered, affectionate ; one of those, upon whom the eyes and hearts of all near, dwell with a feeling of repose.

Her father now began to look forward to his long-cherished hope of introducing her at court ; where he beheld her already attracting his sovereign's gracious notice, and winning the favour of the Queen. He imparted his views to his wife ; adding, that all Ophelia wanted, was a little forming in manner, to render her presentable ; and to that end he intended cultivating for her the acquaintance of a young lady, daughter to a friend of his, the lord Cornelius.

Aoudra ventured the pardonable motherly remark, that their young Ophelia was perfectly well-bred ; a gentlewoman in every particular. "An air of nobility distinguishes her mien ; and the look of unruffled content in the blue depths of those violet eyes, revealing the sweet placidity of her nature, gives a crowning grace of self-possession and ease, that might become a princess. If a court atmosphere, if the royal presence be our child's destiny, she seems fitted for them by nature."

"Ay, ay, by nature. But art may do somewhat. Art may do much. Polish, refinement ; a conventional breeding in manner ; an air of the world ;—are attained only by associating with those accustomed to move in courtly circles. The lady Thyra, daughter to my friend Cornelius, having lost her mother when quite a child, has been early habituated to receive guests, to preside over her father's establishment,— in few, to enact betimes the centre of a distinguishable circle. To promote a friendship between this young lady and our daughter will be to place Ophelia beneath fittest tutelage—in the very school to form her for the future station she will fill."

"Is this young lady Thyra,—unrestricted in her proceedings, choosing her own associates, complete mistress of her conduct and herself,—quite the best associate, think you, my lord, for our daughter ? May there not be risk as well as advantage in the companionship ?"

"What but advantage can there be, good my lady ? The lord Cornelius enjoys the royal confidence. He will rise to highest honors in the state. I foresee,— trust this brain of mine,—I foresee, I say, that when an envoy to Norway shall be needed, he will—but no matter. Where was I? Oh—his wealth is ample; and he allows his daughter well-nigh unlimited command of his means and fortune. What more would you have?"

"No more; nay, not so much. Her power, her position I doubt not; 'tis herself I mean. Is she——"

"Tut, tut, lady mine;" interrupted Aoudra's husband, with a wave of the hand, which she well knew to be of final significancy. "She is in all respects what I could best wish for my girl's friend. The lord Cornelius is as anxious as myself for the improvement of the acquaintance; and it is my will that henceforth the families shall be intimate. Let it be looked to."

"My coach shall be ordered forthwith, my lord; I will wait upon the young lady with our daughter without delay, since such is your wish;" said the lady-wife duteously; adding to herself, "I will hope that it is no more than a mother's anxiety which makes me see a groundless fear in this friendship. The lady Thyra may be all that I could desire, in heart and mind, for my Ophelia's associate. At all events, I shall now see her myself, and judge."

As far as judgment could be formed in a first visit, all that Aoudra saw of Cornelius's daughter that morning led her to rejoice that so pleasant an intimacy as this promised to be, should have been begun. The young lady was evidently the petted child of a fond father, who knew not how to refuse her anything. But this indulgence did not seem to have spoiled her —and that alone, spoke greatly in favor of her natural disposition: She was neither imperious, nor wilful; there was none of the insolence in manner, or impatience of controul, which might have been generated by such a course as hers, of irresponsible self-government. She received the lady Aoudra with much gentle grace; and with a tone of respect in her welcome, which showed, that having been so long her

own mistress had not destroyed that deference which
youth owes to superiority of age and experience.  She
was sprightly, without hardness ; she was easy, without forwardness ; she was self-possessed, without a
spark of self-conceit in her demeanour.  There was a
tone of good-breeding in her every word and gesture,
which showed that she was accustomed to much
society ; but there was that in her manner which
bespoke goodness of heart as well as courtesy of
tongue ; there was an unrestrained freedom in her
mode of speech which told plainly how habituated she
was to the expression of her opinions and feelings
before numbers, but there was something also that
revealed how little need there was for reserve in any
of her thoughts or sentiments.  She was obviously
kind-natured, as well as complaisant ; affectionate as
well as affable ; amiable as well as polite.

As for Ophelia, she was charmed with her ; and
the young lady Thyra, seemed no less won by the
modest sweetness of Aoudra's daughter.  A mutual
and strong attraction at once subsisted between the
two girls ; and after their first introduction to each
other, they became as rapidly and completely intimate, as the fathers could have desired.

Soon, no morning was spent apart ; and Thyra,
intent upon enjoying her new friend's society unin-
terruptedly, made a point of receiving Ophelia alone,
and of appointing her usual visitors in the evening
only, henceforward.  She could assume a pretty
tyranny—a kind of playful despotism, when she
chose.  It sat well on her ; and her friends submitted
to it,—well-pleased,—as only another grace, in the
graceful Thyra.  There was so much of feminine ele-
gance in what she did and said, that it seemed her
natural prerogative to have all yield to her.  She was
not wilful ; but she liked to have her own way ; and
it was so pleasantly asserted, so inoffensively insisted
on, that no one dreamed of denying it her.  She was
so winning while she dictated, so obliging in the

midst of her exactions, so really thoughtful of the feelings of others while she affected to be thinking only of her own, so truly kind, while so pretendedly selfish, that all loved to obey her behests ; and indeed, it was generally found, in the end, that they were prompted by a consideration for the general pleasure, as well as for hers in particular.

" You know, sweet friend, we could not find the way to each other's hearts, were we to meet in a crowd every day, instead of thus familiarly, unrestrainedly, doing and saying exactly what we please, while together. As we do now ; do we not ?" said she to Ophelia, as they sat together, in Thyra's pleasant room—her own peculiar room, which was fitted up with every graceful luxury a young girl's taste could suggest in its adornment, and looking out as it did upon the gardens by which her father's mansion was surrounded,—its windows shadowed with trees and flowering climbers, it was in all respects the ideal of a lady's bower. " Besides, I mean you to know something of the people you will meet, before you come among them, since you have owned to me, with that charming simplicity and frankness of yours, that you feel some awe at the thought of encountering strangers."

" I have so little seen of strange faces ;" said Ophelia. " My father's guests are chiefly men high in office, counsellors of state, grave and dignified personages ; and my dear mother, thinking one so young could not as yet derive advantage from their conversation, allowed me to keep our own apartments, when there were visitors."

" You shall hear all about mine, ere you are introduced ; and then they will be no strangers to you when you see them. You will be acquainted with them beforehand ; and it's a great advantage, let me tell you, to have this key,—knowledge of the character,—previously to looking upon the face. Those, who have none of your novice modesty, would often be fain to get possession of such a treasure as this same key.''

'' Is it quite fair that I should have the advantage you speak of, Thyra ?''

'' Never fear, thou dear scrupulous novice ! Those very people, could they know that their characters have been discussed, would be the best pleased. So that we are but thought of, talked of, our self-esteem is satisfied. To be unnoticed—to be of such insignificance, as to be left uncriticised, that is the sting most difficult for human pride to endure.''

'' Then pray indulge them and me by some of your strictures ;'' said Ophelia, smiling. '' Let us hear what biting things your amount of malice can allow itself to utter. And yet your lip slanders itself if it be a slanderer of others.''

'' Nay, no slander ; truth, nothing but truth. Come, with whom shall I begin ? Methinks I'll commence at once with the highest—and so get the most dangerous part of my task despatched first. Our sovereign and his queen have honored my father's house with their presence, but I may not, of course, count their majesties among my visitors ; the king's brother, however, lord Claudius, is not an unfrequent guest here, and he——''

'' You have been presented to their majesties ? You know the king's person—the queen's ; tell me somewhat of them.''

'' The king is a grave-looking man ; warlike and noble in his bearing ; full of dignity and command ; and looks,—as he indeed is—the accomplished soldier and ruler. The queen is very beautiful, both in face and person. Graciously condescending in the kind notice and encouragement she accorded to myself—a young girl undergoing her first presentation.''

'' And what of the prince, their son, lord Hamlet ? I have heard my father speak of him as a student of great repute ; he says, that he has won high academic honors ; and that if he were not of royal birth, he

could make himself illustrious, as a man of learning.''

"Nay, he's even too much of the scholar, for my
taste ;'' said the lively Thyra. "He has dark reflective eyes, which would be beautiful, but that he
allows them to become absorbed in musing and specu-
lation, instead of letting them discourse agreeable
things. He has a handsome mouth, which he resigns
to a meditative idleness, when he might give it its
natural action in pleasant converse. He is thoughtful,
when he should be amusing ; he is absent, when I
want him to be attending to what I say, or to be inventing something to say to me. All this is owing to
his studious habit, which, moreover, will, if he don't
take care, spoil his figure—for he's inclined to fat ;
and a fat gentleman, thou know'st, even though he
be a prince, can never form a lady's ideal of a man.''

" What sort of man must he be, to embody Thyra's
idea of manly perfection ?'' said her young friend.

" Nay, I cannot tell, not I,'' replied Thyra, with a
momentary embarrassment ; then recovering herself,
she went on : " Not such a man as my lord Claudius,
assuredly. He comes next to tell thee of. There's
something marvellously unattractive to me, about that
lord. Though he be of blood-royal, he looks not
noble ; and though his lineage be high, he hath naught
lofty in his mien. And yet I cannot tell what ails
me, that I should not approve him. He is full of
suavity, and is assiduous in his courtesies and attentions ; but they are too much on demand, to seem
very spontaneous. You shall catch him gnawing the
hilt of his dagger in moody silence, and the next instant shall see him all smiles and ready adulation.
His face changes too voluntary-sudden for sincerity.
He'll shift you his manner from sad-browed to jesting, from abstracted to attentive, at a moment's bidding. I never feel at ease in his company ; and care
not if he never came here again ; but my father considers the visits of the king's brother an honor to our

house, and so I receive him with as good a grace as I can muster.''

'' Thyra, like a good daughter, makes her own inclinings bend to those of her father ;'' said Ophelia.

'' You give me too much credit for filial submission, I fear ;'' returned she, with a slight blush and a laugh. '' My father has hitherto given such free course to my likings that I can scarcely think he would wish me to fashion them by his. And yet, I know not——'' She paused, then resumed :

'' There is the lord Voltimand ; but he is my father's friend, not mine. His forty-odd years, and his wise head, claim affinity with sager maturity than I can boast. He is no associate for my giddy self. Then there are Marcellus and Bernardo, two young officers of the king's guard ; true soldiers, light-hearted, pleasant, rattle-pates ; with more valour than knowledge, more animal spirits than mental acquire- . ment ; but withal very agreeable companions—and their uniforms are a great help to make my saloon look bright and gay.''

'' You tell me chiefly of your gentlemen guests ; have you no ladies among your visitors, dear Thyra ?''

'' Ay, truly, there's no lack of ladies to make our parties complete ;'' said Thyra. '' But one court-lady is so like another court-lady, that as I was giving you an insight into the character of the people you will meet, I naturally left out those who seldom can boast of much distinctive feature in that kind. But I am waxing impertinent, methinks. There are, in good sadness, some sweet women among our lady-friends, but thou wilt find those out for thyself. They are not among the formidable strangers I had to tell thee of. Let me see ; who else ? O, ay, there are Osric of Stolzberg, and Eric of Kronstein, two lords, whose estates adjoin that of my father ; you will often meet them here.''

'' Are they of the formidable class I may expect to see ?'' asked Ophelia.

" Truly, I know not why I classed them together ;
for they differ in every particular, save in being pro-
vincial neighbors of ours.  When we are in the country they are our constant guests.  But the one is a
youth, the other a man : the one is boyish, the other
manly ; the one has mature ideas ; the other, no ideas
at all.  The young lord of Stolzberg is a coxcomb ;
while the lord of Kronstein is—is—well, perhaps something very near the ideal we spoke of, ere now."

Thyra paused a moment, with a little conscious
laugh ; while she stole a glance at Ophelia's face ;
but she saw it looking so quiet, so girl-like innocent,
that she went on :—

" Perhaps it is from the contrast between these two
lords, that the one appears to me so greatly above the
other.  It is not every one who finds Kronstein so
gifted, or Stolzberg so inane.  One great advantage
in public esteem, the latter possesses over the former ;
which is, that his domains are extensive, his land un-
encumbered, his possessions exclusively within his own
power ; while the other lord has a magnificence of
taste which has led to rather a profuse expenditure,
and it is whispered that his estates are deeply mort-
gaged.  This report has blunted worldly judgment,
and dulled the edge of its discrimination, in awarding
the palm of merit between the two.  General opinion
lackeys the rich lordling, and can scarcely allow the
personal desert of the accomplished, but acre-dipped
Kronstein.  Certain it is, that my father and I differ
widely in our estimate of their respective attractions.
He favours the one while I——"

" While you judge the lord of Kronstein to be the
superior man, however he may be the poorer lord ;"
said Ophelia, simply ; filling up the pause in her
friend's speech.

" Yes, dear novice ;" rejoined Thyra, with another
smile and shy glance at the quiet unconscious face.
" I must call thee novice, dear Ophelia, thou seem'st
to me so nun-like new to all worldly thoughts and

ideas.  Thou art a very child still, I do believe, though that grave face, and sedate air of thine, make thee seem a woman.   I'll wager now, thou hast scarce obtained the dignity of teens ?"

" You guess my age accurately, dear Thyra ;  I have scarce seen years enough to give me a claim to equality of friendship with you, who must be well-nigh half a dozen summers riper in wisdom than I ; but I can make up in loving respect for thee, what I lack in befitting qualities to give me claim upon thy liking."

" We will love and confide in each other entirely, as friends should ; and be of all the greater mutual benefit, for what there is dissimilar between us ;" said Thyra.   " My social experience shall help you in learning to face strangers ; and thy novice candour shall teach me the beauty of unworldliness.   Let me commence the lessons I am to give, by initiating you in the mysteries of chess,—now the most fashionable of games."

" Is it so much played ?   I knew you were fond of it, for I see the board stand ever ready ;—but I knew not it was in general favour."

" Yes.   For some time, it was banished from court, after that fatal game, famous in our Danish chronicles, when the sovereign dynasty was changed by a choleric blow with a chess-board ; but of late, the taste has revived ; and the game is pursued with greater zest than ever.   We have some skilful players amongst us.   The lord of Kronstein is masterful at it.   He was my instructor.   When we were last at my father's country seat of Rosenheim, we played together daily."

" Then you are, doubtless, now, a well-skilled player yourself, dear Thyra.   I fear you will find me an un-hopeful scholar ;" said Ophelia.

" You are ingenuous, you are artless, you are un-suspicious, dear girl ;" said Thyra, looking at her earnestly, with affectionate admiration ; " and those seem unpromising qualities for attaining proficiency in a game where stratagem and contrivance are main requisites ; but vigilance, patience, are also wanted ; and these you have, for certain. Your noticing that my chess-board is always at hand, bespeaks an observant eye ; and watchfulness may secure success, when over-eager craft rushes into the jaws of an unespied check-mate. But come ; let us begin.''

At this moment, an attendant entered. '' I can see no visitors to-day ;'' Thyra said impatiently, as she ranged the pieces on the board, signing to the servant to withdraw. '' See that I am denied to every one ; and say that I receive, this evening.''

'' I stated such to be your ladyship's orders ;'' said the attendant ; '' but my lord would take no refusal ; he bade me carry up his name, and beseech that your ladyship would see him, for that he hath news which——''

'' Then why dost not announce his name, sirrah ?'' interrupted the young lady. '' Who is it ?''

'' The lord Eric of Kronstein, madam ;'' was the reply.

The colour flushed into Thyra's face ; but she said in a composed voice—that composure and command of voice which courtly breeding teaches, '' Give entrance to my lord of Kronstein ; he doubtless brings intelligence from Rosenheim—from my father.'' Then, as the servant quitted the room, she added :— '' I make an exception in this visitor's favour, dear Ophelia, because I think thou wilt feel curiosity to see one of whom we have been speaking so much.''

'' Your report was too favourable not to induce a wish to know him ;'' replied she ; '' I shall be glad——''

'' He is here !'' said Thyra. Her manner showed so much agitation, so involuntary a delight, such blushing joy, that it could not have failed betraying her secret to one more versed in such tell-tale symptoms than her young companion. But Ophelia perceived in it only the pleasure and animation with which a friend preferred to others for his estimable qualities, would naturally be welcomed.

Besides, her attention was principally engaged by the new comer. Not only did the description she had recently heard, cause her to look at him with in-terest, but there was something in his appearance which struck her with a singular impression, as of some-thing remembered—something long since seen. She continued to gaze upon the face and figure, as though they were a pictured image of some shadow in her memory. So complete was this effect of his appear-ance upon her, that she kept her eyes fixed upon him with almost as unreserved a regard as if he had in-deed been a portrait, instead of a living man.

For him, he was too much engrossed by the greet-ings that took place between himself and Thyra, to perceive the attention with which the young lady stranger was looking at him.

Presently however, her friend, recollecting her duty as hostess, performed the ceremony of introduc-tion. He bowed courteously ; and was about to re-sume his conversation, when something, in the cursory glance he had bestowed upon Ophelia, seemed to strike him, also, with a vague sense of recollection. He hesitated ; looked at her ; but seeming to obtain no confirmation of his passing fancy from what he saw, upon this second view of the tall slight figure be-fore him, he went on with what he was saying to the lady Thyra.

He asked after all their mutual town acquaintance ; told her how dull Rosenheim had appeared after she had left it for Elsinore ; but said that he had made a point of paying his duty there regularly to the lord Cornelius, who had charged him with loving messages for his daughter, on hearing that he was about to ride to the metropolis.

" My lord, your father, desired me to say that he trusts many days will not elapse ere he joins you here in Elsinore ; but meantime, as I am returning to Rosenheim, he bade me ask you for a packet of papers, which——''

'' You return to Rosenheim, my lord ?  When ? How soon ?'' was Thyra's hurried enquiry.

'' Immediately—I am compelled—indeed, I must—my presence, just now, is indispensable at my own poor place ;'' he said, in reply to the mute reproach conveyed by her eyes, and by the tone of her voice ; '' but it will not be so, for any time ; the estate erelong reverts incontestably to——''

He paused in the low toned but eager explanation he was pouring forth ; but Thyra seemed satisfied with these few broken .words ; for adverting to the packet he had mentioned, she said :—'' But these papers my father requires, my lord ; did he say where they were to be found ?''

'' He bade me tell you, you would find them in the ebon cabinet, by his study-chair, lady ; this sealed packet, with which he charged me for you, contains the key, together with more precise directions for your guidance.''

'' I will seek them at once, my lord, since your return must needs be immediate.  But remember,'' she added, with a resumption of vivacity ; '' your friends in Elsinore will look eagerly for your coming soon among them again.  Your stay at Rosenheim must be brief as may be.''

'' My own wishes will limit its duration to the shortest possible span, believe me, lady.  They abide in Elsinore, even while necessity chains myself elsewhere.''

His eyes followed her, as she withdrew to fetch the packet ; and when she disappeared, he turned, in an abstracted manner to the table on which the chessboard stood ; and played mechanically with one of the pieces, twirling it round and round upon its circular foot.  Suddenly he seemed to remember that he was not alone, and that he owed some courtesy of attention to the young lady who sat there so silent, and so

still.  He was about to address her with some slight
remark, when, upon raising his eyes towards her, he
found hers fixed upon his face.

Her look was so steadfast that it perplexed the gentleman, man of the world as he was.  He took up the
chess-man, and idled with it against his lip, in embarrassment of which he himself hardly understood the
source.

A slight incident will sometimes prompt a struggling
memory, while vainly striving to help itself by recalling more important clues.  The form of the ivory piece
caught Ophelia's eye ; and suddenly she exclaimed,
" The knight !  The white horse !  I remember, the
wood—lord Eric--ay, that was the name.  I recollect
it now.  It was you, then, who———"

" Hush !  Can it be possible ?" was the hasty exclamation, as he looked round to see that no one was
near.  " 'Sdeath !" he muttered ;  " the unopened
rosebud, by all that's strange !  How came she here ?
How came she to be there ?"

" You never returned, after Jutha became so
altered—so ill ?  You never knew that she died ?"

The lip blanched to well-nigh the whiteness of the
chess-man that had lately touched it.

" I knew you would be sorry for her, when you
came to hear of it.  You were kind to her ; you liked
her.  Poor Jutha !"

" Be silent, I conjure you, young lady.  Do not
speak that name again—it can do no good—it may do
fearful harm.  Mischief—misery—more evil than you
can conceive, or could ever repair."

He looked round again, in great agitation and
anxiety.  " Do not name her here, I entreat, I im-
plore———"

His manner, so earnest in its hurried supplication,
had its effect upon Ophelia.  But she answered in her
own quiet way " I have never mentioned her ; she is
unknown here.  She had almost faded from my own
thought, as had your face and person.  I hardly re-

membered you. I was a little child then ; at nurse, in that remote country place."

Her ingenuous look, her simple unconsciousness, as she spoke, plainly told the man of the world that this innocent girl had no suspicion of the share he had had in the unhappy Jutha's fate. His dark secret was safe, could he but hope that she would never revive his victim's name ; never repeat the tale of his forest-visits, to others more clear-sighted, more experienced, than herself.

He summoned all his address to his aid. He told Ophelia how she herself had grown out of his knowledge ; that he should not have recognized the little rustic she then appeared, in the beautiful maiden—the young lady of noble birth and distinguished air, whom he at present beheld. He added some flattering allusion to her family ; said that her father, the lord Polonius, was known to him by reputation, as a statesman whose services were of the highest value to his country ; and concluded by adroitly making it his request that she would never allude to any circumstances of their former meeting, as it was important to him, for reasons which he could not immediately explain, that he should not appear to be already known to her.

Before Ophelia could well signify her acquiescence with his wish, Thyra reappeared.

Eric of Kronstein tarried not long after he had received the packet from her hands. Promising to deliver it faithfully and speedily, he took a graceful leave of the two young ladies, and withdrew.

They both remained silent for a considerable space ; each occupied with her own thoughts. Then, Thyra, rousing herself from her reverie, said, " Forgive me, sweet friend, that I am such dull company—so ill fulfil my part of your hostess and entertainer. Come ; now for our first study of chess."

The quiet chess-mornings, the brilliant social evenings, enjoyed with Thyra, made Ophelia's time speed pleasantly away ; while she could not but observe, that at all seasons, at all hours, Eric of Kronstein was ever the favorite guest of her friend. When others were excluded, he was admitted ; before others arrived, he was already there, and after others had retired, he lingered ; and always, his advent and his stay were welcome. By his adroit management, this was not markedly apparent to the world ; but to one in such close companionship as Ophelia, it could not escape notice.

Once,—it was an evening when there was no assemblage of friends, the young ladies were deep in the absorbing interest of Thyra's favorite game, while the lord of Kronstein stood by, as was his frequent wont, leaning over the back of her chair, watching the lesson she gave, suggesting the best moves on either side, and aiding the fair teacher with his superior knowledge.

It grew late, and the game was not yet ended. Their excitement strengthened with every moment ; for in the interest of the trial of skill, Kronstein had insensibly come to prompt Ophelia's moves exclusively, so that, in fact, Thyra and he were now playing against each other. Her cheeks were heated, her eyes sparkled, as a chess-player's will, when the antagonism is at its height.

At this moment the lady Ophelia's coach, with Reynaldo, her father's confidential servant, and Guda, her own woman, to attend her home, were announced as having arrived.

"Can it be so late ?  I had no thought of the hour. My lord, however unwillingly, you must be inhospitably bidden good-night.  We must play out the game to-morrow ;" said Thyra.

"We cannot leave it unfinished ; sleep would be impossible, with the fate of that game undecided !" exclaimed Eric impetuously.  "The lady Ophelia will give orders that the equipage shall wait."

"My mother especially bade me return without delay, when she should send for me this evening ;" said Ophelia. " It is my father's intention to take me with him to the palace to-morrow, to present me to their majesties ; and he desired that I would be with him to-night, ere he retired to rest, that he might speak some words of counsel he had to impress upon me. I may not tarry. Good night, Thyra. Good night, my lord."

Thyra in returning her leave-taking, evidently expected that the lord of Kronstein would retire at the same time ; but he, declaring that the game of chess must be played out, in order to let Ophelia know its decision, on the morrow, threw himself into the chair she had just quitted, showing that he was resolved to stay.

Thyra in pretty, blushing confusion, partly eagerness and pleasure, partly hesitation, submitted to his arrangement, and reseated herself at the chess-table, bidding her friend be sure to let her see her immediately on her return from her first court-visit.

In one of the large apartments of the palace, on the following day, sat a lady, surrounded by her attendant ladies, working at a tapestry-frame. In a deep embayed window, at some distance from her, stood a man, leaning just within the recess, regarding her earnestly from beneath his bent brows, and drooping lids. Not a bend of her handsome head, not an inclination of that polished throat, not a sweeping line of those white falling shoulders, not a curve of those voluptuously rounded arms, or a single movement of her ample but finely moulded figure, as it inclined over her work, escaped the eye so 'greedily noting every particular of her luxuriant beauty. Sensual admiration lurked in the looks with which he stealthily devoured her person, while all the while, his attention was apparently devoted to feeding and playing with a hawk, which sat upon an ornamented perch, in the recessed window where he leaned.

The man was Claudius, the king's brother. The lady was queen Gertrude.

The weather had been unusually warm. The soft afternoon air crept in by the open windows ; and through the apartment there reigned the silence that grows with a sense of enjoyment and refreshment. It had for some time been preserved unbroken, save by the drawing through of the tapestry stitches, and the occasional restlessness of the hawk, pecking and biting at the teasing finger, when one of the attendant ladies exclaimed : " His majesty, the king ; madam."

Gertrude rose to receive her royal husband. He came to tell her of letters that had arrived from Wittenberg ; bringing news of fresh academic honors attained by their son, Hamlet ; one from himself, containing loving and duteous greetings to his parents, with tidings of his health and welfare ; and other despatches from the royal forces engaged in a northern warfare, which had terminated in conquest to Denmark. The king concluded, by saying that so much happy intelligence arriving on one day, deserved marking by some token of remembrance ; and that he had brought one in the shape of a gemmed bracelet, which he prayed her to wear as the gift not only of a proud and happy father, and of a rejoicing monarch, but as that of a loving husband. As the king fondly leant over the beautiful arm presented to him, that he might clasp the jewel upon it, a sharp inward groan burst from the lips of Claudius.

" My brother !" exclaimed the king. " I did not perceive your presence. Are you not well, my Claudius ?" he added, approaching the recess where he leaned. " That cry you could not suppress—your change of color—your face is pale, man ; you are in pain. I have more than once noted that ashy hue steal upon your face. Tell me, tell your brother, what you ail."

" An old wound, a hurt,—'tis nothing ;" he answered, looking down. " Or if," and he turned to the king, with a ghastly attempt to smile off his embarrassment,—" 'tis but what reminds me that I have been a soldier, and long for an occasion to efface the old rankle with a few new scratches.''

'' It has scarred over, ere properly healed. It must be looked to ;'' said the king.

'' It will never heal ;'' the other muttered, bitterly ; writhing, as he withdrew from the hand laid in brotherly kindness on his shoulder.

'' Our own leech shall examine it ;'' the king said, in his gentle but earnest manner. '' You must not thus neglect health most dear to us.''

'' Your grace shall pardon me,—no leechcraft may avail,—'tis beyond the physician's skill,—I have learned to think it cannot be relieved. I will school myself to more patient, more silent, endurance. You shall hear no more such weak betrayals.''

'' Sweet Gertrude, come hither ; use you your womanly persuasion, with this refractory brother of ours, to have his hurt examined. I will not believe it beyond cure.''

As the queen advanced in obedience to her royal husband's bidding, and approached the spot where they stood, the king took her hand, and placing it on his brother's arm, said : '' I expect no less from the gentle power of my Gertrude's words, which as her loving husband I am free to confess,'' he said, as he regarded her with an affectionate smile, '' than that I shall find, on my return, they have won our brother to our wish. The summer afternoon wooes me forth, to walk awhile in mine orchard. Meantime, prosper you in your suit, my queen.''

He left them standing thus, beside each other ; Gertrude's hand, where he had placed it, on his brother's arm. But when the king had left the apartment, she withdrew her hand, and retired a pace or two from her close vicinity to Claudius. He breathed hard, and there was almost a fierceness in the tone with which he uttered the words, '' He bade you sue me, madam. Your suit ? Your will ? What have you to urge ? Let me hear you plead. *You* plead to me ! But come, what is't ?''

"Your wound, my lord. Consent that it shall be looked to ; there might be relief——"

He turned abruptly, and looked at her, as he said, "You would have it relieved—cured ?"

"Assuredly, my good lord ; our leech is renowned in skill. He will, I doubt not——"

Again he interrupted her : "I speak not of the leech. But this old wound of mine—this deep-seated, scorching pain, here ; this corroding torture, ever gnawing in and in, till vitality itself is the prey, would you have it relieved, cured—if relief and cure were in your own gift ?"

He dropped his voice to a whisper, as he uttered the few last words ; though the whole conversation had taken place in a low tone, which could not reach the spot where the attendant ladies sat, round the tapestry frame, at the farther end of the room.

Gertrude said, in a manner as natural and unconcerned as she could make it, "Can you doubt it, my lord ?"

Wilful misunderstanding sometimes betrays deepest consciousness.

Claudius felt this, as he looked at the varying cheek which belied the assumed composure of manner ; and saw that she knew his full meaning. "Then pity me. This wound is probed to the quick, its festering smart is tented past concealment of the anguish I endure, when he makes me the witness of his licensed endearments ;" he hurried on, hissing, serpent-like, his torrent of scarce-suppressed passionate words. "Can I calmly see him fondle that arm which I so many times have thirsted to press to these throbbing lips. A 'loving husband,' forsooth ! Why, his is a tame affection which can leave a wife, to go sleep in the shade of a cool orchard, while mine is a burning passion that consumes me. Ardor such as mine befits a 'loving husband ; ' not the puling caresses of that dotard."

"My lord ! Remember you of whom you speak ? Of your brother, your king, my husband !"

" Ay, madam—your husband—your ' loving husband !' '' He ground his teeth, muttering a curse.
" The very hem of your garment stirs me to more
adoring warmth than he is capable of feeling, from the
possession of all that he hath in right of loving-husbandship ;'' he presumed to add, as he clenched within his
hand the end of. a light drapery, which formed part
of her attire.

" You presume on my forbearance, my lord !" exclaimed the queen. " You cannot believe that I will
listen longer to such rash speech.'' She would have
withdrawn from the recessed window ; but perceiving
that a portion of her robe was within his grasp, she
feared lest the movement might attract the attention
of her ladies to this circumstance, and so betray to
them what was passing. A veriest trifle, such as this,
will suffice to sway the conduct of a weak-souled
woman.

At this moment, an attendant entered to announce
that the lord Polonius and his daughter, the lady
Ophelia, craved audience of her majesty.

" Conduct them to the presence-chamber ;'' said
the queen ; " I will receive them there.''

The edge of robing was still detained for an instant ;
then she felt it suddenly released, and she was free to
go. She moved away from the side of Claudius,
without suffering her eyes to look towards him ; and,
attended by her ladies, she left the apartment.

As she proceeded along a gallery of the palace, on
her way to the state-chamber, one of her train of ladies
exclaimed, lifting the end of the embroidered drapery
which floated from the queen's shoulders ;—"See
here, madam ; some treacherous doorway hath torn
away a fragment from your majesty's attire ; the
piece is fairly wrenched out. Alack ! the beauty of
the robe is marred !''

" Get other tires ready. I will change these anon,
when my lord Polonius shall have taken leave ;'' said
queen Gertrude. " It must needs have been some

unheeded violence of a closing door, or other like accident.   'Tis no matter.''

"A passing sweet temper hath her majesty, to regard the wreck of such embroidery as that, without so
much as a fretful word ;'' thought the lady-in-waiting.

"And so, you found our queen no less gracious than
I had painted her to you ;'' said Thyra to Ophelia,
when next the two friends sat together, to discuss the
grand event of court presentation.

"She was, indeed, all that a young creature could
desire, of considerate and encouraging ; she con-
descended to make it her express desire, that my
father would bring me frequently to the palace in
future.''

"And while thou hast been basking in the sunshine
of royal smiles, and court favor, poor I have been
yawning in the vapid atmosphere of foppery and folly,
of coxcombry and pretension.''

"Ah, I can tell, then, who hath been thy guest this
morning, Thyra.   Young Osric of Stolzberg ;  was't
not ?   He hath never thy good word, I know.''

"Doth he deserve one ?   Is he not an insufferable
froth ?   An intolerable bubble of emptiness ?   He
thinks to play the accomplished gentleman by affecting
modish phraseology, and adopting fashionable whims
of speech.   See how he minces his mother-tongue,
in his mispronouncings.   Ler me arrange your la'ship's
men for you ; the knaghts, bashops, pones, and so.
You shall take none other than the red,—a blushing
foil to your la'ship's fingers.   Your la'ship advances
your king's pone ?   'Tis well ;  the forward varlet
suffers capture in a trice, for his presumption.''

"In ' a trace ! in a trace ! ' '' interrupted Ophelia,
laughing at her friend's imitation of the young lordling's manner.

"True ; ' in a trace, for his presumption.'   This
same game of chess your la'ship favors with so much
of your la'ship's good laking, is exceeding dainty
sport ; of ingenious devace,—very subject to con-

travance,—very suggestive to skill,—a most pleasing
pastime, and of very exciting encounter. But your
la'ship is playing adly. Have a care! 'Twill be a
drone game!' and thus was my morning droned away,
with his foolish buzzing, and wasplike impertinence."

"Nay, he is but a butterfly. 'Tis thou who art
waspish, Thyra, to be vexed with so harmless an in-
sect. He does but flutter to and fro, displaying his
gay painted coat, vainly, and vain; but leaving no
venom, inflicting no sting."

"But I tell thee, Ophelia, there is a sting in his
presence, for me. My father hath, I know, set his
heart on bringing about a match between this silly fly
and myself. Now, though I do not believe that
young Osric hath one thought of the kind, for all his
hoverings round me, yet I fear lest an inkling of my
father's wish should generate that which his own brain
could scarce originate,—an idea; and that idea, the
one of wooing me to be his wife."

"Thou dost not desire to be a wife, Thyra?"

"I say not that;" said Thyra, blushing; "but I
desire not to be Osric's wife. I will tell thee honestly,
dear girl. There is a man whose wife I could wish to
be—whose wife I hope to be. A man whom I love,
and who loves me; a man whom it is an honor to
love; and whose love it is a pride to have won.
But this man cannot ask me to become his wife, until
the redemption of his patrimony from mortgage, shall
give him a right to claim me openly of my father;
and meantime, you cannot wonder that I should wish
to keep all suitors at a distance, who might win his
consent, before my lover himself dare come forward
to seek it."

"And this lover is—— ?"

"No other than Eric of Kronstein. You surely
must have guessed our attachment. You who have
seen us so much together, dear friend?"

"You forget that I have inexperienced eyes—that

I am (as you call me yourself, dear Thyra) quite a novice in such matters ;" said the smiling Ophelia.

" You are innocent simplicity itself, sweet friend ; as a girl of your years should be. Still, I thought you must have seen how it was with Eric and myself. We have exchanged hearts. We are plighted to each other by the most solemn vows. He has more than once told me he looks upon me as his affianced bride, —his wedded wife ;—I regard him as my husband, and feel that no power on earth should make me give myself to any other than Eric of Kronstein. He tells me that less than half a year will see him reinstated in full possession of his estates, and that then he can ask me of my father with good hope of success. Until that period, therefore, 'tis of the utmost importance our secret should not transpire ; but—I could not have felt true to the confidence I have professed in my friend Ophelia had it longer been withheld from her."

The young girls embraced lovingly and heartily, as Thyra received the assurance that her secret should be faithfully preserved.

Some months had elapsed since the last conversation. One evening as the friends sat together, the hours grew, and with them the impatience of Thyra. She was expecting lord Eric, who had promised to come ; but still the time for his appearance went by, and he came not. His visits now, were generally at a late hour ; but night drew on, and yet he came not.

Ophelia's attendant arrived, with the coach to fetch her home. And she left her friend pacing to and fro in the grounds, by starlight, unwilling to abandon the hope of his coming, even then. But as Ophelia reached the garden gate, and was about to step into her coach, she perceived Trasco, lord Eric's servant. He entered the grounds, and she could see him deliver a letter to her friend ; who, placing it in her bosom, hurried back to the house.

Next morning, at an early hour, Polonius entered

the apartment where his wife and daughter were, and by the ostentatious perturbation of his manner, evidently desired that they should ask what was the matter. The lady Aoudra dutifully did so.

He told her that he had that moment received intelligence, of a circumstance which had occasioned great consternation in certain quarters. It was reported that lord Eric of Kronstein, whose affairs were long suspected to be in an embarrassed state, was discovered to be utterly ruined ; that he had accumulated debts of large amount, that he had gambled away his patrimonial estate, that he was not worth a farthing, and that in order to escape from the crowd of demands which pressed upon him, he had, last night, under favour of darkness, embarked in a vessel bound for the Archipelago. His creditors were outrageous ; and Polonius added, that he had reason to believe many gentlemen of high rank were among the most furious against him, on account of the numerous debts of honour which were thus left uncancelled.

" I confess I cannot feel much concern for them ; they are probably, for the most part, little better than himself,—gamblers, and spendthrifts ;" said Aoudra.

" My dear, your virtue makes you hard upon fashionable follies ;" said her husband. " Conscious of our own integrity, we should be lenient to others more exposed to temptation. You can scarcely judge of those which beset young noblemen of spirit, and with means at their own disposal."

" But their spirit sometimes leads them to use means not at their own disposal. This lord Eric of Kronstein, when he staked at the gaming table sums that were not in his rightful possession, was guilty of more than folly ; he acted basely, unjustly. Besides, if my memory serve, I have heard this same lord of Kronstein accused of even worse vices than gambling. It is whispered that he is a libertine,—a practised seducer."

" My good lady, how often must I caution you

against giving credit to whispers, and hear-say, when they affect the character of those in high station. It is the vice of the envious, to slander those with whom they cannot aspire to be equal. Besides, you are too strict—too austere in your judgment of such matters. These are scarcely more than pardonable errors,—faults and follies to be expected in a handsome young fellow of his rank and age.''

"As I have understood, this Kronstein is not so very young. He has reached years that ought to be of discretion, very long since.''

"Ay, well, it may be so. I know not of my own personal knowledge. But I must not tarry here ; I must away to a privy-council meeting that sits this morning. His majesty laid his gracious commands on me to let him have, without fail, the help of this poor brain of mine. He is pleased to think it of some little avail in weighty questions that concern the state. Well, well ; it may be so. It may be so.''

Away hurried the courtier ; and the silence that ensued after his departure, was first broken, by Ophelia's asking her mother, '' what did you mean by calling lord Eric of Kronstein a libertine ?—a seducer ? I never heard the words.''

The lady Aoudra looked at her daughter with a tender earnestness. '' The better for mine innocent child, that she has never heard them, never known their meaning. Better still could she have remained in ignorance evermore of their evil import. But my Ophelia will soon be a woman ; she will mix with the world ; she will encounter the ill, as well as the good, that exists there ; she will find that men's natures are compounded of vice as of virtue ; that they are capable of sinful and harmful deeds, as well as highest and most meritorious actions ; that they ofttimes work mischief instead of benefit ; woe instead of weal ; and that guile frequently lurks beneath the most specious seeming. To guard her against such sinister assailants, 'tis needful she should know the nature of her danger ; a danger most imminent in the sphere to which she is destined,—a court.''

Gradually, then, and very heedfully, did this tender mother lift the veil from her young daughter's mind. She told her how the selfishness of man, frequently under the pretence of love for his victim, sacrifices her innocence, blasts her good name, betrays her to shame and misery, and then leaves her to ruin—to utter perdition. '' Disgrace, pollution, wreck of fair honor, peril of body and soul, follow in the track of such a villain's footsteps, wherever his fatal admiration chances to alight ;'' said Aoudra, vehemently. '' And such deeds are called fashionable follies, and pardonable errors of youth ! The world is charitable in the allowances it makes for the worker of all this evil, though severely tyrannous to the injured party. But let the multitude be tolerant as it will to the titled libertine, I, for my part, must ever hold deliberate seduction as one of the most heinous of crimes, and continue to manifest my abhorrence of the seducer in proportion with my estimate of his guilt. I hold it to be a base guilt—a cruel guilt ; 'tis the advantage taken by knowledge of ignorance,—by selfishness of generosity ; 'tis the infliction of deadly injury, beneath the mask of feigned love. 'Tis cowardice and treachery in one, and in the vilest form. Shame, double shame, on the betrayer rather than on the betrayed !''

'' But such a betrayer,—a libertine—a seducer,— you believe lord Eric of Kronstein to be.''

'' Such I have heard him described ; by one too, who thought she was doing him honour—fixing another feather in the cap of his gentlemanly qualifications—in ascribing to him such a character. A man of gallantry is, I believe, the polite term. A gallant action, truly, to win the trust and love of a poor maid, and then requite her with destruction.''

'' My poor friend ! And this is the man she deems worthy of all esteem and liking. To whom she has

given her whole heart !'' exclaimed Ophelia.   '' 'Twill
be best kindness to her now, to reveal her secret to
you, my mother, that we may have your experience
and counsel to aid her.   Can we not save her from
committing her fate irrecoverably to such a man's care ?
But he is gone !   Still, the knowledge of his worth-
lessness, will help to console her for his loss.''

Hastily she told her mother of Thyra's attachment
for Kronstein ; of all she knew of him herself ; of her
former meeting with him ; of his request that she
would not revert to it ; and then, as the story of Jutha
was unfolded, owing to the recent better knowledge
she had acquired, it struck herself with a new significance, while to the lady Aoudra it revealed a fearful
tale of sorrow and wrong.

. '' I should have been with thee, my child.   Told at
the time, as it occurred, and as it then struck thee, to
a mother's ear, all might have been well.   A child
should ever have at hand, her, to whom every scene,
every event, together with the ideas they may en-
gender, can be confided.   But even yet, much mischief may be prevented.   We will hasten to your
friend Thyra—to warn her against the evils she can
avoid ; to comfort her in the grief she will have to
endure.

On arriving at Cornelius's mansion, they found from
her attendants, that the lady Thyra had not yet left
her room.

'' She lies late, ordinarily, dear mother.   Let us seek
her in her chamber ; her friend Ophelia is privileged
to come to her rooms at all seasons,—even when she
is, as now, a slug-a-bed.''

She went at once to the sleeping apartment.   She
saw at a glance that Thyra was not lying there ; but
as she was retiring, a something within the curtains,
at the bed's foot, caught her eye.   It was the figure
of her friend, half hidden among them.   Ophelia
went gently forwards, to embrace her ; but as she extended her arms to wrap them about Thyra's form, it

swung heavily away from her, a mere heap of inanimate matter—an image,—a corse ! It was the dead body of Thyra, hanging, where her own desperate hand had stifled out life. Near to her was afterwards found, a paper, with these words :—

" My father !—forgive your lost child. Oh, lost, lost, indeed,—every way lost ! You destined my hand to one whom I could not love. I pledged faith, affection, honour,—all, to one whom I loved only too well. He whom I so fatally trusted, has proved false. He fled. What is left me, but to die ? Deal indulgently by my memory, for the sake of what I was to you, when,—an innocent child at your knee, —your blessing rested on my head. Let the thought of me, as I was then, be all that shall live in your remembrance of                                   THYRA."

When Ophelia was lifted from the floor, where she had fallen prostrate, she was in strong convulsions. The shock she had received, produced a severe illness. For a long space she lay in the utmost danger, now wandering in delirium, now sunk into a heavy stupor. From one of these deep sleeps, she once awoke, stretching forth her hand feebly, and uttering a faint word or two. Her mother, who had never quitted her side, perceived the movement, and bent over her, to catch the sense of the murmured sound.

" Is the king dead ?"

" I trust not, dear one. He is absent in Norway ; and the last despatches brought intelligence of his safety."

" Methought I saw him, dead ;" said Ophelia. " I have been dreaming strangely."

Her mother spoke soothingly ; striving to compose and divert her attention from dwelling upon this. She smoothed and arranged the pillow beneath the feverish head ; she put some cool beverage to the parched lips, whispering the while, loving, cheerful words. But Ophelia reverted to the theme ; and her mother, finding her inclined to speak, and that she did so with none of the agitation which marked her words when she wandered, let her muse on, thus, half aloud.

" He seemed dead, as I saw him—though he moved before me, waving his arm toward them.  He pointed to them, as each appeared."

" Of whom do you speak, dear child ?"

" Of those figures—those women.  It was down by the brook—among the reeds—beneath the willow ;— not the stream in the wood—but the brook yonder, which flows into the castle-moat.  That solitary spot —all rush-grown, and shadowy—where the water creeps on sluggish and slow, margined by rank grass, and river-weeds,—you remember ?"

Her mother gave token of assent.

" It was there she sat,—the first figure I saw.  The night was obscure ;  the clouds scudded athwart the sky ;—the moon's light struggled feebly through them ;  there was a veil of haze upon tree, and shrub, and brook ;  but I saw her plainly, and knew her at once, though her long hair fell drooping over her knees as she sat.  I knew her, before she shook it back, and wrung her hands, and moaned over the little white face that lay upon her bosom.  It was Jutha, mother !"

The lady Aoudra would fain have prevented Ophelia from proceeding ;  but she feared to do harm, by checking her in her evident desire to speak on.

" I would have gone toward her, but my feet were rooted to the spot ;  while, close behind me, there grad- ually shaped itself into substance a form that seemed to grow out of the shadowy night air.  It became the distinct semblance of the king, as I saw him ride to the Norwegian wars, in coat of armour, and with truncheon in hand, not long since ;  save, that his face, in lieu of being lighted with hope of conquest, life- like, and animated, was pale and all amort—ghastly, and set in death.  He turned this wan visage full upon me, as he pointed to the figure of her who sat lamenting ;  and then she vanished."

" Dear Ophelia, thou shalt not recall these sad images ; let me tell thee, dear one, of thy father, who——''

" But there were two others, I saw. One was my poor Thyra. I knew her by a terrible token.'' And Ophelia's voice became nearly extinct, as she added : —'' her livid throat, mother ; and there was a space between her feet and the ground, as she glided past me.''

A moment's pause ; and then Ophelia went on.

" But she faded out of my ken, also, as the mailed figure again stretched forth his pointing hand. The wind sighed amid the reeds. The heads of nettles and long-purples were stirred by the night breeze, as it swept on mournfully. The air seemed laden with heavy sobbings. Then I saw one approach, whose face I could not see, and whose figure I knew not. She was clothed in white, all hung about with weeds and wild flowers ; and from among them stuck ends of straw, that the shadowy hands seemed to pluck and spurn at. The armed royalty waved sternly, but as if involuntarily, commanded by yet a higher power than his own will ; and then the white figure moved on, impelled towards the water. I saw her glide on, floating upon its surface ; I saw her dimly, among the silver-leaved branches of the drooping willow, as they waved around and above her, up-buoyed by her spreading white garments.''

The mother shuddered, as her eye fell upon the white night-gear of her child, telling the vision. But, at this moment, Polonius softly entered the room, having heard from Guda, that his daughter had awakened, better ; and that she was talking more collectedly, than she had done since her illness. He was soon busily engaged, in his half fussy, half kindly manner, chiding Aoudra for indulging Ophelia with too much license of speech ; and making many remarks equally sapient and facetious, on women's love of talk, their proneness for confabulation and gossip.

" They will let each other talk—rather than not have talk toward," said he ; " but you, lady-wife, and you, my girl, must be patient yet awhile, and let rest and perfect silence do their work. Quiet is restorative. Give it its full trial, 'beseech you.''

Thanks to Aoudra's tender nursing, Ophelia was restored to health. But a more severe blow, than any she had yet sustained, now awaited her.

Death, which had spared herself, took her mother from her. It is true that the anguish of sudden separation was not theirs. For some time Aoudra lingered ; hers was a gradual decay, without pain, and without loss of faculty. She was able to give her child those counsels which should best protect her in her approaching entrance upon the world's experience ; while the daughter was permitted the comfort of yielding the gentle ministerings—the loving tendance which best alleviate sickness and suffering. The anxious mother would often recur to the nature of the perils which most peculiarly threaten a young maiden introduced for the first time to the society of men of the world ; men, her superiors in rank, as in artful experience ; and from the exercise of which art to her prejudice, no conscientious scruples would deter them. The mother thought it behoved her in an especial manner to guard Ophelia by this pre-knowledge of the dangers that would environ her, when left alone as she felt her child soon must be, with no female guidance, no other protection than her own heart. And how was this heart to counsel her, were it not previously fortified and instructed by an understanding of its probable hazards, and of its best sources of defence against them ? Aoudra deplored the necessity that existed for thus forestalling in her daughter's mind an acquaintance with the existence of vice ; but she felt it to be a necessity, and she did not shrink from the performance of her duty. She consoled herself, also, with the reflection that to learn the nature of vice is not to become acquainted with vice itself, or the prac-

tice of vice ; that to know of evil is not to know evil ;
and that to perceive the perils of sin, is no allurement
to sin.  On the contrary she felt that a virtuous nature as instinctively shrinks from the pollution of crime,
as purity recoils from mingling with impurity,—there
subsists mutual repugnance to combine.  She therefore hesitated not to point out evil to her young
daughter, as the surest means of averting it.  " But
not only, my child,'' Aoudra once said, " have I to
caution you against the viciously-disposed among men.
Even with their best simulation, there is something
that betrays itself of such men's real propensities, to
act as a warning and a repellant to one of pure in-
clinations.  There is Claudius, the king's brother, for
instance,—a licentious unscrupulous man ; who, unless my instincts have played me false, and done him
grievous injustice, would be restricted by no consideration of honour or duty in the pursuit of his desires.  From such coarse homage as his, were it
offered to her, my child's own delicacy and native
good-feeling would at once prompt her to shrink.  It
is the good, the gentle, the refined in manner, the accomplished in speech and deportment, the cultivated
in imagination and intellect, against whom my daughter must also learn to guard her heart, lest such qualities betray her into a premature gift of that heart,
fatal to her peace of mind.  Tell me, my child,—it
is to your own mother you are speaking, remember,—
tell me if you know one thus distinguished.''

Ophelia was standing behind the large chair in
which Aoudra reclined, so that her face was unseen ;
but as she leaned over, and kissed the wan cheek, her
mother felt the glow she could not behold.

" Since I have heard that his highness, the lord
Hamlet, has returned from Wittenberg,'' said
Aoudra, " I have always believed that you, dear child,
could not fail to note in him the maturity of those
excellences, of which I remember he gave such fruitful
token in earliest youth.  Even then I could foresee

what the future man would be, from the nobleness of nature, which shone conspicuous in every word and deed of the young prince. He was in truth a royal child—a noble boy ! And as he grew into manhood I still marked, on each of his successive returns to Elsinore, how worthily he fulfilled the promise of his boyhood. Such a mind and heart as his, seen as they are through those dark expressive eyes,—now full of intellectual fire, now softened by sensibility ;—seen as they are through his most beautiful smile—a smile peculiarly his—so gentle, yet so arch, so pregnant of meaning, so persuasive in its sweet fascination—can scarcely fail of winning for him the favor of any woman whom he should seek to interest.''

'' But must the yielding him her favorable thoughts, be so fatal a surrender, for the woman whom he could love ?'' whispered Ophelia.

'' For her whom he could love,—truly, and in truth, love,—no, assuredly no ;'' said Aoudra. '' Were a woman well convinced that she had indeed become possessed of his true affection, she would but exchange a mutual treasure in the full bestowal of her heart's best feelings upon such a man as Hamlet. But let her be sure—entirely sure—of his love for her, ere she permit her fancy to engage itself *too* fondly with his image. Let her beware that his thought is as deeply fixed upon her, as hers could be upon him, ere she allow her own to occupy itself too curiously with his merits. Let her securely know that his heart is firm-set in constancy and truth towards her, ere she weakly suffer her imagination to become enamoured of excellences only too well calculated to inspire a passion, which if hopeless, would be fatal to her peace of mind.''

Thus it came, that—from her mother's warning, at this time, as, from her father's and her brother's admonitions, at a subsequent period,—Ophelia had the perils which awaited her, in her future life at court, peculiarly impressed upon her mind.

After the lady Aoudra's death, both the king and the queen made it their study by their tenderness and almost parental kindness of attention to the motherless girl, to lighten the affliction of her loss. They were, in their behaviour to her, rather like affectionate and gracious friends, than her sovereigns. They showed by their eagerness to have her as much as possible with them, that they would fain act the part of loving relations by her ; and she soon learned to regard them with as fond an attachment.

The prince Hamlet joined his royal parents in their attempt to soften the grief of Ophelia ; and in this gentle task, his own growing preference for her, gained strength and fixedness of purpose. His kindness and sympathy were enlisted in her behalf ; his refined taste was attracted by her maiden beauty ; his delicacy of feeling taught him to delight in her innocence, her modesty, her retiring diffidence ; his masculine intellect found repose in the contemplation of her artless mind, her untaught simplicity, her ingenuous character ; his manly soul dwelt with a kind of serene rapture on the sweet feminine softness of her nature. As time went on, tokens of his increasing regard, awoke a responsive feeling in her breast towards him. But while this fair flower of love was springing up between them,—near to it lurked in unsuspected rankness of growth, the foul unwholesome weed of a forbidden passion.

It happened that a courser of matchless breed was sent from a distant court, as a present, to that of Denmark. The king bestowed the gift on his son, Hamlet ; and one morning, queen Gertrude, and Ophelia, were leaning from the balcony of a window over-looking the court-yard of the castle, that they might watch the prince, as he went through the varied paces, and tried the several merits, of the high-mettled horse. The interest of the sight absorbed them wholly ; their eyes were riveted upon the animated scene below, and

they were unconscious that any one was in the room
near to them, when Claudius stepped close to where
the queen was bending forward ; and, standing just
within the open window that led on to the balcony, a
few paces behind her, he murmured :—" This hath
slipped from your majesty's arm."　She turned, and
saw that he had just picked up from the floor, her
bracelet, which he held towards her, but not within
reach.

" Will your grace receive it at my hand ?" he said,
without tendering it any nearer ; but holding it as it
were, in manner of a lure, that she might step within
the room from the balcony.

She did so, saying :—" I thank you, my lord, for
the pains you have taken, that I should not lose what
I prize so highly."

" You may requite them ;" he said.　" Yonder
silken trifle,—that heaving ribbon, blushing and fra-
grant,—a carnation set 'midst lilies," he continued,
pointing to a crimson knot she wore upon her bosom,
" shall be rich ransom for the jewel."

" Were it not for the young girl so near to us, for
whose innocent sake I indulge you with this lowered
voice, my lord, you should not dare speak thus ;" said
Gertrude, glancing towards the balcony, where she had
left Ophelia.

" I rejoice in her presence, or in aught else, that
procures me this concession,—this chance.　Could
you know the fever of solicitude, with which I have
watched for such a precious moment—could you know
the anguish of seeing you ever near, yet ever removed
from my——"

" My lord—I entreat—I insist ; no more !" interrupted the queen.　" Give me the bracelet."

" Not without its ransom.　The last token was torn
from you ; this, I am resolved, shall be yielded of your
own grace, accorded to me by your pity.　That
womanly heart, could it only know how sorely I need
comfort, would not refuse me its compassion,"

He saw that she could not hear unmoved, an allusion to his unhappiness,—offspring though it was, of a criminal passion. In such a woman as Gertrude, the sight of the influence her beauty had upon his senses, excited involuntary interest. There was that in her voluptuous nature, which responded instinctively to the luxurious ardour of the passion he had dared to conceive and avow. Instead of in her heart resenting, and by her manner repelling the boldness of his warmth,—instead of resisting its effect upon herself, and repressing its expression in him, she could not help yielding to the secret guilty pleasure of knowing it to exist. She allowed herself to contrast its unhallowed fire, with the pure love of her wedded lord ; and, sensually judged, the one seemed superior in fervour to the other.

The wife, who admits such thoughts, so judging, is already adulterate in spirit.

Yet still her feeble soul struggled to preserve a show of virtuous indignation at the insult of his admiration.

" Know you to whom you speak, my lord ? Do you remember that I am a wife ?" she said, in reply to his last speech.

" Too fatally,—and that you are not mine." He struck his forehead with his clenched hand.

" Cease, sir ; think that I am your brother's ;—your queen. You strain our patience."

" And do you owe me no indemnity for that which I have shown, in my long-silent torture ? Let me have the token I covet ; or I keep the gem."

" You abuse your advantage, my lord."

" Misery breeds selfishness ;" he replied. " I have abided too long in bitter, hopeless misery, to neglect the one poor gain within my power. Grant me the silken toy."

" I dare not let my husband miss his gift from my arm ;" said the queen, hastily detaching the ribbon.

" Neighboured as this has been, a thousand times

more precious !" he exclaimed, as he snatched the breast-knot to his lips, and returned her the jewel.

Within a week of that time, the realm of Denmark was thrown into dismay, by the sudden death of its monarch. The good king,—so it was reported,—while sleeping, as was his afternoon wont, in the orchard which formed part of the palace-grounds, had been stung by a serpent ; and, from the venom inflicted by the wound, he had instantly sickened and died.

Ere the nation could recover from its consternation ; and while the rightful heir to the crown was plunged in filial grief, Claudius seized the crown, and caused himself to be proclaimed king. So artfully had all his plans been laid ; so resolutely and so promptly did he carry them all out, that he established his claims to the succession, or rather, fixed himself firmly in the possession of his usurped dominion, before the public voice, on behalf of its lawful prince, could be upraised to dispute his pretentions. Scarcely had this first bold step been securely taken, when it was followed up by the solemnity of coronation ; and shortly after, by the ceremonial of marriage between the reigning monarch and his late brother's widow.

The habitual acquiescence with which royal proceedings are for the most part regarded by the populace, could hardly restrain the expressions of amazement, and dissatisfaction, which these events excited. But they occurred in such rapid succession, were carried with so high a hand, and were executed so peremptorily, that they passed without open murmurs, without attempted opposition. Moreover, the lavish splendour, with which the two rites of royal marriage and coronation were solemnized, had their effect upon the vulgar mind, in causing them to be regarded with curiosity and interest, rather than with reprobation. Claudius knew the full advantage of investing his royal proceedings with the glare of pomp and ostentation, as a means of dazzling the public eye ; and he omitted no circumstance that could blind its judgment  He caused the rumour of the surpassing magnificence which was to mark the approaching ceremonies at the Danish court to be spread far and wide ; and, among the many attracted from a distance, to witness so gorgeous a scene, young Laertes, Ophelia's brother, came from France, that he might be present.

He was pleased with this opportunity for spending some time with a sister whom he so tenderly loved ; for though during their life they had been much separated, yet in those intervals that they had been together, he had learned to appreciate and love the modest worth, the affectionate nature of this gentle being.  Besides, they had been in the habit of corresponding with one another by letter ; and thus the attachment between them had been maintained and cemented.  To this means of intercourse, he reverted, when,—the regal pageant concluded,—Laertes prepared to return to France.  As he bade her farewell, he prayed her to let no long time elapse ere he should hear from her.

And she, in her own quiet, though earnest way, in her own simple sincerity of manner, replied :—

"*Do you doubt that ?*"

---

" What to this was sequent thou know'st already."

# ROSALIND AND CELIA; THE FRIENDS.

## TALE IX.

# ROSALIND AND CELIA ; THE FRIENDS.

" We still have slept together,
Rose at an instant, learn'd, play'd, eat together ;
And whereso'er we went, like Juno's swans,
Still we went coupled, and inseparable."

*As you like it.*

" 'Tis a pretty sight, neighbor, is't not ?"

This question was asked by one of two women, who stood together beside a cottage entrance, on the borders of a wood, enjoying an afternoon gossip. The speaker pointed towards the cottage window, upon which the rays of the western sun were pouring their beams, tempered by the green leaves and boughs of the surrounding trees through which the light made its way. She who was addressed, advanced towards the casement, and looked in. Within the room, were two ladies, seated near the open window. One of them had her eyes fixed upon the other, on whose lap lay two infants,—a babe on either arm, both cherub faces closely pressed against her bosom, while both at once, drew thence their sweet milken meal. The eyes of the one lady expressed tenderest interest in the gentle task she watched, mingled perhaps with a shadow of regret that it could not be hers to share ; while on the face of the lady who nursed the babes, there sat that divine expression, which no other earthly task inspires, of so pure, so holy, so benign a character. The little ones themselves looked steeped in that rosy, cosy, slumbrous content, betokening fulness of happiness,—or that happiness of fulness, which

forms their summit of felicity.　Their rounded
dimpled limbs lay crossed and intertwined in loving
co-mingling upon the cradle-lap ; the little fingers of a
hand of each, lay curled and clasped together ; the
same pretty murmurs of satisfaction, the same soft nestling warmth of cheeks, the same comfortably imbedded
noses, the same lazily opened, lazily closed, lazily
raised, lazily drooped eye-lids, told how complete was
the sympathy between the two happy little rogues in
the enjoyment of their dual repast.

The peasant woman who had peeped in, to look upon
this picture, stepped back to the cottage entrance ;
owning it was, in sooth, as her neighbour had said,
‘ a pretty sight.’　And then, she went on to ask her
how it happened, that these ladies and babes came to
be her inmates.

The two gossips sat down side by side, in the porch.
The one nursing her little girl, Audrey ; the other
holding by the hand, her young son, William, a shy
boy of about six years old ; while the former told how
all had fallen out.　She said that one evening lately,
her husband, who was a wood-cutter, had been, as
usual, hard at work in the forest close by, when he
heard the sound of wheels on the road that threads its
skirts.　This road being little frequented by travellers,
the good man had hurried to see whose could be the
rare approach ; when what should he behold, but a
grand coach, drawn by four horses, and surrounded
by several horsemen,—attendants, and outriders, all
betokening the equipage and retinue of some great
personage.　Two gentlemen rode among the mounted
horsemen ; they were leaning upon the coach-windows,
and holding gay converse with the ladies seated with-
inside ; so that, as the cavalcade passed, it left a sound
of laughter and good-humour behind it upon the air.
But the last echo of the mirthful voices, and of the
trampling horses, had scarce died away ; the last
glimpse of the bright housings, and trappings of the
equipage, were still visible through the cloud of dust

that environed and followed it ; when the wood-cutter
saw it come to a sudden halt, and the whole retinue
seemed thrown into confusion. It was evident that
some accident had happened. The little-used forest-
road was in so neglected a state, so full of deep ruts,
so strewn with huge stones, so rugged and uneven,
that when the wood-cutter reached the spot, he found
that the springs of the coach had suddenly snapped,
and that a wheel had come off. The vehicle lay on
its side ; the horsemen were all dismounted ; the attendants hurrying to and fro, attempting to render
what assistance they could, while the two gentlemen
were anxiously endeavouring to extricate the ladies
from the overturned coach. One of them had fainted,
or was stunned, from the violence and suddenness with
which she had been thrown forwards ; while the other
was equally unable to move, from a strain which her
ankle had received, in trying to save the child on her
knee from falling. At length, however, both ladies
were rescued from their perilous situation ; and the
wood-cutter, proffering the shelter of his cottage as
the nearest at hand, they were removed thither, borne
carefully in their attendants' arms. The babes,—for in
the coach, each lady had had a child upon her knee,
—were unhurt. Thanks to the impunity that most
frequently attends the unresisting way in which baby
muscles yield in tumbling about, and to the protection,
regardless of self, which the muscles of those who hold
children invariably and instinctively afford in the moment of danger, the little creatures had escaped all ill
effects from their fall.

Not so with the two mothers. The one lady had a
severe sprain ; while the other, on recovering from her
swoon, found that the shock had banished from her
bosom the power of yielding nourishment to her babe.
The sense of her own deprivation in this calamity, was
lost in anxiety for that of her child ; and her sole concern was how to find one who might replace herself in
the sweet office, which she would so reluctantly, yet

so joyfully, now see performed by another. There
seemed a prospect of the poor lady's solicitude being
relieved, when it was discovered that the wood-cutter's
wife was herself also a nursing-mother ; but no sooner
was this hope espied, than it failed them ; for nothing
would induce the babe to partake with the infant rustic ; the patrician child cried for food, but seemed to
disdain it from a plebeian source. In the midst of her
distress, the mother could scarcely help smiling to see
the pertinacious way in which the little one maintained
its refusal ; while the other lady laughed outright to
see, as she said, the insolence of birth, conquering
even the pangs of hunger,—the proud stomach prevailing over the famishing one. But her own babe
was taking its rightful repast in happy comfort—and
she on a sudden bethought her that her sister's child
should share with hers. She held out her arm to receive it ; and then, there was fresh amusement, to see
with what a willing eagerness the saucy urchin partook
of the kindred and aristocratic meal.

These ladies were not, in fact, sisters, but the wives
of two brothers. They were sisters in rank, and in
affection. They were sister-duchesses, and sister-
friends. The lady Aurelia was married to Gaston, the
reigning duke of the neighbouring province ; and the
lady Coralie to his brother, duke Frederick. They
had been spending some time with their husbands, at
a beautiful country seat, called Beaulieu, belonging to
duke Frederick, and were returning thence to the
court residence, when their carriage was overturned.
Beaulieu was situated on the other side of the forest,
which was some twenty miles from the court ; and the
ladies had suffered too severely from the accident, for
them to be able to travel on. After seeing them safely
established at the wood-cutter's cottage, therefore,
the two gentlemen had proceeded on their journey,
promising to return frequently during the interval
which must elapse before the ladies and their babes
could be removed.

All this the good woman of the cottage told her
neighbour, as they sat in the shady porch together ;
the narrative being only now and then interrupted by
the bashful advances of the boy William, towards es-
tablishing an intimacy with the little Audrey ; which
she returned, as she sat enthroned on her mother's lap,
by graciously kicking him under the chin, slapping his
face, tweaking his nose, tugging his hair, and occasionally thrusting her fingers into his eye.   He seemed
to take all in good part, however, and to receive her
repulses as so many favours ; holding out his broad
cheeks for her to smack, placing his ears within pulling distance, submitting his locks to be wrenched out
by handfuls, and meekly suffering her to claw and poke
into his eyes as she listed.   '' Be still,—be good,
Audrey ;'' said her mother, drawing her back from an
onslaught on William's mouth, which seemed made
with a view to seize some of his teeth out, but which
ended in such a vigorous clutch at his nether lip, that
the imprint of her nails was left ; '' thou wilt anger
him at last ; he's only too bearsome with thee.   Ha'
done, then !''

'' And so the worshipful ladies have bided with ye,
ever since, Nicole ?   And the one has gone on making
twin sucking-babes of her own and her sister-in-law's
bearn ?   And how oft have ye seen his honor, the
duke, and his honor, the duke's brother ?   To think
of such right royal company in the forest—and in
your own cottage, neighbour.   Well, it's enow to
make a poor body stark wood wi' pride.''

'' But the wood-cutter's wife will ne'er be wood enow
to be proud with an old friend and neighbour, let who
will come to her poor house ;'' said Audrey's mother ;
'' Nicole will always be glad to see her good friend and
gossip, Jeannette, though all the dukes and duchesses
in Christendom were to harbour beneath her roof-
tree.   But as for the two dukes, it must be owned,
'twixt you and me, there's a main difference between
them.''

"Ay. How so?" said Jeannette, with all a gossip's keenness.

"Marry, the one's a pleasant-spoken, easy kind of man. He'll lean you against that porch, and talk by the score minutes together, just as natural as though he didn't know what a court meant, and had never answered to the name of duke no more than my good man. And to see him pat my little Audrey on the head!—You'd think he was her own father.—Not a bit as if he was doing her an honor,—only a kindness. And then he's so fond of his own little one; and so gentle to his wife. He might be a labourer instead of a lord, for good manners,—he has such a feeling heart, and such a pleasant way with him."

"And the other, thou say'st, differs vastly from him?" said Jeannette.

"Ay, in sooth, doth he," answered Nicole. "We have good cause to be joyful that my lord Gaston is duke over us, instead of his brother. Why, duke Frederick may be a very good gentleman for the court, and for all the grand folks there, and to live among them, and be liked by them; but he's not what I call a pleasant man. He looks another way, while he talks t'ye; he's thinking of aught else but your words, when you talk to him; he asks questions without waiting for the answer. He's mighty polite, but never kind. He's too courtly with his wife to love her in truth; and I'm much mistook, if she live not much in his thought as his lady, his duchess, and not by her christian name. I've a notion, that, to him, his brother is the reigning duke; and even his own little daughter, is but his heiress. He's a lordly man, and I believe his thoughts are all lordly,—certain it is, that his ways and his manners are lordly,—passing rude and disagreeable." The wood-cutter's wife said this as if she had fixed the crowning stigma on duke Frederick's behaviour. She went on to say:—
"As for his wife, poor thing, the lady Coralie, she can't see a fault he hath, so blindly doth she affect

him.  Well for her, poor soul !  When a husband's faults are past mending, a wife's eyes are best kept closed by a doting seal."

"And it's acting no friendly part, to seek to remove it ;" said her neighbour, nodding her head. "I owe goody Theresa no thanks, but a grudge ever since, for showing me how ill William's father treated me, when he went and listed for a soldier, after drinking away all our poor havings at the ale-house.  But God ye good even, neighbour Nicole.  Come your ways, William, and leave hankering after little Audrey, who'll none of ye, ye see."

For some time yet, Aurelia and Coralie continued to linger in the woodman's cottage, well-pleased with its pretty situation, its quiet, and its retirement, so well fitted to the loving domesticity of the task they had in hand.  The pleasant rambles in the forest, when the ladies had regained strength to walk abroad ; the neatness of the rustic homestead ; the purity of the air ; the dainty country diet, of dairy, garden, and orchard ; the absence of all restraint and ceremony in this sylvan life, made them willing to protract the period of their stay amid these simple pleasures ; while the visits of their husbands, who constantly repaired thither, prevented them from being deprived of congenial society.

"For my part, dear sister," said Coralie to Aurelia one morning as they sat beneath the shade of a spreading oak, with their babes, enjoying the balmy freshness, "I could be well content to return never again to a court life, this sweet seclusion pleases me so well. Here, methinks, we could taste the pure delights of a golden age, when shepherds, and shepherdesses, rustic swains and foresters, careless maids and happy damsels, had the wide world—the world of Arcady—to themselves.  Here, e'en the courtier may learn to rest his ambition, and perceive how vain an exchange his anxieties are for the peace of such a spot as this. Poor seem the fretful solicitude, the carking moil for place and honors, set against the open-air freedom, the liberty of range, the breathing-space for heart and mind, that here may be his.''

'' 'Tis woman's thought—a lowly-natured, unaspiring woman's fancy, sister mine,'' replied Aurelia. '' What would manly opinion say to such a rural grave of all his darling hopes, his lofty aspirations, his projects of glory and renown ?  Could a man be content, think you, to barter away all his projects of advancement in the stir and activity of life amid his fellow-men, for a dreaming existence 'neath bough and sky ?  I'll ask my lord what he says to a shepherd's crook, or a forester's bow, in lieu of his ducal insignia, and thou shalt ask thy husband a like question.''

'' For my brother Gaston, I could well believe that his contemplative spirit might feel the repose of such a life of nature, nowise unsuited ;  his philosophic temperament, his reflective habits, his pure tastes, would teach him to find delight in a recluse and pastoral existence ;  but for my Frederick, I know not ;  there is that in his ardent, high-reaching character, that might dispose him to scorn the inglorious ease, and tame inaction, as he would probably consider it, of forest retirement.   And yet it is precisely on his account that I could wish this present peaceful life of ours to endure.''

'' That is scarcely the wish of a duteous wife ;  who has always hitherto preferred the fulfilment of her husband's will to that of her own.   Why condemn Frederick to a crook, if he have a liking for a sword or a baton of office ?'' said Aurelia laughing.

Coralie attempted to respond to her sister's gaiety of manner, but there was involuntary sadness in the tone with which she said :—'' Because I sometimes have my fears, that his eagerness for such things will one time or other imperil him.''

'' But a wife's jealousy for her husband's honor, will preserve her from a too cowardly alarm for his safety. She will learn to forget his danger in the prospect of his success.''

'' It is because I am jealous for his honor,—his true honor, that I would have him achieve it without the hazard of things even more precious. I mean not life and limb ; but conscience, self respect—they are sometimes risked in the desperate stake for honor— worldly honor. My Frederick is noble, virtuous, —but he hath ambition in that daring spirit of his ; and we know how, little by little, the towering growth of that passion o'ertops and crushes all else. In a court life is a perpetual recurrence of temptations to the aspiring nature ; and it is therefore I could wish, we were to dwell ever in this wood-land content.''

'' You view things too seriously, dear sister ;'' said Aurelia. '' You are scarce recovered from your late weakness, sure, to yield thus to vague alarms. My brother Frederick's ambition will but secure for him and for you, honorable distinctions, worthy eminence ; and your gentle monition ever at his side, will best preserve him from undue aims.''

'' It is because I too surely feel that I shall be early removed from his side, that I have allowed myself to breathe my anxieties for him to your sisterly ear, my Aurelia. Since I have begun to open my heart to you, let me do so entirely. Listen to me with calmness, for I am calm myself, even under the full conviction that I must soon leave you, my husband, my child. I commit them to your loving care, my sister. Well have you already proved how truly you can perform the part of mother to my babe—my little Celia. She will be no less a daughter to you, I know, I feel, than your own Rosalind. Weep not, my beloved Aurelia, my sister ; could you know how resigned, how entirely satisfied my own heart is, in the comfort of entrusting her to you, you would feel no bitterer regret at this near prospect of my quitting life than I myself do. What is there, after all, dear friend, to dismay me in the thought of yielding earth, in the humble hope of

Heaven ?   My Aurelia, I am more than content, I am cheerful, I am happy.   Look upon me, and see if my eyes confirm not my words.''

Through her tears, Aurelia looked into her sister's face, and beheld the truth of her soul, serene in its immortal trust.

Ever after, the manner of the lady Coralie was so uniform in its composure, so constant in its unaffected cheerfulness, that her sister learned to think the prognostics of that morning were but a passing impression, from weakened health, and lowered spirits.   She never alluded to the subject of their conversation ;  but seemed by the animation with which she entered into all the projects for enjoying their present life, and all the plans for their future existence, which Aurelia, Gaston, and Frederick, formed in the happy elation of youth and health, to express her entire sympathy, and unmisgiving concurrence.

Sometimes in their forest-walks, her failing strength would betray that she was unequal to accompany them to such distances as their greater vigour led them to undertake ;  but she would sit down and rest, or beguile them into loitering, while she stole a moment's recline against a tree, and thus be enabled to proceed. Once they found a spacious cave, where the whole party stopped to repose, and to enjoy the beauty and delicious coolness of the spot.   It was tapestried with moss ;  and though lofty, completely shut in, and protected from the weather.   It was so sheltered as to form a cool retreat in summer, while perfectly warm and snug in the winter.   They were enchanted with the place ;  and entertained many a gay proposal of coming to spend here a hermit old age, when the pomps and vanities of a court life should have lost their charms for them.   Aurelia cast a furtive glance at her sister's countenance, to see whether it betrayed any symptom of her late secret avowal ;  but Coralie was on her guard, and no look revealed how unshaken was her belief that she should never reach old age.

But when, after spending still a few more happy days at the woodman's cottage on the skirts of the forest of Arden, the two ladies accompanied their husbands to their ducal home, the tokens of how fatally true had been her foresight respecting her own decline, were no longer to be concealed. The disease proclaimed itself unmistakeably, and before many weeks were gone, the lady Coralie had passed into eternal rest.

At first, her husband, duke Frederick, felt her loss bitterly ; but he was, as his wife had truly known, an ambitious man, and in the ceaseless weaving and prosecution of his schemes for the advancing of his fortunes, and for the obtaining of preferment, he was not long in forgetting his grief.

To his infant daughter, the lady Aurelia well replaced the mother she had lost. From the first tender office she had performed towards the little creature, when she had taken her with her own child, to her bosom, bestowing its gentle treasures of love and nourishment on both babes equally, she had known no difference in affection for either. Celia and Rosalind were alike dear to her. Had they been twin-born her own offspring, she could not have felt a more perfect and undivided fondness for them. She thought of them together, cherished them together, she nurtured them together, she held them in her arms together ; and when her arms no longer sufficed for their resting-place, she let them share the same cradle ; she let them bathe in the same bath ; she clothed them, fed them, and bred them, alike and together.

Between the little ones themselves, the affection grew to be as strong, and undivided, as that which the mother felt towards them. As they grew older, they learned the same lessons, and played at the same games ; they studied, as they sported — together. They not only cared nothing for their pleasures, if they were not mutual ; but they were also unsatisfied, unless their pains, their little vexations, their youthful

troubles, were borne together.  It was almost droll to
see the implicit way in which they made every event
—whether welcome or no—a double one.  They
seemed to take it for granted, that nothing could befall
either, solely.  They appeared not to be able to comprehend anything happening to each alone.  All was to
be between them, scrupulously apportioned to both,
equally.  If a gratification were accorded to one, she
expected a like favor to be bestowed upon the other.
If a treat—even a reward, were granted to one, she
stayed to enjoy it, and the other waited as a matter of
course, until a parallel indulgence came.  Just so was
it with a rebuke, or a punishment.  If the one were
reproved for an error, the other stood ready for correction at the same time.  If the one incurred blame,
the other seemed to think it her right to be censured
likewise.

Once Aurelia had occasion to find fault with her little girl, for some juvenile misdemeanour.  But she had
no sooner banished Rosalind into the corner, to stand
there with her face to the wall, as a fitting shame and
disgrace for such giddy behaviour as she had been
guilty of, than Celia stepped up beside her, and demurely turned her face away too.  Aurelia could not
help smiling at the matter-of-course way in which it
was done ; and it amused her still more, to see, how,
gradually, the companionship in exile prevented its
being any punishment.  For soon the arms stole round
each other's neck ; the two little curly heads got close
together, and there was such a whispering, and tittering, and undertoned sympathy between them, as totally
to do away with the notion of penance.  Aurelia put
on as grave a countenance as she could, and told them
to turn round, and look at her.  The two little heads
faced about ; but where was the contrition, the
abashed regard, the disconcerted air ?  There were two
smiling-lipped, roguish-eyed, merry little wags as ever
met a mother's attempted frown ; looking precisely as
if there were no such things as faults, or punishments,

or repentance in the world,—as if misdeeds were unheard of, penalties needless, and compunction out of the question. There was nothing for it, but to call them to her, bid them promise they would be good in future, while she gave them a hearty kiss of forgiveness a-piece.

Another time, duke Frederick, who was in his way a fond father, but apt to be irascible, and capriciously severe ; strict by fits and starts, but carelessly indulgent in general, took violent offence at some fancied disobedience of his little daughter's ; and he pronounced as her sentence, that she should be left at home, upon occasion of a forthcoming festival, to which the children had for some time looked forward. It was a grand entertainment to be given in honor of duke Gaston's birthday, in the pleasure-grounds of one of his nobles ; and, as an especial treat, the children had been promised that they should be present. The disappointment was very great, when poor Celia found that this was to be her punishment ; and she could not help crying bitterly. Rosalind was of course keeping her company in her tears ; but she suddenly brightened up, and said she would devise such brave amusements for their day at home, that they should not need to regret the festival.

"But you are not to stay at home, Rose ;" said Celia. "It is only I, whom my father has forbidden to go."

"Not to stay at home ! Not forbidden to go ! We'll soon see that," exclaimed Rosalind, starting up from the low seat on which they had both been weeping side by side, and running off to seek her uncle.

She came back, her face glowing, her voice trembling. "It's too bad ! It's cruel ! He says I shall go, if it be only to make you feel your being left at home the more mortifying."

"O, but that it will not ;" replied Celia ; "the only thing that could make me glad, would be to know that you are enjoying the sight, though I can't."

" But I shan't enjoy it—I can't enjoy it, without you, Celia.  You know it well.  Stay, I know !" she paused ; and clapped her hands.  " I know how I'll do.  Trust me, I'll manage."

Her cousin tried to make her say farther ; but she only skipped about the room, and finally skipped out of it.  A moment or two afterwards, Celia heard a crash ; and in a moment or two more, Rosalind came skipping back.

" Huzza !  It's done !  Huzza !"

" Rose !  What have you done ?"  Celia went up to her young cousin, who was much excited, clasping her fingers tight in one another, then loosing them ; her eyes sparkling, and her cheeks flushed.  As Celia questioned her, the colour subsided, and she became rather pale, but still looked eager and resolved.

" Rose, dear Rose, is it possible you have broken that porcelain vase my father values so much ?"

" Yes, I threw it down.  Was it not for lifting it off the marble ledge, contrary to his desire, that my uncle forbade you to go to the festival Celia ?"

" It was.  I did not know that he would not allow it to be touched ; but he thought I knew his orders were strict about that vase, and so he was very angry when he found that I had taken it down."

" Well then, he'll be still more angry, when he finds I've knocked it down.  I'm sorry to have destroyed my uncle's vase, but I'm glad he'll be angry with me ; now he'll punish me as I wish ; he'll give me my own way about staying from the festival, at home with you."

Celia looked rather frightened at this bold step ; and so to tell the truth, did Rosalind, when she came to think upon what she had done.  But she had no wish to recall it ; and the two little girls felt more than ever bound to each other, the one for what she had had the courage to dare on behalf of Celia, the other for what she owed to the daring of Rosalind.

Finally, the good duke Gaston, by the timely gift

of a rich vase, with which he replaced the broken one, and by the good-humoured representation which he made of the children's delinquency, obtained from his brother a remission of their sentence ; and they both, after all, were permitted to go to the festival.

While Rosalind and Celia were still children, the duchess Aurelia took them with her, one summer, on a visit to a friend of hers, the countess de Beaupré, who had been left a widow with a young son and daughter. They lived in a beautiful spot called La Vallée. It was situated at about the same distance from the court, as duke Frederick's country-seat of Beaulieu, but in quite another direction ; La Vallée lying to the north, and Beaulieu to the south of the ducal residence.

In the society of her friend, the countess, Aurelia spent some very happy time ; while the two children made pleasant acquaintance and companionship with little Flora de Beaupré, the widow's daughter. They did not like Raoul, the son. He was a haughty, dictatorial boy ; and treated the three girls with a sullen disdain, as his natural inferiors and understood vassals. He even seemed to entertain considerable scorn for his mother ; a mild woman, who treated him as the heir of the family, while he was yet a child ; and regarded herself as merely an interloper on the estate,—the dowager tenant, until such time as he should be of age to claim his rights, his lawful inheritance. He was a complete feudal lord, in spirit as in fact : and beheld but serfs in all who surrounded him. He would kick and cane his men-servants ; and let his little sister kneel to fasten the clasp of his shoe. He would rave and swear at the women-domestics, and suffer his mother to set him a chair. He would take as a matter of course all waiting upon him. His mother might stand with his hat in her hand, his sister might run and fetch his fallen arrows, they might either, or both, be in constant attendance upon him, but he rarely stretched forth his hand to take what they held, until it perfectly suited his own convenience. Raoul, count de Beaupré, was his prevailing thought, as the impersonation of supreme authority ; and all created beings else, ranked as mere slaves, ministrant and subservient to his will. There was one person, the especial object of his tyranny, the recipient of all his domineering humours. This was a boy called Theodore, a poor relation—a cousin ; nay, some said that he might have claimed even nearer kindred to the late Count de Beaupré than that of nephew. Certain it is that his likeness to the young Flora, who was the image of her father, was singularly striking. He was nearly of her age—had the same delicately cut features, the same transparent complexion ; and were it not that her hair was golden, and his jet black, the same head and face seemed theirs. This girlish-looking child was a convenient toy for the young heir. Now his butt, now his plaything ; now his lackey, now his laughing-stock ; but in all characters, buffeted, jeered, cuffed, mocked, and ill-used as the caprice of the young lord of La Vallée might choose to dictate. No one seemed to think it hard or strange—not even the victim himself ; it was so thoroughly an understood thing, that submission was the only thing with which the insolence and tyranny of Raoul de Beaupré were to be received.

Even little Flora, the only one in the chateau of la Vallée who possessed any thing approaching to spirit, never dared remonstrate with her lordly young brother on his behaviour to their cousin ; she merely contented herself with showing the boy, in her own person, all the kindness which might compensate for the treatment he received at the hands of Raoul. The affection thus engendered between the two younger children, became a means of their better enduring the despotism of the elder. Theodore, in his gratitude to Flora, learned to bear her brother's insults for her sake ; while she forgot her own contemptuous usage in sympathy with the harshness and ignominy to which this boy was subjected.

Altogether, Rosalind and Celia felt it a relief, when the period of their return home arrived ; for the conduct of the heir, which from daily habit was scarcely felt by the inmates of La Vallée, oppressed them with a sense of cruelty and malice constantly exercised against unoffenders in word or deed. With the exception of Flora, between whom and themselves there had arisen a strong liking, they regretted nothing there ; but the mothers had promised that there might be a correspondence kept up between the little girls by letter, which would furnish good exercise for their faculties, as well as a means of innocent entertainment. The duchess Aurelia, with her usual eagerness to promote the happiness of her two little ones, said that a messenger should be appointed to carry the epistles to and fro between them and their young friend.

Some years passed by in happy study, in increasing improvement ; in ever-growing, ever-strengthening attachment between the two cousin-friends ; but just when they reached a time of life, most, perhaps, needing the gentle presence and guidance of a mother, Aurelia, that tender monitress, that indulgent guardian, was removed from them by death. Her loss made one more strong bond of union between the two girls ; it was a mutual bereavement. It was a mutual source of regret, as of consoling thought ; they both knew her worth, they could sorrow together, as they could comfort each other, calling to mind her excellences, and promising that her image should abide evermore with them, a virtuous, a strengthening, a holy memory.

Duke Gaston, always of a quiet, passive disposition, sank into deep despondency on the death of his wife. Even the love of his daughter, Rosalind, had no power to arouse him from the stupor of grief to which he yielded. He shrank from all society ; and hers seemed especially painful to him. He shut himself up in his study, to brood alone. In the hope of giving his affliction its own chosen way to seek healing, she yielded to her uncle's wish that she should accompany his daughter Celia to Beaulieu for a time. Here, in country retirement, amid the beautiful scenes of all restoring Nature, the two young ladies gradually recovered their serenity, and eventually, the blithe spirits proper to their time of life, and to their happy temperament in particular.

Through the spacious grounds of Beaulieu, the two cousins would wander arm-in-arm, indulging many a pleasant fancy, weaving many a bright romance, picturing all kinds of glowing visions. They peopled the glades with dryad shapes, and old pagan stories. For them fauns and satyrs lurked amid the trees, and peeped from thicket, and copse, and bosky grove ; for them, the panting Syrinx rustled and cowered among the reeds, shrinking from him who drew but mournful music where his lips had sought warmer response ; for them the margins of cool brooks were haunted with the smooth white forms of bathing nymphs, or long-tressed naiads ; for them the fresh morning air rang with the shrill horns and baying hounds of Dian, and her huntress train ; for them the rills and fountains murmured echoes of the fates of Arethusa, of Acis, and of fair Cyane ; for them, thatched cottages were Baucis and Philemon roofs, sheltering highest Jove in his wanderings ; for them, each scene had its mythical as well as actual significance,—a classic grace, no less than an intrinsic beauty. Their reading had been such as high-born ladies, in those days, took delight in ; and their thoughts and associations were naturally thus coloured. The lore of the poets, the history of old Greece and Rome, the traditions of bygone ages, with their creeds of imagery and imagination, had stored their minds with ideas which refined and elevated each object in existence. To them all the realities of life possessed the added charm of ideality. They viewed even Nature herself through the purple light of a poetic medium.

After a season, however, the desire of Rosalind to
see whether her presence might not now conduce to
her father's happiness, led her to urge her cousin, that
they should quit the delights of Beaulieu, and return
to what she hoped might prove the duty awaiting her
at court.   Celia ever one in thought with Rosalind, as
soon as that thought found utterance, agreed.   On the
day appointed, just as they were setting out, they received a letter from Flora de Beaupré, in which she
confided to them her anxiety respecting her cousin,
Theodore, who was suddenly missing from La Vallée.
"My brother Raoul is much incensed at his flight;"
thus concluded the letter; "he has spared no pains
to obtain traces of the fugitive; but as yet none have
reached us.   Since our dear mother's death, I have
observed a kind of ill-smothered fire take the place of
the old submissive patience with which my poor cousin
used to bear the slights and harsh treatment of his
lot.   I tried to preserve forbearance between them as
long as possible.   I endeavoured to moderate in one,
his exercise of power, and to maintain in the other, his
passive endurance of evils he could not avoid.   But it
seems that this endurance was at length taxed too far.
He must have resolved to fly from a tyranny, from
which there was no other escape; and is doubtless, by
this time, equally beyond the reach of Raoul's ven-
geance, and of my regret.   Poor boy!   Dear, dear
Theodore!   Shall we ever see each other again?   That
you will pity me, I know, dear friends; for you knew
his gentle qualities.   What he was, as a mere child,
when we were all children together, he has grown up
still to be,—good, uncomplaining, full of humility, and
all kindliness."

"Poor Theodore!" echoed Celia as she closed the
letter.   "Ay, he was ever, only too full of humility,
too kindly, too gentle.   Had it been my lot to dwell
within the reach of such a tyrant arm as the odious
Raoul's, I should never have submitted; I should
either have faced my injuries, turned upon them, and

resented them, or shown them a fair pair of heels long
ago, as he has done at length.''

" And, poor Flora, I say, as well as poor Theodore !'' said Rosalind, " How deeply the affectionate
girl regrets him.''

" Ay ; perchance too deeply,'' said Celia.   " Dost
not think that it may be, Flora regrets more than
a cousin, in Theodore ?  Is't not too possible, that
amidst all that sympathy, and interest she felt for him
while beneath her brutal brother's power, and with her
constant care to screen him  from its worst inflictions,
a warmer liking than cousin-love may have sprung up
in her heart ?  If so, ' poor Flora,' indeed !''

" I  do  not  believe  it ;''  said  Rosalind.   " She
speaks not of  him in terms such as women use, when
naming  him they love.   What woman ever called her
lover ' Poor boy !'   No, no, trust me ; Flora regrets
Theodore with  but  honest affection ; with but simple
cousin-love.''

" True those words ' poor boy ' warrant Flora's
heart free from all but cousin-love, as thou say'st,
Rose.   But tell me what is there, after all, truer,
stronger, or warmer than this same cousin-love ;'' said
Celia.   " I verily think, I shall  never love lover with
any love half so worth having, as that with which I
love thee, coz.''

" But we are more than cousins, we are friends, thou
know'st,'' said Rosalind.   " Relationship hath some
delicate natural links of its own, doubtless ; but there
is a voluntary affiancing of two kindred beings,—kindred in more than blood, kindred in spirit, in heart,
in mind, in soul,—that welds them together into one.
All  the  sledge-hammers  of  the  world,  with their
weight  of  envy, malice, or detraction brought to the
assail, would fail in sundering such  steeled affection.
They but the more finely temper it.   The materials
would  give  way, ere that which incorporates them ;
the  two  hearts  would break, sooner than the bond
which unites them.''

The two ladies were pursuing their way homeward, as they conversed thus. The weather was so very lovely, their road, skirting the forest, so beautiful, that they preferred the freedom of horseback to the confinement of a coach. They accordingly rode, attended by a proper retinue, such as beseemed their rank.

The afternoon sun enriched the scene with its warm glow of beauty, while the shade of the trees, which fringed their road on one side, formed a welcome screen from its ardour. They paced on easily, walking their horses, and talking to each other ; when they neared a spot they had often stopped to admire. It was a kind of well, or rude stone fountain, celebrated for the sparkling purity of its waters, which flowed from a moss-grown rocky recess ; it was situated on a grassy slope, was bowered in with festoons of brambles, wild-rose, and woodbine, and over-arched by a thick umbrage of tall and spreading trees.

As the ladies approached, they perceived a figure sitting by the side of the well. It was that of a stripling. His head rested on the stone brink ; his limbs were stretched forth in the attitude of thorough weariness ; his dress and shoes were covered with dust ; his whole appearance betokened that he had come far, and that he slept the sound sleep of fatigue. The trampling of the horses on the turf failed to arouse him ; and he stirred not from his position. His face was partly hidden upon his folded arms, as he leaned against the well-side ; but one of the grooms, dismounting, to obtain a cup of the fresh fountain water for his young mistress, touched the lad on the arm, and asked him if he had no better manners than to lie lounging there in the presence of ladies ; and then the countenance revealed to view, shone with good-humour, though he affected to be angry at being disturbed.

" My lady may desire a draught of cold water,'' he said, " but her need must be great, 'an it equal mine for rest ; my weariness against her thirst, for any sum

thou lik'st to name.  I fear me, though, the stakes
would be all on one side, like an ill-built paling ; for
my pocket is free from trouble,—it hath not a cross
to bear.''

" I am sorry thou hast been awakened on my account, good friend ;'' said Celia.  '' Sweet rest is too
precious to be interrupted for an idle wish, that scarce
amounted to a want.  Besides, the cup could have
been filled without disturbing thee.''

'' A lady's caprice has broken many a rest, madam,
ere now ;'' returned the youth, glancing up at her with
a merry look, while he removed the cap from his head,
as he stood before her to reply to her kind voice and
words.    '' But in truth, there are some faces well worth
losing sleep for ;  and had I not awakened to look
upon the one I now see, I had lost a sight better than
twenty such naps—sweetened though mine was, by
hunger and way-faring.''

 '' Thou hast walked a long distance ?'' asked Celia.

'' All the way from Chateau Fadasse, madam, which
lies some score miles eastward of this.  To tell your
ladyship heaven's truth,—and there is that in you
which forbids a man to think of uttering aught else,—
I ran away from that very Chateau, no longer ago than
this morning.''

'' Chateau Fadasse ?''  replied Celia, musingly.
'' I have heard my father speak of a baron of that
name.''

'''Ay, madam ; the same, doubtless,'' replied the
youth.  '' I was born there ; and bred there, if that
may be called breeding, which was rather a breaking-
in to live  upon ill-usage and broken victuals.  In the
baron's household, my father filled the office of jester
until Death called him to a better place, promoting
him from the Fadasse service to that of the King of
Terrors.  Though service be no inheritance, yet I
succeeded to my father's, and served the baron for a
fool,—as I was, staying so long to be made a fool of,
and to be kicked and cudgeled like an ass.''

"A breaking-in, truly ; one less gentle than befalls a horse ;" said Celia.

"Not one of the baron's stud but was envied by his jester, madam ; they were snugly stalled, full fed, and caressed ; while the only privilege I enjoyed, was, that the chevalier, the young heir of the house, made it his sport to treat me like a kind of human foot-ball, on which to exercise the toe of his ill-temper. At last I bethought me that I might take it as a hint that I was kicked out ; and so set forth with a broad prospect before me, if not a fair one,—the wide world."

"And now thou hast no home, my poor friend ?"

"If your ladyship call me so, or, better still, be a friend to me, then have I no great need to bewail, what is, after all, no great loss. To draw upon those few drops which every man hath a scant store of from his mother, and to waste them in bewailing a home such as that—which was no home,—but rather a house of bondage to me, is extravagance and spilth,—a casting away of good eye-water."

"But hast thou nowhere to lay thy head ?" pursued she, amused with his replies.

"No other pillow than holy Jacob's, madam,—a stone. But that which brought a dream of angels to a patriarch wanderer, may well serve an erring youth like myself. Nor no snugger hangings than the blue canopy yonder ; but many a better man than I, hath had as spacious a bed-tester."

"Thou hast not wherewithal to eat a meal, hast thou ?" she asked.

"To say sooth, madam, no daintier food than hog-fare,—beechmast and acorns ; with mayhap, hips and haws, and such odd bird-berries ; but the hedge and the brook have furnished meat and drink, ere now, to famishing scholars, why not to a starving fool ? The teeth of youth are sharp and sound, as its appetite is sharp set ; and these are main helps to digestion. Nothing like the animal spirits and light heart of under-twenty for imparting a relish, let the victual be ever so tough and unsavoury. Hardest fare comes scarce amiss, to years not yet of discretion.''

'' I like this fellow's spirit, well, Rose ;'' said Celia turning to her cousin ; '' 'tis a cheerful spirit ; one that will take him his bites from the cheery-cheeked side of the apple, through life. What say'st thou ? Shall we bid him come with us ? We'll provide him a home ; and he shall supply us with mirth.''

'' A fair bargain, and a kindly ; thou'lt do well to strike it, coz.''

'' Art thou content to follow me ?'' said Celia, again addressing him.

'' Ay, lady. Find but a stepping-stone beyond this round, slippery ball, the earth ; an' you set your foot on it, mine shall scramble after. There is something in that look, which puts willingness, e'en impossible feats into heart and sinews of him that should be thy follower.''

'' Then, mount ; and come with me. Gaspard, bring forward the sumpter-mule, that this lad may ride with us. And give him a ration from our store ; for it's ill beginning new service by fasting.''

'' And my stomach hath struck a hollow sound for every hour I've spent in the forest since I entered it ; which was at daybreak this morning. I thank your ladyship for the timely thought.''

'' And now tell me thy name, good fellow ;'' said Celia, as he fell in with the cavalcade, a little to the rear of her side.

'' I was called cub, lout, hound, or cur, idle varlet, lazy swine, and such like, for the most part ; though, in good sooth, none of them was my rightful style and title, as your ladyship's discernment will have already told you. But, truly, I care not now to be known by the name I bore when blows and privation were my daily having. Yonder well-brink, where I rested my head, being the stone on which turned my good fortune, I'll call myself, henceforth, no other than Touch-stone. 'Tis the name given me by a fine brain of in-

vention ; and that may e'en stand in lieu of godfather
and godmother, gossipry, and apostle-spoons.''

" If it be the saving of apostle-spoons, it may yet
need thee a long spoon, in the close quarters to which,
through lack of a christian name, thou may'st be
brought with the Prince of Darkness. Thou know'st
the old proverb.''

" Marry, the meeting with yourself, lady, is the silver spoon in the mouth of my new-born fate. I'll
look to have no other.''

" Nay, I think thou'lt furnish the spoon thyself.
Thy pate will be thine own wooden ladle.''

" It shall furnish my lady with a plentiful dish of
merry conceits, skimming for her the froth of folly, and
the cream of jesting. Thus the fool's treen spoon may
indeed help himself, while it serves his mistress. It
keeps his own heart light, and her in good humour.''

" To be kept well stored in good humour, is both her
benefit and his ;'' said Rosalind. " See thou that
thy humour be good, fool, and I'll ensure thee thy mistress's good-humour.''

On their arrival at the court, Rosalind's first care was
to enquire for her father. She was met by the young
lord Amiens ; who was not only by blood related, but
by affection deeply attached to duke Gaston. He told
her that the duke still kept himself in strict retirement ; that he evinced the same disinclination to see
any one, or to take interest in the active concerns of
life. He mentioned that even a visit from a very dear
old friend of the duke's, had failed to rouse him from
his profound melancholy, though (Amiens added) he
believed this friend had spoken very urgently. The
friend was a country gentleman, a worthy knight, sir
Rowland de Bois ; and from the well-known attachment that subsisted between him and the duke, it had
been hoped, that his remonstrance would have produced a salutary effect. The good knight had left his
country mansion, and come up to the court, where he

had not been for some years, expressly to see his sorrowing friend, when he learned into how baneful a despondency he had sunk.   In the private interview which took place between them, sir Rowland left no argument unurged that his honest heart could devise as likely to move the duke.   He besought him to remember his duty to his people, who could not fail to miss his wise and temperate government, were this ceasing to take part in public affairs prolonged.   He implored him to beware, lest in yielding so utterly to his grief, he might not be guilty of a weakness, a selfishness unworthy a ruler who had the happiness of others to consider ; of others whose welfare depended on, and had been confided to, his paternal care, as their lawful sovereign. He even hinted to him that advantage might be taken of his absence, while preserving so complete a seclusion and inaction ; that a sinister influence might be at work to dispossess him of his dukedom ; that his own deed would allow conspiracy and enmity to effect his ruin ; and that, in short, he more than suspected much evil had already been the result of this protracted seclusion, by the scope and opportunity it afforded to unscrupulous ambition in attempting to usurp his rights. Duke Gaston had replied to this, that he knew his old friend's warmth of zeal ; and however he might feel bound in gratitude to the love from which it originated, yet that he knew too well the strong prejudices which it engendered, to believe there was any ground of fear from the quarter to which sir Rowland's hints pointed. He said he knew that they referred to his brother Frederick ; that the knight had always avowed doubts of his integrity ; but that he could not allow himself to entertain unworthy suspicions of one whom he had known from childhood.   The knight murmured something about " lived with, but not known ;" and of " a transparent nature fancying others as clear as itself, and believing that it can see through a dark one." But he went on to say, that there was still one other consideration which ought to have weight with his friend Gaston ; and that was the happiness of his young daughter, Rosalind, which would be seriously affected by seeing that of her father irretrievably lost.

The father said it was among his few comforts, to know that the love which subsisted between his child and her cousin Celia, prevented her happiness from being too fatally involved in his ; and to know that this innocent affection preserved her from sharing, in all its poignancy, the affliction which overwhelmed himself.

"But let it not destroy you, my friend ;" said the hearty old knight in conclusion. "Be your own noble self. Strive against this poisonous sorrow. Its indulgence is a wrong to yourself, and to your people, your friends, your child, and even to her whom you mourn. I loved my own wife deeply and truly,—she brought me three fair sons,—and when she left me and them upon earth, I felt that what I could best do to deserve joining her in heaven hereafter, was to be the best father I could to her boys."

Duke Gaston wrung his old friend's hand, and in a broken voice promised to think of his words. They parted ; and Amiens said that since sir Rowland's visit, it had been touching to see the ineffectual efforts made by his unhappy cousin to banish at least the external evidence of his grief. He said that the duke's endeavour to assume cheerfulness was even more moving than his usual self-abandonment to depression. The one was natural, and had its own sad solace ; but the other was forced, and most painful to witness. The young man added, that his grace had signified his willingness to listen, when he offered, as he had so frequently done before in vain, to sing him some of the old airs once loved so well ; but that the attempt had been followed by such a burst of anguish, that he had never since ventured to repeat it. Rosalind, with tears, thanked Amiens for his tender sympathy and care towards her father ; and felt in her heart grateful, not envious, that this young man's presence was an

accepted comfort, where her own was too keenly
associated with her mother's image, to render it en-
durable.

When he had seen her restored to composure, he left
her to return to the duke.

As Amiens retired, Touchstone, willing to divert
Rosalind's thoughts by a sally which he saw she could
now bear, said :—" That gentleman hath a warbling
face.  I take it, his voice is sweeter to sing, than his
wit is keen to speak. "

" He hath a true heart, fellow ; which is better than
either sweet voice, or keen wit ;" replied she.  " He
is a loyal and a loving friend to my dear father ; let
that ensure him thy respect."

" I cannot fail in it to whomsoever your ladyship
favors ; which will answer for the large amount I
mean henceforth to pay to myself,—your fortunate,
though unworthy servant.  Self-respect is noble, and
now I am to be a courtier, and to live among nobles,
I intend laying up a store."

" Courtiers live by paying respect to others, fool,
not by cultivating self-respect.  They too often lose
it altogether, in seeming to pay a servile homage to
those who have no superior claim to regard, beyond the
power of bestowing a ribbon or a vacant garter."

" Garters and ribbons are pretty knacks enough, in
their way ; but they show paltrily, methinks, against
a few sterling things we wot of ;" said Touchstone.
" I cannot think the gewgaws are worth deforming
soul as well as body.  A cringing spirit, a perpetual
stoop in the shoulders, and ever-crooked back and
knee, are scarce compensated by a star on the breast.
The power to hold up your head, and look every man
straight in the face, I hold to be the higher order of
privilege."

Here, the princesses' gentlewoman, Hesperia, entering to offer her services, the two ladies retired to
their room, to take off their riding gear.

The next letter from Flora de Beaupré not only confirmed her young friends in their conviction that she regretted Theodore as her cousin, the companion of her childhood, the object of her sympathy and pity, merely, but it also discovered many other matters. She told them that the fugitive had contrived to send her secret intelligence of his welfare. That he had resolved upon finding his way to Rome, in order to satisfy his ardent thirst to behold the glories of Art there treasured ; and that he was not without hope of being able, by diligent study and perseverance, to win for himself an honorable career as an artist.

Theodore had, from infancy, manifested extraordinary talent for limning natural objects ; and though this gift had had little opportunity for developing itself under the ruffian treatment of Raoul, yet it had been secretly indulged ; as the walls of his own narrow chamber could testify, being covered with myriads of rudely-scrawled sketches and designs. This had inspired the thought of earning an independence, could he but once free himself from the thraldom of his life at La Vallée. He had lately asked himself why he need continue its endurance ; and had resolved the question by flight. His only regret in leaving the spot where his unhappy childhood had been spent, was the not being able to take leave of her who had been its sole joy amid so much misery ; but he had not dared to risk the discovery of his plans, or to compromise Flora, by imparting them to her. He was brooding on his regret, when he came to the end of his first few hours' journey from La Vallée. The sun was high in the heavens ; and he had stopped to rest during the fervid hour of noon beneath a small grove of trees, just within a park fence. He had not been lying there many minutes,—stretched at length upon the soft cool grass, and indulging the pleasant feeling of liberty, although mingled with the regret concerning Flora,—when he beheld a young gentleman approach, whom he knew to be Victor St. André, the owner of

the domain, from having seen him once or twice at La
Vallée.   There had been a slight intimacy between
Victor and Raoul, as owners of neighbouring estates ;
but the little assimilation which existed in the respective characters of the two young men, would have
prevented farther advances towards friendship on the
part of Victor, had it not been for one other person at
La Vallée.   In the sister, Flora, he soon learned to
feel a potent attraction for him, that far outweighed
the power which Raoul's qualities had to repel him.

There was that in Victor St. André's frank countenance and generous bearing, which inspired a feeling
of trust and liking in the heart of the poor fugitive
youth.   Although he had seen him but seldom,—for
the subordinate position filled by Theodore at La
Vallée did not permit of much communion with its
guests,—he suddenly resolved to confide in this young
gentleman, and to make him, if possible, the medium
of farewell to his cousin Flora.

His story was soon told ; and as promptly met with
sympathy, and friendly offers of assistance from the
hearer.   Victor St. André warmly expressed his approval of Theodore's resolve to seek freedom and independence ;  he besought him to prove that he believed him sincere in his earnest desire for his success,
by accepting a sufficient sum to carry him to Rome ;
adding that it was, in fact, but an advance which he
made, in payment of the first picture he should paint,
to secure its possession for himself.   The boy looked
up with a smile at this kindly augury.

It was this very smile of his ; it was his voice, so
like hers ; which,—besides the interest that the lad's
own sad story had inspired in the generous breast of
Victor,—caused him to speak so warmly, and to take
so active a part in assisting her poor cousin.   That
brilliant complexion, those soft appealing eyes, brought
the face of her he loved so forcibly before him, that
his offered help was scarcely less a delight to himself
than to the young lad.

Then Theodore went on to beg he would contrive means of conveying to her his farewell message ; he entreated him to be the bearer of it himself, that it might reach her securely, and without the knowledge of her tyrannous brother. And then Victor felt as if the eagerness with which he undertook the charge, must betray his joy in having to devise means of speaking privately with Flora ; but the boy had no thought beyond that of sending his gentle cousin tidings of himself, to relieve the anxiety which he knew must be hers, when his absence should be discovered.

With earnest thanks to the friend he had so fortunately encountered, Theodore proceeded on his way ; and Victor St. André lost no time in repairing to La Vallée, that he might execute his welcome commission. On arriving there, he found that Raoul de Beaupré was just mounting his horse to ride over his estate, and superintend some improvements that he was planning. He proposed to Victor to accompany him ; but finding him show no great disposition to do so, he said :—
" Pray use your own pleasure ; if you have a greater fancy for wearing away an hour in rest after your ride, pray walk into my poor house. You will, I know, waive the ceremony of my dismounting to accompany you in. My presence is absolutely needful yonder."

St. André, secretly congratulating himself upon the haughty young gentleman's necessity for absence, in a few courteous words, begged he would not think of deferring his ride upon his account ; and in another moment had the satisfaction of seeing Raoul set spurs to his horse, and gallop off.

Seeing a page in the fore-court, Victor beckoned to him, threw him his rein, and bade him send some one to enquire of the lady Flora de Beaupré whether she had leisure to receive one of her brother's guests.

In the interview that ensued, not only was Theodore's message delivered, but Victor's love was told. No sooner had Flora's heart been put into a flutter by the unexpected approach of her brother's guest, unaccompanied by that brother, than it was relieved, on her cousin's account, by the tidings she heard of him ; but then no sooner had the poor little heart been so far set at rest, than it was made to beat more quickly than ever, by the avowal of St. André's passion ; and it had hardly become aware of that secret, ere it learned another,—that of its own feelings ; and it had not recovered from the agitation into which that dis-covery threw it, before it was asked in exchange for the proffered one of Victor ; and it was still in the tumult of all this emotion, when it gave itself as it was asked—frankly and fondly to him for ever.

After the first raptures of the lover, he was as eager for Raoul's return, as he had been glad to see him depart ; for he longed to have the gift confirmed ; he knew the feudal privileges of a brother, in disposing of a sister's hand, and he could not rest until he had obtained the young count de Beaupré's sanction. Flora, at the thought of Raoul, turned pale ; and mur-mured a timid dread of his displeasure.

But Victor would hear of no reason for alarm.  He was conscious of no just cause of impediment to his suit ; and he could not think that mere haughty ca-price would influence its denial.

The event proved that he was right in his hope. Raoul, who knew that Victor St. André was a gentle-man of good lineage, a man of unblemished reputation, 'and a soldier of honorable renown, signified his con-sent to these proposals for a union with Flora ; merely stipulating that some months should elapse before the marriage took place, as his sister was still so young.

Rosalind and Celia heartily rejoiced at these happy prospects of their friend, Flora de Beaupré ; but shortly after, events happened, which still more nearly affected them.

The good old knight, sir Rowland de Bois, had not over-estimated the mischief that was brewing, in con-sequence of his friend Gaston's fatal self-absorption. This long withdrawal, this total abandonment of all

state duties, had given duke Frederick the occasion he
had so long warily sought. At first he merely sup-
plied his brother's place ; ostensibly conducting the
affairs of the realm during his temporary absence ; and
carrying on the offices of government until such time
as duke Gaston should have recovered from the grief
in which he was plunged. Then gradually, he suffered
his zeal to warm in its displays ; he allowed himself
to utter regrets that the lawful sovereign should be so
engrossed in self-commiseration as to be incapable of
fulfilling the duty he owed his people. He contrived
that these regrets should find an echo elsewhere ; he
artfully sowed disaffection and displeasure among the
populace towards their rightful sovereign ; he managed
that his own administration should contrast advantageously with his brother's conduct as ruler ; who, shut
up with his sorrow, was unconscious of all this.
There were many faithful partizans of duke Gaston's,
who would not have failed to plead his cause with the
people, and endeavour to represent his abandonment of
their interests in its most favorable light ; but the
schemes of the ambitious Frederick were so subtle, so
carefully planned, so deep-laid, and so cunningly carried out, that the evil was effected, ere it was well suspected to exist. Accordingly, when quite secure that
all was ripe for his purpose, he caused his brother to
be arraigned on the charge of neglecting his dukedom's interests ; he procured his conviction, his con-
demnation to exile, and his own nomination to the
ducal supremacy in his stead. Duke Gaston was banished ; and the usurper succeeded to his throne.
Before the people could well know whether they were
pleased or displeased, their old ruler was expelled, and
the new one installed. By several popular acts, duke
Frederick strove to gain popular favour ; but though
the multitude were appeased, and vulgar clamour was
silenced, yet the voice of the faithful few murmured
against his arrogated authority. But these, when he
found they were not to be won over, he quelled, by

having them attainted as disloyal subjects.    They whose only fault was being too loyal, were treated as traitors—their property confiscated, and themselves banished the dukedom.    Thus, many worthy gentlemen followed their late sovereign into exile ; among the rest, Amiens, duke Gaston's cousin, whom reverse of fortune only attached the more closely.    Duke Frederick, in his paternal consideration for Celia, would not allow the sentence of banishment to include Rosalind.    He knew that to separate them would be to break his daughter's heart ; and Rosalind had the comfort of knowing that her father was accompanied by a true friend, who would supply her place to him.

Had not the old knight, sir Rowland de Bois, died at this crisis, he too would doubtless have joined those who followed duke Gaston in his exile.

After a time, Rosalind had the joy to learn that his vicissitude, so far from having increased the weight of her father's sorrow, had had the unhoped for good effect of arousing him from his stupor of despair ; that he had seemed to gather strength under adversity, and to have attained a degree of philosophic composure, and even of cheerfulness, such as his friends at one time had not dared to think could ever again be his. Hearing this, his child could scarce regard that as a calamity, which had brought about so blessed a result ; and when she thought of him as a happier man, she almost forgot to deplore that he was no longer a duke.

Meantime, her own life was made a happy one, by the fast friendship that existed between herself and her cousin Celia ; whose affectionate nature, and tender love for Rosalind, besides her native sprightliness of disposition, inspired her with an ever-charming flow of spirits, which served to keep them both gay and blithe-hearted.    It was an especial delight of Celia's to beguile her cousin into that mode of feeling, when a smile was too faint a token of gladsome fancy ; when nothing save a hearty laugh—that sweet ringing laugh of Rosalind's—would serve to express the exhilaration of spirit, the innocent joy of heart, which sprang from youth, health, and goodness, needing but Celia's playfulness to call it forth.

Then Celia would say ;—" What a delicious thing it is to hear thy laugh, Rose !  If I am high fantastic melancholy, its most distant music will suffice to set my heart to dancing-measure."

" Thou melancholy !  It must be high fantasy indeed, that would persuade thee thou had'st thy spirits tuned in that low key.  Leave all such affectations, I prithee, to the gravity-mongers, who have no better claim to be thought capable of thought, than the putting on of a moody brow.  A pretended melancholy is the shallow device of a wiseacre to get a character for wisdom ; and a real melancholy befits scarce anything but guilt.  'Tis one of the merriest-conceited of jests, when such as thou,—good-conscienced people, —play at melancholy.  Good conscience is not the stuff to breed genuine melancholy out of, believe me."

" How know you that I have a good conscience ? What makes you so boldly pronounce upon me ?"

" Marry, by those sure tokens ; pleasant and infallible.  Thou sleep'st sweetly o'nights, a sound token ; thou wak'st cheerily and fresh o'mornings, a strong token ; thou'rt ever free to note the thoughts of others, a good token ; thou hast no brooding secrets of thy own ; thou hast a hand frank and ready to relieve the wants of those who need thy help, which denotes thy own few cares.  Thou can'st eat thy meat without peppers and sauces, a wholesome token ; thou car'st for no wine in thy fountain draught, a pure token ; thou ne'er stick'st pins awry, a pointed token ; ne'er wear'st unbecoming colours, a vain token, an' thou wilt, but e'en let it pass for a woman's token ; ne'er goest slatternly in thy garments, a neat token ; or slipshod, a standing token ; or neglect'st thy mirror, a clear token.  Thou sing'st, and sigh'st not, when lost in thought, a glad token ; thou seek'st thy bed with a step untired, and a spirit as alert as when thou first arose, a confirmed token ; and thou art almost as soon asleep as a sailor, when once thy head touches thy pillow, a token upon which thou may'st set up thy rest that all I have said is true."

" Trust me, coz, I think, in the matter of an un-bruised conscience, we may both thank the gods for having cast our fortunes in such happy mould, as to have given us no cause to lay the burthen of self-reproach on our souls ;" answered Celia.

" 'Twould be a step in charitable judgment, if the favored among mortals thought of this when holding their moral heads above others less cared for by the blind woman on the wheel ;" said Touchstone.

" Thou art there, art thou ?" said Celia. " Hast thou carried our messages to those ladies I bade thee call upon, this morning, in our name ?"

" Ay, madam. But truly, it demands some of the fool's philosophy,—videlicit, laughing at that which we cannot mend,—to enable a man bravely to face such insufferable moppets of silliness as some of these court ladies are. One will build you her reputation upon an arm or an eye ; and then you shall be fanned into a fever of admiration, or ogled out of counte-nance. Another will make a stand upon the beauty of her ankle, and then you must abide all the shock of display, for she will receive visitors no otherwise than reclining on her couch, playing a thousand pretty angers, saucy petulances, and pouting, the while, with her foot. A third sets up for a wit ; and then, pray for Heaven's mercy on your patience and ears, for she will have none. A fourth——"

" But can'st thou not find a favorable word for one amongst them all ?" interrupted Celia, laughing. " Wert thou not favorably received ?"

" Nay, the pretty peats were only too favorable in their graciousness towards your poor servant, madam ; 'tis of their favor I complain. I care not for it, I vow. A sophisticate woman pleaseth not me. There is madame Lucretia. You shall scarce see her her own natural self, though you took her in her night-cap. She's farded inch-thick with affectation. She's perfumed to suffocation with the musk of pretence. The color on her cheek is part paint, part mock-modesty. She leers and ogles by rule ; sighs and languishes on system. Her smiles are calculated, her frowns prescribed. A simper is her heartiest laugh ; and no genuine tears spring to her eyes but those that belong to a yawn."

" What think'st thou of madame Christine ?"

" Ay, there now ! What a piece of pinched pre-cision it is ! Those thin, compressed lips of hers, look like an owl's beak, with its tight-held pretence of wisdom."

" If our court-ladies fare so hard in thy esteem, how stand the men in thy good liking ?"

" Faith, madam, I can scarce call them ' men.' Had you said court-gentlemen, I could have answered better ; for your courtier seems a different kind of creature from your man. He bends so low, when congeeing and making a leg to the idols of his wor-ship,—place and power, that he seemeth a link in Nature's animal creation, somewhere between human biped, and base quadruped."

" Thou art hard upon court-sins. Hast no growing sympathy that can teach thee tenderness for the foibles of thy fellows, now thou art become a courtier also ?"

" Madam, 'tis a trick of sageness, and conscious weakness, to censure those who are given to such errors as we ourselves have a leaning towards. So shall we 'scape suspicion. Moreover, 'tis well to affect slight regard for advantages within reach. Now that I am at court, court-vices, court-pleasures, court-benefits, are to be held as things of nought. Were I amid rural beauties, then, a life of nature and simplic-ity, should be my theme of disdain, while clowns and boors should wince beneath the edge of my scornful wit."

" As thou wilt ; e'en let courtliness feel some of its

keenness now. What other cuts hast thou for our court-people ?"

" Why, madam,—to return to the court gentlemen, —there is young monsieur Le Beau, with those tuzzes of hair on his cheeks and chin, and those furzes of hesitation in his moral courage. He'll tremble to shake hands with a man out of favor ; and put off associating with him until they meet in the company of angels. He dare as soon be seen conversing with the arch-fiend himself, as with a poor genius ; and he will turn his back on a saint in disgrace, to curry favor with a coroneted sinner."

" But are not some of them lively companions ? How say you to that facetious gentleman, the young lord Dubadin ?"

" His gestures are flippant nimble as a squirrel ; but his ideas are heavy in their dull monotony as a caged bear, lumbering, ceaseless, to and fro, behind his bars. Bruin, as I have seen him in the court-menagerie, shouldering out the hours of his captivity, grudgingly indignant, ever stolidly striving against his own ponderous incapacity, is fittest emblem of my lord Dubadin's struggling thoughts. The companionship of such a fellow is among the most intolerable of pains."

" All pain is hard to bear ; 'tis well to find philosophy for the endurance of a dull coxcomb, among other diseases we have to encounter," said Rosalind.

" Aches and pains are of divers degrees and qualities, madam ;" replied Touchstone. " There are some pains more difficult to bear with,—morally as well as physically,—than others. Is there any one that feels not the degradation of owning to a colic ? And who shall be so hardy as to crave sympathy for a cut thumb ? The bravest of us would not dare bemoan himself for it."

" Therein are yet women better off than our lords and masters. While sovereign man is denied the privilege of so much as a wry face—we may weep, tear our hair, sigh and lament ourselves to our hearts' content. But, come, your list of tolerable and intolerable pains. Give us your catalogue."

"Imprimis, there is your headache, which is an intellectual pain ; then there is your heartache, a sentimental pain ; there is the ache from gouty toe, a wealthy pain ; there are the aches from sabre and sword thrust, from pistol and gunshot wounds, all esteemed honorable pains. None of these, men account it shame to endure ; but few care to encounter the obloquy, as well as smart, of a plebeian pain, such as starving ; an undignified pain like stomach-ache ; an abject one, like sea-sickness ; or a paltry pain, like finger-ache, though its claims to distinction were fester or whitlow. But see ! There is your ladyship's messenger ; with a despatch from La Vallée."

The letter from Flora de Beaupré was a long one. It told of the period of happiness she had enjoyed while her promised husband was still near her. But then came the bitterness of parting, when he had to leave her and join his regiment ; and after that, came the dreariness of absence, during which her brother Raoul's morose humours, and cold arrogance, had seemed more painful to bear than ever, from the contrast they presented with the qualities which distinguished her warm-hearted lover. Since then, however, worse had arisen. A certain chevalier Fadasse had taken a hunting-seat in their neighbourhood ; he had formed an acquaintance with Raoul de Beaupré, which acquaintance had ripened into a strong liking, while this liking was still further cemented by a violent passion which the chevalier had chosen to conceive for Raoul's sister. When the count de Beaupré found that the chevalier Fadasse was the heir of a wealthy and powerful baron, the circumstances seemed at once to obliterate all recollection of Victor St. André's claims ; nay, even to efface all memory that his own promise had been already given ; for, upon the chevalier's applying to him for permission to address his sister Flora, he had at once granted it, with every expression of satisfaction at the prospect of seeing her united to his excellent friend Fadasse.

Poor Flora's dismay may be conceived, when she discovered how far matters had already gone, before she had had so much as a simple suspicion of what was brooding. Even had not her heart been wholly preoccupied, it could never have been won to any liking for the chevalier. He was a consummate coxcomb; one whose profound sense of his own merits nothing could disturb or destroy. He was incorrigible in vanity; invincible in self-conceit. He had the most overweening estimate of his personal, as well as worldly advantages; he entertained the most unmisgiving belief in his consequence as a handsome young bachelor, a chevalier, and the heir to a barony. How could he suppose that the individual in whom concentered so many attractions, could by possibility be an unwelcome suitor to any young lady, whom he should chance to favor by his preference? The smirk with which he professed to lay himself and fortunes at Flora's feet, told how perfect was his conviction that they would not lie there long; and that no other than the proper amount of maidenly diffidence which a young lady was expected to show on such occasions, could prevent her snatching them up at once, with ill-concealed exultation at the prize she had won.

When therefore, in surprise at seeing him kneel before her, thus professing, she started back, averse and displeased, he only saw what he expected,—the usual affected reluctance of a young damsel at the first avowal she receives of that which she would fain hear; and he said:—" Sweet queen of flowers, in beauty, as in name, this timid denial is but an added charm. Far be it from me to brush with too sudden-rude a breath the bloom of modesty from the gift which you now withhold, only to bestow with added grace. Let it come at your own sweet time; grant that gentle heart to me in all meet season. Blushing, and coy as you will, be your yielding ; it befits your honor, and the delicacy of my passion. Thus let me thank my sovereign lady.''

But as he attempted to raise her hand to his lips, Flora de Beaupré summoned spirit to reply :—'' I know not what I have granted, sir, that deserves your thanks. If it be your suit, that is yet unconceded, as it is yet unmade. I have heard no suing, though much assuming, sir.''

'' The dignity of your feminine reserve, lady, shall have all due observance from me. I reverence too highly that charm of your sex—delicacy, not to give it the full amount of ceremonial it hath a right to ex-act. You shall have all the form of entreaty, of humble petition, of devout prayer, that so lovely an idol deserves. Your surrender shall be as tardy as your most exquisite sense of maidenly decorum shall demand—but let not your adorer—captive and con-queror in one—languish too long. Be generous in your season of appointed power.''

'' Sir, you mistake me altogether. Let me be ex-plicit. I desire not your subjugation ; seek not mine. I have no wish to see you enact the part of a slave ; leave me no less free.''

'' Fairest bud of beauty, Flora, imperial blossom of blossoms,'' replied the imperturbable chevalier, '' this pretty simulation of inexorableness pleases me,—as a part of your lady right ; but the next time I shall plead, let me hope to see its rigour abated, and some slight show of favor substituted, on which I may live until such time as you shall see fit to let me behold the whole treasure of my possessions in that gentle heart.''

'' You will not apprehend me, sir. Understand this ; the heart can never be yours.''

'' Your brother has promised me that it shall, lady. I know you will ratify the pledge ;'' he said with his most insinuating, and most satisfied smile ; '' but let it be at your own time and pleasure. Meantime I may not, I will not, I cannot despair,''

The chevalier withdrew ; leaving Flora biting her lip, half in vexation at his impertinent self-sufficiency, half in amusement at the mode in which it was displayed.

But soon she found no cause for smiling. The affair became only too serious. All her protestations to the chevalier were treated in the same way,—as mere feints to veil her glad acceptance ; while all her remonstrances with Raoul failed in moving him one jot from that which was now too evidently his settled purpose. Her love for Victor St. André gave her courage to brave her brother's ire, by reminding him of his pledged word, passed on a former occasion ; but he set aside all her urging, by saying that he had chosen to recall that word, for good and sufficing reasons ; that he did not consider himself bound by a promise thus made ; that he knew the power which feudal rights gave him in the disposal of a sister, still a minor, in marriage ; and that he gave her to understand, once for all, that it was his intention to avail himself of that power, by bestowing her hand on the chevalier Fadasse. He concluded by haughtily desiring her to conform to his will without a murmur, as he was resolved to enforce her obedience, if she were not wise enough to give her compliance.

The chevalier, without a misgiving of all this, retired to his chateau of Fadasse, to prepare for the reception of the bride. After his departure, the scenes between the brother and sister were terrible. As Flora beheld all her hopes melt away beneath the stern unrelenting of Raoul, she became only the more frantic in her entreaties that he would spare her the misery of becoming the wife of one man while her soul was given to another. As the time drew on for the chevalier's return to claim her, and to wed her in the chapel belonging to the mansion, the fear that all would be so privately and peremptorily carried, as to effect this detested union in spite of all her struggles to prevent it, drove her to despair, and in agony, she flung herself at her brother's feet, and besought him to kill her on the spot, rather than condemn her to what was far worse than death itself.

Enraged to find such pertinacity where he had expected nothing but instant submission ; exasperated at resistance, where he thought to meet none other than the ready yielding which till then had followed his lightest demand, he spurned her from him, declaring that nothing should alter his determination to have her married, at the conclusion of the month then begun, to the chevalier ; adding with a solemn oath :— " I am so resolved you shall then be his, that, if the last day of this moon pass, and you are still unmarried, you may e'en wed Victor St. André himself. I have sworn it, and nothing shall move me from my vowed decision. Though I retract my word, I will not break my oath. But in order that there shall be no chance of your evading its fulfilment, I shall lock you up, young mistress, in the turret-chamber, whence I think e'en your own hot love will scarce furnish ye with wings to escape."

Flora de Beaupré had swooned there, where she lay, at her cruel brother's feet ; but he, nowise moved by her extremity of anguish, had raised her in his arms, borne her to the turret-chamber, and locked her in, scarcely waiting till she was restored to consciousness. Here she had remained ever since ; alone, save when her jailer-brother brought her, in sullen silence, some daily food. She had beguiled her solitude by writing an account of her misery to her friends Celia and Rosalind, though with scarce a hope of the relation reaching them. But one evening she had been so fortunate as to observe their appointed messenger in the garden, beneath the turret-window, looking about, as if in quest of her. She contrived to attract his attention ; and by means of some ribbons knotted hastily together, she had succeeded in lowering her own letter, and raising the one brought for her.

Her friends gave her hard fate their cordial sympathy, and talked over many a plan for aiding her to escape from her imprisonment, and from the worse fate which was to end it ; but none of them seemed feasible, none of them seemed to offer the remotest chance of success.

" See, here she says, that the window of her turret-chamber is strongly grated ;" said Celia ; " I think I remember hearing that it was originally used as a dungeon for refractory feudatories. Out upon him ! To use his sister no better than a serf. Even could we succeed in gaining access to the outside of her window, by some one who should scale a ladder planted for her to descend, I know not how she could be drawn through those close-set iron bars."

" Minerva, mother of mother-wit, though thyself motherless, inspire me with thy inventive wisdom !" cried Rosalind with sudden glee. " God Phœbus with his light, Dan Mercury with his cunning, lend me their several aids ! For methinks, I have a scheme seething here in my brain, which perchance may prove a goodly one for our purpose. The gods delight in sacrifices ; but surely not in such a one as this,—the offering up of an unhappy virgin on the altar of a detested wedlock. Let us invoke them to further a plot which shall prevent poor Flora's immolation."

" Right willingly ;" said Celia ; " tell me thy scheme, that I may help thee, heart and soul, with prayer for its success, even if I cannot assist thee in its planning."

" Let us to our room, then ; where we may talk, secure from all chance of eaves-droppers."

The chevalier Fadasse was walking one evening in his orchard. He paced backwards and forwards, and seemed employed in pleasing meditation, for he not infrequently smiled. The subject of his thoughts might be guessed from the complacent glances he ever and anon threw upon his white hand, as he spread it in divers positions ; now extended, now bent ; now with the little finger erect, now with all of them curved gracefully over the thumb ; now held sideways, that he might see its shapely joining on to the wrist ; now upwards, and open, that he might trace the delicate veins and lines within side. This new and curious kind of palmistry, was varied by an occasional downward look of approval at his foot, or an appreciative regard at the calf of his leg, as he caught a sidelong glimpse of it, turning in his walk to and fro ; and more than once he stopped to observe the fall in his back, or the carriage of his head and shoulders, distinctly marked in the shadow of his figure, thrown upon the gravel-path. At the end of this path, too, there was a marble basin, holding water ; and in this natural mirror, he could see clearly reflected, what to him formed the most interesting, and most admirable portrait in the world. He was startled from a profound contemplation of this object, by the sudden appearance of a strange figure. It was a man masked, and muffled in a dark cloak, who stood immediately in his path.

"What mummery is this ?" asked the chevalier with a frown.

The figure stood for a moment, immovable, with folded arms, looking fixedly upon the chevalier Fadasse, without a word. Then he slowly raised an arm, stretched it forth, waved it, and dropped again into his former position.

At this signal, six men stepped forward, from behind a hedge, or thicket, near at hand, which formed one of the boundaries of the orchard. They ranged themselves three on each side of the chevalier, and then stood stock still ; awaiting, as it seemed, the bidding of him who had summoned them.

" What would you with me, gentlemen ?" said the chevalier in a supercilious tone.

The six merely bowed in silence ; and turned their faces, which were singularly wooden and meaningless, towards the masked man. He seemed to be the di-

rector of their movements ; which were, to the full,
as mechanical, and void of any spontaneous appearance, as their countenances.

" Will your worship condescend to explain ?" asked
the chevalier of the masked man. But the mask
mutely bowed, also ; with the added courtesy, of laying his hand on his heart, which said, as plainly as
gesture could, " Excuse me." Then the mask produced something from beneath his cloak ; and before
the chevalier was aware of his purpose, advanced
briskly upon him, and whipped something over his
head and ears ; by which means the chevalier found
himself blindfolded. He raised his hands hastily, endeavouring to snatch off this something ; but he found
it to be a kind of iron head-piece, securely fastened by
clasps, or springs, impossible to undo.

He uttered some violent exclamations ; but they
were totally unheeded. No word was spoken in reply ;
but he could hear a sound of horses' feet, surrounding
him ; and presently he felt himself lifted up in the arms
of the six, mounted, and a rein placed in his hand.
In a fury, he flung himself off, blindfolded as he was,
at the risk of breaking his neck ; but he soon felt the
six busy about him again. They forced him into the
saddle, and held him there, three on each side.

Feeling his utter helplessness, he made up his mind
to submit ; resolving to shout an appeal to any passengers they might chance to meet.

Presently he found the horses put in motion ; and
himself riding on between the six. For some time,
they proceeded thus ; he hearing nothing all the time
but the trampling of eight steeds. He tried to form
some conjecture of the road they were taking, but
there was nothing which could guide him to any
definite conclusion. He thought the ground gave a
soft and muffled sound occasionally, as they passed
along, as if, at such times they were proceeding over
turf ; he fancied once or twice that he heard a bird
singing ; at another time he distinguished the lowing

of cattle, and at another, the barking of a dog, all which made him believe that they were still in the country. No token could he perceive of passers-by, which confirmed him in the thought that they were conducting him through by-ways and unfrequented paths. Once he was aware that they passed close to some trees, for he could hear the rustling of the branches, as some of the party brushed by them. He could form but a vague idea of the progress of time ; yet he guessed by the freshening of the air, and the coolness of shadow that seemed to fall upon him, that the sun had set. After what must have been a some hours' ride they came to a halt. He could feel that the horse he rode was checked by another hand than his own, laid upon the bridle-rein ; then some food was held to his mouth, and the monosyllable, " Eat !" was pronounced. He listened keenly to the voice, that he might learn whether it was one known to him ; but it struck him, even in the utterance of that single sound, to be a feigned one.

" I care not to eat ;" he said.

A can was proffered at his lips, and the same voice exclaimed :—" Drink !"

" Nor to drink ;" he rejoined. But he thought that this halt for refreshment betokened an inn ; and he called out suddenly, and lustily, " Hallo ! House ! Within there ! Is there any one at hand, willing to help a gentleman, betrayed by rascals ?"

But no sound replied, save the echo of his own words, which rang loudly out, and then died away. Soon after, they resumed their journey ; and soon after that, he felt his horse strain at the curb. The chevalier gave him his head ; the animal stooped ; and the chevalier could hear him drinking. They were crossing a ford, then. It suddenly occurred to him that they must have been coming round and round, over the same ground ; for he thought he remembered the same thing having occurred, more than once before, since they set out. But the interval of time and distance between each recurrence of the ford, showed him that the space they must have traversed in their round, —if round it were,—must be considerable.   He took care to watch for this circumstance, carefully ; and became convinced that they again returned to the same spot, where his horse, each time, made an attempt to stoop and drink.   He could hear the peculiar sound, too, as the eight horses splashed through the shallow water—some brook probably, that crossed the road. He tried to recollect, if there were any such ford, in the part of the country about chateau Fadasse ; but none could he remember.   They must have travelled many miles, from the long time that seemed to have elapsed ; when, at length, the whole party came once more to a halt.   This time they all dismounted ; and then, the six gathered about him, three on each side, and assisted him out of a saddle.   He felt them lead him by the arms, up some steps ; a door seemed to open ; he found himself entering beneath a roof ; he heard the door close behind him, some bolts drawn, a key turned in a lock, and other sounds of fastening, which fell heavily on his ear, as denoting incarceration. He prepared himself for some dark dungeon, or gloomy cell ; for solitude, for bread and water, for all the usual horrors of captivity.   What then was his surprise, when, the mask, stepping forward to unfasten the iron head-piece, enabled him to see the place in which he really was.   His eyes, long blindfolded, could scarce encounter the blaze of light which burst upon them ; and at first he could distinguish nothing clearly in the excess of splendour which surrrounded him. Gradually he could perceive that he was in a spacious apartment, hung entirely with rich silk hangings ; at regular distances, chased silver sconces projected from the walls, bearing branches of wax-lights ; a huge candelabra of the same metal, depended from the ceil- ing ; a tripod of classical design, filled with flowers, stood beneath each sconce ; and figures of sculptured marble, gleamed in snowy contrast against the deep crimson of the hangings, among which they were tastefully disposed, at set spaces from each other. In the centre of the apartment, stood a table, spread with delicacies. At one end, was placed a large chair ; on either side, two others ; and the table was laid with covers for three persons. As he observed this last circumstance, the chevalier Fadasse could not help wondering what sort of fellow-prisoners were to be his —if fellow-prisoners they were.

The masked man had withdrawn ; but the six advanced, made some slight final arrangements in the disposal of the supper-table, and then stood waiting. There was a short pause. Then, a portion of the hangings at the other end of the room, was drawn aside, and disclosed a door (not the one—so it seemed to Fadasse—where he had entered), through which presently appeared two veiled ladies.

"O ho !" thought the chevalier, "a gallant adventure ! That's quite another affair. I am now in my element. Fadasse, my dear fellow, thou art at home and at ease, now ! See that thou carry'st thyself with thy usual address in such circumstances. Yet, poor sweet souls, I cannot but pity them when I think how small a share my heart can play in the attentions I offer them. That is devoted solely, in its faithful worship, to its sovereign queen, my Flora ! But, pardie ! I must not allow my becoming a married man to render me a boor. I must not let these dear creatures languish in the shade of my coldness and neglect. Allons !"

He approached the veiled figures, addressing them with some high-flown compliment. They each made him a profound curtsey ; and then motioned him to take the head of the table, while they seated themselves on either side. He hastened to do the honors of the banquet, by carving, and by helping each of the ladies to some of the dainties spread there in such tempting luxuriance ; for he remembered that in eating, the veils must be raised ; and he was dying with curiosity to behold the faces which must needs belong to such figures of grace and beauty. He passes to each, her plate, and she bows graciously, as it is placed before her. He watches them keenly. A small white hand is raised by the lady on his right ; whom he distinguishes from the other, by observing that she is the taller of the two. The lady on his left also raises a fair hand ; but in lieu of putting back their veils, they merely lift the plate from before them, and give it to the one of the six who is standing behind their respective chair.

"Fair ladies, you use me barbarously to decline eating with me. You first deign me the beatitude of your presence, to cheer my solitary meal ; and then you crush my enjoyment by disdaining to share it. Is this one of the bewitching but tormenting caprices of your sex, with which you are accustomed to rend and torture our too-susceptible hearts ? 'Tis scarce hospitable. How may I know the cates are not poisoned, if you forbear to taste them ?"

At a signal from the lady on his right, one of the six—who seem automatons rather than men, so like machines do they move and act—places another cover at the opposite end of the table ; sets a chair ; disappears for a moment ; and then returns, bringing back with him the masked man, who takes the seat opposite to Fadasse, bowing low, and laying his hand on his heart. The chevalier can no longer complain of any lack of zeal in the performance of the part of tester. The newcomer fulfils his office with such right good will, that he swallows enough for three—the ladies, and himself.

He also goes through all the duties of hospitality,— even of joviality,—with great diligence, though in dumb-show. He pledges the chevalier with evident (though silent) cordiality, when he drinks, which is not seldom, or in stinted draughts. He passes towards him the bottle, with earnest (though mute) signs that he should help himself. He recommends various

dishes to the guest, not by uttered words, but by un-
utterable relish on his own part ; and by an active example, even more than by significant and courteous
gesture, presses him to partake of the good things before them.    He lolls back, after the meal, with an easy
air of satisfied repletion ; seems to be meditating, in
a careless, pick-tooth kind of way, and now and then,
while playing with a little dessert-fruit, has the air of
interchanging some light after-dinner remark, so perfect is the pantomime with which he plays his part of
entertainer.

There is something in this self-possessed enactment
of the host, on the part of the mask, which the
chevalier feels to be peculiarly provoking.    He frets
beneath the assumption of equality,—nay of superiority, which it indicates.    He winces at the unwar-
ranted freedoms, as he thinks them, which this kind
of behaviour permits.    He has more than once tried
to frown them down ; but resentment against silent
insults is difficult to evince ; there is something almost
ridiculous in its display, and the greater the endeavour
to mark it, the more absurd it becomes.

Fadasse gave up the attempt, by resolving to take
no more notice of them, or of the impertinent who
chose to play them off.    He addressed himself, therefore, once more, to the veiled ladies.

"Fair creatures," he said, "indeed you treat me
ill.    You set me down to a feast, it is true ; but you
deny me that which makes the charm of a feast,—fes-
tive intercourse ; which gives zest to the viands, flavour
to the wines !    That magnate of the eastern story,
who in a fit of fantastic humour, chose to try his
guest's temper by a wordy vision of described dainties,
in lieu of actual cates, was less tyrannous than my fair
entertainers, who pamper my grosser appetite, while
they starve my intellectual palate.    Ladies endowed
with wit such as doubtless adorns your speech, when
you permit it to bless mortal ear, should not thus
cruelly doom to famine your expectant listeners.    Sat-

isfy my impatient hearing no less generously than you have regaled my other senses. I have savoured delicious food, provided of your bounty ; I behold yourselves, graceful and shapely ; I touch this hand of cygnet down——"

He was about to take the hand of the lady seated on his left, as he spoke these words, but she withdrew it.

" Nay, fair Cruelty, why so cold ? I touch this hand of swan-like whiteness and softness," he resumed, attempting to take that of the lady on his right,—when one of the six stepped forward, and touched him on the arm, with a warning gesture.

" A strange household this !" he exclaimed, as he fell back in his chair, rebuked ; and lifting a glass of wine to his lips to conceal his chagrin. " What companionship is there in silence ? Call it churlishness rather. As well drink alone, as drain none but mutely-pledged wine-cups."

" You shall not deem us churls, sir chevalier ;" said the mask. " Rather than you shall have just cause of complaint, in being compelled to the imbibing of unsocial draughts, myself will be your boon companion ; a man, as it seemeth me, more fitly fills that office than a lady."

" And yet poets have told us ere now, that women and wine combine for man's delight ;" said the chevalier.

" Trust me, they are but scurvy poets—rascal poetasters, rather—who desecrate beauty by associating its inspiration with that of the goblet ;" said the mask.

" But Jove, the omnipotent had the good taste to make the budding vernal Hebe his cup-bearer ;" answered the chevalier.

" Jove, good sir, was Jove,—king of gods and men. It behoves us petty mortals take heed how we rashly challenge comparison with the Thunderer, or ape his doings. Moreover, sir, bully Jove repaired his uncourteous blunder, by taking Tros's son to be his tapster, when he saw his error of turning the goddess of Spring into a barmaid."

Fadasse recognized the mask's voice for the same as that which had uttered the two monosyllables during his blindfold journey. It still struck him as being a feigned one. There was, besides, somewhat singularly perplexing to him in the tones of this voice. They seemed an echo of something that perpetually mocked his endeavour to retrace where, or under what circumstances, he had heard it. They were suggestive of something subordinate ; something that ought perforce to be deferential and respectful ; and which, therefore, the more vexatiously grated upon his ear in the inflections which it now assumed of ease and familiar equality. He felt galled and embarrassed, each time they sounded ; but he strove to preserve his appearance of imperturbability.

" May I crave your worship's name, since you favor me with your converse, sir ?" rejoined the chevalier.

" Far be it from me to limit your desires, sir ;" replied the mask. " Crave, as much as you please. But permit me to give you this warning. There are certain things here, which you may have a wish to question ; but to which you may chance to receive no replies."

" Is your worship's name among the forbidden enquiries, pray ?" said Fadasse.

" Sir, had you duly noted my words, you would have perceived that in the matter of demand, there was no prescription. You are at full liberty to ask what you think fit ; but whether the satisfaction of answers will be yours, is yet an unsolved problem."

" May one know if your own name is to remain a mystery ?" persisted the chevalier.

" It is one of those mysteries that may not only be fathomed by your profundity, but may be revealed by my willingness to gratify your curiosity. Know me, sir chevalier, for your friend, Pierre La Touche."

There was nothing in this name that reminded Fadasse of any one he had ever known.

"Good monsieur Pierre La Touche," he said, "I am beholden to your courtesy. May I farther own myself its debtor, by your informing me the names of these fair ladies?"

"I would fain oblige you, sir. But, for all that regards those fair enigmas," said the mask, bowing, and placing his hand on his heart, "I must refer you solely to themselves. What they will vouchsafe for your contentment, I know not. But whatever it be, it must come of their own unurged goodness ; it must be conferred of their own free and bounteous will."

"I am but too glad to derive my hope of favor from so promising a source ;" said the chevalier, with an insinuating look towards each of the veiled ladies. "I cannot fear I shall languish long, when I look upon these feminine forms. A tender heart must belong to such exterior softness."

"You see those women, and fear no protracted holding of tongues, I ween ;" said the mask. "You build,—as most men do, in their views upon the sex, —on their soft hearts, and love of talk. Sad betrayers, both, of poor maidens. But we shall find how long silence will prevail, where a whim of will holds natural inclination in subjection. It remains to be seen whether Will, or Speech,—both so dear to female heart,—shall conquer. Meantime, sir chevalier, these ladies take their leave ; wishing you, as I myself do, the complacent dreams, such a gentleman must needs enjoy. Good night, and fair rest t'ye, sir."

"Fair Cruelty, fair Rigour," said the chevalier, bowing to the ladies as they rose from table, "for so must I distinguish you, until you deign to acquaint me with your truer, because softer, names, I wish you the undisturbed sleep, which may not be mine while you remain inflexible to my prayers."

The two veiled ladies made a profound reverence ; and withdrew, through the small door at the farther end of the apartment, followed by the mask, and four of the six automatons. The two, who remained, lifted up the hangings opposite, and discovered another door, which they threw open ; inviting him, by a gesture, to enter. He did so, and found a luxurious sleeping-apartment, no less superbly hung and adorned, than the saloon where he had supped. He was sufficiently wearied by his long ride, to hail the prospect of repose with eagerness ; so that he devoted but half the usual time to his night-toilette ; which it was his custom to perform with the scrupulous care of a fop.

He slept long and soundly. When he awoke, he was surprised to see the moon-like lamps with which the bed-chamber was hung, still burning. He felt refreshed and wakeful, and had all the sensations of one who has slept for many hours ; yet no sign of morning could he discern ; so, believing that he must have been mistaken in the lapse of time, he turned round and went to sleep again. It was but a short doze. He felt that he had slept long enough,—that it was time to get up,—that it must be morning.

" I forgot those thick hangings ; they exclude the light, doubtless ;" thought he, as he leaped out of bed, and drew back the heavy crimson drapery. There was a window-space ; but no window, visible ; the shutters were closely shut and fastened. He en-deavoured to undo the fastenings ; but they resisted all his efforts. He went to another window, but with no better success. He hastily opened the door which led into the other apartment ; but found the same blaze of light there, as when he had first entered it. The sconces had been replenished with wax-candles ; and the candelabra that hung from the centre of the ceiling, also. He drew back a portion of the hangings in one of the spaces between the flower-bearing tri-pods. There was a window ; but close-shuttered and fastened. He found another, and still another ; but all were alike impervious to the day-light, and impos-sible to undo. He tried to find the door, through

which the ladies had made their appearance. He
found it readily ; but it was fast locked. He searched
for the one through which he thought he himself must
have entered ; and which seemed to be at the other
end of the saloon. He found that likewise ; but it
was immovably barred and bolted.

He noticed that the table had been cleared of the
previous meal ; and that it was now laid as if for
breakfast. He observed, too, that it was laid but for
one person.

"Corbleau !" he exclaimed, " they intend carrying
on this farce of disdain yet awhile longer. 'Tis a
shallow pretence, a poor affectation that cannot deceive
me. Why should they have brought me hither ? Is
it not clear they affect me ? Why, then, delay avowing what is so evident ? But 'tis like the silly vanity
of the sex,—the palfrey of power, of which they are
so fond. Allons ! Let us indulge the sweet souls
with their fancied supremacy ; 'twill not last long.
Let us be tolerant of their weaknesses, which after all,
have their peculiar advantages for us gallants."

Smiling, and confident, he went through the rites of
morning-toilette, taking, if possible, more than
ordinary care in the adornment of his person. When
he once more came forth into the saloon, the six automatons entered, bringing hot chocolate and other such
requisites for making the first meal of the day, as were
at that time almost exclusively confined to royalty, or
the highest nobility.

He was assiduously waited upon, while at table, by
the six ; whom he did not fail to interrogate, with the
endeavour to elicit something that might enlighten him
on the subject of his present position ; but their
wooden, expressionless faces, let him say what he
would, made it a matter of doubt whether they might
not be deaf and dumb, instead of only voluntarily the
latter.

After breakfast, they cleared the table, and withdrew.

The chevalier was seized with a fit of yawning.  He cast his eyes round the room, wishing that among its rich adornments, mirrors had not been omitted.  He strolled into the bed-room, and amused himself for a time with the toilette-glass ; examining his tongue ; twisting and coaxing his whiskers ; smoothing his moustaches ; paring and trimming his nails, rearranging his rings and other ornaments.  But even the most interesting employments will pall, at last ; and he sauntered back into the saloon.  In one corner, to his great joy, he found a merelle-table, a chess-board, dice, and a pack of cards.  In a recess opposite, a lute, a viola, a viol-de-gamba, and a few other musical instruments.  With these he entertained himself for some hours ; until, just as he was beginning to think it must be dinner time, in came the six, and began to spread the centre table.

In this manner, he now went on.  He could form no idea of the lapse of time.  He had not the slightest notion whether he might not be, in·fact, taking his noontide meal at set of sun, breakfasting in the dead of night, or supping at day-break.  He only knew that his different refections were served at about the same intervals from each other ; after he had himself regulated his breakfast-hour by coming forth dressed for the day from his sleeping room.  Whether the moon and stars were then shining, and making night glorious ; or whether the sun were high in the heavens, shedding its golden beams through the blue sky, and lighting up·all earth with its splendor, he had not the remotest means of judging.  The same blaze of wax-lights from the candelabra and sconces in the saloon ; the same tempered radiance from the lamps, in the sleeping-room, kept him in total darkness,—as to the progress of time.  Once, a sudden light (of conjecture) broke upon him.

" Aha !" thought he, " my kidnapping and bringing hither was not enough ; my detention here was not sufficient !  It is requisite that I should be kept in ignorance of the passing of time, that I may not know when the thirtieth of the month arrives ; that I may be absent, lost, nowhere to be found, on that day ; that I may be made involuntarily to break my engagement with Raoul on that day ; that I may not be married to his sister, in short, on that day ! Pardie ! The pretty rogues have laid their plans well ! But which one of them is it, I marvel, who has so set her heart upon having me ? I would give this diamond solitaire to know ! Is it my fair Rigour, that tall, graceful beauty, whose eyes shoot perilous sparkles of light, e'en through the thickness of her veil ? Or can it be that sweet little dove, my fair Cruelty ? For after all,—they cannot both wed me. One has doubtless, for the sake of the other, generously sacrificed her own passion. Or perhaps they wait but until the fatal day which was to have seen me lost to them for ever, shall have safely passed, and then they will leave to myself the decision between the two ; the rejected one content to yield me to her rival sister, though not to a stranger. For sisters they must be. How else could woman's love,—mutual woman's love—be found firm and true enough for so fearful a sacrifice ?. Dear souls ! It racks my heart to be constrained to grieve them by a knowledge of the truth. But it must be told. However painful the task, I will be ingenuous ; and tell them, I can never make any woman my wife but Flora de Beaupré. I will not, to spare theirs, break her heart. She has a right to my faith ; it was first given to her. I will not drive her to distraction by forfeiting my word to her. They are fascinating creatures, 'tis true ; still I cannot be false to my poor little Flora, even for their sakes. Methinks, I long to see them again, if it be but to disabuse them of their fatal error.''

But many breakfasts, many dinners, and many suppers succeeded to each other, ere his wish was gratified of seeing covers laid for more than one. At length, he perceived that the six prepared the supper-table,—

or what, by its order of meal-succession, should be the
supper,—for three persons.   As on his first arrival,—
a chair was set for him in the place of honor, and one
on either side.

As before, also, after a pause, the two veiled ladies
made their appearance through the same small door ;
and, with a profound curtsey to the chevalier Fadasse,
took their seats at the table, while they entreated him,
by a courteous gesture, to take his.

"Fair ladies," he began, "I am far too happy in
this gracious return of yours, to greet it with a reproach. Otherwise I might, perhaps, with justice, ac-
cuse you of a too-cruel austerity, in having thus left
me to pine so long for the delectation of your presence.
But I taste it now.   We will suffer nothing to mar its
perfect enjoyment.   Let me help you to some of this
exquisite-looking dish ; 'tis wild-fowl of some kind,
daintily held captive in savoury jelly, and needs no
condiment to aid its own surpassing relish, I warrant
me.   Or to some of this farced peacock ?   The gar-
nish of its natural plumage, so glowing, so beauteous,
imparteth an air of longing to fly towards the plates of
those so worthy in beauty to give it acceptance."   The
ladies bowed ; received what he carved for them ;
then gave their plates to the attendants to be carried
away.

"Still implacable ?   Still relentless ?   Can I never
hope to win a word,—a smile ?   May I never look to
soften those obdurate hearts ?   Will they never accord
me the grace of avowing, what I may venture to guess,
from acts that have spoken, perhaps, eloquently
enough ?   Will not those lips confess the sweet secret ?
Will they not let me have the bliss of knowing from
themselves that which has been so flatteringly and
convincingly owned, in the fact of my spiriting hither ?
Will they not let me see them in their ruby loveliness
aver, that which has already been spoken in deed ?
Will they not let me hear their soft accents murmur
confirmation of my happy fortune ?   Will they not

let me thank them, as only rightly they can be thanked, for their gentle yielding ?''

In the eagerness of his suit, the chevalier had extended his hand towards the veil of the lady on his right ; but a touch on the arm from one of the six, warned him not to proceed.

'' Foi de gentilhomme, this is pleasant !'' he exclaimed, petulantly. '' You bring me hither, ladies, to play the gallant, and then forbid me the use of my tongue, by resolutely holding yours ; and deprive me of the use of my limbs by those confounded living wooden statues of yours, who rap me on the arm if I do but so much as offer to take your hand. You have me carried off, as Hylas was borne away by the enamoured river-nymphs : you secrete me here, with all loving cherishment ; and then would fain have me believe that you care not a jot for me, by all this killing coldness of behaviour. You teach me your kind meaning by capturing me ; you warm me into rapturous hope by having me seized and brought hither ; but you waywardly repress all expression of my passion, by this chilling and inviolable silence on your own parts. Surely this is beyond the licensed privilege of feminine caprice.''

He observed that the lady on his left hung her head a little ; and thinking she was duly abashed at the justice of his remonstrance, he resumed.

'' Come ;'' he said, in a less captious tone, '' I will not be severe in my animadversions upon the foibles of the dear sex. You shall have your fantasy of wilfulness out. You shall maintain your chariness of speech, your frigid reserve and distance. But you cannot hinder me from drawing my own conclusions from the one fact of my seizure and imprisonment by you. It is but right, however, that you should be informed of one thing in return. It is grievous to me to be compelled to give fair ones like yourselves the pain of knowing your love is placed on one who never can return it in honorable kind. But I must be frank.

I can marry neither of you. I am promised, bound to another ; and to her I must preserve my fidelity."

Both the ladies gave unmistakable evidence of being violently shaken by emotion of some kind. He thought them weeping ; and hastened to console them.

" Sweet creatures," he said ; " believe me, it gives me anguish to afflict your gentle hearts thus ; but I deemed it due to my own honor, and to yours, that you should be made aware of this fact. Now, if contrary to all prudence, you rashly persevere to love me, —the peril be on your own heads ; I can say no more."

The ladies drew forth their handkerchiefs ; and beneath their veils, the chevalier could perceive them wiping away the irrepressible tears.

" My heart is saddened, oppressed, by the sight of your grief, lovely ones !" he said ; " would that it were in my power to assuage it ! But Fate has willed otherwise ! Take courage, dear ladies ! Be comforted. Believe that I pity, though I cannot marry you !"

The two ladies abruptly arose ; cast themselves for a moment into each other's arms ; and withdrew in a burst of uncontrollable agitation.

" Poor souls ! Poor dear souls !" he murmured compassionately. " My heart bleeds to behold their agony. But it was my duty ; and I have performed it. Let that be my consolation." He helped himself to a glass of Tokay, and drank it off ; gave a deep sigh ; poured out another glassful ; and after swallowing that, ejaculated :—" Allons ! we must resign ourselves ! I suppose, now that they know there is no hope of marriage, they will release me. Had they not persevered in keeping me at that chilling distance, —given me that proud silence in return for all my eloquence. of pleading, and nought but avoidance for all my tender advances, I could, perhaps, have been content to have idled away some time longer here, in pleasant dalliance with these fair enslavers ; but as it is, I will now hope that I may be detained no longer from the fulfilment of my promise to Raoul and the beautiful Flora. I trust I may yet be in time. I wonder what the day of the month is ?"

The next time he was conscious of thinking, he was wondering what the hour was. The wax-lights were burning low. The six were busily employed clearing the supper-table. He found he had been dozing in his chair. Once more murmuring " Allons ! we must resign ourselves !" he made his way to the sleeping-apartment.

But many more breakfasts, dinners, suppers, followed each other in succession ere he was gratified in his hope of release. At length, after one of these breakfasts, just as he was about to engage in a game at merelles, with as much of excitement and entertainment as could be derived from a match against himself, he saw the mask enter, accompanied by the six ; who, as usual, looked like wooden figures moving on springs.

" Ah, my worthy Pierre La Touche, welcome !" exclaimed the chevalier. " 'Tis dull work, playing alone. I shall be right glad of thee for an opposite. Come, take thy seat ; arrange thy men. I hear the savage British islanders have a rustic imitation of this, our gallic game of merelles ; wherein they mark lines on the ground, for a board ; have paltry pebbles, in lieu of our neat pieces ; and give this, their bungling simulation of our sport, the title of nine men's morris. Hast thou heard of this Boorland version of a gentlemanly recreation ?"

" Not I, sir chevalier ;" replied the mask. " My conversation and intercourse lie but little 'mongst clods. My tastes lead me to herd with my fellows. As it is the nature of sheep and goats to flock and follow,—and of bulls and deer to scorn mingling with baser cattle, so doth the cavalier of refinement, disdaining the company of rude clowns, consort solely with his kind. But my present business is not with nine men, or nine gentlemen, but with one, even with yourself, sir chevalier ;" added he, stepping briskly forward, and placing the iron blindfolding once more over Fadasse's head.

He felt the six gather round him. He heard the door unbarred and unbolted. He found himself led forward.

"Stay, good Pierre La Touche !" he exclaimed ; "I would fain bid farewell to those veiled beauties, ere I quit their enchanted palace,—as I opine I am about to do,—for ever. Lead me to them—Let them know I am being torn from them—Let me assure them that I leave, even more unwillingly, than I came hither."

But without any heed to his exclamations, the six hurried him on ; mounted him ; got into their own saddles ; and soon the whole party were riding in the same order as formerly.

There was the same long journey ; the same indistinct traces of its being performed round and round in a given space of some considerable extent ; and, at length, came the halt, the dismounting, and the final withdrawing of the iron head-piece.

The chevalier Fadasse looked hastily round. He was in his own grounds again ; on the exact spot where he had been walking when these men first accosted him. They were now scouring off, with the led horse upon which he had himself ridden, between them. Last, went the mask, bringing up the rear of the party.

"Villain Pierre ! Rascal mask ! Scoundrel La Touche !" shouted the infuriated chevalier ; "be assured I shall live to have my revenge of thee for this foul trick !"

"I have already lived to have mine for the one thou play'dst me, master Fadasse, once upon a time, for many a long day together !" laughed the mask, in his natural tone, as he scampered away ; and was soon, with his companions, out of sight among the trees.

"Peste !" cried the chevalier, "'tis no other than that truant imp, the old jester's son ! Who should

have dreamed of his turning up again at Chateau Fadasse ?  I was in the mind, more than once, that I
knew some of those pert tones.  A murrain on the
varlet's impudence !  To treat me, his old master's
son, forsooth, with such airs of equality.  But who can
those ladies be, in whose service he hath employment ?
The mischief is in it, when two roguish women, and
a discarded page-jester and knave, set their heads
together to outwit one !  Malédiction !''

He bit his lip, and stood plunged in vexed meditation.  The scene, the hour, were precisely similar to
those when he had last been here.  The afternoon
shadows fell all as sunnily upon the gravel-walks ;
the water in the marble basin shone clear and still as
before ; the leaves and blossoms of the orchard were
rich and bright-coloured as ever ; but where were the
glowing and complacent thoughts that filled the chevalier's fancy on the former occasion ?  Vague feelings
of resentment,—of moody anger,—of baffled will,
possessed him now.  He stood there the conscious
victim of some knavish trick, some arch piece of dupery,
expressly played off to make game of, and torment
him.

A serving-man crossed the court, and approached
the orchard.

"Hallo !  Sirrah Jacquot !  Come hither !''

"My young master !''

The servant was about to hurry away again, to
carry the news of the chevalier's return to his father,
the baron ; when Fadasse called him back.  "Before another word, tell me what day of the month it
is ;'' he said.

"Good lack, master !  Why, the fifth, sure.''

"The fifth !  Then the thirtieth is past and gone !''

"The thirtieth !  Of course it is ;—of last month.''

The chevalier Fadasse uttered an imprecation ; but
stayed to question no more.  He hurried to his stable ;
bade one of the grooms saddle his horse ; mounted,
and rode off at full speed in the direction of La Vallée.

It was many miles' distance ; and he did not arrive at the mansion until too late an hour to seek an interview with Raoul. There was no house of entertainment near ; but he was spent with fatigue, and felt that he must seek rest and a roof at all events ; and, if possible, food. He approached a cottage, which he imagined must belong to one of the Beaupré tenantry. He found it to be a sort of lodge to the park ; and, fortunately for him, was inhabited by an old woman, not inclined to be hospitable, but communicative. She told him that the great house was all in confusion ; that there had been a many worrits there, lately. That first there had been a terrible ' tripotage ' about mademoiselle Flora, who had vowed, poor lamb, not to marry some rich abomination of a man whom her tyrant brother had insisted upon her having, instead of that charming monsieur Victor, whom everybody loved, as well as mademoiselle Flora. That then her ' villian loup ' of a brother had shut her up in the turret-room, swearing a horrible oath that she should not be let out until the ' abomination' of a ' prétendu ' came to marry her. That the ' poor lamb ' had pined and pined in her solitary confinement ; while all the time, preparations were making for her sacrifice at the altar. That the chapel had been re-decorated ; the saloons newly hung ; the house generally made gay, against the expected wedding. That as each day brought the one fixed for the nuptials more near, the young count de Beaupré had been heard to express fresh impatience and wonder at the non-arrival of the bridegroom. That at length the fated thirtieth had dawned : but still no bridegroom,—that is, no ' abomination' of a bridegroom. But in his stead, who should make his appearance but Victor St. André, the first lover, come to claim his betrothed wife. That then certain facts had transpired. How that Raoul's oath had specified a clause, in favour of which, Flora, if not wedded on the last day of the month to the ' abomination,' was free to marry him to whom she had been originally promised. That the 'loup' full of sullen ire against the truant ' abomination ' had given a grim consent to the nuptials of his sister with the man of her choice, and that they had actually taken place on the very same day which was to have seen the ' poor lamb ' united to the detested ' prétendu.'

The chevalier had contrived hitherto to conceal the personal interest he took in this narrative ; but at the last fatal piece of intelligence he muttered a deep curse.

The old crone, who was rather deaf, and did not comprehend the import of his exclamation, went on to say, that the young couple were no sooner joined, than they were separated ; for that immediately after the ceremony, Victor St. André had been compelled to quit his new-made wife. He had obtained leave of absence from his regiment but for a few hours ; that he had travelled without drawing bridle-rein, to be at La Vallée at the requisite point of time ; and that it was all he could do to be back with the army in time for an engagement which was forthwith expected to take place with the enemy. The young officer had only received leave of absence from his general, for these few precious hours ; and now, his honor demanded his immediate return. He went, leaving the ' poor lamb ' still within the power of the ' villain loup ' of a brother ; for the young husband had not even time to remove his Flora to the protection of their own house. All Victor could do, was to beseech Raoul to remember that she was his orphan sister, until such time as he himself could return to claim her as his wedded wife.

But it seems that no sooner was Victor St. André gone again, than Raoul resumed his old tyranny. There had been nothing but a succession of ' tripotages ' since, the old woman said. Nothing but recrimination and reproach on the one side ; with tears, and wringing of hands, and swooning, on the other.  Until at length, on that very yesterday, it was discovered that mademoiselle Flora, ' poor lamb,' had strayed ; she was missing, was nowhere to be found, was lost, was gone.  She had fled from her brother's house, no one knew whither ; and Raoul, half in rage, half in affright, had taken horse, and set off from La Vallée to seek her.

" Then the count de Beaupré is no longer here ?" enquired the chevalier.  He had to repeat his question, before he could make the old woman understand what he asked ; and then, finding that it was indeed too true, and that neither Raoul nor Flora were now at La Vallée, he resolved to stay no longer.  He took his departure even yet more deeply mortified than he had arrived.  He now saw plainly that he had been made the object of a well-concerted scheme to keep him out of the way until the period of Raoul's rash vow should have elapsed ; thus affording an opportunity to Flora of effecting the only means of escape in her power.

Piqued at her evident disinclination for himself, which the whole affair discovered, he was the less wounded by the loss of the young lady ; but his pride could not endure this defeat ; he was enraged, too, that the brother had it in his power to reproach him with his failure in appearing on the day appointed, even though this non-appearance was involuntary. His self-love revolted from the humiliation of having to vindicate himself to Raoul ; who would probably disbelieve the whole story of his kidnappinganddetention.

He resolved therefore, that he would altogether avoid the vexatious reminiscence of these late circumstances, by leaving the scene of their occurrence for a time ; and accordingly set out upon a journey of some months into Spain, to try what travel and change of scene would do towards obliterating the memory of these mortifications.

Rosalind and Celia were spending a pleasant season

of retirement at Beaulieu.  The former little thought
she was so near the spot chosen by her father for his
place of exile.  She had not yet learned, that it was
in the forest of Arden he had withdrawn with his
faithful friends ; that in the very cave where he had
once in happy youthful days with his lost wife, laid
sportive plans for a future hermitage, he had found
safe shelter in the present storm of his fortunes ; that
in the very scenes where he had once strayed with her
in gaiety of hope which nothing yet had chilled, he
was now acquiring the cheerful philosophy and resig-
nation of spirit which should best enable him to endure her loss as but a temporary earthly separation.

His daughter, all unconscious of his vicinity, was,
as usual, happy in the companionship and perfect love
that subsisted between her cousin Celia and herself ;
and, one bright spring morning, at this time, the two
were pacing up and down the broad terrace-walk of
Beaulieu, thus conversing :—

" Ay, 'tis all well ended, so far ;" said Celia.
" Flora's hasty letter brought me word that the marriage had happily and surely taken place ; that she
was, beyond all fear, the wife of him she loved.  But
this compelled separation from her young husband—
now her proper protector ; this inevitable return to the
guardianship of her unnatural brother, fills me with
fears for her.  Matrimony, in tales we read, is ever
the happy ending ; but in poor Flora's case, I fear
me, 'tis but the commencement of fresh troubles."

" In tale-telling, the false rogues of writers would
fain have us believe wedlock is the blissful goal ;" replied Rosalind ;  " if we are to credit realities, 'tis
too frequently the prelude of care.  Well for Flora,
that her troubles commence not where a wife would
least have them spring,—from her husband.  The
young couple can scarce pick conjugal quarrels, apart
as they are."

" Absence ofttimes breeds anxiety and doubt ;
which can scarce arise between two who truly love

each other, when together ;" said Celia. "But we
will not meet cares half way. Time enough to consider how they may best be provided for, when they
arrive, and we are forced to house them. I will not
suffer myself to dread ill-usage for her, from Raoul.
He will not dare maltreat her, sure, now she is a
wife, and beyond the lawful pale of his authority.
Let us rather content ourselves that she is safe married
to the man she prefers, and safe from marriage with
the man she abhors."

"' Abhor' is a strong word ;" said Rosalind,
laughingly ; ' yet 'tis scarce too strong to speak the
feeling aroused in a woman's heart 'gainst such a self-
sufficient fribble as Fadasse. How chivalrously he
sought to protect us from our own weak hearts !
How generous his compassion for our love-sick grief !
How tender his considerations for our disappointment.
What a noble self-abnegation did he display towards
his enamoured captors ; and with what disinterested
candour did he not break to us the groundlessness of
our hope. But I would wager aught that should not
imperil mine honor, that had the two veiled fair ones,
not kept him at such arm's length as they did—he
would have indulged their foible for his sweet person,
though he chose not to give either of them a wedding-
ring right to its exclusive possession. Out upon the
conceited coxcomb !"

"My sport in the device was, to see how the fool
had the wit to pay off old scores, by treating his
former tyrant as his puppet ;" said Celia. "Touchstone as the masked man, matched the chevalier for
making him, as a boy, his foot-ball."

As Celia finished speaking, she found herself suddenly in the arms of some one, who clasped her close,
and imprinted several kisses, in rapid succession, upon
her lips.

She struggled to free herself ; and to her indignation perceived that it was a strange youth, who had
burst from a thick-pleached arbour at one end of the

terrace, and whom, at first, she did not recognize.

"How now, young sir !—What ruffian behaviour is this ?" she exclaimed.

Rosalind said laughingly :—" Do you not know him, coz ?  Do you not perceive it is Theodore, Flora's cousin ?"

" I know not how that entitles him to accost me thus—I should rather say, to assail me thus ;" said Celia, with a sparkling eye, and a tone that showed she was much hurt and offended.

" Cast thy glance upon him once more, ere thou pour forth all the vials of thy virtuous wrath upon the poor youth's head ;" said Rosalind, still laughing.— " See here, what think'st thou of this, as a warrant for the innocence of his assault ?"

Celia saw her cousin draw down from among the short black clusters of hair which peeped beneath Theodore's broad hat, a long bright golden ringlet. Rosalind drew it to its full shining length, in a sort of smiling triumph of proof ; then let it go ; and as it sprung up from her finger and thumb, in a wavy elastic curl against its owner's glowing cheek, it proclaimed that owner a very woman,—Flora de Beaupré herself.

" Dear Flora ! you here ! in this dress ?  How came you hither ?  How came Rose to know of your presence—of your disguise ?"

" I contrived to let her into my secret first, in order that we might try its effect upon you securely.  For it is of all importance that my disguise should be unsuspected, as I am about to take shelter with you, until my husband returns to take me to my future home."

" With what a pretty air of wifely pride doth she talk of ' my husband,' and ' my future home ! ' " said Celia, looking at her with a loving smile.

" But will you harbour me till I can claim them with as open a pride, as I now may show to you alone, dear friends ?" said the blushing Flora.

" You know how right willing we shall be to have you with us ;" answered they.

" I do know it ; and in this happy confidence, I made my plans. I will not tell you how cruelly I was made to feel that I could no more abide under the roof where I was born. Suffice it that I felt I no longer possessed a brother in one who seems to lose all natural affection in his rage of thwarted power. I bethought me of taking refuge with you ; but I knew that your father, Celia, might object to his daughter openly receiving a runaway sister. Could I conceal my identity for a time, and remain with you quietly here at Beaulieu, where I learned you were staying, I might be safe until Victor's return. I therefore provided myself with one of my cousin's suits ; stained my eyebrows black ; and by good fortune found a peruke of the same hue, which had once at a masked ball, served my mother. Thus disguised, I stole from La Vallée under shadow of night ; made my way across the country through bye-ways, and least-frequented paths ; and this morning, without a single misadventure, reached Beaulieu in safety. I was fortunate enough to stumble on your faithful follower, Touchstone (whom I had determined to take into my secret, knowing that it would be fruitless to attempt concealment from his sharp eyes) ; him I begged to take my message to Rosalind, who came to me, welcomed me warmly, and afterwards stationed me in this close arbour, whence I might steal out as Theodore, and take you by surprise in the graceless style I did. Forgive me the alarm I caused your modesty, in consideration of the assurance it gives us, that my disguise is beyond suspicion perfect."

" Thou art a dear fellow ; and as proof I forgive thee thy saucy attack, I give thee this embrace of my own accord ;" said Celia, giving Flora a hearty hug as she spoke.

" How will your ladyship's father take it, if he chance to see you clasping a young gallant about in

that free fashion ?'' said the voice of Touchstone,
who came up at this instant.

''My father !   What say'st thou ?   What mean'st
thou, sirrah ?''

''I say that he is here.   I mean that he is arrived.   I saw his grace's coach enter the great
gates of the park but even now ; and hastened hither
to acquaint your ladyship thereof.   It is high time
for timely warning when a woman's arms are wrapt
round manly doublet, and father or husband approaches.''

''Dear Flora, what shall be done ?   Will you risk
meeting my father's eye ?''

''I have no fear ; I have complete faith in my disguise, since I have proved upon you its efficacy of de-
ceiving.   Besides, the likeness between my cousin and
myself is well known.   Present me to the duke as
Theodore, and all is safe.''

The experiment proved completely successful.
Duke Frederick spent a day or two at Beaulieu ; with
no other thought than that the youth he found there
on a visit to his daughter and niece, was Theodore
de Beaupré, whom they had formerly known when
they were all children together at La Vallée.

On his return to court, the duke found Raoul awaiting an interview with him.   The young count came
to ask whether any tidings of his sister had reached
her friends, Rosalind and Celia ; as he had immediately suspected that she would seek protection of
them.   But duke Frederick, with the utmost confidence in the truth of what he asserted, assured him
that they knew nothing of Flora's whereabout.   He
was going to add, that Theodore had returned from
Rome for a holiday-visit to France ; and that he had
grown into a tall stripling, with the same remarkable
resemblance between him and his cousin Flora, which
had formerly been apparent ; but remembering that
the lad had fallen into Raoul's displeasure, by his
abrupt departure, some years ago, from La Vallée,

the duke refrained from mentioning the circumstance of his being now at Beaulieu.

There, the three ladies spent some pleasant time together. Flora would have been quite happy with her young friends; had it not been for her anxiety respecting Victor, of whom she heard no direct tidings. Rumours of continually recurring engagements between the two armies, occasionally reached her retreat; but no certain news.

Her friends sought to cheer her, by hopeful prognostics; but she could not altogether forget her fears for his safety.

"'If he should be wounded,' madam?" repeated Touchstone one day, overhearing her murmured expression of dread lest such a chance should befall; "if he should, why, more shame for him not to have been crouching in a ditch. Serve him right, I say, for his folly. A man's a fool to become a soldier at all; but a thrice double fool, not to duck when bullets are flying about him, and blows are aimed at his head. Wisdom knows better. Bravery's little better than foolery, believe me."

"Thou speak'st foolery, like a fool as thou art, fool;" said Rosalind. "She would not have her husband other than the brave man he is, for all her coward speech."

"The fool speaks according to his nature, lady; well if all wise people did the like. Folly and light talking are as becoming in cap and bells, as learning from philosophic lip. 'Tis a trick of prate, both. But the jester's art cometh the nearer to nature, being mother-wit."

"Thou confound'st wisdom with learning, fool. Wisdom is as truly the offspring of mother-wit as jesting."

"Nay, madam, 'tis your schoolmen confound them, not I. The bookman who crams his brain with the musty thoughts of others, claims credit for them,

as though fresh-born of his own pia mater. He chews
the cud of other men's fancies, and reproduces them
with the grave visage, and solemn complacency of a
ruminating cow. 'Tis ever the craft of pedantry to
confound erudition with knowledge. No duller dul-
lards than your pretenders to wisdom.''

'' Pretenders of all kinds are wearisome, fool.
Pretension, ever-straining, and full of effort, must
needs tire itself and others. But true wisdom,—like
genuine mirth, like all things true and genuine,—is
always fresh and welcome.''

'' Yonder comes a pretender of one kind,—a pretender to virtue. One that makes a sour-faced scare-
crow of sweet-visaged virtue, by her own crabbed pre-
tensions to be its votary. How will she be welcome
to your ladyships ?''

'' 'Tis madame de Villefort, Rose ;'' said Celia.
'' Let us go in and receive her. I see they are usher-
ing her into the saloon.''

Their visitor proved to be the lady in question. The
marquise de Villefort was a rich widow, whose estate
adjoined the Beaulieu grounds. In right of country
neighbourship, she instituted a kind of inquisitorial
visiting acquaintance with the young princesses, Rosalind and Celia ; and in right of her reputation for
strict virtue, she contrived to make her visits as odious as possible. She was always critical ; always
censorious ; full of animadversion upon others ; had
an ever-crammed budget of misconduct to tell ; was
never without a supply of news, slanderous, detrac-
tive, mysterious, calumnious, conveyed in innuendo
and affected commiseration.

She was so over-good, that she made goodness hateful. She was so fastidious and scrupulous, that she
made scruples an impertinence. She was so oppres-
sively virtuous, that she made virtue a bugbear. In
short, the marquise de Villefort was a prude. Many a
coquette, by nature is a prude by circumstance. Her
advances are slighted, and she takes refuge in reced-

ing.  Not encouraged to be forward, she revenges her own want of charms, and the insensibility of mankind, by being ultra-backward.  She haply owes her immaculacy to a plain set of features ; but unwilling to derive it from so mortifying a source, she gives it a voluntary air by repulsive manners.  Her homeliness preserves her from solicitation ; but by demure conduct, she hopes to have it thought that only, which keeps wooers at a distance.  Nature has made her looks forbidding in a personal sense ; she hopes by art to make them seem forbidding in a moral sense. She is unattractive in herself ; but in order to screen this, she assumes unattractive behaviour, that admiration may appear repressed, not unyielded.

This prudish widow had a pet dog, that she always carried about in her arms ; and on him she lavished those caresses which she was supposed to withhold from mankind.  She would frequently expatiate on the intimacies to which she admitted this canine favourite, while they were denied to his human brethren, with a minuteness and an emphasis, that had anything but the severe delicacy which she fancied herself pourtraying.  She would often declare that Cher-ami alone should share her couch ; while no second husband might ever hope to win her to another espousal. · She would press her lips to the muzzle of the little animal, fondle him against her bosom, and let him lie for hours on her lap ; while she held forth on the inflexibility with which she should frown away all presumers to her hand.  This lady it was, who now came to pay a neighbourly visit at Beaulieu.  She entered the saloon, bearing Cher-ami, as usual, curled within one of her arms, just as Rosalind, Celia, and Flora, approached from the terrace, coming in through one of the windows that opened on to the ground.

 " A fair morning to you, young ladies, and to you, young sir.  I see you are still at Beaulieu.  How comes it that your studio in Rome allows of so protracted an absence ?  Will not art languish, while you are giving your time—I will not say idling your time —here, with these fascinating princesses ?  Beware they do not bewitch you into an utter oblivion of your vowed mistress—Painting.''

Flora addressed some suitable reply, in her character of Theodore ; and by a well-turned compliment to the widow herself, contrived to divert her attention from the subject she had chosen for discussion.

'' What do you think I have heard, sweet ladies,'' said . the marquise, turning to Rosalind and Celia, '' concerning that young gentleman in whom you took some interest, I think, on account of his marrying a friend of yours.  I speak of Victor St. André.  It is said, that he is in high favor with his general officer ; not only on account of his gallant behaviour in the late actions against the enemy, but from the assiduous court he is paying to the general's daughter. She is an only child, a rich heiress, and no bad ' partie ' for a young lieutenant ; but it is really scandalous behaviour in Victor to pay attentions to this young creature, when he is already a married man. He perhaps considers himself hardly such ; for I have heard—you can tell me if it be true—that he was compelled to leave his bride at the very altar.  A bride and a wife are very different personages ; and after all, men allow themselves strange license ; still, I think he cannot venture either to befool the general's daughter, or to betray the young lady between whom and himself a legal ceremony has certainly taken place.''

'' Victor St. André will never do anything unworthy, I dare avouch, madame la marquise ;'' said Rosalind firmly.

'' It is impossible to conjecture what young men will attempt ;'' returned the marquise ; '' their principles are, alas, too often sadly lax on such points.  They take a latitude of privilege, that we poor women dream not of.  He may not be able to resist the temptation of a match with one who is reported to be lovely, wealthy, and not insensible to his merits ; and moreover, an alliance with whom will at once secure his military promotion. But tell me, my dear, did he, as it is said, quit his scarce-married wife in the very hour of their nuptials ? This point makes an important distinction in the view I take of his conduct. I am, I will own it, perhaps over-nice in my notions of what is due to feminine honor."

" Over-niceness allows itself to pry into matters that simple modesty leaves unapproached, e'en in thought ;" replied Rosalind. " But jealous as I am for my friend Flora's honor and happiness, I will not believe, for an instant, that they are imperilled by having been committed to the keeping of Victor St. André. He is her husband, madam, and will never act otherwise than consistently with that character."

" My dear princess, you are warm ;" said the marquise, charmed to find that she had excited a sensation by her news. " I see your cousin has so taken to heart these tidings of Victor's treachery——"

" Treachery, madam ! Is it thus you stigmatize a man's acts, on a mere idle rumour, that has doubtless exaggerated a passing courtesy to his general's child, into an offer of marriage ?"

" My dear, I trust it will prove so. I only know that he was seen bearing her in his arms to a litter that was waiting in a sheltered lane, one evening ; and that she seemed nowise averse to be so supported. But all this is hearsay, probably. Pray be easy ; I dare say all is as it should be. Only, I was about to say, your cousin seems to be so much affected by these reports of her young friend's husband having forgotten the ties that bind him already, that she has withdrawn. And leaning upon the arm of that youth, too. I must caution you, my dear, as a friend to your cousin, that if she wish to avoid having awkward conclusions drawn from the familiarity with which she treats that young fellow, she should keep him at greater distance."

" Never fear, madam.   Celia regards Theodore for
her friend Flora's sake.   You may have perhaps heard
that he is madame St. André's cousin ; and the poor
youth was doubtless affected by what he heard you
tell of the whispers which have gone forth concerning
her husband's alleged inconstancy."

" Now I think of it, the young gentleman's cheek
did grow pale as I went on.   He even seemed much
agitated as your cousin led him away ; but still I
think she consults not her own dignity in taking so
evident an interest in master Theodore's uneasiness.
Tell her so, from me, my dear, as a friend who feels
a sincere anxiety for the unspotted preservation of her
good name."

" I will not fail, madame la marquise ; though I
have no fear but that my Celia's own unprompted delicacy will suffice.   Ay, even in spite of evil tongues
that are ever busy ; and of misconstruction and mis-
representation, that are ever on the alert ;" said Rosalind, as the marquise de Villefort rose to take leave.

The prude's morning tattle had done its pernicious
work.   Flora was very miserable.   This poor young
creature had been brought up in such complete subjection, that it had made her diffident of her own
merits.   She could not help attaching some credence
to this tale of Victor's having forgotten her, in the
dazzling prospect of a union with a young, beautiful,
rich girl, the daughter of his general, and who, it
seems, was not indifferent to him.   She secretly fretted ; accusing herself of a too credulous vanity, in
allowing it to persuade her that she could seriously
attach such a man as Victor St. André.   But she
rallied, before her friends ; she affected false spirits ;
she assumed the indifference of resentment ; she tried
to speak as if she felt only a growing coolness towards
him, in return for his neglect of her.   Rosalind and
Celia were not deceived by this show of braving it, on
her part ; they saw her feverish suffering through her
apparent gaiety ; they knew her to be deeply wounded

beneath this exterior unconcern ; they knew her assumption of spirit to be but a courageous attempt to dissemble how much she was inwardly hurt ; but until they could give her the only effectual consolation, that of knowing Victor to be still true, and unswerving in his faith, they let her carry it off thus with seeming indignation.

" I would he could obtain leave of absence, were it but for a day ;" said Celia once. " Could you but see each other—could you but hear him explain this, as he doubtless can, to your satisfaction, all would yet be well."

" Why should I see him ? I desire not to see him." Flora's trembling voice belied her words, as she uttered this treason against the love that lay hidden in her heart—" Why should I listen to explanations, which he, like the rest of his sex, is well able, no doubt, to pour forth at will, in the most plausible style, to the beguiling of us poor credulous fools of women."

" Beware how you let your anger make you unjust as well as bitter, dear Flora ;" said Celia. " Think if you can recall one instance wherein Victor spoke otherwise than truly, acted otherwise than nobly. We should judge friends in absence by what we know of them, not by what we hear of them."

" He had the gift of seeming true and noble ; but how know I, he was what he seemed ?" said Flora, with a vain struggle to speak without faltering.

" Here are some unseemly drops gemming your worship's vest ;" said Rosalind, pointing to the tears which fell fast and thick upon the front of Theodore's doublet. " What, man ! let not your woman's eyes rain their own betrayal."

" They are tears of anger, not of weakness. Do not think they spring from a tenderness unworthy of a forsaken wife. I am no spaniel to fawn on him who spurns me ; I cannot crouch to a reluctant affection. If Victor desire to forget me, I will show that

I can forget him. Why should he come to renew the tie between us, if he have wished it broken. Why should he return to excuse and explain ? I would not see him—I would not hear him—I could not bear to have him frame shallow pretexts, utter hollow assurances, aver and protest a thousand untruths. It would break my heart.''

" I doubt it not—were he to do so—but I do not think he would. He would speak nothing but truth ; plead nought but right.''

" He cannot ; he cannot. Right and truth are his no longer ;'' said Flora in vehement agitation ; then mastering it, by an effort, she added decisively, " I would not see Victor so degrade himself. I would not see him, if he came hither.''

Touchstone had more than once heard madame St. André express herself thus peremptorily on the subject of declining to see her husband should he come to Beaulieu. He had his own secret opinion on the matter ; but he felt bound to abide by her avouched determination. This it was, doubtless, which made him act as he did, one evening, when as he was crossing the park, at some distance from the house, he chanced to meet the very gentleman in question,— Victor St. André.

" Hist ! good fellow ! Hear me !'' called Victor aloud, as he saw the jester turn away into another path, as if he had not seen him.

" Whom call'st thou fellow, pray ?'' replied Touchstone. " I would have thee to know I hold fellowship with no strangers. I give not my countenance so easily, as to let a man call me one of his brotherhood, until I know him to be a true man. Prove me your claim to the title, ere you name me anything but Touchstone, which is my rightful style and denomination.''

" I would have thy kind offices, good Touchstone, to lead me where I may speak with thy ladies, the two princesses.  My business is urgent, and will not bear delay.  Test me this gold, good Touchstone.  Prove its value, by accepting it.''

'' Sir,'' said Touchstone, drawing back, '' I am bribe-proof ; although a namesake of the transformed Battus.''

'' Is that a hint to double it ?  Battus, thou know'st, yielded to the second offer.''

'' When the silly old shepherd of Pylos gave way at the instance of him who filched the flocks of Admetus, he knew not his man.  But I have a shrewd suspicion of mine.  I take it, you are no disguised god-head, like the sly Hermes ; though you may well be one of his disciples—a thief, sir.''

'' How, sirrah ?''

'' You steal hither in the night, sir ; or, to speak more accurately,—in the dusk ; is not that the act of a thief ?  You would rob me of mine honor, by proffering a bribe which shall induce the betrayal of trust ; doth not that prove you a thief ?  I find you furtively, fraudfully, stealthily, surreptitiously—not to say, burglariously, seeking to effect an entrance into a dwelling-house against the owner's will ; is not that the proceeding of a thief ?  Truly, I think you are no better than one of those said Mercury's minions.''

'' I'll tell thee what, fellow ; lying as well as thieving is, I believe, among their attributes.  But as I am a gentleman and no thief, a true man and no liar, I lie not, when I promise to break thy head, an' thou do not my bidding.''

'' Marry,  sir, that promise shall hardly suffice.  An' bribes could not succeed with me, threats shall not ; and where gold failed, the tempting offer of a broken head shall scarce prevail.  I scorn propitiation.  Give ye good night, sir.  Sleep where you will, you house not here.''

Turning on his heel, Touchstone left the spot, and went straight to the saloon where he knew the two princesses were sitting, with their friend, the seeming

Theodore. They had deferred having the tapers of the sconces illumined, that they might luxuriate as long as might be, in the delicious air of evening, and its softened light. The windows that opened on to the terrace were all set wide, and commanded a lovely view over the trees and lawns of the extensive park. A crescent moon was just rising ; its silver line clearly defined against the tender azure of the sky, which was still tinged with the last faint lingering golden and roseate hues of sunset ; and a few stars twinkling forth, lent their diamond sheen to the mild radiance of the whole scene.

"You should see, dear friends, how firmly I would behave," Flora was saying, as Touchstone entered the room ; "I would not betray myself, were he close beside me. Until not a doubt remained upon my mind that his love has never wavered, I would not let him guess how foolishly faithful, how weakly strong, my affection has been, and still is, for him. His very presence should not shake me from this resolve."

"The meaning of that, is this,—which though no rule in grammar, is a good phrase in logic ;" said Touchstone, stepping forward. "Your meaning is, as I understand it, sir madam, that you would be adamant, in case your husband besought you to hear him. 'Tis well that I forbade him the house, when he would fain have paid you a visit but now."

"How say'st thou ? 'But now !' Hast thou seen him, good fellow ?" gasped Flora.

"A goodly adamantine aspen-leaf ;" cried Celia, laying her hand upon the trembling Flora's sleeve ; "but sit thee down in yonder corner, and recall some of thy firm resolves, to harden thee against aught that may bechance."

"Victor here ! you jest, man ;" said Rosalind to Touchstone.

"As a jester should, madam."

"Nay, nay, leave thy quips now, and let us have sober verity."

But just as he was about to tell her how he had met
Victor St. André in the park, he saw the figure of the
gentleman himself appear on the terrace ; and pointing
to it, he said :—'' In sober verity, then, he is here.
Behold him !''

Rosalind signed to Touchstone to be gone, while she
herself approached one of the open windows.

The figure came onwards ; and seeing the lady,
hastened his steps towards her.

'' This is what I hoped ;'' he said, as he raised his
hat, and advanced to address her.  '' I hoped that I
might be able to find my way to your presence un-
guided, since guidance was denied me.  I beseech you
to believe that I should not have used this scant ceremonial in approaching you, had not my state absolutely
required secrecy.  With the hardly-wrung sanction,
or rather, with the connivance of my general officer,
I have stolen hither to obtain if possible, traces of my
Flora.  A rumour suddenly reached me that she has
quitted La Vallée, and the protection of her brother ;
that she has fled, no one knows whither.  You, dear
lady, who are one of the two friends dearest to
her, can surely inform me if this terrible news be
true.''

'' It is but too true ;'' said Rosalind.  '' I pray
you, walk in, sir, and let us speak of this farther.
My cousin Celia and I have been sitting here in the
twilight, with a young friend of ours, until we forgot,
in the interest of our talk, which was on this very
theme, to order that the wax-tapers should be lighted ;
but by your leave, we can continue our converse by
starlight, rather than have the interruption of the attendants.''

'' It best suits my condition, which must shun curious eyes, while I am a deserter from my post ;'' replied he.  '' But in pity to my anxiety, lady, let me
know all you know of my Flora—my wife.''

'' Why did you not stay to see after your wife yourself, good sir, instead of leaving the task of caring for

her to others," said a person who had hitherto remained somewhat in the shadow of the apartment.

" That voice !" exclaimed Victor in sudden amazement.

" Ay, that voice, good sir ; the voice of Theodore ; which probably strikes upon your conscience, from its likeness to that of his cousin, the woman whom you, with so much of the insensibility ascribed to a husband, left, after an hour's marriage. You must be gifted with more than the usual amount of conjugal indifference, if you found time to tire of her in that short space."

Victor gazed upon the youthful figure which stood there. The faint light fell upon the same face and form which had once before so powerfully impressed him with their resemblance to those of her he loved. There was the same transparent beauty of complexion ; contradicted by the pencilled jet eyebrows, and the short thick raven clusters of hair. There were the same vibrating tones, so like hers in their fulness and sweetness ; but mingled with a pert, peremptory inflection, that brought to mind the querulous sadness of the boy's accents, who had accosted him that morning on the skirts of his own domain.

" I remember you, now ;" he said, with a deep drawn breath ; " you are the lad whom I met on your road to Rome, are you not ?"

" 'Tis of a piece with the rest of your delicacy towards our family, to remind me of the service you then did me ;" replied the youth. " But I trust I shall live to requite it—to repay the money you then lent me. I disdain to live under obligation to one who has behaved to my cousin—my poor Flora, as you have done."

" You know not how little there was of slight in my leaving her when I did, young sir ;" said Victor. " You would not have had her the wife of a recreant soldier—a dishonored man—which she must have been, had I tarried one hour longer away from the army at that perilous moment. I loved her honor, which was then become involved in the preservation of mine own, even better than herself.''

" And truly your love for herself can be but of sorry quality, when we learn that it hath melted away in the fire of a newer liking ;'' said Theodore.

" My love for my wife can never melt in heat of liking for any other woman ; and can only be extinguished by death itself ;'' said Victor firmly. " I forgive your rude questioning of myself, for the sake of the affection it denotes towards her ; and I answer for that reason with more patience than I otherwise might.''

" How doth your assertion of love for my cousin, agree with the attentions you are now reported to be paying to your general's daughter ?''

" Ha, ha !'' laughed Victor ; " so that silly tale hath reached you, hath it ? On the eve of one of our engagements, the young lady you speak of came rashly near the field, to enquire of her father's welfare. He, in the very moment of giving directions for the attack, sent me with his message of entreaty that she would retire from her dangerous vicinity, and also bade me leave no arguments unurged which might prevail with her to obey his desire. A litter was in readiness ; and after much eagerness of solicitation on my part, she yielded, and permitted me to convey her to it, that she might return home. This interview, I afterwards learned, was misinterpreted by some chance witnesses ; and the general and I have had more than one laugh, since, at the absurd credulity which gave to a simple entreaty that a lady would remove from danger, the significant importance of a love-scene. The general is about to unite his daughter to a gentleman of birth and virtue. He knows well that I am married. Nay, it is because of his sympathy with my present anxiety respecting my wife, that he has given me tacit permission to absent myself from the army while there is no immediate prospect of an engage-

ment with the enemy.   But, alas, if she have indeed
fled from La Vallée, how may I trace her ?"

"How know you that she would have you trace
her ?   How know you that your desertion may not
have extinguished love in her heart for you ?   Mayhap, in the absence of the neglectful husband, some
brisker gallant hath found the way to persuade her to
bestow upon him, that which Victor de Beaupré held
not worth the having."

"But that your voice, uttering my name, moves me
in mine own despite, I would not tamely hear you
speak thus lightly of her ;" said Victor St. André.

"Peradventure, her flight is in company with this
gallant, whosoever he may be.   Why not seek them,
and assert your conjugal claim ?   By prior right she
is yours, you know.   Why should you care whether
her heart hath strayed irretrievably, so you recover
herself ?"

"Were it possible she had so swerved, and become
the fallen thing your words describe, I would not hear
you utter them ;" said Victor.   "But being as she
is, I firmly believe, the soul of unspotted truth and
honor, wherever she may be—and however fatally lost
for a time—you shall not malign her unpunished.
Come forth into the park with me, young sir ; these
ladies shall not protect you by their presence, from
the chastisement due to so shameless a tongue.   Whatever advantage your youth and unequal height may be
supposed to give me, will be made up to you in the
disarming power of your voice.   I am unmanned while
I hear it."

"You would fain have me believe you feel the echo
of her voice, yet you would kill her cousin because he
tells you your own desertion has made her a false
wife."

"I will fight even with that face—these eyes—
those lips—if they couple falseness with her name !"
exclaimed Victor, passing his hand across his eyes for
an instant, as if to shut out the sight of what caused

him such deep, such bewildering emotion.   Then, in a
sort of fierce rallying of his determination, he half drew
his sword, repeating " Come !  Follow me, young sir !"

But at the first glimpse of the blade, the seeming
Theodore sprang forward, and clinging to his arm, exclaimed—" Don't hurt me, Victor !"

" Coward, as well as slanderer !" he cried, and was
about to push the youth off ; when Rosalind stepped
forward, twitched away the black clusters of hair, and
revealed the fair ringlets of Flora, exclaiming :—

" Have a care, master Victor, lest in your rough-
ness to Theodore, you injure Flora !"

" Flora ! my wife !"

" Victor ! dear husband !"

" Let us leave this foolish pair to fight out the rest
of their quarrel, after their own fashion ;" said Rosalind, leading Celia away.   " Clubs won't part them
now."

" Ay, marry ; they're close engaged ;" replied she.
" But, certes, their fair encounter needs neither um-
pire nor witnesses ; so have with you, coz."

On the following morning, the happy party of four
friends were all walking on the terrace together ;
Victor trying to assert his marital authority, in forbidding his wife to think of carrying out a resolution
she had formed, of accompanying him to the army as
his page, rather than again be separated from him.

" Help me, sweet ladies ;" he said, to Rosalind and
Celia ; " help me to persuade this dear unreasonable
against so wild a project.  She knows not the risk of
'noyance that would be hers ; she dreams not the difficulties, the perils, she would have to encounter, in so
hazardous a position.  I speak not merely of personal
dangers,—her wife-errantry might give her courage to
confront those ; but of the perils to her modesty, to
her nice sense of propriety, which such a situation
would entail.  Besides, how could her husband perform his duty as a soldier, with so fruitful a source of
alarm ever at his side ?  The thought of her, and of

her thousand perils, would make a coward of his heart, and take all virtue from his sword."

"You bid her prove herself a worthy wife, rather than a fond wife ;—a hard task for a young wife, but one, which if she be a wise wife, she will learn early, that she may ever after be a happy wife ;" said Rosalind.

"Theodore shall stay with his friends at Beaulieu ;" said Celia ; "until such time as Flora's husband can fetch her to St. André ; though to say sooth, I hardly know whether I shift not some of those perils to modesty you talk of, from your wife's hazard, to mine own ; for my reputation hath already run some risks, I fear, in the favor shown to this pretty youth. His welcome here,—the intimacy between us,—hath given scandal occasion to hold a fan before her brazen face, and to whisper a malicious aside. But I am content to abide the issue, if Theodore will still give us his company."

"Scandal would be content to hold her tongue, I fancy, could she but change the object of Theodore's intimacy ; her malice would be discreetly dumb, were he to offer his gallantries to herself instead of to you, coz ;" said Rosalind.

"Oh, I know whereabouts you are ! Poor madame la marquise ! She is your impersonation of scandal, with her lifted brows, and pursed lips ;" said Celia.

Flora laughed. " I could find it in my heart to avenge the heart-ache she gave me by her despiteful story of my husband's inconstancy. I've a shrewd notion you are right ; and that Theodore would have little difficulty in thawing the prude's icy punctilio. Betake yourself to your defences, madame de Villefort, for the youth hath a mind to try his bonne fortune."

"Cry you mercy, good folk ! take me with you, I beseech you, or I am left darkling ;" said Victor St. André. "Of whom are you speaking ? Who is this marquise de Villefort ? and how doth her name affect my Flora ?"

" Nay, she nowise affecteth Flora ; but we are much mistook, if she affect not Theodore passing well ;" said Rosalind. " She hath thrown glances of favour on him—furtive, but manifold. She grudges his attentions to others ; she hath fifty pretty feints to engage them towards herself. She passes bickering comment on his deeds and words, in the company of others ; but she makes amends by casting him sweet eye-liads when no one is looking. She twits and gibes his youth ; but contrives to let him see she thinks him a very pretty fellow ; she sometimes praises, sometimes makes a mock of his beardless bashfulness, thereby letting him understand that a little more saucy enterprise in his manner would not only be becoming, but welcome. She laughs at his shyness, and rallyingly commends his diffidence, showing that forwardness would be encouraged, as well as forgiven. She pretends to censure his awkwardness, while she lets him know and feel that in her eyes he is never amiss."

" I plead guilty to the truth of all this, on the part of madame la marquise ;" said the laughing Flora. " Should I not succeed, think you, were Theodore to attempt giving her a lesson in return for the pang she caused your poor little wife ?"

" No doubt of it, from what I hear ; and I dare say she richly deserves that you should stay and read her such a lesson ;" replied Victor.

" Ah ! ' Stay ! ' That is what I cannot bear to do, since you must go !" said Flora ; all her smiles fading away at the thought.

Just then, a man on horseback, whose uniform proclaimed him an aide-de-camp, rode up the park approach, towards the house ; but seeing the group on the terrace, he made his way across the sward in their direction.

" It is a soldier ! He has seen you, Victor ! We are lost !" said Flora.

" Fear nothing, love ; I told the general where he might hear of me, in case he should desire to summon me—to communicate with me."

Flora's cheek grew paler and paler, as she saw the horseman deliver into her husband's hand the missive which was to call him from her ; but she strove to be collected and firm, while eagerly perusing his face, as he read the letter.

To her surprise she saw joy sparkle in his eyes.

" Dear Flora ! See here ! Read this !" he exclaimed. " We need not part. Henceforth, my honor, my duty, are one with my delight. They alike call me to my home with you."

The general's letter congratulated Victor on an amnesty which had just been ratified between the long-contending armies. He bade him take his new-made wife in triumph to St. André ; and there joyfully to celebrate the proclaimed peace, by proving himself as good and happy a citizen in this period of the realm's tranquillity, as he had hitherto shown himself to be a brave and faithful champion in its time of war.

Rosalind and Celia were in the midst of offering their felicitations, when a visitor was announced,— madame la marquise de Villefort.

" We will attend her in the saloon ;" said Celia, to the attendant. " Or rather tell madame la marquise, we are with some friends on the terrace, if she will do us the favor to join us here."

" Now, master Theodore," said Rosalind, " muster all your forces. The lady is at hand, upon whom you are to try the courage of your impudence. Let it not fail you, for the love of true modesty. Her pride of prudery deserves a fall."

Flora was so elate, so full of glee at the news she had just heard, that she could not by possibility have been in better humour for the gay task proposed. She played her part so well ; she led the widow into such bewildering belief of her being struck with her ; she entangled her in such a maze of banter, compliment, playfulness, adulation ; she so thoroughly impressed her with the notion of Theodore's enamoured fancy, and desperate liking, that the prude was fairly bewitched,—enchanted,—charmed out of all her artificial frigidity, into the coquetry natural to her. She was trapped into seductive looks ; betrayed into alluring words ; her freezing reserve unconsciously melted into blandishment ; her malice merged into kindness ; her sarcasms became covert flattery ; and her usual severity was insensibly exchanged for the most captivating softness. Her scruples were foregone ; she lost sight of all her reserve. The strict decorum exacted from others, she forgot to observe, when she herself became the object of admiration ; the rigid adherence to propriety, so often insisted on in judging imprudent women, she left unheeded, when there was a pressing suitor in her own case. The rapture of finding that this youth was dazzled by her beauty, blinded her completely ; and his simulated passion proved an irresistible bait to her vanity. The conventional prude stood confessed the native coquette.

Rosalind, Celia, and Victor, quietly enjoyed this comedy, played off for their amusement by Flora ; they felt no compunction for the object of the plot, since she merited her unmasking.

Towards the end of her lengthened visit, the marquise had admired some beautiful exotics, which filled a vase standing on the table of the saloon, whither they had adjourned from the terrace.

" They are gathered from a plant, which my father's indulgence has placed in the conservatory here, for me ;" said Celia. " I will send your ladyship a branch of them, since your taste so approves them."

" Sweet princess, I am greatly beholden to your courtesy. But whom will you find, worthy to be their bearer ? Such flowers as these, should have none other than hands of highest desert, and nicest charge ;" said the widow, looking full at Theodore. " No hireling page is fit to be entrusted with them. It should be some gentleman, whose refinement and good taste would ensure their safe conveyance."

" I am sure my friend Victor St. André would have great pleasure in bringing them for your ladyship to Villefort ;" said Celia demurely.

" Rather call him your cousin's friend ;" replied the marquise with emphasis, though sinking her voice to a half whisper. The princess Rosalind is really un-blushing in the display of her preference for monsieur St. André. You would do well to advise her, as a friend, to be more guarded in her conduct. So open a show of liking for a young man, is scarce seeming, in a young maiden of her years and rank. Her own dignity demands greater discretion. But to return to the flowers. If you yourself, my dear, can spare that other young gentleman from his perhaps imprudently close attendance on your steps, I would ask you to let him bring over your kind gift to Villefort. 'Twill give the youth consequence, you know, poor lad, to find himself the trusted envoy between two ladies."

" It will be received by him as valued encourage-ment, I doubt not, madam ;" said Celia, with a smile.

" Jealous, poor little thing !" thought the marquise.

When madame de Villefort took her leave, Rosalind, Celia, Victor, and Theodore, all bore her company through the park, as far as the great gates, where she said her coach was awaiting her.

Theodore and she, by mutual contrivance, kept side by side ; and as the party strolled on beneath the trees, these two gradually fell into such exclusive interchange of words and looks, that the others lingered some way behind, leaving them to themselves.

" I overheard your charming arrangement with the princess Celia, that I should be the favored bearer of your flowers ;" said Theodore to the marquise, with an animated look of gratitude and delight. " I could not misconstrue its generous condescension—its flatter-ing import. Thus let me thank my goddess ;" and the youth raised her hand to his lips. " You intoxicate me with your goodness ; you transport me with your gracious indulgence ; do you indeed select me to bring those flowers to your house—to come to Villefort—to visit you—and alone ?  You will receive me alone ?'' And Theodore acted the insinuating wooer with his eyes, to perfection.

'' These youths are so foolishly explicit ;'' muttered the widow.   Then she added aloud, with a tender glance :—'' Come ; and trust to my friendship for you. I want to have your counsel respecting the best mode of arranging the princess's gift.   So come early, that we may have daylight for our task, in the disposal of the flowers.''

'' So marked a proof of confidence from your ladyship, deserves equal trust on mine.   I will tell you a secret, madame la marquise ; one that concerns my future existence,—on which depends my very being. Have I your permission to reveal it ?''

'' Can I not perhaps guess it ?'' murmured the widow, with a languishing look.

'' I think not ; you will never suspect me of having taken such a daring advantage of your kindness,—your encouragement.''

'' Nay, speak out ;'' said the marquise, with a smile as unlike the forbidding austerity she had taught her lip to assume for its general wear, as a ripe cherry is to a wilted crab-apple.

'' Thus emboldened,'' stammered the blushing, but roguish-eyed Theodore, '' I find courage to own to you that I am not what I seem ; that I am,—that, in short,—I am—a—a—woman !''

'' A woman !'' exclaimed the widow, with a gasping shriek.

'' Ay, madam, at your ladyship's service ;'' said Flora, doffing her broad hat, and with it the mass of short black hair ; so that her own fair curls fell around her face, and down upon her shoulders, while she glanced into the prude's face with those smiling rogue's eyes of hers.   '' Command me in aught that

can avail you.   I would bring the flowers over to Villefort this evening—but I have an engagement to go with
my husband to St. André.   Nay, he should have
brought the flowers, and enacted the part of your ladyship's adviser, which he would doubtless have filled
with far abler grace than Theodore, poor youth ; but, I
know not.   'Men allow themselves strange licence,'
you know.   I, as his wife, you, as a severely virtuous
lady, will think it best, perhaps, that he should keep
his duty-appointment at St. André, instead of the
pleasure-engagement, — the   assignation, which you
vouchsafed to me.''

"Assignation ?   Insolent !   I know not what you
mean, madam ;'' said the marquise, as she flung from
her, and advanced to step into her carriage, which by
this time they had nearly reached.

" Of course not, madam ;'' replied Flora.   " None
are so conveniently at a loss to discern a meaning, as
you ladies of quick apprehension.   Your squeamish
purity sees a latent sense of evil in simplest words and
deeds ; but becomes dull as ignorance, where it suits
you to understand nothing.   Farewell, madame la
marquise !   Commend me to Cher-ami ; and may his
innocent slaver continue to compensate you for the
despised caresses of false men, and still falser youths !''

When their friends Victor and Flora quitted them
for St. André, Rosalind and Celia also left Beaulieu,
and returned to court.

About this time, Rosalind had her thoughts much
drawn again towards her father.   She learned where
he had taken up his abode ; she found it was the
pleasant forest of Arden that he had chosen to make
the scene of his exile ; she heard of the cheerful philosophy, the happy serenity which had become his, in
this charming spot ; she heard how he drew inspirit-
ing lessons from everything that surrounded him in
this woodland life of peace and contentment.   She
heard too, that many more of his friends had lately

joined him ; that several lords had voluntarily banished themselves to bear him company. His faithful cousin Amiens was, of course, still with him. All this was of sweet comfort to her ; and yet she could not but occasionally suffer her heart to sink a little, as she felt the natural longing of a child to be with her father, that she might give him her loving care, cheer him with her company, and make him and herself happy in their mutual affection.

Her uncle treated her very kindly ; although his feelings towards her were of a mingled complexion. He loved her for her own sake ; he could appreciate her brilliant qualities ; he knew how much they added to the lustre of his court ; and he was therefore anxious to retain them there ; he also liked her for his daughter's sake, who he knew tendered her no less dearly than her very self ; but in addition to these favorable sentiments with which he regarded her, there lurked, besides, certain misgivings with respect to the place she held in popular esteem ; a sort of jealousy of the people's commendation of her many virtues and excellences, and a kind of uneasy association of her presence with the injustice he had done her absent father. Nevertheless, the prepossession had hitherto prevailed over the distrust ; which lay smothered, in self-unconscious existence, until some occasion might arise which should call it forth into an open evidence of displeasure against her.

The friendship between herself and Celia, had even increased with their growth, and strengthened with their added years. It had acquired the maturity and solidity of better knowledge of each other ; and together with this higher appreciation of the qualities of either had come a truer acquaintance with their own capabilities of loving. They were sisters in heart. Celia, in her generosity of soul, saw that in Rosalind's mind, which she delighted in, as something she gladly confessed superior to her own powers of wit and fancy ; while Rosalind beheld in the affectionate gentleness of Celia's nature, that which she reverenced as above even intellectual gifts. The perfection of feminine attachment was theirs.

But it was under the impress of a passing shadow of regret concerning her father, that Rosalind, one day, seeming less gay than was her wont, caused Celia to say :—"*I pray thee, sweet my coz, be merry.*"

To which Rosalind answered :—"*Dear Celia, I show more mirth than I am mistress of; and would you yet I were merrier? Unless you could teach me to forget a banished father, you must not learn me how to remember any extraordinary pleasure.*"

And now this story ceases, that it may have its proper termination in the play (be that, however, ' as you like it ' !), and " end in true delights."

# PASSAGES IN THE PLAYS

### IN RELATION TO

## FACTS, NAMES, AND SENTIMENTS,

#### WITH WHICH IT WAS REQUISITE THE TALES SHOULD ACCORD.

---

### TALE VII.

Page 8,
line 21.

' Bollitura ' is a kind of thin drink, or decoction, for sick people.

Page 10,
last line.

" Signor Baptista may remember me,
*Near twenty years ago, in Genoa.*"
TAMING OF THE SHREW, Act iv., s. 4.

Page 20,
line 23.

We are told that " Saint Macarius happened one day inadvertently to kill a gnat that was biting him in his cell ; reflecting that he had lost the opportunity of suffering that mortification, he hastened from his cell to the marshes of Sceté, which abound with great flies, whose stings pierce even wild boars. There he continued six months, exposed to those ravaging insects ; and to such a degree was his whole body disfigured by them, with sores and swellings, that when he returned, he was only known by his voice." Of St. Simeon Stylites we learn, that " he erected a pillar 6 cubits high, and on it he dwelt four years ; on another, 22 cubits high, ten years ; and on another, 40 cubits high, built for him by the people, he spent the last twenty years of his life."

Page 22,
line 24.

There is a singular inconsistency in the feelings of the Italian people towards friars. They reverence their holy calling ; but it is reckoned unlucky,—or, as the Scotch would call it, 'un-canny,'—to meet a friar in the streets. They make a particular sign towards him, stealthily, with the fore and middle finger, called ' jetta-tura,' which is supposed to avert ill-conse-quences, from the ' evil-eye,' or other ominous encounter.

Page 34, line 38.

'Pignoli' are pine kernels ;  a kind of nut much in favor with Italian boyhood.

Page 35, line 15.

'Miscetta' is Northern Italian for 'puss.'

Page 35, line 38.

'Cedrata' is a drink made from citron ; ' Limonata' from lemons and 'Semata' from lemon seeds.

Page 69, line 33.

'Battuto' is made by laying a stratum of cement, strewn thickly over with marble broken into small pieces beaten hard with iron flats, and polished into a beautiful, smooth, mosaic-looking floor.

Page 107, line 28.

When Bianca finally jilts him for Lucentio, Hortensio says :—

"I will be married to *a wealthy widow*
Ere three days pass ; which hath as long lov'd me,
As I have lov'd this proud disdainful haggard."
    TAMING OF THE SHREW, Act iv., s. 2.


## TALE VIII.

Page 114, line 13.

Those who remember Goethe's uncandid re-marks upon Ophelia's songs, in his Wilhelm Meister, with the prurient deductions he draws from them in estimating her character, will see the gist of Botilda's fleer.

Page 132, line 27.

In one of her ravings (HAMLET, Act iv., s. 5), Ophelia exclaims :—" O, how the *wheel* be-comes it !  It is the false steward, that stole his master's daughter !"  The commentators differ about the significance of the ' wheel ' alluded to ; some believing it to be the spinning-

wheel of the girl whose song Ophelia has just
quoted ; others affirming it to mean "the
burthen of the song," *rota* being the ancient
musical term in Latin for this.    In the tale, it
has been assumed that the 'wheel,' was the
instrument of torture, upon which the false
steward was racked, in becoming punishment
for his crimes.

Page 146,   Another of Ophelia's wandering sentences,
line 35.   in the same scene, is :—" They say, the owl was
a baker's daughter."

Page 157,   See the colloquy with Reynaldo, at the com-
line 29.   mencement of the second act, for this peculiar-
ity of Polonius's.    Some of these short scenes,
omitted in stage representation, afford subtlest
instances of the Poet's mastery in the develop-
ment of character and manner.

Page 159,   The stratagems of sending Ophelia to Ham-
line 25.   let, and of placing himself, the king, and the
queen, where they may witness the interview
unseen, with the one of hiding behind the arras
to overhear what passes between the prince and
his mother in her closet, are both devised by
Polonius.

Page 163,   *     *     *     *     " we here despatch
line 1.   You, good Cornelius, and you, Voltimand,
For bearers of this greeting to old Norway ;"
HAMLET, Act i., s. 2.

Page 182,   The reader will remember Hamlet's banter of
line 26.   Osric's affected style of speech and pronuncia-
tion, in the fifth Act.    The word 'impawned'
is spelt 'imponed,' in the folio edition.    " Why
is this imponed, *as you call it ?*"

Page 199,   *Laertes.*                    " My dread lord,
line 7.   Your leave and favour to return to France ;
From whence, though willingly, I came to
    Denmark,
To show my duty in your coronation ;
Yet now, I must confess, that duty done,
My thoughts and wishes bend again towards
    France,
And bow them to your gracious leave and par-
    don."—*Ibid*, Act i., s. 2.

## TALE IX.

Page 204,   For Audrey's obsequious swain, William, see
line 19.    the scene at the commencement of the fifth Act,
in the play of As YOU LIKE IT.

Page 212,   The duke says to Orlando :—
line 25.    * * * " the residue of your fortune,
Go to my *cave* and tell me."

As YOU LIKE IT, Act ii., s. 7.

Page 214,   *Cel.* * * * " know'st thou not, the duke
line 20.    Hath banish'd me his daughter ?

*Ros.*              That he hath not.

*Cel.* No ? hath not ? Rosalind lacks then
the love
Which teacheth thee that thou and I am one :
Shall we be sunder'd ? Shall we part, sweet
girl ?
No : let my father seek another heir.
Therefore devise with me, how we may fly,
Whither to go, and what to bear with us :
And do not seek to take your change upon
you,
To bear your griefs yourself, and leave me
out ;
For by this heaven, now at our sorrows pale,
Say what thou canst, I'll go along with thee."

*Ibid.*, Act i., s. 3.

Page 220,   The classical colouring given to the diction
line 32.    of both Rosalind and Celia, by the poet, is
striking. It is in exquisite keeping with the
tone of the drama ; and forms a tasteful and
natural characteristic of these two charming
heroines. Instances might be multiplied, to a
remarkable extent, of the mythological allusions
that occur in their speeches. To cite one of the
first that occurs,—where Celia asks her cousin
what she shall call her in her man's disguise,
Rosalind replies :—

" I'll have no worse a name than Jove's own
page,
And therefore look you call me Ganymede."

As YOU LIKE IT, Act i., s. 3.

Page 222,    We hear of Rosalind and Celia in the first
line 27.    scene, "never two ladies loved as they do ;"
and afterwards ; "their loves are dearer than
the natural bond of sisters."—*Ibid.*, Act i., s. 2.

Page 226,    *Ros.* "But, cousin, what if we assay'd to steal
line 11.    The clownish fool out of your father's court ?
Would he not be a comfort to our travel ?

*Cel. He'll go along o'er the wide world with me;*
Leave me alone to woo him."
*Ibid.*, Act i., s. 3.

Page 227,    Duke Frederick says to Orlando, youngest
line 34.    son of Sir Rowland de Bois :—
"The world esteem'd thy father honourable,
But I did find him still mine enemy."

And Rosalind says :—

"My father lov'd Sir Rowland as his soul,
And all the world was of my father's mind."
*Ibid.*, Act i., s. 2.

Page 229,    The duke addresses Amiens thus :—"good
line 33.    *cousin*, sing."—*Ibid*, Act ii., s. 7.

Page 236,    "There's no news at the court, sir, but the
line 5.    old news ; that is, the old duke is banished by
his younger brother, the new duke ; and three
or four loving lords have put themselves into
voluntary exile with him, whose lands and
revenues enrich the new duke ; therefore he
gives them good leave to wander."—*Ibid*, Act
i., s. 1.

Page 240,    Le Beau says to Orlando, when he announces
line 7.    him to Duke Frederick's displeasure against
him :—
*    *    *    *    "Sir, fare you wel !
Hereafter in a better world than this,
I shall desire more love and knowledge of you."
*Ibid.*, Act i., s. 2.

Page 260,    That Celia is the shorter of the two lady-
line 10.    cousins, Shakespeare has noted in more than
one passage of the play ; and Rosalind herself
says :—

"Because that I am more than common tall."
*Ibid.*, Act i., s. 3.

Page 264,
line 24.

"Merelles, or as it was formerly called in England, nine men's morris, and also five-penny morris, is a game of some antiquity. Cotgrave describes it as a boyish game, and says it was played here commonly with stones, but in France with pawns, or men made on purpose, and they were termed merelles; hence the pastime itself received that denomination."— STRUTT'S SPORTS AND PASTIMES.